Pretty Something Book One

Pretty Good

Aneka Bailey

Mental Health Boundaries

Reading Limits

This book contains themes and elements that can be triggering such as: *Drug abuse and use, physical assault and abuse, harassment, brief mention of sexual assault/abuse, alcohol use, anxiety, attempted murder, emotional abuse, profanity, PTSD, sexually explicit scenes, physical injuries, and abandonment.*

Kinks: *Breath play, choking, degradation, rough sex, spanking, cum play, water sex, barebacking (unprotected sex), begging, clothed sex, oral sex, dirty talking, slight edge play, voyeurism, public play, exhibition, orgasm denial, praise, and degradation.*

If you find any of these themes triggering, please do not force yourself to read further.
Your mental health matters.

The Mental Health Hotline at 866-903-3787

Dedication

For the Black women and readers that enjoy found family,
diverse characters, dark themes, and spice,
I saved a seat for you.

Playlist

Band's Playlist
All Time Low - Clumsy
Get Scared - Give Up My Ghost
Bad Omen - Just Pretend
Coldrain - Bloody Power Fame
Emotional Oranges - Personal (Isaac's and Ebony's duet)
Kelly Clarkson - Happier Than Ever
Jordy - Trevor

Party Playlist
Stray Kids - Taste
Nightlife - Fool Me Once
Olivia Lunny - Think of Me
Bad Bunny - El Aragon
Beyonce - Cozy
Paula Abdul - Straight Up

Ebony and Kane's Playlist
Justine Skye - Collide
Mahalia - Bag of You
V (BTS) - Christmas Tree

PRETTY GOOD

Jay Sean (Feat. Rick Ross) – Mars
Alina Baraz – Maze
Elhae & I.M – Need to Know
Ella Mai – Found

1

Ebony Young

Last Semester

A heavy blackness surrounds me as I attempt to stumble somewhere. Anywhere. I'm not sure how blackness can be heavy, but this one is. I can barely move.

The bass of the music pulsates beneath my feet as I stumble towards something, anything.

I'm lost, blinded by the grogginess that's creeping through my body. All my senses fading by the minute.

A firm, sturdy hand grabs my arm and relief floods through me.

"Hey, you okay?" someone asks.

Their hands brace me as they attempt to steady me. My lungs begin to burn as I feel my head lean against a hard surface. A wall maybe. I try to shake my head, but someone else interjects.

"She's just drunk off her ass," they snicker before leaving my side. Accompanying the darkness is cold. Brutal, frigid cold that rests deep in my bones and all around me.

Please. Please help me.

Struggling to my feet, I stagger into my darkness with seeking hands that only feel a cool surface to my right. I stumble over something and fall to what I assume is the floor. The fibers of the carpet bite into my skin confirming my thoughts. I try to crawl, but my limbs and brain aren't communicating properly anymore. Intermittently, my body gives me strength just to be zapped of it moments later.

Dread sets in when I realize this isn't my normal drunk. My thoughts are scattering around as I attempt to retrace my steps to remember something that could help me if anything happens to me. I just have to move.

There's a feminine voice in the distance, which is impossible because I can feel their body heat right beside me. I know this voice, the heat that's surrounding me. The intoxicating smell of citrus that makes up their essence. All of it belongs to my partner. I manage to move my hand over towards them. Relief blooms in my belly.

I'm safe.

A sound mixed between a mumble and a sob escapes my mouth as I try to talk to them. Seeking comfort and solace in my safe space within them.

"Shhh. You're okay," their soft voice reassures me. Warm hands circle around my torso as they help me to my feet, shushing me the entire way.

Our bodies move, shifting as they counterbalance my weight with their own. I stumble over my dragging feet and they pause. With quick, steady movements, they shift my weight on them, then proceed to move us in some direction.

Metal on flesh resonates in my ear as my body leans forward. They shift, and a click from the mechanism greets me. I silently rejoice at being out of this hell, but the cool air of spring doesn't come. My mind panics.

The voice in the back of my mind is telling me to run, bolt, but my body isn't working with me.

Something squeaks and I'm placed on a soft surface. The room reeks of sex, weed, and vomit. I gag, but nothing comes up. My body won't budge as I try to sit up. The weighted blackness pushing all of its heaviness on my limbs, muscles, and nerves.

My eyelids resist as I try to open them. I fight myself just to attempt to move again. To my luck, I'm able to roll and land on the uncomfortable carpet below.

I whack my head on the cushioned floorboard and groan involuntarily. The pain doesn't come.

Why does this not hurt? It should have fucking hurt.

Panic rises in my chest as I hyperventilate, filling my lungs with wasted breaths. A wheeze passes my lips as I attempt to call out to my partner or anyone within hearing range. Helplessness straddles me, taunting me as the music downstairs continues to thump. When did I get upstairs?

"I thought you put her on the bed!" A gruff voice punctures the silence.

This voice, although familiar, is one I'm not accustomed to. We may have spoken a few words to each other, but nothing more than that.

There's a moment where the two bicker, but I focus on my need to get my body moving. I put what's left of my energy towards my big toe in an attempt to wiggle it. Something I saw in a movie once when I was a kid, but nothing happens.

Please let me make it safely out of this.

I realize two things. One, my partner was helping someone keep me here, and two, I can't call for help if shit goes left. And in my mind, shit's going left. This realization doesn't help the rising panic attack, but it helps me open my eyes. I blink rapidly, happy to gain some form of control in my body.

But everything is blurry. Colors mix and smudge together like I'm on those spinning tea cups at an amusement park. There may be a window or a bathroom door in my line of sight, but I can't be sure.

Come on, Ebony, move.

Rough hands grab me and throw me back on what I assume is a bed. The springs squeak and groan as I land. There's something moist on my back and I whimper.

"Shut her up," the masculine voice growls closer to me.

Leon? Joel? Samson?

The name escapes me as I reach for my partner. I know they're here. They brought me in here. Even if I shouldn't trust them, they're all that I have in this moment. And maybe, just maybe, they'll change their mind and get me the fuck out of here.

The bed shifts quickly. Their hair brushes past my face, a dull tickling sensation making my skin tingle. Maybe it's the drugs.

"Hi, baby," they coo in my ear, but their voice isn't sweet nor is it soothing. Knots form in my stomach as my mind fights hard to record everything going on.

I barely feel their lips on my forehead as the edges of my vision begin to turn black. "Just relax. Everything will be okay. You'll be asleep in no time."

My body is heavier now and my heart pounds viciously. I try to plead with them, but only whimpers escape past my lips, still fighting hard to move.

Warm palms touch my face as thumbs brush under my eyes — a sensation that's fading quickly despite it seemingly going by so slow.

"Don't cry. I promise you'll be okay," my partner's voice continues to coo. "Tell him she's almost ready," they say, void of all emotions, their hands still caressing my face.

I try to open my eyes one last time, but the blackness consumes me. The tightness in my throat is the last thing I feel as I fade away. The sounds, smells, and sensations are gone.

"Somebody help, please," I finally manage to whimper, hoarsely. But then I'm swallowed whole. A body of nothingness.

I don't want to die.

2

Ebony Young

Present Day

The bass of the club thumps while my band and I get ready in our respective dressing rooms. I check my make up, slip into my high top Converse, and shake my locs before rearranging them the way I want. Knuckles tap at the wooden door.

"On in five, Ebony," a masculine voice on the other side of my door calls out.

"Thanks!" Tugging at the frayed edges of my navy blue and white 'Knight University' midriff, then at my high waisted jeans, I give myself one final look. Satisfied, I grab my guitar and walk down the dark, smokey hallway. I slip down a secret passage and meet my band mates behind the small stage of the club.

A small black curtain separates me from the people on the other side. Voices mingle together just beyond where I am creating a cacophony of sounds. A chill shoots through me as I think about the audience.

"Alright guys," the lead guitarist, Liam, starts.

Liam is about six feet tall with pale skin and choppy brown, mullet like hair. He attempted to do a butterfly cut last week and this was the result. He says he likes it, we say he needs his eyes checked. He's cool for the most part. Like a big brother I never had and didn't ask for. I make sure he knows it every time he lectures me. He knows it's all love.

Liam's voice is a bit raspy from screaming lyrics, probably with the wrong technique, and smoking for so long. I don't know exactly how old he is, but I know that he frequents my school's campus every now and then. When we ask why, he always says he's a drifter, staying close to his alma mater. A Knight through and through. Weirdo.

"E, you're on background vocals until we get to the ballads, then it's all you," he confirms.

I nod my head, focusing on my breathing. I may have performed a handful of times, but I still need to talk myself down from a panic attack.

Liam addresses the other members of our little band. A low murmur mixes in with his voice and captures my attention every now and then. Attempting to take a peek, I shift slightly out of my band's huddle and look through the tiny sliver between the curtain and the wall. I stopped liking large crowds since the night I barely remember.

Even if I can't recall what happened, my body does and starts to shut down. I feel bad. I'm holding the band back, but they all reassured me that they're happy playing anywhere. Even here at my Gramp's bar.

"You get that, E?" our bassists, Clint, asks.

Clint's gray eyes are now fixed on me. Shame blooms through me as I shift uncomfortably in my spot.

Clint is a stocky guy with broad shoulders and a hard face. He looks aged due to a hard, stressful life despite him being two years older than me. He's my cousin on my father's side. More reserved and cautious making him quiet and introspective. There's a power to his voice when he does speak.

His dark brown skin glows under the dim lighting backstage. He keeps his hair short except for the beard he started growing last year. Something he prides himself on because it's thick, full, and gets him laid. Gross.

"No. Sorry. Repeat that for me."

"Your Femme Fatale act is going on after our set when Gramps leaves. Don't forget your set list. They should have your costume or whatever in the back." He cringes a bit, still not used to me being open to sexualize myself. My older cousin also wants to keep me safe, especially after having to watch me cope since last semester.

My heart accelerates. I remember begging to do another femme fatale performance since the last one was a huge success, but since my Gramps owns the bar, there's nothing I could do. Until today, someone found a work around. I nod excitedly.

"I'm so fucking excited!" Isaac, our drummer, whisper-shouts when Liam and Clint begin talking to each other. "And who knows, maybe Zeke is sitting out there like he's been promising you."

Isaac is one of my closest friends from my first year in college. He stands a few heads taller than me. His dark brown eyes glitter in the light as he beams. The red lights that trickle in from somewhere off stage make his brown skin glow enchantedly. He should be a model. His chiseled jaw making him more handsome, his incredible skin care routine also helps.

I roll my eyes. Zeke Marín is a random friend I made after *that night*. His hair is usually shaggy, curly, and black. He's tall, about 6'2, with a bulky, muscular body. He plays football for Knight University. He and his friends are powerful and basically dominate the school. Anything they don't like is usually gone the next day. They have that type of power. That type of money. Fucking loaded.

"He was at the last one when I did my femme fatale act," I comment with a slight smile.

"Well, he needs to come back."

"Curtain in one minute," a guy rushes past us saying. He checks our equipment and cables before disappearing on the other side of the curtain.

Cigarette smoke snakes behind the curtain and dances in the air. I watch the curls of the smoke slither through the air before vanishing into the lights overhead.

"Show time," Liam says with a wide grin snapping me back to reality. We get in our spots and wait for our cue.

When the curtain opens, the bar patrons sit at various tables scattered around the room. The dingy wood floor is dull and scuffed with puddles of beer and other liquid. A yellow caution sign sits by the newest mess, which was haphazardly cleaned. The room concept is open, spacious. Tables and chairs line the outside of the dance floor, which is just an open space with a spotlight.

The in-house lights are dim, but I can make out enough

faces to cool my nerves. Regulars. Each and every face is warm, familiar. My shoulders relax a bit as the room quiets down except for the occasional clacking of the pool balls from the back of the room.

"I want to thank you all for being here," Liam's raspy voice drones through the microphone as his finger strums a few notes. I join in, already hearing my in-ear monitors counting us down. Isaac taps his kick pedal into the bass drum getting us started.

My fingers press on the strings of my guitar, feeling the vibration as they sing. I start moving to Isaac's beat, avoiding the eyes of the crowd. The faces may be familiar, but I still don't want to be aware of *who* is staring at me.

The first song ends and I take a long swig of water. I turn and look at Isaac, who's spinning his drum stick.

"Killin' it, babe," I mouth when Isaac looks at me. He smiles and winks.

Liam's voice rumbles through the speakers as he explains why we chose the songs we did. It gives us time to adjust, drink water, anything to help make sure we're playing our best.

I look over at Clint, who adjusts his bass strings and switch-es out his pick. He nods towards me before I face the crowd. Looking in the audience, I see Zeke. His goofy smile greets me as he nods, acknowledging me.

I joke that he's got the personality of Beast Boy. The one from *Titans*, he kind of looks like him too.

He isn't alone this time. Even sitting under the lighting, his friends, Zeus, Freya, Sanjay, Rainn, and Kane, are perfectly beautiful. They radiate a power so intimidating and alluring, I see why people fall at their feet just to be in their aura. And anyone who's anyone knows them.

Zeus, a huge beast of a man with wavy brown hair and pale skin, sits next to his girlfriend, Freya, who looks like a goddess. Tall with a slender nose and full lips. Piercing, yet soulful hazel eyes peak from light brown skin. Her dark brown hair is cropped to her shoulders, accentuating the angles of her face. Beside her, Rainn tosses her strawberry blonde hair over her shoulder. She's a beautiful, curvy, plus-sized woman with pale skin. Her face is decorated with a labret piercing that sparkles in the light. Her boyfriend, Sanjay, drapes a thick arm around her. His naturally tan skin is reddened by the lights, a boyish grin on his youthful face.

Then there's Kane, the ladies' man. He's about 6'4 and every inch of him is muscular. Not in a body builder kind of way, either. His muscles are defined, with a softness to them. They have a purpose. Probably from years of playing football and working out.

His black hair falls at his shoulders and flips out slightly. Stubble of a forming mustache and beard ghost across his face, only making him more sinfully attractive.

A cross chain dangles from his neck, glittering against the light. I'm sure if I got closer, small black gauges would be in his ear. The darkness hides the tattoos that kiss both of his arms.

He looks a little uninterested until a girl walks past. He does little to nothing before she slides him something. He pockets it with a smirk before looking back at the stage, crossing his arm over his broad chest. The toned muscles of his arms bulge, making me think of how they'd feel pressed against me.

Despite his reputation, I've always had a slight crush on Kane. We've never really talked, but always happened to be in the same places and would greet each other every so often. We also had a few classes together from freshman year till now.

The rapping of Isaac's sticks pulls me back from letting my eyes roam any longer. Liam and I start strumming our next song, shifting my shoulders as my guitar strap digs into my arm. With a gentle roll of my shoulders, I manage to shift the position of my guitar. Once comfortable, I swing my hips to the beating of Isaac's drum finally getting back into the music.

Liam sings the first verse into the mic passionately and I join in attempting to avoid the gazes of onlookers now.

"Three more songs, then femme fatale," my in-ear crackles out as I back away from the mic. My guitar sings and I watch my pick strum out the melody, then harmonize with Liam.

Fixating my eyes on the back wall, I continue playing along. A slight shift from the pool tables catches my attention as some people stand, pool sticks in hand, watching us perform.

I look over to Liam and he gives me the cue. I sing a separate part of the chorus on my own a little closer to the mic. My eyes look towards the edge of the stage, where someone stands. I continue to move my body to the rhythm as I sing to them. She smiles, placing her hands on the edge of the stage swinging her hips until we play the final chords. Then, she bounces back to her friends with a giggle.

Clint tosses me a bottle of water and I catch it, crack it open, and take a long grateful gulp. It's fucking hot under these lights and my anxiety isn't helping it. I roll the knots in my shoulders a bit.

"Damn, E. Don't show me up now," Liam teases.

"Not hard to do," I say by the mic with a laugh, some people in the crowd joining in.

"Cocky are we?" He lifts an eyebrow.

I give him a pointed look with a sassy shoulder shimmy just as my hair tie pops. My hair comically falls over my face causing more laughs. I stare down at it, my shoulders shaking with my embarrassed giggles. I toss my hair out of my face and kick the broken band to the side of the stage.

We usually do a bit like this. Liam giving me a compliment and me shooting him something sassy back in response. People enjoy it, we enjoy it with them.

"That's what you get, Eb," Isaac says into his mic and I flip him off with a smile.

"Love you too," I retort back a little closer to the mic.

My eyes lock on Zeke, who smirks at me with a wink. I shake my head and hide my smile. Zeke is a flirt.

We finish our bit, then perform our second to last song. I feel the sweat running down my chest. I curse the lights as I finish off my second bottle of water. I shake my arms and legs as the nerves creep back.

"Hey, E," Isaac starts into his mic. I turn to look at him leaning into my mic getting ready to respond. "Save some of that ass shaking for when you perform later."

There's a loud whistle from someone in the back as the

audience cheers loudly. Claps rumble from various corners of the place.

"Fuck you, Isaac," I retort with a laugh, shaking my head.

"In my wildest dreams." I flip him off again, but give a little hip wiggle just to play along.

"Mine, too!" someone from the audience shouts. Probably Zeke, it sounds like him anyways. I cover my face, hiding my blush.

"Now kids," Liam says with a laugh.

Clint shakes his head laughing a bit, which means our little bickering is amusing him for once. The crowd is more engaged, laughing with our bickering back and forth.

"Sorry, Daddy," Isaac says seductively.

Whistles, cheers, and loud laughs echo through the bar. More people fill in the spaces laughing. This is how our shows go. We start with little to nothing, but we end up getting more before the show's done.

Liam tucks his lips, his shoulder shaking as he tries not to laugh. "These fucking kids," he pretends to groan looking at Clint.

"Are awesome, yeah?" I say looking over at him crossing my arms over my chest, arching my brow, and tapping my foot.

Liam shoots me a playful 'I'll kill you' look. "Love you, too, old man." I blow him a kiss.

"I'll kill—" he starts and I begin playing, stepping away from the mic to laugh. Liam stays put, laughing while he adjusts his guitar then plays along with me.

I chance another look at the audience and breathe. People sway and mouth the words to the songs. Zeke and his crew drink, the girls bob their heads to the beat, but the guys just stare.

Awkward? Very much so.

Liam thanks the crowd as I hand off my guitar and rush to the back. My dressing room is already open when I make it back there and I change quickly.

"Alright, E," DJ Shel starts. She's a short woman with a fade and dark brown skin. Her brown eyes are warm and remind me of home. Her voice is a bit deep and soothing.

She closes the door and pulls out her clipboard. "You're going to mix and mingle a bit and we'll play Jackson Wang's 'Blow.' When you leave, there should be some cool little gadgets that will let you blow out smoke. Then we'll do your cover for Dove Cameron's 'Boyfriend.'"

She hands me waivers with comments on it for me to look over while she keeps talking. "After that, your cover of Chloe Adams' 'Dirty Thoughts', and we'll end with you lip syncing Rosenfield's 'Do it For Me.' Sound good?"

"Can we do 'Dirty Thoughts' last? And I want to sing 'Do it For Me' live." I throw my soggy bra off, do a quick wipe down before putting on another. I glance down at the waivers and stare at one particular waiver. Zeke's cursive handwriting all over it. I smile, putting it with two others and hand them to DJ Shel.

"Yep, let me make those adjustments while I have you." She sets her computer down and does a few clicks. The lights on the screen replicate the swiveling and shifting that happens in the bar. Gramps got them updated when we started performing freshman year.

"This looks great!"

"Perfect!" She gathers her stuff and heads for the door. "Two minutes. I start with or without you," she adds with a smile.

The door clicks closed behind her and I rush to get ready. Slipping into a black lacy bralette that has my breasts spilling over the top. A pair of black "too little" shorts that hug my curves, at least that's what Gramps calls them. I pull on a form fitting black suit jacket that's designed to be a short, form fitting dress and suede thigh high stilettos. I put on long lasting red lipstick, check my teeth in the mirror, then rush out with my mic in my hand.

I walk down the dimly lit hallway and wait for my cue. Excitement bubbling in my stomach and chest. I close my eyes and focus on my breathing.

3

Kane Yamada

I don't know why Zeke has us sitting here watching a cover band play. I only came because: booze, girls, and pool, but he insisted we sit and watch the performance. I question his judgment. Don't get me wrong, they were fairly good and the girl would most definitely be on my roster, but other than that, I'd rather be schooling Zeus and Sanjay at the pool table.

"E usually does this performance that's sexy as hell. I talked to a little birdie to make sure it happens tonight," Zeke says with a smile.

Zeke and I stand at the bar, which is close to our table. He grabs his drink and leans against the dull wooden top. The bartender slides me a beer, I give him a nod and take a long grateful swig.

"A sexy performance?" Freya asks.

"Yeah. Think… burlesque, but with a little more clothes and more *hands on* approach."

There's a hummed acknowledgement from the table as everyone looks around the room drinking. Sanjay and Rainn duck their heads together, their fingers linked as they talk to each other. Dude is whipped.

"I gave her the rundown on everyone. She won't bother

17

you love birds," he adds, getting their attention, then blows them a kiss. Four middle fingers respond to his comments. I laugh, taking another drink of my beer.

"She's not gonna try to set us on fire or some shit is she?" I ask, crossing my arms over my chest. I stretch my legs out in front of me.

"You'll see," he says with a knowing smile.

He's hiding something. He's been my best friend all my life and I know that he's either hiding something we're going to absolutely love or would want to kill him for. I'm hoping for the latter.

Suddenly, the lights get dimmer and a song starts pulsating through the speakers. People start cheering and we look to the stage. There's anticipation lingering in the air. Everyone's excitement changing the somber mood that was settling into something more charged. The energy starts to make the hairs on my arms stand up.

"Give her a second," Zeke says before he downs his beer and fists a new drink. His smirk still etched on his face like he was born with it.

Then, she comes through the crowd, brown skin fucking glowing under the lights, round hips swaying, and her shoulders flowing to the rhythm. She owns this shit.

Black thigh high heels squeeze over thick ass thighs. Her suit jacket kissing all the right curves and barely covering that fat ass. Fuck. I'm already drawn to her and the performance just started.

I adjust my dick, watching as she approaches Zeke. Her full, red lips mouthing the words to the song.

He sits in the stool behind him and leans back smirking at her. Cocky fucker. How the hell does he know her? She shoots him a wink then struts my way.

She eyes me seductively, taking in every inch of me, but not the way she needs to. Trust me, I have plenty of inches she can take.

I already made a plan to get her out of that outfit and bent over the bathroom sink in two seconds once she's done.

She steps on the bar of the stool I'm sitting on, leans into my ear.

"Suck," she whispers seductively.

I think that's something I'd rather you do.

She puts something to her mouth, places her small, soft hands on my throat giving it a gentle squeeze, then blows smoke directly into my mouth. I suck in and watch as her head falls back slowly. The rest of the smoke comes out in a thick cloud of herbal goodness.

The beat kicks back in and her hips start swaying like she's giving me a lap dance. My lungs begin to burn before I blow the familiar smoke out of my mouth watching her dance. I hold myself back from pulling her closer so she can feel what she's doing to me. I focus on enjoying the buzz from the weed she shared with me.

She walks back to Zeke, grabs his hands giving him a little "private" dance. Her hips hover in the small space she keeps between them.

He gets closer to her, grabbing her hips and moving with

her. She pushes him back, stands on her tiptoes, and blows the smoke in his mouth before handing a blunt over to him. She saunters back into the crowd as Zeke blows out the smoke, takes another drag, then passes it to me.

She sways her hips in the empty space seductively dancing. Hands sliding down her body as the tight suit dress shifts giving glimpses of her lace covered tits. Her eyes looking over at me as she runs her hands back up, squeezes her tits, then clenches at her throat. She rolls her head back swinging her hips from side to side.

I. Am. Fucked.

My dick is stiff as fuck in my pants and the fact that she smells like Valentine's day candy, doesn't help. And I'm not talking about the cheap Valentine's day shit, I mean the expensive strawberries and chocolate kind. Warm and sweet once your tongue touches it. I wonder if she tastes that way too. I hope she does.

I grab my beer, taking another drink knowing damn well I shouldn't be thinking these things.

Zeke nudges me with his lips upturned and his tongue sticking out. This asshole is amused by the reaction I'm having watching her. Yeah man, she's fucking gorgeous.

We sit back at our seats while our other friends laugh at my face. I must have been in a daze because that damn vixen of a woman. Whatever was in her weed, I want more of it. Maybe it's just her. Either way, it's fucking intoxicating.

The song goes off and a slower melody comes on. She brings the mic to her lips and eyes someone. Her eyes are alluring with a bit of a warning to whoever she has her sights locked on. Her hand touches the back of the polished wooden chair she's standing near.

Instead of talking, she starts to sing, dragging the chair slowly behind her. It scrapes against the wooden floors, but barely makes a sound. Hell, the only one making a sound is her as she sings.

She sits in the chair in the middle of the floor. Then struts that sexy ass over to the woman she's been eyeing. She takes her hand, intertwines their fingers, and pulls her over to a chair.

She gently pushes the woman down and eyes her on some fem domme shit. *Yes, ma'am I'll do whatever you want, ma'am.* Her voice is siren-like as she sings close to the woman's ear.

E's small hand caresses the woman's arm making her shake. A blush rapidly spreads across her pale skin. E doesn't even have to touch anything but her thigh and the lady is already quivering.

Zeke looks around the table with a smirk. We're all glued to her. Trapped like bugs in a Venus fly trap, moths to a flame. Transfixed on this entertaining and beautiful sight.

She knows how to use her sex appeal and isn't afraid to get a few people hot and bothered in the process. A tease that will do whatever and whoever she wants in this moment.

We watch, leaning forward at our table, as E grabs the woman's legs and pulls her gently to the edge of her seat. The woman is steady, but stiff. Something I'm sure every guy in this place can relate to. Save the two at the table with me.

She straddles the woman, ghosting her juicy ass over the

woman's thighs. E swivels her hips and puts the woman's hands on her exposed thighs, then guides her hands up.

My palms tingle as I picture my hands on her exposed skin, imaging how warm and soft it is. How the taste of her sweet, sticky sweat would make every nerve on my body ignite. I have to drink my beer to keep from fidgeting.

She leans into the woman's ear, whispers something to her then slowly stands and lets her tits brush past the woman's face. The woman's tongue slides out of her mouth hoping to get a taste of E's skin, but E moves back, toying with her.

Her sultry voice comes out of the speakers like warm butter. Combining with the sexy sounds of the music, keeping everyone's eyes fixed on her and the show she's giving. A few people strain their necks for a better view. My eyes flick back to the performance not wanting to miss a second more.

E gets on her knees, a move that damn near makes me cum in my pants, and kisses the lady's thigh. I swear the lady must have had an orgasm right then because her head goes back and her chest vibrates as she pants. Her fingers grasp the edge of the seat so tight that her knuckles lose the color in them.

E grabs the woman's waist and pulls her closer. Their hips touching in the most intimate way that I almost think a very different show is about to take place. E's hand is firmly at the back of her chair before she tips it back and gives a few slow body roll-like thrusts.

"Ladies and gentlemen, E," Zeke announces as the song ends.

Applause fills the quiet space as E uprights the lady who's

still shaking. E speaks to her softly before escorting her back to her seat and kisses her on the cheek making the woman flush more. As E walks away, the woman's friends fan her as she smiles bashfully at them.

"She's gonna have my balls on E tonight if she comes over here again," I mutter as the bass drowns out my voice. Thankful Zeke didn't hear. He'd never let me live it down.

"Happy birthday to the birthday girl," E speaks into the mic with a soft laugh. Her voice is full, alluring as it resonates around us. She gestures towards the woman she was just all over and the spotlight illuminates the birthday girl in question.

I don't look or clap for the birthday girl. My eyes are glued on E as she walks around in those killer heels. She takes a drink of water and nods at someone off in another direction. Another song comes on and E looks over her shoulder.

She waggles her finger beckoning them forward. From bashful and sweet to primal. The lady slowly stands and E walks over to get her with a smile.

She sings into the mic as she places the woman's hands on her body. The woman does a giddy little wiggle before rubbing her hands up E's front. E throws her head back, rolls her head around then looks in the woman's eyes.

The woman kneels before E, sputtering something as E pins her with a dominant stare. She moves her hips from side to side and the woman moves closer to her. Her face only inches away from E's pussy.

E slowly puts her leg over the woman's shoulder, grabs a fist full of hair from the nape of the woman's neck and gets in her face. *She's flexible.* The sputtering stops and she just stares in awe.

"I feel like I shouldn't be watching this, but I can't help myself," Rainn mutters.

E puts her leg down, guides the woman to her feet and spins her around changing the hold she has on her hair. The woman bends forward and E slowly thrusts her hips seductively. She rolls her head back and closes her eyes.

I lean back in my chair and steady my breathing, catching E's attention. Her eyes are blazing when she looks at me. No longer the innocent and sassy girl in the band, that part of her is tucked away. Those eyes are now filled with sin. This woman could eat your heart out and make you want to get another one for her.

I'm willing to toss out all the numbers I got tonight just to fuck her right now. I don't care who's watching at this point.

She lays the woman down on her back and crawls over her as the music blares. She dives close to the woman's belly button and slowly snakes her way up to her face with her ass up in the air. She runs her hands down the woman's body and turns her on her stomach.

E whispers something and the lady arches her back and E taps her ass with a smirk. "Good, girl," she says in the mic, her voice sensual, raspy even. She smirks, giving the woman's ass another slap.

Using her hand with the mic to brace the woman from underneath, E gives another slow thrust. She grabs her hips, slowly rolling her hips until she places her chest against the woman's back.

She whispers the background lyrics in the woman's ear as the swell of the music takes over. E places the mic down and grabs the lady's throat softly. Finger tips brush down red flesh as E runs her hands up the woman's side.

I put my hand over my mouth chewing on my cheek. The image I have of her in my head in that position would have my parents ashamed of me.

As the last notes of the song end, she's back to her innocent looking self as she helps the lady up and back to her seat.

The woman's skin is flush, and she's breathing heavily. I guarantee if E asked her to fuck, she'd be more than willing to jump in line too. She better know I was first, second, third, and last in that line at this point.

She squats down with her knees together talking to the lady as she interlocks their fingers. The woman, so damn red, is nodding and giggling.

The drummer from the set before rushes out with water and E kisses the woman on the forehead. A sweet, kind gesture that has the woman turning even more red.

"Holy fuck," Freya says from behind me. "She's good."

The next song comes on after the lady sits down and E's eyes fixate on me. She takes a slow step and lets her eyes roam over me from head to toe. No longer a curious look, but one that looks like she's planning something.

Game on, baby. Come to Daddy.

She struts over without breaking eye contact, but sits on Zeke's knee. She looks at him singing the first verse to him, caressing his face. His hungry eyes devour every inch of her. His hand brushing up her thigh slowly, then her eyes cut to me as she sings the chorus.

She grabs another chair and takes a seat in front of me. Then she gets to her next verse, she crosses her legs revealing her smooth brown skin that I want to mark up in the most delicious ways. She puts her elbow on her knee and her chin on her palm. Her eyes dance between sweet and innocent to the devious and sinful like I saw earlier.

As she gets to the part about being good-looking naked, her eyes roam over me before she smirks and nods. I lick my lips with a smirk.

Damn right I do.

She grabs the middle of the chair's seat and stands, her ass pointed towards the table behind her. She moves the chair and places a heel between Zeke's legs as she sings the chorus to me. His hand rubs up from her calf to her thigh before she walks over.

Her fingers crawl over my shoulder. When the rhythm of the song changes, she grabs my thick, black hair and pulls it back softly.

My tongue rolls around in my mouth as our eyes lock. Fire burning right behind her brown orbs. Her eyes trace my face, stop on my lips, then take their time coming back to mine again.

Kicking her leg over my thick, toned legs, she straddles me, placing her round ass on my thighs.

My hands immediately grab them, sliding up her silky skin. I know she can feel how hard I am as she grinds against me, throwing her head back. I try to stifle my groan as she pushes herself closer.

Her mic still in her hand as she pushes her tits against my chest and sings softly in my ear.

I can't help the slight grind I give back as her hips circle around again.

With her hand on my neck, she tips my head back, then licks from the base of my throat to my ear giving the lobe a little nip.

I squeeze her thighs hard and continue slowly grinding against her the entire time.

She gets up, pushing herself off of me, then saunters off. Hips swinging and ass naturally jiggling.

I grab my beer and throw back what's left, but it doesn't do shit. I look in the direction she walked off to, ignoring my friend's laughter.

The room fills with applause and whistles.

"The Ebony effect," Zeke states, looking at me wiggling his eyebrows.

"Yeah, I bet," I say dryly looking in the direction she walked off. I wonder if I could find her dressing room if I really tried.

4

Ebony

"Holy shit, E!" Isaac gushes as I get changed. "I don't know how you fucking do it, but you did that."

I laugh, wiping down with a damp cloth then pulling on a tie up top and baggy 'boyfriend' jeans. A stark contrast compared to the sexy outfit I wore earlier. I throw on my Converse after stretching my aching toes.

"And the fact that Kane fucking Yamada looked like he wanted to fuck you on that table. Zeke, too. Ma'am. God gave you gold."

"Is that really a compliment though? Kane and Zeke get around," I comment.

I don't care that they get around. I've had my share of hookups. A lot of my shares actually. I just don't think them wanting to fuck me was as much as a compliment as Isaac thought. Don't get me wrong, I'm flattered that Kane was *very into* my performance. But what ladies' man wouldn't like a half-naked woman that sings about sex?

"Like you wouldn't let him hit?" Isaac crosses his arms and looks at me with an arched eyebrow.

I roll my tongue around the inside of my bottom lip and hide my blush.

Busted.

Let me clarify: me thinking him wanting to fuck me wasn't a compliment and actually wanting to do the deed are two completely different things in my eyes.

"Exactly!"

He squeals and kicks his legs excitedly. "You dry humped him!"

I remember. My skin warms thinking about how his hands gripped my thighs. I squeeze them together remembering how hard he was. The gossip doesn't do him any justice in that department. Mans is packing.

I normally don't scoot closer to customers or even pick men out of the crowd. It always felt wrong, but the way he stared at me when I walked out sparked something in me. I wanted to push him. I wanted to see what would make him tick. It also helped that Zeke set him up for it to happen.

Isaac sits in a chair and looks at me. "Let the party girl back out, E. Have fun. Have threesomes again."

I snort at him trying not to laugh. Party girl E was wild. That is until I decided I needed extra protective measures that involved very little "fun." Sex included.

I finish getting dressed and adjust my pants, getting distracted at how my body looks in my jeans.

I'm not the skinniest girl. More like midsized. Get the right pants and I feel like the sexiest woman in the world, get the wrong style and I feel like I look sloppy. I constantly battle my thoughts on how my body looks, but performing helps—especially when it's sexy. Tonight, these jeans only accentuate my ass. That's a win for now.

"I'm going to the bar up front after this, wanna come?" I ask Isaac after catching his eye in the mirror.

"No. Zeke is there and I'm not going to cheat on my boyfriend. He won't even let me use a hall pass despite him using his."

I roll my eyes and walk out of my dressing room with Isaac. Despite Zeke being popular, Isaac just recently laid eyes on him at a party. After that, he's always been infatuated with Zeke. It amuses Zeke more than anything. He's a flirt that likes to toy with people, but he means well. Sometimes.

"By the way, what did you have them shotgun out there? Didn't look like the play smoke we used last year for Halloween."

I wiggle my eyebrows at Isaac and giggle. I'm willing to bend rules to make our performances better. No one usually gets hurt and if anyone does, it's me. It was just weed and I needed a little extra courage.

"They're going to kick your ass out if you do it again!" Isaac swats at my arm.

"It's cool. Zeke says they smoke. He's been wanting a shotgun from me for a minute. Made his dream come true."

"But your Gramps ain't cool with it." Isaac rolls his eyes at me. "I'll catch you later. Keith's outside waiting on me. I told him Zeke is here and he's freaking out on me."

"That's why you don't tell your boyfriend that the guy you have a crush on is here," I nudge him before we part ways.

I see Zeke before he sees me. Giddy excitement takes

over as I run up to him and wrap my arms around his bulky midsection. "If it isn't my favorite slut."

I notice eyes shift to me. Angry, offended, protective eyes. *Well fuck. Remind me to not call Zeke a slut around them.*

"Does that make you my favorite co-slut?" He turns and embraces me.

"I'm reformed," I shrug, then nod with a smile on my face. His hands inch towards my ass and I grab his arm tightly and glare. "Hands."

"What about a kiss then?" He leans in and I dodge him.

"You ruined the moment," I grumble.

He laughs and throws his heavy arm around my shoulder. "Everyone this is Ebony aka E or Eb. E this is… my family." He smiles fondly.

I wave at everyone giving them a soft 'Hi.' They study me closely. The tension from earlier dissolving. They wave while still studying me, but without the protective fire.

"She planned an orgy for me the beginning of last semester. Shit was incredible," he says casually as he offers me his lap. There's sputtering and coughing as my face twists in disgust. Even if he's a new friend of mine, I'm used to the crazy shit that he says. I look over at him and he smiles, patting his upper thigh then outstretching his hands.

"Best seat in the house, babe." He winks.

"Is there ever a moment where that gorgeous head on your shoulders works in interactions?"

"No. I'm pure sex and rage." Zeke pulls me on his lap, not shy to nuzzle his face in the nape of my neck. I edge away laughing. He may be a flirt, but he knows my boundaries. It took time to get here. Time and trust. "I'm willing to give you a taste."

Everyone laughs except Kane. He's drinking a beer and his eyes are fixated on me, roaming over my body. He leans back in his chair, a ghost of a smirk on his lips.

"Wait. Ebony, I think you modeled for my photography class," Freya interjects. "I was trying to think of why you looked so familiar."

"Yeah!" I exclaim. I pop Zeke's wandering hands and stand up, shooting him another glare. "How'd your project come out?"

"Better than expected. I'll have to send you the images sometime!"

I smile at her nodding. Music fills the space as I look around the table. Loud conversations fill the space as Zeke leans his chin on my shoulder. I lay my head against him as he talks to me about an idea he had for a party.

Kane puts his empty bottle on the bar top and slides it away looking around for Clint or the other bartenders. A soft sigh passes his lips before he looks back at me. His mysterious eyes taking me in. Questions hang under them as his eyes go between Zeke and me. I feel Zeke's face shift as he smiles.

"Drinks?" I ask, Zeke nods and lifts his head.

Walking around the bar, I squeeze past Clint who's mixing a drink. I notice the group moves closer together talking amongst themselves. They laugh and Kane's eyes dart over towards me. Heat and tension passing between us. His eyes drink me in before he looks over at Zeus laughing at something he said. *God his smile is beautiful.*

I grab a few beers and start mixing a drink.

"Hey, E?" Rainn asks.

I look up at her, sliding Zeke a drink. His hand grabs mine and I pop it. My eyes shooting over to him to send yet another glare. Zeke laughs, taking his glass and drinks, allowing me to focus back on Rainn.

"Do you normally perform like that?"

I shake my head. "It's rare, but brings in a lot of money." I use a hair tie to pin my locs back out of my face. "Drink?"

She shakes her head, then leans into Sanjay. The two very clearly in their own little world. He plants a kiss on her forehead and grabs the beer I slide him.

"I doubt an orgy is why you two are friends," Zeus interjects with an inquisitive glint in his eyes.

"Well, E here has equal opportunity pus—"

"I will rip your dick off," I cut him off through a gritted tooth smile.

Freya, Rainn, and Sanjay stifle their laughs with their glass. Zeus looks amused at the grin on Zeke's face. Kane looks away with a slight shake of his head, a smirk pulling at his full lips.

He runs his thick fingers through his hair, giving me a better look at the tattoos on the inside of his arm. His sleeve's intertwined and beautifully designed around the contours of his skin and muscles. As he shifts his hand, fisting his beer, I notice the ink on one of his knuckles.

"She's in the rainbow mafia with me." Zeke shrugs.

"See, isn't that nicer than saying what you were going to say?" I look at Zeke warmly.

"No. I still like saying 'equal opportunity pussy.'" He drinks his beer with a smirk. I roll my eyes clearing up the empty bottles from the bar top.

"Is your preference women then? Or is that just a performance thing?" Rainn asks.

I think for a moment, chewing my cheek before responding. "I don't really have a preference dating wise, but performance wise, I prefer women. Some of them are softer, easier to work with. It also helps that I can move the chair with them in it," I laugh. "As for guys, they're like this guy," I point to Zeke, "they don't take directions well. Most that come here always want to be in charge."

Rainn nods thoughtfully. She takes Sanjay's beer, taking a sip then sticking her tongue out at him.

Kane leans close to the bar. A sweet smell of cinnamon sugar and spices rolls off of his skin pulling me closer to him. "So, you picked me because you couldn't resist me?"

Sanjay and Zeus pop him in the back of the head rolling their eyes making him and Zeke laugh.

"I picked you because Zeke paid me extra to get a rise out of you. Did it work?" I brace my hands on the bar as I lean in. A smile deepening on my face as his eyes drop to my breasts then back to my face. Our eyes hold each other for a moment. A knowing look plastered on his handsome face.

"Ebony," Clint calls from the other side of the bar. I tear my eyes from Kane's and look at Clint. "Need some help back here for a second." I tap the counter and look back at Kane one last time before rushing off.

"Hurry back," Zeke shouts with a playful giggle.

5

Kane

Music blares from the speakers around the place, someone must have turned up the volume. Girls brush past me letting their fingers trail against the muscles of my back to get my attention subtly. I glance back for a second then focus back on my drink.

I normally would have chased behind them, but my mind's already planning how I'm going to spend my night.

When I turn back, my eyes land on Ebony. She's elbows deep in the ice machine. Her ass poking out of those jeans. She stands with a mixer full. The top closes with a pop and she starts to shake and my eyes watch gratefully. The big guy that asked for her help rings someone up on the register.

She passes a drink over the counter, takes money, then slides it in the cash register and takes a moment, dancing to the song surrounding us. Someone cheers her on and she laughs, popping the top of a low end beer brand and sliding it across the counter. A large bill is passed to her and she thanks whoever gave it to her and shoves it in her pocket.

The energy between us fizzling, simmering along the surface of my brain waiting for the next interaction. She won't keep her attention on me for long. I'm sure I know why, but

I also have a feeling she's one you shouldn't make assumptions about.

"On your left," the big guy says over the music as he brushes past her with his arms full of liquor bottles.

My other friends left a few minutes ago, leaving Zeke and I alone at the bar, which is becoming crowded. I'm assuming the show sparked a little inspiration in them. Then again, they're always all over each other.

Love struck fuckers.

"E," Zeke calls out to her. "Eb!" he shouts louder.

She turns quickly. The light catches her big brown eyes making them glitter. Zeke holds his glass out towards her and she walks over wiping her hand in a towel she has looped through her belt loops.

"You need to slow down, Zeke," she scolds, fixing his drink. "This is like your fifth in 30 minutes." She slides him a water putting his drink on the counter behind the bar. "Drink this, then you get your drink."

"Aw, you do care about me," Zeke coos. He chugs the water. Then reaches out his hand wiggling his fingers.

She glares at him. "Don't be a dick."

He laughs in turn taking a sip of his drink.

"You want another drink?" Ebony asks me. Her eyes lock onto mine and that charged energy comes rushing back. Her hand rests on the counter after she hands Zeke his drink.

A ring on every finger but one. A large tattoo decorates her forearm on her right arm and two small ones rest in the skin on her left arm.

"I got it, E flat," the big guy says. "Go hang with your… friends." He eyes us suspiciously. "Let me know when you're leaving."

There's a little extra warning he's not vocalizing for her. A silent communication going on between them as she looks at him. The joy seeping from her face for a moment, then she nods, shoving it all down and walks around the bar to join us.

"You should have planned an orgy after this. Shit would have been a huge relief," Zeke slurs looking at her.

He shifts in his seat letting his eyes roam over her body. The look in his eye isn't heated, not like it normally is when he sees someone he wants, but there's a hint of it.

"Zeke," she starts with a laugh, "you have enough people you can call to hook up with."

"I mean yeah, but there's one right beside me that won't budge." He nudges Ebony.

"This big guy?" She points to me trying not to smile.

"Fuck that," I grumble.

Stepping closer to her as the crowd grows, I bask in the warmth of her body heat. Being this close to her makes my head buzz like I'm drunk. I step closer intentionally now, my hips close to hers, hovering the line of giving her no personal space and occupying my own.

"I'm pretty sure he and I would rather have you," Zeke shrugs and sways a bit in his seat.

She startles and reaches for him instantly. The look of concern on her face makes me even more curious about how close they are. Her hands are gentle as she steadies him against the wall beside him.

"I don't think Kane wants to take me home," she laughs after she pops his hand away from her thigh.

"Who says I don't?" Her head whips around and I quirk an eyebrow. If she isn't going to make another move, then I am.

A slight red rises under the deep brown in her cheeks only making her color richer, deeper. A sexy undertone that only compliments her skin tone more.

"And I know you've heard the stories." Zeke licks his lips and slouches against the bar, laughing.

He's completely wasted, so even if I could get Ebony to agree to let me fuck, I'd have to take care of that asshole first.

"Who hasn't?" She looks between the two of us. "You're both sexually infamous on campus."

"All good things I hope," I say to her, finishing my drink, then taking a peek at Zeke. He's two seconds from falling asleep. "Shit. I gotta get him home," I grumble as I step to the side to reach for him.

"Let me help," she offers in a rush.

She lifts Zeke's head and talks to him softly. "Hey, big guy. You gotta get up so you can go home." She brushes his curly hair back out of his face and taps it lightly. He groans.

"If you touch me like that again…" he stops talking, barely able to keep his eyes open. She laughs to herself.

Helping me get his arm over my shoulder, she guides me out the door to the hot summer night air. Crickets screech in various bushes around the building. The yellow light hanging outside the door blinks periodically.

"Do you guys have a car or a rideshare you can call?" She looks up at me.

"We walked." I lean him against the wall and run my hands through my hair, then dig for my phone in my pocket. I press the button a few times and groan. It's dead.

"Umm, wait, I drove. My Gramps hates me being out here late at night. I'll drive you guys."

She rushes back inside the bar before I can deny her offer, not that I would have tried very hard to. I brace Zeke's weight on my shoulder again.

"This would have been a great wingman move if you hadn't gotten shit faced, man," I grumble.

I have Zeke wedged between my hip and the brick wall off to the side, but he still staggers a bit. He grumbles under his breath, but for the most part, he's black out drunk.

I look back towards the bar. My plan? To get Zeke settled in his room with her help, then get her into my room for some additional *help*. Limited clothing, if necessary. And if she hesitates, give her a little taste to make her come back for the full thing.

6

Ebony

I'm not sure how I went from helping Zeke into bed, to a hot make out session in Kane's bed, but here I am with my hands in his soft hair. His front pressed to mine as the TV drones on in the background. He pulls my leg over his, pushing his erection against me, coaxing a moan from my mouth.

Panic rushes through me causing me to push away and roll off his bed. Thoughts and images bouncing through my mind as I look at his flushed face. My chest rising and falling as I catch my breath. Nerves bubbling up.

I'm safe. I'm okay. My mind repeats.

He sits up, pushing himself to the edge of the bed looking at me curiously. "Want to stop?" his deep, husky voice asks. His lips are red, swollen from our make out session.

I look at the closed door, then back at him shaking my head, feeling all my anxiousness slowly unravel. I lean in towards him, sealing our lips together. One of his hands grips the back of my neck as our lips move in sync. Our tongues explore each other's taste as he grabs my thigh, pulling me onto his lap.

The bed springs squeak as I straddle him, his free hand groping at my ass as I shift more on his lap. Strong arms hold me as he turns our bodies to hover over me. He palms my breast over my shirt, groaning into my mouth.

"You're very, very overdressed," he mutters slowly onto my lips.

He trails kisses from my chin down to where my shirt is tied. He unravels the loop, then tosses it to the floor.

"Fuck," he groans, taking a pierced nipple in his mouth. I moan, arching my back to push my breast deeper in his mouth.

We work together to pull his shirt off his broad body and I run my hands up his six pack. I can make out the tattoos on his chest, exhaling sharply as it turns me on more. He flexes with a cocky grin making me laugh.

"Come back down here and kiss me," I sigh, reaching for him.

With a firm grasp, he holds my neck and pulls me back to his mouth. Our lips crash back together as his hand kneads at my breast. His fingers ghost down my skin to the waistband of my pants.

"Need these off," he groans, then helps me shimmy out of my pants. His tongue teasing my lips just as he tosses them to the side.

Aggressive kisses skitter down my throat before he sucks right on the base near my collar bone. His fingers grasp my locs in the back of my head and he tugs firmly.

"Fuck," I moan. A silly, lustful smile on my face.

"I knew you'd like that," he whispers against my hot skin, his hand sliding up my thighs, kneading them as he slowly makes his way up.

My body trembles under his touch. Gasps making my chest

heave. His feathery touches a stark contrast to his aggressive squeezes.

"All that fucking teasing you did," he slides his hand over my clothed pussy before pulling the fabric to the side and pushing his middle finger in me.

"Oh my god." A whimper-whisper escapes from my mouth as my head leans back against his bed spread.

"You can call me that later," he chuckles against my skin, adding another finger. He groans, "so tight."

He kisses me deeply before pulling my panties off and dipping his head between my thighs.

He licks at my wetness before sucking on my clit, making my back arch more. He hums against my clit, pulling noises from my throat I didn't know I could make. My hips grinding against his mouth, fingers digging and pulling at his silky hair as he holds my thighs open, anchoring me to his bed as I chase my building orgasm.

"I'm going to make you scream my fucking name, Ebony," he growls before sucking on my thigh. His hand runs up my body as he trails kisses back to my pussy. "Fuck. You taste so fucking good," he groans into me.

My shaking thighs push and struggle against his strong grip. My breathing becomes labored and rushed as my orgasm titters over the edge. He continues sucking my clit as he inserts another finger, curling and thrusting them faster. His eyes watching me intensely.

"You look sexy as fuck coming undone for me. Such a sexy fucking slut."

I cum hard, my muscles convulsing around his pumping fingers and his name falls from my lips like a secret I can't keep. My thighs vibrate as the tremors start to subside.

He pulls his fingers out of me kissing his way up to my mouth.

"Taste yourself," he whispers over my parted lips.

His tongue diving deep in my mouth. He shifts his lower body, removing his pants and boxers. His dick falling onto my leg, hot and thick. He rolls his hips over mine, coating his shaft in my wetness.

I reach for it, but he grabs my wrist. "Not yet."

His fingers go back inside of my pussy and I moan against his mouth. My mind scrambles as he thrusts and uses his palm to simulate my clit.

"That's it. Cum for me." He leans into my ear. "Your pussy's so fucking pretty wrapped around my fingers like this." His tongue licks up my neck and I shudder. A whimper falling from my lips. "I can't wait to shove my dick deep inside you."

I moan his name, feeling another orgasm rip through me. I grip the sheets, throwing my head back attempting to fuse myself to his bed. Blinding white light fills my eyes and his voice tethers me to this moment.

"Look at that," he purrs. "You should look at the mess you made," he chuckles with a hint of cockiness. He knows what he's doing and I'm putty in his fucking hands.

I open my eyes and catch him tasting his fingers. He nods towards my thighs and I see the wet spot from my orgasm. "You're so good with your hands."

"Just my hands?"

"The rest is up for review." My voice is breathy as I come down from an orgasmic high.

He smirks at me as he strokes himself. His eyes survey me before he stands straight.

"Let me feel how good those juicy lips feel around my dick," he groans.

The comforter shifts under my knees as I kneel in front of him. Getting on my hands, I seductively crawl the short distance to him.

"There she is. I was wondering where that deviant side went," he comments standing.

His dick pulsates in my hand as I grab it, giving it a slow stroke. Pre-cum glistens on the tip before oozing out and rolling down his shaft. With hooded eyes, I slowly lick the tip then run my tongue down the base.

His body shudders with this action and a groan slips past his lips.

Our eyes meet and I give his head a wet kiss before running my tongue from base to tip. I slide the head in my mouth and he thrusts deep.

"Such a fucking tease," he groans as he grabs my hair and angles my head to push his dick deeper in my mouth, making me gag.

"None of that. You're gonna swallow this dick."

I catch up to the pace he sets and I use my arms to brace myself on the bed. I suck deep and attempt to open my throat more as he slides deeper in my mouth.

"Damn," he groans, closing his eyes and shuddering again.

I grab his balls, massaging them gently. My tongue swirls around the tip as he pulls back. I use my tongue against the underside as he pushes back in.

He pulls his dick out of my mouth and grabs my throat, pulling me up to kiss him. I move on my knees, placing his dick between my thighs. "How's my dick taste?"

"So good," I whisper as I rub my clit against the tip of his dick. Soft moans bubble out of me as the sensation increases.

He reaches in his nightstand and grabs a condom from a box. He rips the wrapper and watches me rock my hips against him. I lay on my back, using my fingers to stimulate myself as he rolls the condom on. His weight shifts the bed beneath me as he climbs over me, then pushes deep inside me and stops for a second.

"You're so tight," he growls, putting his forehead to my shoulder for a moment. He nips at my neck as he rolls his hips. His large hands grab my wrists, pinning them above my head, and setting a faster pace.

He fills me completely, stretching me open in ways I've experienced only a handful of times. Our bodies are sticky with sweat as the heat between us increases.

"So fucking wet and ready for me," he groans, thrusting harder, faster. The bed springs begin to squeak under his movements.

I revel in the feeling of his dick sliding in and out of me. The slight pain of his fingers digging into my tiny wrists. His mouth finds mine as we sloppily kiss.

My hips find his rhythm and work against him for more friction. I squeeze my walls around his shaft and he groans in my mouth.

"You're gonna make me cum doing that," he says against my mouth.

He shifts his weight, slowing his pace to pin my hip down with his free hand, then thrusts harder. The sound of his body driving into mine taking over the sounds of our moans and the TV still playing in the background.

"You hear how wet you are? So fucking wet for me," he growls in my ear, getting more aggressive.

Another whimper escapes my lips as his shaky breaths tip me to the edge of an orgasm. He slows down, pulling me from the ledge, toying with me.

His strong hands turn me on my stomach and he slaps my ass.

"Keep that ass up." He plants a kiss on my shoulder blade as I get on my knees, spreading them for him slightly, and arch my back.

He slaps my ass harder, making me moan into his mattress. His hard, rough thrusts send his balls colliding deliciously with my clit.

"So. Fucking. Good." His thrusts emphasizing each word. Throwing my ass back, I match his tempo. "Good girl, fuck me back just like that." His palm connects with my ass again and I moan at the stinging sensation.

I turn my head as he leans back, letting me take control. He watches how his dick enters my body. He looks at me with a sexy smirk, then rubs my clit.

"So damn sexy," he groans, grabbing my hips and pounding into me harder. "This is what you wanted? Hmmm? Humping me in that chair. You wanted me to fuck you like the sexy slut you are?"

Words cease to exist. It is what I was hoping for, and he is delivering it and then some. Moans spill from my mouth as he pushes and grinds his hips against me.

"You take my dick so well," he groans.

He pulls me against his chest, one hand pulling my hair, the other bracing me as he adjusts his position for better leverage.

I wrap my arm around his neck and lean my head on his shoulder as his body slams into mine. His muscles flex against my back as his hips move, pushing deeply into my body.

"Right there, I'm so close," I whimper.

His hand lets go of my waist as he rubs fast, gentle circles on my clit. I shudder, holding on tightly.

"Cum all over this dick, Ebony," he whispers in my ear. "Be a good girl and cum for me."

My body shudders as my pussy clenches his dick and I scream his name.

"That's right. Let everyone know who's making this pussy cum." His breath is shaky in my ear. "I want you to cum one more time for me, Ebony." His fingers still working my clit.

I whimper as I feel it building up again already. My head is swimming higher and higher as his dick swells and spasms inside of me. He groans before biting my shoulder, making me cum again. I grasp him tightly like a lifeline. Our bodies shuddering as strangled groans fill the space. His lips find my neck as he sucks on my flesh before we collapse on his bed.

"Oh my fucking God." My voice is breathy as I pant. His body shifts off of me and he laughs.

"Hell yeah," he pants, pulling me to him and sliding his tongue into my mouth. We kiss for a moment before we relax back on the bed.

My satiated body lays heavy and blissful as I hear him move around. A soft blanket touches my sweaty skin and he wraps his arms around me.

I feel myself falling asleep before I can decide to get dressed and go home.

7

Kane

One Week Later

I'm sitting in a humid office that smells like unwashed ass and rat piss. Sure, the building was updated last semester, but that was just to add a new addition, which sticks out like a sore thumb. The floors are still an ugly muddle of green and yellow. The desk looks like it's been kicked in and patched up a couple hundred times over the last decade. I rest my arms on the arm rest of the rickety, tattered chair I'm sitting in and feel something sticky beneath my palm. I grimace and slide my hands on my lap.

"Mr. Yamada," a woman with salt and pepper hair smiles at me from over the dated wooden desk. "Dr. Sumner will see you now."

I walk past her desk and in through the door on the left without knocking. I'd much rather get this whole thing over with.

"Good to see you, Mr. Yamada," Dr. Sumner, a man in his late forties, greets me. He's balding, but refuses to let it go. He has a small beard on his round face. He's shorter than me by a foot, which isn't saying much since I tower over most people.

"If I'm seeing you, I doubt that," I say with a dry laugh as I shake his hand and sit in a wobbly chair.

"You make a valid point," he laughs, then clears his throat. An awkward silence settles into the air and he clears his throat again. "Mr. Yamada, you're a star student so it pains me to have to meet with you under these circumstances."

He adjusts his tie and smoothes his jacket. I make him nervous. Good. I settle in my chair with that knowledge.

"But the dean and admissions office have made the determination to put you on academic probation," he concludes. He fidgets again.

"One call to my parents and that's cleared up," I say leaning my chin on my fist.

"Unfortunately, your parents agree that this is the best way to handle a situation like this."

"What I'm being accused of wasn't even anything bad," I protest.

He pulls out my file, pulls out a slip of white, yellow, and pink papers, and slides on a pair of gold wire frame glasses. He reads over the documents and verbalizes my offenses.

"Mr. Yamada, you 'replaced the bookstore's URL with a free digital book download site, costing the bookstore close to $100,000 in lost revenue.' It's also documented that you 'destroyed a golf cart by driving it into the campus pond, killing all of the Koi fish.'"

"Allegedly," I add, trying not to laugh.

"You were caught on camera," he looks at me unamused and frustrated. "Which you also attempted to erase, but were caught by Officer Kilter."

Good ole Officer Kilter and I had this thing. I'd fuck shit up and vanish, and he'd be left with nothing. As for the books, they're already more expensive than they should be. The school gets plenty of money, they can stand to lose a few bucks.

When he caught me red handed trying to tape over the archaic footage of me crashing the golf cart, a complete accident by the way, he rejoiced.

No, really. He broke out into a whole dance routine in the middle of the doorway after cuffing me.

I got sloppy. I admit it, but it won't happen again.

"If you won't accept academic probation," he starts.

I sit forward in my seat waiting for something interesting to come out of his mouth.

"You'll be kicked off the football team for the time you remain here. That was a recommendation from your parents."

Well, fuck.

"So, either take the slap on the wrist or deal with the real consequences." He takes a moment staring at me. He releases a sigh and adjusts in his seat. "I know you've been anticipating meeting the scouts this year so you can play pro. I bet you'd rather take academic probation instead of not playing at all."

"Yeah," I say dryly. The second punishment gave me a swift kick in the ass. I didn't think my parents would let something like that happen. Guess they're sick of my shit. "How long will I be on academic probation?"

"For the semester, then the following semester you'll have time to complete the volunteer hours. You'll need to do 35 hours a week."

I knew academic probation sounded too light a punishment. Don't get me wrong, it wasn't a bad punishment for the damages I caused, even though I replaced the golf cart the next day.

I'm no mechanic, but I thought I did a fantastic job getting it to get back into working order. Maybe it was the Koi fish that did them over. I do feel bad about that.

"I'll take your silence as you agree to the terms and conditions?"

I begrudgingly nod. He slides a form over locking me into the deal. With a quick, angry swipe of a pen that barely works, I sign away my trouble making ways.

I hop out of my seat like there's a fire under my ass and head for the door.

"Oh, Mr. Yamada," I stop, waiting for him to continue. "We have discussed with your parents that if there is any more trouble from you at any point in this semester, that you will be expelled. That was the schools only non-negotiable."

A growl rips through my chest as I trudge out of his office, past the front desk.

"Miss Young? Dr. Sumner is ready for you."

Chocolate covered strawberries fill my senses as someone quickly walks past me. I stumble over my feet trying to stop quick enough to see if it's Ebony, but I only catch the office door closing.

I don't know why I wanted it to be her. It's not like she'd let us hook up again.

I can still hope.

I glance at the door one more time before trudging out of the office to get ready for conditioning.

8

Ebony

Two Weeks Later

A record-breaking heat wave rolls through during the first week of classes. And there are no clouds to block the sun's angry rays. I'm forced to scramble and find a sliver of shade to stay remotely cool in the grass of the courtyard, which sits in the heart of campus, surrounded by small cafes, restaurant style fast food joints, and bookstores. The campus is beautiful. Trees that hold brightly colored flowers in the spring line some of the pathways. Benches sit on the edge of the walking path leading to academic valley, where most of the academic buildings can be found, dorms and on campus apartments, and some other campus buildings.

I unroll my lavender yoga mat underneath the shade of a large tree. I pull at my workout shorts and start to stretch. Denise, my best friend since middle school, stands beside me. She's about two inches shorter than me with curvier hips and chest. Her medium brown skin is decorated with tattoos and a septum piercing. She's stunning, glowing. *Beautiful.* Isaac lounges beside her on his own yoga mat with his phone in his hand. He takes a few pictures before fanning himself.

"I understand being zen, but in this heat?" He shades his

eyes from the sun as it shifts in the sky. "I'm all for a good golden hour selfie session, but this sun is beating my ass."

"My therapist says vitamin D and yoga are supposed to help boost your mood," Denise explains as she looks at a book and follows the image on the page.

"You sure they didn't mean getting some D?"

I cackle beside Denise as I sit with my legs tucked beneath me.

"Only you would say that shit." Denise shakes her head with a ghost of a smile on her face.

"It's true." He leans back against the tree he's close to. "Look, the other day I was pissed at Keith. Then we did the do and I'm good."

"I could have gone all day without knowing about any of that, Isaac," I groan, trying not to laugh.

"Well now you know!" Isaac says with a wide smile. "By the way, D, did she tell you about her performance two weeks ago?"

"Barely! Girl's been running around tryna save her peers and shit." She nudges me, her eyes sparkling with pride. She's supportive about the work I've been doing. Always has been. "What happened?" Denise gives up trying to do yoga and sits.

"Girl, she was grinding on Kane Yamada."

Isaac poorly pantomimes grinding before laughing hysterically at my deadpan expression.

"Ooop!" She slaps my leg. "And you didn't tell me!?"

"She apparently left with him and his friend!" Isaac spills looking at me waiting for me to fill in the gaps. "Clint was grumbling the next day about it."

"I did a performance," I said, giving a pointed look to Isaac. "And then I helped him get Zeke home because he was faded as fuck."

"You got Zeke lit?" They ask in unison.

"Yes and no?" I scratch my head. "He was asking for drinks, Clint and I tagged teamed making them for him. He had too many in a short period of time."

"Not to mention you got him high too."

"Damn Isaac. Can I have any of my business?"

"No," he says with an eye roll and a giggle.

"Bitch," Denise sighs. "Why didn't you tell me!?" she whisper-shouts at me. She places her hand on my wrist, looking me in my eyes amused.

"Because it's an in-person conversation. I'd rather you enjoy hearing the story."

"So, you gonna tell me or leave me hanging?" Denise asks, looking between me and Isaac. "'Cause we in-person now, girl."

"Oh! No worries, I got a video of the performance!" He pulls out his phone, finds the video and sends it to Denise. She watches closely.

"Oh, bitch!" she squeals as her eyes grow wide. She flails, letting her hand slap at my arm. A silly, impressed smile grows on her face. "That's my best friend!!" she shrieks.

I look across the courtyard and see Zeke and Kane tossing a football between each other. The sun glitters across their sweaty, exposed arms.

"Bitch!" Denise shrieks again, immediately catching my attention. "You basically fucked him with yo clothes on!" Her and Isaac giggle beside me.

"Didn't I tell you!" Isaac says leaning into her still laughing.

"It's not that serious," I groan, shrinking away from the curious eyes that turn towards us.

I mean, yeah the after math was, but this wasn't the place where I wanted to tell them he fucked me to sleep. Twice. Or that I left feeling some type of way, which makes me feel guilty for even indulging. Especially because I don't do 'feelings' when I know I'm hooking up with someone.

"It's not, but by the way he was looking," there's a look that passes between her and Isaac.

"Face down," Isaac starts.

"Ass up," Denise finishes, then slides down with her ass in the air and shakes it.

"Ma'am, we're in public," I slap her ass, laughing.

"E!" I hear from across the courtyard.

Denise, Isaac, and I immediately look around to find who's shouting. Zeke and Kane are no longer in their original spots.

"Ebony!" Zeke shouts louder and I immediately find him as he waves animatedly.

"Hi, love!" I shout back waving with a goofy grin on my face.

He blows me a kiss then leans over to Kane saying something that earns him a slap to the back of the head. Kane gives a small wave, then shoves Zeke in the opposite direction. He slings his arm around Zeke's shoulder as they walk towards the football field.

9

Ebony

Four Weeks Later

"Okay, class. I know we just started back a week ago, but I've assigned partners for the end of the semester project." A collective groan echoes through the room. "I know, I know. Forced partnerships are gross." Dr. Goodwin mocks us with an amused sparkle in the corner of her eye.

Uninterested in the rest of the class, my chin sits in my palm as I trace idle patterns on the table. Denise flips her box braids over her shoulder, tickling me. I look over at her with my eyebrows raised.

Her body shakes as she kicks her leg, which is crossed over the other. She places a piece of gum in her scrunched up mouth and starts chewing.

"I wish this bitch was joking," she whispers.

"They're passionate about group work," I sigh, leaning back in my chair. "I hope my partner actually does the fucking work."

"Say that shit," Denise agrees, leaning back in her seat too.

"Kane Yamada and Ebony Young. You two are working together," she continues on.

A soft sigh passes my lips as I chance a peek back at Kane.

He flirts with a blonde that sits beside him. Her tits sit on the table propped up for him. He's not shy about checking her out. He looks over at me with a ghost of a smirk. He nods, then gives the blonde his attention again.

I feel the jealousy bubble up in me as I face the front. I can't explain why. It's been a few weeks since we hooked up. No point in being upset that he is what I've always known. I am that way too—was that way.

You know this game well, you play this game. Now get back on your shit.

Even if it wasn't often that I hooked up with someone I've been fawning after for a while, I know the rules of this game.

Denise groans beside me before grabbing her stuff.

"Girl, I do not want to work with Miranda," she said, wiggling her head mocking a peppy tone. I grab my book bag and straighten out my destroyed denim jeans. "It's either going to be glitter galore or excuses. Jesus be a fence."

"I heard she has a pretty good hands-on approach."

"You did not fuck Miranda..." she gawks at me. I look at her confused and shake my head. "Ohhh girl, you had me scared."

"She's not even into girls. I'm not into the sexual exploration phase some women have." We laugh.

The sun's heat beats down on us as we push out the front doors of the building, the gray pavement reflecting the rays back into our eyes. We squint and use our hand to shield as much of our faces as we can.

"Hey, E," Kane calls behind me, stopping Denise and me.

"Ooop." She gives me a shocked look. "'What I miss for you two to be on a 'hey, E' basis?" I roll my eyes at her laughing.

"E, wait up. I'll walk with you," he shouts, trying to walk away from the blonde he was sitting with in class. She pulls him back, wiggling her chest in his face. He looks impatient and uninterested.

"That's my cue to get gone. I'll see you at lunch?"

"Yes! I'll fill you in then?"

"You better!" she pins me with a serious look before smiling and walking off. She shoves her headphones in her ears and slings her braids over her shoulder.

I stop walking and watch Kane quickly approaching me. His large, muscular frame wearing a graphic T that does little to hide his thick, tattooed arms. There's a lazy grin on his face as he approaches me and I feel butterflies.

Where's the pest spray when you need it?

A warm breeze blows, spreading the scent of wild flowers from the flower bed behind me to my nose. A loose strand from my jeans tickles the new tattoo on my thigh as he approaches. I push the strand away and give Kane a small, guarded smile.

"Nice ink," he comments when he reaches me.

He eyes my thigh for a moment then slowly drags his gaze up my body, stopping at two spots he had his head buried before. I shake the thought out of my head as I shift my bag and walk in step with him.

"Thanks," I say with a soft giggle.

My hands grip the thick straps of my book bag as an awkward silence forces its way through the space between us.

Rustling tree leaves and tweeting birds attempt to fill the space, but the awkwardness remains—thick like molasses.

What should I say? 'Hey, what should we do for the project? By the way, I can't stop thinking about your dick down my throat.' Gag, no. There's other things I can say, but knowing my socially awkward self I'd end up saying that.

"So…" he starts. "How'd you want to do the project?"

"Um… We can set up a shared folder on the drive and work that way." I offer, chancing a glance at him. "I'm off on Friday so we can set up a project outline then and get started."

"Alright, sounds good." We stop walking and step out of the path. People walk past calling out to him and he nods, giving a few a slapping handshake. There's a tension building in the air between us as we avoid each other's eyes. A heat that pulls and tugs when our eyes do lock. Images of that night transmuting between each passing glance as I think of all the possible outcomes. "I should get going. I'll catch you around."

"See ya," I wave as he rushes off without a second glance back.

I'm foolish for thinking he would in the first place.

10

Kane

My mind is in disarray as I replay the last face-to-face meeting I had with Ebony. Seeing her in class wasn't new, I was very aware of her presence, her sweet, intoxicating scent. But I did hope that me wanting to walk with her would spark up something. I shouldn't be hoping for anything more. I should consider sex with her a one night thing.

She's still sexy as hell, don't get me wrong, but it was awkward. That "I've seen you naked and tasted you and now I don't know how to approach you" kind of awkward. That's what I get for not really reaching out for a while I guess.

She knows the rules of the game though. She's like me.

Coach's whistle pierces the air, breaking me from my thoughts as we start our next set of drills. I race towards the tackle pads and drive my shoulder in the cushioned center, pushing the device back. I dodge off and run back to our line up.

I stretch and walk using my shirt to dry the sweat dripping from my face. I stand in line trying to keep my breathing even as my mind wanders. Today's topic—Ebony.

"Academic probation?" Zeke questions beside me as we get back in line. "We literally fixed the dang golf cart."

"The Koi fish died," I comment.

"Maybe it was their time to go." He shrugs his shoulders, inching forward as the line moves.

"My mom did say she loved the idea about the books, but everything else she wasn't impressed with," I share.

Zeke helped me execute the plan. We broke into the school's digital records, stumbled on emails with book samples being sent, and decided to upload them. It took a week with the two of us.

Funny to think how most of these instructors use their pet's names, which they mention in class, as their account passwords, not that I'd have any issue getting into their account if they used something more secure.

"So, the punishment for the golf cart that barely worked when we got a hold of it is academic probation."

My parents cleaned up a lot of my troublemaking ways. There was the time an impromptu bonfire got out of control. Yours truly started it and it was fine until some idiot threw a bottle of scotch at the fire.

"They're making an example out of me. My parents are going along with it because the school's donors are pissed. School's afraid to lose the free money."

Zeke and I looked into the school's financial records for fun. We noticed some shady shit behind the scenes. Money being collected, but used in different departments for higher ups. That's originally why we posted all the books online. They had enough stashed away to not even lose an hour's worth of sleep like their students and faculty.

My friends may call me a cocky asshole, and I am to an extent, but I do have a heart.

The whistle trills and Zeke and I charge forward, colliding the musky blue padded dummies hard. We push them back fast and hard before stopping and going back in line.

A moment passes between us as he stretches his arms. I kick and wiggle my legs to release the tension in my limbs.

"Rumor has it, you may or may not have hooked up with E a few weeks ago," he says leaning towards me. He gives me a curious, smug look before inching forward in the line.

"Who says?" my face scrunches up in confusion. I know I'm faking it, but if she hadn't told him, I'll take that as a sign that she doesn't discuss hook ups.

That could explain why she didn't say much earlier today.

"I won't reveal my source until you confirm or deny. I will say… locker room is buzzing though." Zeke cocks an eyebrow at me as the coach releases us to get water. "You should have. That's the only reason why I got drunk." He walks away leaving me to stare at his back in disbelief.

"Terrible fucking move, Zeke," I mutter laughing to myself. That guy's way too smart for his own good sometimes. Then a second realization hits me. This asshole would still need me to get him home.

"Zeke!" I shout. "You were going to make me carry your ass back to our apartment!?"

I sprint into the locker room to find him.

11

Ebony

Howls echo through the cinderblock corridors of the animal shelter I volunteer at. The groaning wheels of the cart alert the dogs that food is coming.

"Okay, okay," I say with laughter in my voice. I grab the keys off the hook and start passing out food dishes and looking in at the dogs. The loudest ones calm down once their bowl is in front of them. Crunching and smacking fill the long room once I finish.

Placing the items back, I sit at a chair in the front and look over my notes. Then, I take my phone out of my pocket and look down at my contacts. I click on my father's and listen to the phone ring as I stroke the cat in my lap.

"You've reached the voicemail of Robert Deed. I can't—"

I hang up after contemplating leaving another voicemail. I send a text instead.

> Hey Dad, haven't heard from you in a while. Everything okay?

> Just busy. Talk later.

"You always say that," I mutter as I slide my phone back in

my pocket.

"Fancy seeing you here," a familiar voice says to me.

I look up and lean my cheek in my hand staring at Vin, the light skin "baddie" and my ex from high school. We parted on "decent" terms, but he still isn't my favorite person. We were TOXIC together, all capital letters necessary. He thinks he's Nathan from *Insecure.* Negative.

His golden face is littered with brown freckles. His brown eyes are dark, almost blending into his black pupils. His bleached brown hair is cut neatly with a small design on the side. His curls are wet, but defined.

He's a lean guy with subtle muscles and surprising strength, the football team's secret weapon. He's fast on his feet and lethal with his hands. Running into him is like running into a brick wall. His hours spent in the weight room are solely to make sure his body works that way.

"No, 'hello'?" he laughs leaning against the counter.

"Hi, Vin. How can I help you?" my dry tone matches my disinterest in seeing him.

We don't usually run into each other except for a handful of times, but this isn't a usual time. No one from school comes here to visit any of the strays.

A fluffy white cat jumps down from the cat tree and walks up to me. He nuzzles his head against my arm before lounging in front of me purring. He blinks at me slowly and releases a soft meow. I smile down at him and rub my hand over his soft fur.

Vin sneezes.

I forgot to mention, he's allergic to cats *and* dogs. So, there's no real reason he's here other than to bother me. At least his allergies will be kicking his ass for the next few days.

"Rumor has it that you hooked up with Yamada." He plays with a pen in the cup holder before stepping away from the white cat in front of me. He sneezes again.

"A rumor you started I'm assuming?" I lean back in my rolling chair. The small gray cat that was in my lap stirs and looks up at me.

No one saw me and Kane go in or out of his apartment together as far as I know. And I know Zeke wouldn't talk about it if he knew, and we never had time to talk beyond 'hi and bye' recently with football season and school in full swing.

He shrugs his shoulders in a lazy, uninterested kind of way. "I'm letting you know people are talking. I want to protect you. I still care for you."

I sigh, shoving down the negative thoughts about Vin. It's possible he does want to protect me, but if he's spreading rumors based on proximity, which is what it boils down to, then this is a possessive kind of thing. He's always been a "once mine, always mine" kind of guy. My eyes search his, looking for the seam of his lie.

"Okay, so you don't believe that." He raises his hands defensively and backs away. "There's a lot of shit we went through, I know."

"It shouldn't be a surprise. Why are you here though? You're allergic to the top two animals here."

"Because I came to warn you." I feel my face scrunch up. "I

know you. You're gonna go all in for this dude and he's going to hurt you. I'd hate to see it."

"For one, nothing is going on with me and Kane. And for two, even if there was, I'm a big girl. I can handle it."

"Like when you got drugged at that party?" Vin spits, giving me a pointed look. "Do you even remember what happened?"

A black cat with green eyes hisses at Vin. His fur stands up on his back and he spits at him. The other two cats near me yowl and dash off into their hiding spaces. I scoop the black cat up and cuddle with him.

"Hey, it's okay Silver," I whisper to him, ignoring Vin's question.

"Silver? Ebs, that's a black cat," he states condescendingly. Incredulously, he looks between me and Silver. He shoves his hands in his jean pockets.

"He's named Silver because he keeps the ghouls away." I glance up. Vin sneezes rapidly, then backs away.

"Disgusting animals," he mumbles. "Look, Ebs, locker room is buzzing and you're the topic of discussion. Either people want to fuck you or they're talking about how Kane is 'railing' you." He actually uses air quotes. "I want you to be careful. Shit's not a good look."

"You didn't have a problem with anyone making me a conquest when it was you 'railing' me," I state back, air quotes and all.

"I thought you let that go," he huffs.

"Kind of hard when my entire reputation was ruined because of you." Silver glares at Vin still. Soft yowls pour from his mouth.

"I told you I was sorry," he says softly. "I was young and dumb and I hurt you."

"Sorry doesn't change what I had to experience because of you, Vin. And the only thing you did was laugh."

"You think Kane would treat you any differently?"

"I'm not even anything to Kane!" I growl frustrated. Silver hisses towards him, catching Vin's attention. He backs up closer to the door. "He's my project partner. Happy? Now can you go back under the critter cluttered rock you were under and leave me alone?"

"Fine. Don't let it get any further with him. He's a good dude, but not the dude for you. Alls I'm saying." He heads to the door then pauses. "Your Dad asked about you the other day when he called me. Give him a call sometimes."

The bell on the door chimes as he exits the shelter. My hand strokes Silver's fur and I sigh. Of course my father calls Vin and not me. And it's no surprise that I'm painted as the avoidant daughter that neglects her aging parents. There's something odd about Vin popping up randomly. Especially since not many people know I volunteer at a shelter that's a few miles away from school, nearly in the middle of nowhere.

An idea sends a chill through me. I don't think Vin would hurt me, but if he decided to, then help wouldn't come as quick as I'd probably need it to. Especially since he had a slight glaze in his eyes like he's been using.

A couple walks in as my mind starts to deep dive and I snap

out of my musing. I give them a bright smile and walk them through the kennel.

One question lingers in the back of my mind: would Vin hurt me?

I don't think I want to find that out.

12

Kane

The library lights are bright as they turn on after the sun sets. I squint, scrolling on my laptop doing research when an email comes through. It's from Ebony. I read it and locate the link to a drive folder for our project and an idea for how to write the proposal.

I click on the folder and see she's already started uploading files. A new one pops up and I contemplate my next move. After a quick glance around, I turn on my VPN and hack my way into the school's system.

It's for the greater good. My Dad has done much worse.

I look up the student records and pull her number from there. I close my computer and close the door to the study room I'm in. My thumb hovers over the green icon before I press it.

Now or never.

"Hello?" Her voice is soft and curious. There's some ruffling in the background then soft music. "Dammit, Silver what are you doing little weirdo." She laughs softly.

"Hey, it's Kane" I lean back in the rolling chair. "Thought it be better if we worked on the proposal plan together over the phone?"

"Oh! Hey!" she laughs to herself. "I was going to email it

to you tonight. I thought you had football."

"I did, it got canceled. Too hot."

There's a moment of silence and I clear my throat.

"I can come to you if that's better?" I say leaning forward in my chair secretly hoping she'd agree.

"Oh, oh, no." She sounds more preoccupied than disinterested. That's a good sign. "I'm looking up something, sorry. I'm not good over the phone when I'm working."

"Then let's try something else." I press the video call option.

When she answers, I notice the loose fitting tee shirt that she has on, hanging off her shoulder. Her locs are pushed to one side of her shoulder and the screens illuminate her perfect brown skin. She's absolutely gorgeous.

"Is this easier?" I ask, pulling out my computer and propping up my phone, starting my own research. I look over at the phone and see she's watching me. Her eyes, moving as she takes me in. She smiles.

"Yeah, this works. No long moments of silence without you being able to see what I'm doing," she laughs again.

I can slightly see her couch behind her. A black cat jumps up and meows at her before rubbing against her head. She reaches up and rubs the cat's silky black fur.

"Hi, Silver," she leans back with a big smile on her face. I'm lost in the interaction as she coos to the little cat. It purrs so loud I can hear it.

"Silver?" I ask with a smile.

"Yeah, because he keeps the crazies away. Ain't that right,

Silver?" she coos into his fur.

"Is it short for Silver Bullet, then?" I give up researching, not that I planned on doing that on the phone with her. If that's what she wants to do, then I'm prepared. But I had to find a way to make her comfortable with me.

I rest my chin in my hands and admire her like some fool struck by cupid's arrow. There's no way I have a crush on this girl. Okay, maybe just a little one. It'll fade.

"Mmhmm," she has a ghost of a smile on her face as she looks at the screen, then a full blown one takes over. "I started volunteering at an animal shelter a few miles away from campus. We've been glued to each other ever since. No one really wanted to adopt him so the shelter owner let me today." She kisses at Silver before looking back at the camera. "Are you an animal person?"

She types at her computer and I see her eyes darting from her keyboard to her computer screen as she does.

"Love animals honestly. I have a husky back home. Her name is Akemi. I call her pretty girl or beauty so she answers to either." I look through my pictures and send her one of Akemi. She looks at it and her face lights up. My heart flutters like a kid in a candy store.

Stop it.

"She really is beautiful! She looks like she's vocal."

"Very. Don't feed her on time and she's waking the entire neighborhood." We laugh together.

Silver darts across the back of the couch and knocks something over.

"Jesus, Silver." She's laughing hysterically. She stands and I get a view of her beautiful legs and that new tattoo she has. A broken down skull with a bouquet of roses, lilies, and baby's-breath.

She sits back down with a glass of wine in her hand. "Silver is on kitty crack. Only explanation I have for how he's acting," she laughs with a shrug.

"He feels safe," I add, moving my phone and getting comfortable. I should be walking home, but I'm enjoying this moment.

"Does Akemi do that when she's comfortable?"

"No, she prances like a little reindeer. I think my sister taught her. I'd send you a video, but then I may send more of her than you'd want." I laugh.

She looks at me in disbelief. "I volunteer at an animal shelter. I would be honored to enjoy your Beauty with you." She pauses. "Not your beauty, but Beauty, your dog. Not saying that you're not beautiful, clearly—" She grabs her cup and takes a long drink while hiding her face with her hands.

Drunk her spills her dark secrets. Noted.

"Don't hide from me," I say softly with a smirk.

What the fuck am I doing? I feel like I'm back in high school flirting with her like this.

She looks at me trying not to smile and shakes her head looking back at her screen. She does a little air guitar as she softly sings the song playing in the background.

We spend more time talking, sharing pictures of our pets, and flirting than we do working on our project.

By the time we get off the phone it's two in the morning. And we've established two things—we need to meet tomorrow to get the proposal and project schedule done and our chemistry is insane.

She feels worth much more than a roster and I'd have to make drastic life changes to make sure she doesn't get caught up in my chaos.

13

Ebony

I sit next to Miya, who is a year younger than me with long, straight black hair. She has almond shaped eyes that are deep brown and intelligent. Her face is soft and angular. We became friends quickly when working on various projects with student life since she's been here. I met her before I met her brother, Kane. The difference between the two is enough to give you whiplash. Night and day those two.

We look over our plans for the rest of the school year and for next. Our polished proposal sits in a project folder beside the plans.

"Miya, Ebony, it's so good to see you two."

We stand together and shake hands with the Assistant of the Chair for student life department. It's unusual for them to take meetings, but because she's worked with the department most of her academic life, they let her get away with it.

"How have you both been?" Grace, the assistant, asks. She's slim and her pencil skirt and button up top only reinforce her size. She's short, about five foot compared to my five foot three inches. She sits at the table and looks at her copy of the documents we have in front of us.

"We've been good. We brought the reports that you've

asked for, and a proposal for a future project that involves the chemistry department," I start with a smile on my face.

"We're thinking wrist bands that test drinks for date rape drugs. It has similar components to the other methods out there, but we plan to make the bracelets reusable. That way, they can be used on and off campus," Miya adds.

"Do you have a sample to show us how it works?" Grace asks.

The department chair slips into the office and takes a seat with a smile on his face. He's in a gray suit that makes his blue eyes pop. Brown hair neatly tamed with a freshly groomed beard.

"They were just telling me about their plans to work with the chemistry department to make bracelets to test drinks for any date rape drugs. Reusable bracelets."

His eyebrows lift in amusement as he looks at us and then down at the documents in front of him. He flips through the pages. "These numbers are incredible. The initiatives you two have taken to shift funding and donations in such a short amount of time has improved sexual assault reports on campus." He nods reading over a few more lines, then looks at us. "Has this been tested yet?"

"Not in an uncontrolled setting," I state. "We have a list of our party dates and we plan to launch at the fall festival party at the beginning of October."

"We do have video of the bracelet working. It's a mix between a mood ring and heat activated jewelry," Miya adds.

She presses a button on the table and a screen slowly drops

down from the ceiling. With a push of another button, the video comes to life on the screen. Several yellow bracelets sit on the table. There are labeled jars behind it to represent the popular date rape drugs. One bracelet dips into each jar and turns a pink color. Then after a few minutes, the bracelet turns yellow. One bracelet is alternated between each jar to show that it can be used multiple times, then the video ends. Miya and I anxiously wait as the two smile to each other.

"That's incredible," Grace says looking at the paperwork.

"Once we get the reports back from your testing in a real world setting, then we can circle back and meet with the Dean. I'll pass the message along to the science and the tech department so we can get some bracelets completed for the fall festival."

"We can meet again at the end of this semester with results? It seems like you'll have plenty of chances to test the product," he adds, giving us both a thoughtful look.

"That's great, thank you," Miya gushes with a big smile on her face.

We stand and shake hands as I thank each of them.

Once they leave, I look at Miya with a big smile on my face. She squeals and pulls me into a hug.

"We did it!" she shouts. "I was nervous they would cancel this project, but oh my God they loved it!"

"It's because we know our shit!" I whisper shout to her with a big grin on my face.

We begin putting our stuff in our bags. Then make our way into the brightly lit hall. We look out the windows to the second courtyard and watch people running around.

"I just don't want anyone to go through anything traumatic when all they wanted to do was have fun, you know?" I say softly.

"They won't. Not if we can help it."

"Are you coming to that party next Wednesday?" I ask as I step away from the window.

"I have a huge Geography test the next morning so I'll have to bow out."

I groan, but give her a small smile. "Fine, lunch. On me!"

14

Kane

I sit in a small coffee house at the edge of campus staring out the window the following morning, grateful for air conditioning. My father told me he'd be around and decided to set up an impromptu coffee meet up. My parents are good people. Kind. Me on the other hand, I like to see what makes people tick. I'm calculative and manipulative to an extent. My mom assures me everyone is, but I've never seen anyone use it the way that I have.

The door creaks and groans against the hinges as it swings open and I stand turning to see my father enter. His dark suit pants and white button up top make him stick out among the college students that trickle in. He's about my height, give or take an inch, and my mother says we are the spitting image of each other. A small nose at the perfect 45 degree angle (this is exactly how my mother describes it. Odd, I know). Medium thickness in lips, and almond shaped brown eyes. We have an effortlessly dominant look when our faces rest. Mysterious, dark, and almost unapproachable. My Dad more on the mysterious side and me enjoying the treasures of the dark side.

He takes long strides to get to me and I bow before embracing him in a tight hug. His hand claps my back before he grabs the back of my neck to kiss my temple. I push away from him laughing.

"Dad," a playful warning in my tone.

"You're my son. If I want to kiss your face in public, I will." He smiles at me and takes his seat. "How's school been?"

I sit across from him. With both hands, I slide him a cup of tea and lean back. "It's good. Easy classes, but they won't let me advance up."

"Schools trying to not show 'favoritism'."

"Or fear," I add.

My Dad looks out the window with a thoughtful head nod.

"I assured them our family has cut ties with the Underground."

"We need them." His eyes shoot to me. Disappointment shines on his face more than anything else. "Miya has been working on this project. Her and her team could probably expose more with the Underground's help."

Miya, my younger sister, is a breath of fresh air for my parents. She's dainty, reserved, and respectful. Always has been. They know exactly where she is and what she's doing. They trust her in a way that they don't trust me. I understand, I wasn't the best kid. Fighting, bullying, selling shit I had no business getting.

My Dad would do anything for his 'princess', and I like knowing that the people who have been around since I was a kid still have access just in case…

"I don't want you wrapped up in that Underground stuff."

I sigh and run my hand through my hair.

"I see the wheels turning. No. We got out of it for good reason."

"I know. They don't hold the same family values as the organization once did, but—"

"No, buts." My Dad sighs, taking a sip of his tea. "Anyone still involved in the Underground, no matter how sincere they are, are no good. It's like a plague."

"Miya needs data that the school's repressing. With me being on academic probation, I can't help her get the sealed records."

"You can't pretend the shit you were doing was for Miya," my Dad says pointedly, crossing his ankle on his knee.

"It wasn't. You're right, but I know that she's at another dead end. And I know I messed that up. But now, I want to be available to help her if the school gives her any push back."

"The school shouldn't," he mumbles, but the look on his face says otherwise. "You think the school would suppress crime report data?"

"The school is a business and you know what businesses do when they want to make more money."

"Under what basis, Kane?"

"Ren," I say their name firmly. My Dad's eyes stare at me. "This could help clear their name."

Ren, a family friend, used to go to Knight University with me until the beginning of this year. The story behind why is spotty, but they said it had to do with drugs and girls.

Their favorite pastime.

I assumed the two are related to Miya's project, but I haven't figured out how related.

"I was called?" Ren's bubbly voice cuts in.

I smile and pull them into a tight hug. They wiggle out of my arm and push me. They embrace my father before taking the chair beside me.

"They're in town and wanted to see you and Miya, but Miya is busy so she opted for lunch," my Dad informs with a smile on his face. He sips his tea. "You can join for lunch."

"I have football right after class," I say, staring at Ren.

They look different. Their long black hair is cropped short and dyed a rosy pink color that makes their face stand out more. Their once round cheeks are more defined.

They tuck their hair behind their ear.

"I heard part of your conversation," they confess. "Do you really think you can clear my name?"

My father looks at them, then at me. My eyes are on him as he sighs, his shoulders rising and falling with the simple action. "Depends on what the records say. We only have the police reports and you say they're falsified."

"They are," they nod rapidly. "I don't know some of the girls that said I sold to them and the ones I do know were getting it from someone else."

"Who?" I ask leaning into the table.

Ren shakes their head. "I want protection before I give names. I want my family safe and I know out of everyone, you two would keep me safe."

They look between my father and I, then swallow hard.

"I won't sabotage my daughter's research opportunity, but

I'll do my best." My Dad gives me a pointed look. "I'll talk to my contacts on campus and give you some wiggle room. Don't abuse that power."

I nod at my father concealing my smile. Relief floods through me as he takes another sip of tea and talks to Ren about their family.

We don't stay much longer. With a quick, warm embrace. I see my father and Ren off before buying two iced coffees.

15

Ebony

Today's a particularly windy day. Bees buzz around the tree I sit under and I watch them closely. A book I have open weighs my lap down. I leave the bees to do their thing and watch people pass by idly. I look back at my book and start taking notes.

I smell him before he says anything—cinnamon sugar and spices. A smile decorates his face when I look up at him. His black shirt crinkles as he sits beside me on my blanket. He wipes his hands on his light denim jeans and moves his Converse covered feet off the blanket. His brand new shoes glow brightly in the sun.

"Wait long?" he asks, sounding out of breath. He hands me a small iced coffee and I take it with a smile.

"No. I was just reading up on some stuff," I answer, closing my book and moving it to the side.

"You look nice today." His eyes roam over me. "I mean, you always look nice, but today there's something different." He takes a moment and laughs at himself.

"Thank you," I blush, laughing with him. I tug at my shorts and adjust the straps of my tank top. "Did you have any ideas for the project?"

"We should do something simple. We're both busy. Let's not complicate it."

"We should complicate it though," I challenge. He looks at me with an unsure look. He crosses his thick, tattooed arms over his broad chest. I sit up straighter. "Listen, I've seen some of your work. It's incredible and your work mixed with what I can do… We'd have the best project, hands down."

He takes a drink of his iced coffee allowing the idea to roll around his mind. He faces me, a contemplative look across his face. His eyes search mine for a moment before he looks away. He doesn't say anything as he takes another sip of his iced coffee.

"So?" I ask moving my head to get a better look at his face to figure out what he's thinking. "We could do a race car or something. Program the codes to have it move like a roomba or something."

"Having a race car move like a roomba doesn't really sound like it fits together."

"It doesn't, but we could make it make sense. That's the point of the project."

"It is, but we don't want to add too much complication with the coding and functionality of everything."

"We absolutely should," I say with a sigh.

A weird look passes over his face and he smirks. "Are we having our first fight?"

I look away from him with a laugh. "You and Zeke are so much alike."

He reaches over my leg and grabs my notes looking over

them. Heat from his body rolls into mine as his smell overpowers the fresh air. A violent chill threatens to run through my body before he leans back into his spot.

He takes a pen from his backpack and adds notes in the margin and keeps reading. "We could do a basic computer. A high-powered one. We can basically make it multifunctional. It connects to an app on your phone and allows you to control virtually anything in the house without being there. Think Home Alone booby traps, but less violent."

"Kane, there are so many apps that do something like that." I sigh, crossing my legs and leaning my head in the palm of my hand. I watch him move. "Why don't you want to challenge yourself?"

"What's the point of stressing out about a project? Based on the rubric, we get what we need done and get a good grade."

I nod and look away for a moment.

"You're not gonna drink your iced coffee?" he asks.

I freeze and look at the cup. I turn towards him and grab the cup and take a small sip. His brows bunch together.

"Don't like it?"

"It's good!" I say with a giggle taking another small sip.

"What's up, Yamada!" Someone shouts from the other side of the courtyard. Kane nods with a smile. "Nice footwork on the field."

I quickly put the cup down focusing on my breathing like my therapist told me. I don't think he'd slip anything in my drink, but I didn't think my ex would either. But thanks to the black spot in my memory and a shit ton of trauma, I'm hesitant to trust anyone. Yay life.

"What's up, Kane? Hey, E" Zeke says, walking up from the opposite direction.

"Hey, you!" I say with a wide smile. He sits beside me pushing me closer to Kane. Zeke engulfs me in his arms. "You smell so bad. The hell have you been—don't answer that."

He laughs as he reaches over and shakes hands with Kane ending it with a snap. He puts his arm behind his head as I scoot down on my back and look at the notes that Kane wrote.

I can see your nipple rings through your shirt.

This is a good idea. You really think we could pull off a drone?

How bad did they hurt? (Re: Nipple piercings)

*Supercomputer is a good idea, I don't know why you doubt our brain power .**

Zeke reaches over me and grabs my iced coffee and takes a drink. I look over the top of my book at him. "That was mine."

"So *that's* why it's making me hard." He nudges me with his leg and I gag, rolling to my side slightly to come face to face with Kane's hand. I notice the veins that slightly protrude out his tan skin. The rings that decorate the knuckles. I roll back over on my back hiding.

"I actually got that for her, jackass." Kane pops the back of Zeke's head. "I'll get you another one, E."

"She doesn't take drinks from strangers," Zeke says, sticking his tongue out, then smiling.

Kane looks down at me. I glance at him and shrug. He leans on his palm closest to me, his knuckle brushing my side and I jolt from the sensation. A soft giggle breaking free.

"You're ticklish?" Kane says with a devious look on his face.

"No," I defend quickly. Both Kane's and Zeke's attention are on me like predators locked on their prey. "No. Look, can we talk about it. Please? *Please?*" I wiggle away and quickly get to my feet backing away. They slowly get to their feet and I bolt. I dodge Zeke and slip on a slick piece of grass before hauling tail back towards my blanket laughing.

I can hear them running behind me and dodge Kane's hands.

"Oh! You're letting a chick show you both up!" I giggle as I keep running. Kane barrels towards me and I scream as he grabs me in his arms and Zeke comes up and starts ticking me. I cackle and thrash in Kane's arms trying to beg for them to stop.

Satisfied, Zeke rubs his hands together and walks back towards my blanket with a shit eating grin on his face. Kane carries me back and deposits me beside him. My chest rises and falls rapidly as I try to catch my breath.

"Who's letting who beat them?" Zeke taunts, barely sounding out of breath. I flip him off laughing.

"You have to admit I had you going for a second," I pant out.

"You almost had him, not me," Kane helps me sit up. Him and Zeke offer me their cups at the same time. I shake my head finally, not panting as hard. A cramp makes me wince. I use my fingers to massage the soreness.

Zeke shrugs, placing the paper straw between his lips, taking a long sip. My eyes catch Kane's, who's basically glaring at me. His dominating look making me shrink back slightly and take a sip from his cup. I grumble, glancing at his smug face.

"Good girl," he mutters and I almost choke.

Zeke whoops. "It's like you two kissed," he laughs, leaning back on the tree. Kane and I exchange a look that makes me blush before going back to plan our project.

16

Kane

The computer lab is one of my favorite places to be. It's usually vacant and quiet. I can access any of the servers in the room beside me, and I can run programs and pretend I'm not breaking into protected systems. That is if I'm smart about the path I take.

I'm pretty good at hacking and coding. My Dad figured it would be the best way to keep me out of trouble. It did, then it didn't. I quickly learned how to find loopholes in software coding, or make one, and break into systems for the hell of it. As I got older, my hacking turned into me exposing sealed records, demolishing business revenue, and a few other things. My Dad always protected me.

I'm lost in a code before I notice Vin has entered the room. The door clicking catches my attention and I look over to him and give him a nod. Vin and I aren't friends, but I do know he's a beast on the field. Ever since the rumors, more like gossip, about Ebony and me started, his name has been tossed in the mix, too. I know they went to school together, Zeke told me that much, but everything else is unknown.

"What's up, Vin," I say, closing down my coding log and giving him dap.

"I just wanted to talk to you about Ebony," Vin pulls up a seat and drops his lanky body into it. I don't like the way he says her name. Like she's a problem that needs to be handled; like a loose cannon ready to explode.

I cross my arms over my chest and lean back in my chair. "What about Ebony?"

"You two are spending time together. I saw you both on campus." He's on the defense. I lean forward a little bit intrigued.

You got a thing for Ebony, Vinny boy?

"Yeah," I say, nodding and rubbing my chin.

"She told me you guys were working on a project together. Either way, just be careful. She's got a lot of… baggage."

"Baggage?"

"Yeah. Mommy issues. Daddy issues." He chuckles to himself softly. "We dated for a while back in the day. She went fucking wild. Thought she calmed down a bit when we got to college, but—" He stops himself lost in thought.

There's a look on his eye that I don't like. One that seems to remember the devious side of E. Amused by the things she does behind closed doors.

"She gets around," he adds.

He's jealous.

"Well, we're just working on a project together," I say, leaning back studying him. I watch as he fidgets and shifts.

"She's a great girl, man. Hella fuckin' fine." He shifts in his seat and looks around. "And her head game is crazy, but you would know if you two were fucking."

I hum looking at him. I feel my face twist in disgust. I've never been one for locker room talk. I also hear the challenge in his voice. He's trying to figure something out.

He wouldn't though. He's not that smart if he's throwing his cards on the table like this. Especially since Ebony and I aren't fucking again, not yet anyways.

Give me time and we will be.

He rubs the back of his neck with a chuckle. His eyes never meeting mine as he nervously fidgets beside me. "Sorry man. I know you aren't one to kiss and tell."

I nod with my brow still arched. No one, other than Zeke, has approached me about E or the rumors. I've heard them every so often, but mostly from Vin.

"You're great on the field and I don't want her to be the reason you don't get scouted or on the scout's list this season."

"I don't think our project would prevent me from being on the scout's radar," I say, keeping a close eye on his face.

"No, but she's chaos wrapped in a fat ass, tight pussy, and a pretty bow. She'll ruin your life and make you think it's the best, euphoric feeling in the world. If you hit, run. Teammate to teammate."

He stands and rubs his hands on his pants and gives a quick nod. He leaves the room just as quietly and quickly as he came in.

I stare at the closed door. He's hiding something. I file that in my brain for later. If I do get my way and fuck Ebony a few more times, he may pose a problem.

Zeke enters the computer lab once I turn back to the screen.

He pulls up a chair and sits beside me.

"What's up my man?" We slap our hands together and snap. "Been looking for you. Thought you may have been chasing behind Ebony like a little puppy."

I shoot him a middle finger, then get back to coding.

"What's that," Zeke asks, sliding his chair over to look at my screen.

"My sister is working with student life or initiatives, whatever that department is called. She's doing this project, but thinks the numbers are flubbed. I gotta make a backdoor code to get in and see what I can find for her."

"While on academic probation for hacking the school's system?"

"My Dad gave the okay. He knows I'm not *that* sloppy. I'm going to move slowly to make sure they don't catch me."

"How can I help?"

My eyes cut over to him.

"Ride or die, bro," he laughs.

"I'll let you know if it comes to it. Right now, it's just a hunch."

"A true hunch." His voice is soft and it catches me off guard.

"True?"

He nods and looks at his phone. "Look, I have a contact that you won't find in the files. The 'perfect victim' that will help whatever point Miya and you are trying to make. I gotta talk to them, convince them to tell their story. Give me time."

"You really are a ride or die," I laugh, cuffing his neck and giving it a shake.

"You questioned it?" He pushes away from me. "I'm hurt."

"Get the fuck outta here," I laugh.

He flips me off before leaving the room.

I grab a piece of paper and take a few notes.

Note 1: Vin is sus.

Note 2: There's a victim that's being silenced and they'll be the one to expose this place.

17

Ebony

I t's hotter than a bitch outside, much hotter than the day before. My body is profusely dumping any water I'm consuming and my shirt sticks to me. My thighs have begun chafing and the only thing I can do to alleviate it is sit my ass in a seat until the sun sets. Too bad that's not an option.

I walk into class miserable and soaked with sweat. I plop in my seat and bask in the glory of the coolness on my burning thighs. A bucket of ice would be heaven to sit in at this moment.

"Did you bring the sun with you, bitch?" Denise asks, sliding away from me. Her chair scraps against the ground as she makes space. I don't have the energy to say anything back so I just grunt. "Your skin is radiating heat."

"If this is what Hell feels like, I promise to be a better person," I groan, laying my head on the desk.

"Too late, girl, He knows the tricks you taught me and he needs a teacher for the heathens down below. He said you or me. Self preservation, bitch."

I attempt to laugh but even that burns up more energy.

"Who says the Devil is a man?" Kane's voice asks as something cool touches my arm.

"Oh my God," I moan. Loudly. Like I'm getting dicked down in the middle of class and I'm on the brink of touching Jesus' hem from an orgasm.

Welp. I'd rather go to Hell now.

Denise cackles beside me. Her body folds over the table as she stifles her giggle fits. I'm glad someone is enjoying my shame.

I let out a defeated sigh looking up at Kane who's looking amused, turned on, and pleased to be reminded what I sound like when I moan. I can't even mouth for him to not start because the entire class is staring at me.

Kill. Me. Now.

He holds the drink up for me to see. "Looks like I'm right on time." His deep voice has an edge to it. A hint of an offer lingering behind every word.

He sits the iced coffee on the table still looking at me with a smirk on his face and I shake my head.

Denise sits up with giggles still bubbling out of her every once in a while. She has the nerve to wipe a tear from her eye.

"Thank you," I say, taking the drink. He watches me with an arched eyebrow and an expectant look.

I take a slow drink and stifle a moan as the ice cold liquid flows down my throat. My eyes roll back as I drink more. Vanilla dances on my tongue, cooling me from the inside out. The coffee is smooth, creamy and the perfect temperature. Heaven in a cup.

When I open my eyes, Denise is in another fit of laughter and there's a dark look in Kane's eyes. They're challenging me.

Taunting me to give him a reason to drag me out of this room over his shoulder. It doesn't help that he does a quick adjustment below the belt when he sits in a chair that he pulled up.

And the only reason I know what that look means rests on that one night. I swallow hard pushing the images away while crossing my legs.

"So, who says the Devil is a man?" he repeats. I know that's not what he wants to ask and I appreciate that he leaves that question lingering behind his eyes.

"Oh, that's easy," Denise pipes up. Kane's eyes stay on me for a second longer as he looks me up and down before leaning on the table to give Denise his attention.

"The concept of hell is torture and revenge. You didn't follow the rules so you get to live in constant turmoil. Compare that to some guys' inability to take rejection and you have the concept of Hell, for women."

I nod, taking another grateful sip of my coffee.

"And not many men understand the concept of care," I add.

"Care?" the guy at the table in front of us asks. I think his name is Josiah. I nod. "That's bullshit."

"I said 'not many', not 'all' for one. For two, as a woman, we tend to be a little more softer by nature. Not all. Some."

"What would you know about women being soft to others besides your skewed perception because you are one."

"Because I've fucked plenty of women," I say flatly before tilting my head to the side and taking a sip of my coffee with a smile.

Josiah's jaw drops. His eyes wide like saucers.

Kane stifles a laugh as he rolls his tongue around his mouth amused. He covers his face as his shoulders start to shake with laughter.

"Plus, women talk to each other," Denise adds. "It's like locker room talk, but real."

"I didn't… I thought you were…" Josiah sputters.

"I like every gender," I laugh.

"Is that what you noticed when…?" he asks softly.

"I want to know that, too," Kane teases leaning forward again. He's dangerously close to me. I squeeze my legs a little tighter.

"For the most part," I shrug. "Look at it this way, if someone says they want aggressive sex, what do you think about?"

"Slapping, choking," Josiah answers, turning his seat. A small crowd gathers.

"Spanking and biting," Kane says with a suggestive smirk.

I avoid his eyes. He continues to remind me exactly why he and Zeke are best friends.

"Okay, Josiah?" He nods. "How do you choke someone sexually? I'll let you use me to demonstrate." I lift my head. Josiah hesitantly grabs my neck and I push his hands off shaking my head.

"First problem, you're going to crush your partner's windpipe. Make a 'v' with your hand, apply pressure on the sides. Let me show you." I pause and look around.

Kane's eyebrow is up. He gestures that I can use him, but I cut my eyes to Josiah who gives a subtle nod.

Touching Kane would result in me being in a bathroom

stall with his hand over my mouth and another part of him in me, making me see colors that don't exist. I know me well enough to admit that much. I may have said I was reformed, but I'm very willing to fold for him again.

"Breathe in," I say with my grip on Josiah's neck. As he breathes in I squeeze, count to five, then release. He breathes again and I squeeze again and hold for a second longer, then release. "How was that?"

His pupils are dilated and he stares at me like he wants to ask for more or maybe I unlocked a new badge in his treasure trunk of kink.

"Are you okay?" I ask, a little more concerned.

He snaps out of his daze and nods quickly turning and shoving his book bag on his lap. An awkward silence hangs in the air before Denise claps her hands together and slices through it.

"And that's it for sex facts with E! You'll be charged for any additional tips and tricks."

Everyone scurries away, but there's a murmur in the air. Various people look at their hands practicing the technique and of course, there are a few laughing and mocking me.

I glance at Kane who looks slightly disappointed and annoyed. He stands and pushes the chair back, mouthing "You are trouble" to me with a cocky grin.

"Good afternoon, everyone!" Dr. Goodwin calls out as everyone shuffles back to their seats.

"If I didn't know any better, I'd assume you two are either planning on fucking or already have," Denise whispers to me staring at the teacher. "And I don't think he's the sharing type."

She glances behind her shoulder and I pretend to go through my bag to do the same. Kane stares daggers at the back of Josiah's head. He opens and closes his hand ignoring the bubbly blonde to his right.

18

Kane

After practice, E invites me back to her apartment since we got the green light on our project proposal. The one I barely helped on, not by choice. She basically popped my hand and told me to chill, which led to us play fighting in one of the study rooms in the library. We only stopped once we realized the compromising position we were in. I wouldn't mind, but the flicker of fear that passed in her brown eyes was what made me stop and help her up. I can be a gentleman—sometimes.

I kept my hands to myself after that, especially now as I sit in her living room on her couch. Silver sniffs around me, then darts off. I try to coax him to me, but he wants no parts of my bullshit. I feel the furry little fella. That's the way I felt watching my woman choke that random guy in class.

Reel it in, Kane.

She walks out the kitchen in leggings and an oversized sweatshirt, and I thank the Gods and the creator of leggings for this sight. She's holding two glasses of water, then passes me one. She sits on the floor and pulls her computer out, messing with the end of one of her locs.

We've been working for a few hours getting a lot done, but I'm pretty sure we both would rather take a break.

Silver darts across my foot and nuzzles past her before climbing into her lap.

"She said it was fine that the product was vague?" I ask putting my computer back on the table scrolling through the comments the instructor left. Using my thumb, I spin my ring around my index finger looking through the document.

"She didn't really say much. I don't think she cares what we make, as long as it's good. And not a basic ass supercomputer," she looks at me like she's annoyed, but there's a ghost of a smile tickling the edges of her full lips.

"A supercomputer is far from basic," I challenge, looking at her.

I grab a nacho from the table and put it in my mouth. Silver walks over to me sniffing once again. Hopping up on the couch, he sniffs before laying beside me. Slow blinking green eyes stare up at me as he tucks his paws, then purrs into the silence.

"I think I passed the vibe check," I laugh, running my hand over his silky fur. He purrs louder. "Definitely passed the vibe check."

There's a thoughtful look in her eye as she looks between Silver and me. "I guess you're not all *that* bad," she mutters.

"You thought I was bad?"

"Not completely," she admits.

As I look in her eyes, our sexual tension forces its way through the room, much heavier than when we play fought. Her eyes do this thing where they gradually get a little dark. She's thinking something and based on her response, she's thinking of all the "bad" things that make her feel good. That make her body vibrate and float into other dimensions before I bring her back down and tether her to me, just to do it again.

Fuck a spark, there's an electrical current at this point. Maybe even an electrical storm if shit collides too fast. So, I brace myself for what happens next. And you better believe I want a next in this moment. We'd be a perfect storm.

She looks down at her computer screen instead and I find myself muffling a sigh.

"So, that thing with Josiah a couple days ago," I start. "You think he understood?"

I swallow down my jealousy, toeing into the conversation. I wanted to gauge why she picked him over me without going off. I don't have the right to.

Why him, Eb? What kept you from choosing me?

A laugh bubbles out of her. She puts her computer down as her body shakes. "I think I broke him," she laughs out.

I shake my head joining in with a soft, tense laugh making a feeble attempt to mask my true emotions.

"His face was frozen, Kane. Fro-zen." She grabs her water and drinks. "Normally, he'll say something to D or me, but today he was quiet. Not a word. Not a glance."

I may or may not have threatened him after class. Not a full-fledged threat. It's not because I like her. I just thought his reaction was weird and he was always staring at her.

You do it, too.

"Why do you look so angry?" she asks.

A soft, thoughtfulness lingers in the confines of her face and I let my eyes trace her features before stopping back at her eyes. Hers dart to my lips and I lick them. She shifts, but the thoughtfulness lingers.

I shrug, scratching the back of Silver's ear. How exactly do I answer that question?

"Don't let the rumors get to you," I settle on while looking at her. I don't answer her question. I don't want to, not yet. Not until I know why she's got my world doing this topsy-turvy thing. A flash of confusion takes over her expression. "About us."

She laughs softly. "This wouldn't be my first run with rumors. I don't give a damn enough to stop them." She grabs her computer and starts scrolling again.

In my attempt to read her, I notice there may be something else that she's not saying. Maybe it was the stares? She always did turn heads, but I've noticed a few more people watching her now that we're working on this project together.

And flirting out in the open. Be real.

"I didn't say anything," I admit looking back at my computer.

"I know," she says softly. I feel her hand come near mine as she rubs Silver's fur. "Such a pretty, pretty boy," she whispers to him as she gazes at his snoozing face.

This could be your life, Kane.

The thought has me scrambling. Too real, too fast, and too fucking intense.

There's a panic rising in me. I'd ruin her before she ever got to feel my love. And my love is just as violent as everything around me. I. Don't. Do. Love.

"I gotta go. I'll add what I finish on the drive," I say, jumping up startling Silver who glares at me. She looks up at me confused. "I'm sorry, Silver."

She sits back on her legs laughing. "You apologized to a cat."

I look at her and stop shoving my computer in my bag. The smile on her face brings those domestic thoughts back.

Get her a big ass diamond ring. A dope ass mansion. Take her to places like Bali and claim her on the balcony of every resort. Have her tell the world she's yours and yours alone. Then give her all the kids she can handle.

"You look at me like that and I may think you're in love with me," I say cocky as ever trying to redefine the line that I'm an arrogant asshole. She scoffs and rolls her eyes standing up.

"Right. You don't do love," she jokes. "Let me walk you to the door."

But I wish I did.

"So chivalrous," I tease.

"You know me, Ms. Chivalrous," she flips me off as she opens the door for me. I chuckle as I step over the threshold and turn to face her. Silver peeks at me from his cat tower.

"Bye, Silver," I call over her shoulder, then my eyes fix on hers.

I could kiss her right now. I should.

And kissing her leads you to taking her to her bed. It's right through that door.

She breaks eye contact and looks back at Silver. He's still peeking at the both of us. Only little green orbs in the shadow of his black cat tower.

"Talk later?" she asks looking back up at me.

"Missing me already?" I say with a cocky grin.

"Bye, Kane," she laughs, waving me away. I step back and she closes the door, locking it. I stay there for a moment grabbing on to the frame of her door breathing.

What's the worst that can happen if you let go?

19

Kane

I don't know how E has time to plan any of these parties, but I'm always impressed when I come. They're wild, but controlled. People are relaxed and having fun, much like they are at tonight's party. The place is fucking packed and people are grinding against each other. Weed smoke fills the room and the smell of sweat accents the odor. I take in the crowd before I spot her. Sandwiched between some guy and girl, a red solo cup in her hands. She takes a drink and laughs as the guy whispers in her ear. I grow agitated watching them. One of his hands grabs her waist, while the other is on her inner thigh and trailing up. She grabs his wrist, stopping him.

Good girl.

I follow behind Zeke as he digs through the crowd to get to her. She sees him and lights up instantly. She was happy before, but when seeing him, she's a different kind of happy.

I'm not jealous that my friend makes her this happy, but I am bitter about it.

"And you don't want to do that on me, E!" Zeke whines looking at her.

"You came!" She launches into his arms and hugs him tightly before gripping his wandering hands. "Hands, asshole."

She smiles at me, but it's different. Guarded despite knowing that I know how she tastes, the sounds she makes when she cums, and how she looks sleeping after being fucked thoroughly. Working together on the project is different, there's a reason for us to interact. Here in this space, anything can happen. I can see that it has her on edge.

Stop obsessing.

"You still performing tonight?" He's holding her by the waist. His mouth is a little ways away from her ear, but he still has to shout a bit over the music for her to hear him. She smiles and nods. "Should I get a chair ready? I'm sure me or Kane will happily give you a ride." He wiggles his eyebrows making me laugh.

"Singing lead? Yes. Dry humping anyone in this room? No." She laughs keeping a strong hold on his arm.

I'm a bit disappointed that she wouldn't grind in my lap again, but I shake the feeling off. It's not that big of a deal.

Who are you trying to fool?

I take the time to check her out. Her light washed jeans are tight around her thighs and ass, but flair out towards the bottom. Beat up Converse peek from underneath. A tight, ripped shirt hugs her upper body and displays her tits. A smidgen of skin peeks out between the waist of her jeans and the hem of her shirt. Her locs are pulled up and a few pieces fall in her face.

"E!" someone shouts from the other side of the room. It's Isaac. He waves her over and she kisses Zeke's forehead before getting lost in the crowd of bodies.

"Let's get a drink," Zeke says, going over to a cooler and

snagging two beers.

"You knew she'd be here?"

"Yeah, she's at all the parties she plans. Liam, the guy that sings lead, decided they needed to play. That's what she was telling me." He pauses. "You were too busy checking her out, weren't you?"

I shake my head and take a long drink. He's right. I couldn't keep my eyes off her enough to hear them talk. I'm surprised he can.

"Let me know man. I can set it up. I know she's been into you for a bit."

"She's not into me." I look around the room and catch a few flirty eyes.

Zeke snorts at me before looking back at the stage. I ignore him, still gazing around the room, checking out a few girls and shooing others away.

After that night with E, none of these girls seem to do it for me. Don't get me wrong, I've tried, but never let it get too far. My doctor said I'm fine. I want a second opinion.

She surfaces on a makeshift stage, her purple and white guitar slung over her shoulder, dead smack in the center of the stage. She smiles at the guys around her and someone in the crowd.

Liam takes the mic from her. She shoots him the most impressive "go fuck yourself" look making me laugh. She makes her way to the other mic stand and adjusts it.

Atta Girl.

"Liam always needs to be in the spotlight apparently," she

jabs after his long spiel about success and hardwork. She gives him a pointed look and he glares at her and mouths 'bitch.'

I lean forward and notice Zeke shifting too. We exchange looks knowing good and damn well we'd beat his ass if he does that shit again.

She motions to the back of the room towards a window. Someone slides it open and cool air helps clear the smoke while cooling the packed place down. The smell of chlorinated pool water drifts in. Better than the smell of musky, sweaty bodies and sex I guess.

A song swells into the air, I notice it's a song my sister likes by that group Stray Kids. The bass of the song named 'Taste' makes the crowd sway.

Her body moves hypnotically slow as her lips mouth along the melody of the song. She looks back at Isaac, getting him to join in. Kneeling to the edge of the stage, her body moves to the song's beat.

She walks to the other side of the stage, then does her signature hip sway. She teases the crowd by lifting her shirt slowly and someone starts a "take it off" chant.

She laughs and shakes her head before looking back at Isaac, who's approaching her with his mic in his hands

Isaac sings a line, then puts the mic to E's mouth.

She seductively whisper-sings the response. Her hips hover near his and his hand glides up her thigh.

The urge to punch him in his throat intermingles with the urge to claim her on that stage and let everyone know who makes her scream when she cums.

You haven't done that in a while though. Chill.

He starts rolling his body and pulls her closer, closing the small space between them. Their bodies move in sync as they dance seductively.

She bends at the waist and rotates her ass to the beat against him. When she stands back up, she grabs the back of his neck and she sings the backup vocals on the chorus.

I feel my jaw clench and I release it. Cheering surrounds me, even Zeke the damn traitor.

A wad of money gets tossed on the stage and she smiles in the general direction it came from. She points to Isaac, then herself and gives a thumbs up. She grabs the money and tosses it to Isaac and he smiles, tucking it in his pocket.

My shoulders relax as she laughs with someone in the front of the crowd. I crane my neck for a better look and see her friend D.

Liam starts playing before her and Isaac are settled in their spots. She rushes to get her guitar on and then joins in visibly annoyed.

What an asshole.

She starts singing as her shoulders move to the rhythm with her guitar hanging behind her. I watch in awe as the crowd dances and sways with her. This girl can command a room full of people. The fucking power she holds is way more than the power I have over anyone.

Her hand is bracing her guitar so it doesn't swing around and throw her off balance. She sings the second verse of Olivia Lunny's "Think Of Me" before pulling her friend Denise up on stage to dance with her.

The band plays as they dance and she looks at me singing the last bit of the chorus.

I'm a goner.

The look in her eyes unleashes a feeling in me that's unfamiliar. I scoot closer to the edge of my seat with my eyes still on her.

Her and her friend continue dancing and she breaks eye contact once the song ends. I take a swig of my beer, letting the liquid warm in my mouth before I swallow it. I grimace at the lingering taste. I hate warm beer.

Liam motions to Isaac and the click of Isaac's drum sticks starts a countdown. The speaker gives a little whine as she grabs her mic and they start playing a new song.

Her shoulders move as Liam sings the intro. She mouths the words only coming in when she needs to. Her eyes are closed and she's completely in her element. Her fingers strum her guitar and she leans into the mic.

As she sings the chorus, the crowd joins in with her. She steps away and focuses on her guitar. Her and Liam's guitars sing in unison before she belts the chorus again.

The crowd basically eats out the palm of her hand. Hands are up reaching for her and she intertwines her fingers with someone and sings to them. The crowd cheers as she removes her guitar and another song takes over the speaker.

She sips out of her water bottle as Issac whispers in her ear. She laughs, almost spitting on everyone. She covers her mouth with one hand and extends the other to apologize nonverbally.

"Spit on me, E!" someone yells. She looks at them then grabs her mic.

"Don't threaten me with a good time."

She laughs as people scream completely surprised by their reaction. The guys on stage with her laugh, except the big guy, he shakes his head looking disgusted.

Zeke shifts beside me, breaking my focus from the stage. "You look like you want to punch someone."

I shake my head and take a swig at my beer before grabbing Zeke and I another one.

"Just admit you like her, man," he says with a nudge. "I won't be too lonely in the single pool."

"Zeke," I warn.

"I've seen that look before." He laughs.

I huff, glaring at him as I flip him off, leaning back in my chair. "You got it wrong."

"If you say so," he winks at me and chugs his beer.

20

Kane

The night starts to wind down as I sit outside looking at the stars. Something I've never really done until tonight. I feel body heat beside me and the smell of chocolate covered strawberries has me ready to pounce. I look at her, letting my eyes take her in.

"What's up," she says softly. She takes off her shoes and socks, rolls up her pant legs, then puts her feet in the frigid pool water. She sighs as she lays back on the pavement. "Best way to cool off quickly."

I laugh, still watching her. "You did good in there. Why didn't you tell me you were performing?"

She shrugs. Her eyes close for a long moment before she opens them, staring up at the sky.

I lie beside her, then move a bit closer. Her eyes are on me now. She studies my movements closely, then lets her eyes explore my face.

I can feel her body heat from where I am. The soft skin of her hand leans against my own for a second before she pulls it away and rests both on her stomach.

"Zeke says you have a thing for me," I tease.

"I'm going to fucking kill him," she groans. She looks at me hesitantly. "It's nothing. I've always had this pull to you. And you're fine, but you've always had at least two girls with you. Plus, someone said you always smell like sex."

"I smell like what?" I laugh.

"Sex," she says, looking into my eyes laughing. "I hope you know that takes talent."

"Tell me," I say lower. "Do I smell like sex now?"

She shakes her head looking at me. "You smell like cinnamon sugar and spices. Baking." She leans close to me and smells my neck. The simple action turns me on more than it should. "You remind me of my grandma's house for the holidays." She lays back a bit wobbly. I can tell she's a bit drunk.

"So, you think I'm fine?"

She laughs and nudges me. "I can tell you're very aware of how fine you are."

"I like hearing you tell me though."

"Don't lie," she rolls her eyes at me with a small smile on her face.

We stare at each other for a moment before we both move closer. Her nose touches mine.

My heart pounds in my chest as I close the distance between us, placing my lips against hers. The warmth of her breath rushes out as her she sighs. Her tongue grazes my lip and I suck it in my mouth, teasing it with my own before biting at her bottom lip. Smooth palms graze past my cheek before I feel her fingers dives into my hair and grips it tightly.

She tastes like strawberry lemonade and vodka. Sweet, strong, and flavorful.

I pull her closer, deepening the kiss just to taste her more, but she slows the kiss down. Her hand on my chest, adding a light pressure to separate us.

Is she scared of what comes next? She shouldn't be. I wouldn't intentionally hurt her, not if I can control it.

I give her another tentative kiss and look back into her eyes.

"I think you've ruined me for anyone else," I admit with a soft laugh as I ease away from her.

She searches my eyes and smiles a little.

"Right, just one night and I've ruined you," she laughs, dryly and looks back up at the sky. "A whole four weeks later."

"I didn't know that was bothering you," I state, still watching her face.

She shrugs. "You're Kane Yamada. You get pussy."

We laugh.

There's a brief moment that passes. The crickets sing around us as the party music turns into a slow medley.

"And if I say I want yours?"

"Been there, done that." She dismisses my comment with a wave of her hand and another tense laugh.

"Enjoyed it and want to do it again."

My confession catches her by surprise. Her head quickly turns towards me, then her bright brown eyes search my face. "and again…" I inch my face closer to hers. Her tongue wets her full lips and I'm already wanting to dive back in to taste them. And I know she'd let me.

Her eyes still search mine as she moves a little closer. She's guarded and searching for something that I don't know exists. Something I don't know ever existed. And for some reason, I silently pray that I'm wrong and she finds it.

She inches closer to me and our lips brush against each other. And right as I put my hand on the back of her neck to seal our lips together, someone hurls right beside us into the pool. She shrieks, yanking her feet out of water as I pull her up with me laughing. She idly grabs my arm as we stare at the person hunched over emptying their stomach in the pool, surrounded by people trying to soothe them.

"I guess I'm cool enough," she says sarcastically, stifling a laugh.

She bends over grabbing her socks and shoes and my eyes trace the silhouette of her body, then her delicate profile.

Yeah, Ebony Young. I'm completely fucked.

21

Ebony

"Hi, Z!" I say brightly as I slip into the booth beside Kane, catching them both off guard. Voices intermingle in the café as Isaac and I make space for ourselves at their booth. I glance over at Kane and nod at him before snatching a hot fry from his tray.

"That's mine," he says with a playful glare.

"Come get it," I say tilting my head more. A smirk tugging at my lips as I attempt to fight it. His body shifts as he leans closer to me, his eyes fixed on mine.

"This is great and all," Isaac starts sounding uncomfortable. "but you promised me food, E."

"Come on man," Zeke groans.

I move away from Kane giving Isaac and Zeke attention. Zeke's hand gesturing between Kane and me as he glares at Isaac.

"I respect that. Truly, I do, but she promised me food."

"I'll get you food," Zeke groans with an eye roll.

"No, I got it. I'm going to steal this one for a bit," Kane states, lifting his hips and digging in his pockets for a moment. Pulling his hand from his back pocket, he slides a wad of cash towards Isaac. "Good?"

"You want a sugar baby?" Isaac asks as he counts the cash.

"Isaac!" I place my hand on my head trying not to laugh as my friend shrugs his shoulders before shoving his loot in his pocket.

"Fine. Take her," Isaac says. "Guess it's you and me, Zeke."

"Joy," Zeke groans looking between Kane and I.

With a gentle nudge, I climb out of the booth catching Kane's smile to Zeke before he nods towards the exit.

It's quieter outside and less crowded as we walk the flower lined pavement.

"Where are we going?" I ask after a few moments of walking.

"You remember Dr. Goodwin said there was this really nice museum around here?"

"With the old tech projects?"

"No," he chuckles. "A real art gallery."

"I didn't take you for an art guy," I comment, laughing softly.

"I'm not," he smiles over at me. "Let's go. We'll grab something to eat after."

"If I didn't know any better Mr. Yamada, I'd think you're taking me out on a date," I smirk at him. We walk in step, heading towards student parking.

"I am," he confirms with a dazzling smile. "For the project of course."

"Just the project, right?" I ask, chewing at my inner cheek.

"What? Scared you'll fall in love?" he asks as he leans against the side of his fancy, black car. The sun glitters off the smooth, sleek surface.

My eyes trace the lines as I stare in awe of it. Then, my eyes lock with his as he smirks at me. He gives his head a gentle nod towards his car.

"Now or never, E," he coaxes as he swings his keys around his long index finger.

"Okay," I say with a slight giggle. "Let's go on a project date."

He smiles wider at me before rushing to the passenger side of his car. He opens the door, ghosting his hand over the small of my back as I ease in. He closes the door, then takes long strides to the driver's side beaming.

"Ready?" he asks with the same smile he entered the car with.

"Absolutely," I smile back, caught in his infectious happiness. I secure my seat belt and lean back as he eases his car on the road.

It's a quick drive to the art gallery downtown, but it felt like a blink with Kane. Not because he drives a little faster, but because being with him feels… easy.

I stare up at the building as he opens my door and ushers me out of the car. Advertisement flags fly in the breeze, slapping against the bricks that stack up the three story building.

Kane takes my hand, gently pulling me with him.

"I've never been here before," I mutter as I fall in step with him. His palm is warm against mine for a minute before I ease my hand out of his with a mumbled apology. He looks over at me, an arrogant smirk on his face.

"Glad to be the first to take you," he says, stopping at the counter. "Two tickets please," he pulls out his wallet.

"Oh," I breathe, pulling out my wallet. "How much is it?" I ask softly as I study the pamphlets.

"Paid for," he whispers to me. He gives a slight nod to the attendant before placing both of his hands on my shoulders. He leads me through the large, wooden double doors with designs carved deep into the brown, polished barrier.

"Tell me how much to send you," I say over my shoulder, not realizing how close his face is to mine. I feel the warmth of his breath on my cheek and shy away from his searching eyes. I never realized how long his lashes were until that moment.

"No," he states firmly. He steps away from me with a smile, then nods towards one of the large cases with different mechanical equipment.

I study the metal bracelet-like bands and different devices. "Are you thinking of something other than a drone?" I ask looking up at him. "I think a digital watch would be cool. Similar to another project I'm working on actually."

"What project is that?" he asks, looking in the case.

"Can't talk about it yet," I whisper, stepping away from the glass case. "Hasn't been fully approved by the school."

"School has you on a NDA?"

"No," I laugh, wringing my hands. "I think it's bad luck to talk about projects too early."

He hums his acknowledgement, following beside me. "Never thought you'd be superstitious," he laughs.

"I'm not that superstitious," I shrug.

"Can't be if you have a black cat," he smiles at me as we make our way to the next set of stairs. "When'd it start?"

"When did what start?" I ask as we reach the landing.

"The project superstition."

"Middle school," I answer with a laugh. "Don't tell me you don't have some superstition or ritual when playing football."

"I feel like that's different," he laughs. "Gets my head in the game."

I glance over at him as he stares at me. A thoughtful, pensive look on his face as his eyes scan my face for a moment. I shy away from his eyes as I walk ahead of him, trying to force myself to admire the art, but he catches up, standing beside me at each painting. It takes us about an hour to see everything and by then, we find a comfortable banter as we talk about each painting. Occasionally, talking about our project and how to make it memorable.

"I'm starving," I sigh as he escorts me out the front door. The sky is a faint orange as the sun sets.

"I know this really low key restaurant. And I promised you food," he comments with a small smile. He holds open the passenger side door and I slide in.

"As long as the food's good," I counter, looking up at him.

He leans close to me. His smell overtaking the natural fragrance of the world around us. His nose inches closer to mine and I suck in a small, lungful of air.

Kiss me...

My stomach growls loudly and we both separate laughing hysterically.

"Okay, okay," he says, closing the passenger door and driving us to a small restaurant not far from the gallery.

22

Ebony

After the first project date with Kane, he's managed to convince me to go out more "for research." His words, not mine. However tonight, I managed to convince him to focus on our project. I shovel pasta in my mouth as I scroll through my computer. My hand scrawls notes that I barely pay attention to until I check to see what I wrote, then my eyes search the computer screen again. The old blue carpet in the library digs into my legs as I sit surrounded by notes and printouts of diagrams. The faint musky odor of mildew drifts in the air as the fan turns on.

"I can't find anything that can connect these two conductors to make this run with your programming," I groan, putting my bowl in the trash and rubbing my eyes.

I stretch out my legs and look over at Kane who sits typing at his computer. He finishes what he's typing then looks over spinning the chair to face me.

"Then we'll have to figure out a different build." He sighs. "I thought you said this one would work?"

"It's supposed to," I say defensively, grabbing a paper with bright yellow highlights and passing it off to him. He takes it and looks it over.

"Okay, so, let's go to the server room at some point and try testing the computer chip pairings. If everything else is right, then the only thing we need to try is a new chip."

"Maybe," I say looking back into the screen. My teeth tug at the dead skin on my lower lip as I read what's on my screen.

"E," he calls softly. "Ebony."

I look at him frustrated. "Yeah?"

"We should call it a night. It's late. Don't you have class early tomorrow morning?"

He looks at me compassionately, but I can see the exhaustion lingering underneath. We rushed over right after class and started hammering away at researching.

Technically, we were way ahead of our plan, but we both agreed that it would be best to finish early and test until the deadline.

"Okay." He looks at me in disbelief and I throw my hands up. "Okay!" I laugh, closing my laptop and bundling the papers together.

"I built a computer when I was 10. My Dad showed me a trick to it. We'll get this project done in no time. Don't sweat it."

He uses his finger to spin a pen around his thumb. An anxious habit I've seen a time or two since working with him.

"I keep thinking that maybe the product shouldn't be a computer. I know you have football and your full load of classes, but I really think we could do something better."

The pen stops spinning.

"What should the end product be then?" He leans back in

the chair with his cheek resting on his fist. "That drone you wrote down earlier?"

"That would cost more than I make in tips." I stand up putting the papers and a folder in my bag neatly. I grab my computer and slide it in my bag.

"What if I said money wasn't an issue?"

I pause.

"We'd need to build a blueprint... That might put us behind," I say, chewing on my lip as I think.

"I think we can get it done. A drone would be better anyways," he confirms, grabbing my bag. "We'll talk about it while I walk you to your apartment." He shoulders my book bag and waits for me to walk out the room with him.

"I knew you would agree with us doing something more complicated," I state with a small smile on my face. He throws his heavy arm on my shoulder shaking his head laughing softly.

"Let's go." He uses his hip to nudge me forward out of the study room. We pass more study cubicles before exiting the building.

"By the way, there's going to be a fall festival and a Halloween kind of party. Are you going?" I reach for my bag and he shifts his shoulders out of my reach. "It will also help with some testing I have to do for another project."

"Do I have to sell myself at some bachelor auction or something?"

"No," I laugh. "Just wear a band to both and I'll take it from there."

"One more question." His face is serious as he stares at me.

"Are you going to be there?"

He looks at me with a smirk as we walk towards my apartment. He eyes me up and down. "Yeah, I'm usually at all the parties. Just behind the scenes."

We climb the steps and get to my floor. I unlock my door and reach for my bag. He hands it over and steps closer to me leaning in. "I'll be there. Just don't be so behind the scenes."

I roll my eyes with a blush. "Bye, Kane." I step in my apartment and close the door. Rushing to the window I open my curtain to peek out at him walking towards the parking lot. The wind blowing his black hair as he walks with his hands in his pocket. He looks over his shoulder for a second with a ghost of a smile on his face.

I sit on my couch with Silver in my lap purring. The faint scent of him lingers on my clothes and I sniff slightly, before getting up to take a quick shower to clear my head.

Once out, I grab my computer and start looking up something for our project, then get dressed, make a cup of tea, and sit at my bed uploading documents that I've found to the drive I share with Kane.

My phone beeps beside me and I see a message from Kane.

shouldn't you be asleep?

Maybe...

Go to sleep. We'll look at this stuff tomorrow.

> I found what we needed. I think you much rather that than have work piling up.

> I'd rather be kissing you.

> Kane…

> I like the way you say my name.

I smile to myself chewing on my thumb nail, watching the dots pop up indicating he's typing.

> Especially when you get frustrated with me for being stubborn.

My smile gets bigger as I laugh to myself. The text dots pop up as he types more.

> and when you cum. Yum…

I roll my eyes with a scoff. My thumbs typing my response quickly.

> Night, Kane.

> Night, beautiful xx

I unfortunately spend the night using my toy to get the dirty thoughts of Kane out of my head before going to sleep.

It only makes me dream of him even more.

23

Kane

Miya rushes into the computer lab and plops her small body in the chair beside me. She shoves her hand through her hair to smooth it out of her face before spinning the chair towards me. Her arms cross over her chest as she glares at the side of my face. She huffs to get my attention. I glance at her, then continue typing the code I'm working on.

"Spill it," I demand as my fingers type quickly.

"Dad *finally* told me you plan on 'helping' me. I don't need your help, Kane," she grumbles.

"It's not just to help you. It's to help Ren, too."

"Help Ren? Why would they need help?" My sister spits. She's never really liked Ren. She couldn't explain why, but the tension between the two was enough to snuff a fire or start one. They can tolerate each other if they have to, but beyond that would be asking for a fight.

"Yes, Ren was expelled for being attached to something related to your project."

"I'm sure they know and they're just not telling you. We both know Ren isn't the most up front."

I shrug. "Neither are we when the situation is necessary."

"Do you hear yourself? What part of them potentially being

a part in some drug scandal makes you think lying to anyone, especially you, is worth it."

"They have their reasons," I huff. "And I don't think they are lying. They have no reason to lie to anyone."

"Maybe, but something has always been off about them, Kane. I need you to believe me."

With a sigh, I stop typing and look at my younger sister. I run my hand through my hair and lean my face on my hand.

She chews on the inside of her mouth as she watches me. Her leg bounces as she moves the chair from side to side.

"Did you find something out?"

She shakes her head and sits forward. "It's a hunch." She takes the chair beside me, logs in, and starts a quick search on a database. An article pulls up and I look it over.

"Ebony, the lead on this project, showed this article to me when she pitched the idea for the project we're working on together."

I think for a moment. My sister mentioned when she started the project that the lead was pretty cool and the two became close friends. I just didn't know it was Ebony.

Small world.

I lean forward reading the headline.

"An unnamed woman on this campus claims there's a drug trafficking group on campus," I read aloud. "Okay?"

"Has Ren mentioned this article to you?"

I shake my head looking at the article again then looking at my sister. "Are they the one that brought it to the journalist's attention?"

My sister shakes her head in turn. "Ren's named a suspect by one of the survivors interviewed."

"That's nothing new," I state leaning back.

"Their name is connected with another one I can't locate anywhere else. Both the writer and the survivor are adamant that someone named Eva, who is connected to Ren in another article, has something to do with the operation or knows who has a hand in it. I think Ren and Eva were working together and got caught."

"Okay, Nancy Drew, where's the proof?"

"In the documents that are sealed. I've been working with the office to get physical copies, but they got real sketchy."

"Not gonna work. If the school is covering it up, it's going to be on a digital database or locked in one of the basement's filing systems. So, you do need my help."

Miya sighs, leaning back in the chair.

"How did Ebony find out about this?"

Miya shrugs. "I never really asked. I assumed she just stumbled on it in her initial research."

I rub my chin as the silence rests between my sister and me. I look at my code idly. I contemplate the possibilities of Ren not really being innocent and the additional work that they'd have to do to find the unnamed woman.

"So," my sister's voice cuts through my thoughts. "Are you and Ebony gonna be a thing?" she finishes slowly.

"Why?" I ask her slowly.

"Because if you are, just save the typical 'pretty boys break hearts' bullshit for after my project with her. I need her."

"What about me?" I look at my sister feigning hurt. She laughs.

"You're my annoying big brother. I'll always need you. She just seems to have information the school won't give me." Miya sucks in a huge breath and lets it out. "I want to do more research before I tell you my theory."

"Don't trust me?"

"I do, but I don't want to add any fuel to the gossip mill. It's like the school has secret ears. It freaks me out." My sister stands and ruffles my hair before leaving the computer lab.

I watch her. She's right. A lot of information has been flying around this campus like the rooms have ears and eyes. I pull out my paper and add it to my existing list.

Note 3: Is the school bugged?

24

Ebony

There's a buzz on the campus as Denise and I sit on a bench near the Art Annex drinking smoothies. Bent and dingy note cards sit between us underneath a heavy book. I check my lip gloss in the mirror and adjust the position of my hoop earrings.

"I'm just saying Eb. The way he looks at you in class now, that man wants you," Denise says looking at me. "And normally I would say leave the dark, brooding, bad boys alone, but that one has something going for him."

"Because he's tall, muscular, and good looking?"

"Exactly," Denise confirms. "Not to mention he's a beast on the football field. You should go to a game and watch."

"Vin plays on the team," I say, scrunching up my nose.

"Fuck, Vin," Denise scolds rolling her brown eyes. "I'm saying. You're getting back to you. Angela Bassett in *How Stella Got Her Groove Back* kind of comeback. You weren't just a party girl before all that shit happened."

I nod. We tiptoe around the conversation. We don't know how to navigate it, but it's a Pandora's box that I'm told I should open and explore. No, but thank you for the consideration.

My phone buzzes in my pocket and I pull it out while

136

Denise digs in her bag.

U eat?

Not yet. Studying with D.

Good. I have something for u.

Fuck..

???

You're sexy as fuck all the time, but right now… drool…

I look around quickly, then back at my phone reading the message again.

C me yet?

Don't be creepy.

Never creepy.

2 u're left

He sends me a selfie with a panty dropping smile and I roll my eyes blushing. Turning to my left, I see him, leaned against the light post across the courtyard with his head leaned against it. He waves, then approaches me with a smirk.

All eyes are on him as he bypasses girls that stop and gawk at him. I don't blame them one bit, man is the epitome of sexy.

He holds a bag of takeout in one hand and drinks in another.

"Girl, is that…" Denise conceals a squeal as she slaps at my arm. "He got it bad."

I shush her swatting at her, laughing and standing. I adjust my pleated black skirt and my loose button up that hangs from one of my shoulders.

"Hey," he greets us with a smile, handing me the bag. "Thought you and D could use some food. Got it from the burger joint a few blocks over."

"That's my favorite place!" Denise squeals, grabbing the bag from me. "Keeper."

"You didn't have to."

"Wanted to. I feel like I've been slacking on the project."

Denise makes random noises behind me. I glance back at her and mouth. "Can you relax?" She shakes her head as she puts french fries in her mouth and tilts her head to the side. I turn back to Kane and smile, trying to mask my blush.

"You want to sit with us?"

He laughs adjusting his bag on his broad shoulder.

"I actually have class in a little bit, but I heard you were around here somewhere." He looks over his shoulder and nods to someone. "You look good." His eyes scan my body.

"Ya girl here had an interview with the dean office for some student life stuff. You wanna know how she did?"

"How'd she do D?" he asks with a small smile on his face. Denise shoots me a 'I like him even more look' and he laughs.

"She nailed it!" Denise says with a mouth full of fries.

"Really? I'm not surprised. A little hurt that you didn't tell me." He places a large hand over his heart and pouts. I push him gently, rolling my eyes. "What are you going to be doing with student life?"

"Using donations to get more entertainment on campus."

"She's sick of partying," Denise pipes up around me. She shakes the ice in her cup.

"D," I look behind me to her. "You just gonna tell all my business?"

"I'm just saying!" She holds her hands up and looks between me and Kane with her lips pursed trying to hide her smile.

"She's partly right. It's kind of a selfish reason." He quirks an eyebrow and shifts his bag again. "The goal is to lower petty crime statistics on campus. Giving people more to do also means we can lower those rates."

He thinks about what I said for a moment then smiles at me. "Smart. I like that idea. Let me know if I can help with anything. My parents donate to the school and I know with my sister and me going here, they'll love to contribute more to make campus safer, for her at least."

I smile at him and feel Denise poke me.

"I gotta go. Class. Text me. We can work on the project when I get out of practice."

I nod and wave as he walks away.

"Girl," Denise mocks with a smile on her face. I roll my eyes and snatch a fry from the bag, shoving it in my mouth.

"So, when did it happen?" Denise asks with a knowing look that makes me laugh nervously. "Thought you could hide it, huh?" She giggles not pushing the subject.

I check my phone and shoot my parents a text.

> Hey! Great news! Working on a big project and got another level of it approved by the school. Hope you guys are good. Maybe we could meet for dinner? I really miss you guys. Love you.

I slide my phone in my bag and grab another fry.

"Still nothing?" Denise asks me.

With a small smile, I shake my head.

"These fries are so good," I say lightly, hiding my face from her as I dig in the bag.

She hums in response, but not pushing the issue. One of these days, she'll get sick of me hiding from her. Will she leave me, too? Will Isaac? Zeke? Kane?

I look at her and lay my head on her shoulder.

"Have I ever told you how much I love you?"

"Uh-uh bitch don't get me to start crying," she gushes pushing me off of her with a laugh.

I don't even want to find out.

25

Kane

Her floor is soft below my body. There's talking from a movie we put on, but we aren't watching. Silver's bell jingles as he attacks his scratching post. Purchased by yours truly. Ebony lays beside me on her stomach. Her pencil makes scratching noises, then she erases feverishly. She groans and lays her head on her paper and pretends to cry. I look over at her pushing my hair back out of my face.

"I can't draw," she groans. She rolls over on her back and dramatically throws her arm over her face. I peek at her picture and stifle a laugh. "Are you laughing at me!?"

"Yes," I say, trying to hold my laugh, but succumbing to it anyway.

She grumbles at me as she gets up and adjusts her clothes. "I need a drink. Want one?"

"What you got?" I ask as I get up, following her to her small kitchen. I lean against the white fridge and watch as she struggles to reach the middle shelf. She looks around for something, then tries again.

"I have wine, but I can't find my stool to get it." She braces her hands on the counter to lift herself up when I approach. I put my hand on her shoulder, reach over her head, and grab a bottle of red wine. Sitting it carefully on the counter, I look down at her as she turns to me. She's so close. So. Fucking. Close.

Fuck. Fuck. Fuck. Fuck.

I told myself on the way over that I would behave. I wouldn't try to kiss her, touch her, anything. Being this close poses a problem for that effort. Now all I can think about is doing all those things to her and more.

Her eyes are soft as she looks up at me. Conflict battling behind the brown depths. Maybe she's thinking the same. Forcing herself to be restrained when the inner parts of her just want to run wild, free to do and feel whatever in this moment.

I step back despite not wanting to and lean back on the fridge. Crossing my arms over my chest, I stare at her from where I am. Her eyes are still on me as she releases a shaky breath. She turns away, reaching on the lower shelf.

"You feel it too, don't you?" I ask softly. I don't mean to say it out loud, but I do. And now that it's out, I'm going to go with it.

She puts two wine glasses on the counter and rolls her shoulders. She glances back at me before fixating on the glasses. She's tense now, guarded because she wants to resist and it looks like her resolve is just as thin as mine.

"Don't know what you're talking about, Kane." Her voice is soft as she pours us both a drink. She chugs her glass and fixes another.

"Bullshit." I walk towards her smoothly. My fingers grasp her arm and I gently turn her to face me. "You wouldn't have downed that damn wine if you didn't know what I was talking about."

My mouth hovers over hers and I feel her unsteady breath on my lips. She braces herself on the counter. My hands rest on either side of her body as I move a little closer. Our bodies are only a hair apart. Heat cascades off hers, pulling me in closer.

She swallows hard as her eyes dart from my eyes to my lips. She shifts, bringing her body closer to mine. I can tell it was unintentional by the way she steps back into the counter. The lower cabinet door clatters as her foot hits it.

I smirk watching her scramble mentally to figure out what to do. It's like a game of chicken. Who's going to back down first?

"Want to get back to the blueprints?" I lean in closer to her mouth. I tilt my head to the side slightly with my eyes locked on hers. She can seal her lips to mine if she wants. I'm just a breath away.

"No," she says softly, then she closes the distance.

The kiss is hard at first, needy. Then she softens it as her hands grab my waist, pulling my front to hers. My mouth immediately moves with hers as I put one of my hands on her waist and the other on the back of her neck. I lift her on the counter and push myself between her legs.

She sighs with the movements. The tension releases from her body with each stroke of my tongue against hers.

Her arms wrap around my neck while our tongues explore each other's mouth. Soft moans spill from her as I suck on her bottom lip. She nips at mine in return. Using her thighs, I pull her closer to me, then slide my hand up her tank top. I grind my hips into her.

"Kane," she whisper-moans against my lips.

I hum in response, slowing the kiss. She starts teasing my mouth with her tongue.

"You're trouble," I whisper against her mouth with a smirk. Her breathy laugh fills my mouth as I plant a hot kiss on her lips.

"No," she states, shaking her head. "I'm just really fucking horny."

I lean back and look at her. She licks her lips before sliding her hand down my pants and grabbing a handful of my dick. I groan pushing into her hands.

"So are you," she whispers, leaning into my neck to suck on it. She strokes me slowly brushing her soft thumb over the head then back to the base.

My breathing is shaky as I fix my eyes on hers and pull my pants down enough to expose me for her to see. She plants a kiss on my lips before nudging me back. I make space for her to slide off the counter on the floor. She gets on her knees for me, wedging her body between me and the cabinets.

She licks from the base to the tip before shoving my dick to the back of her throat and I moan.

My hands gripping on the counter to keep my balance while she gags and slurps on my length.

I move my hips trying to get her to swallow me whole and groan as she relaxes her throat enough, letting my dick slide further in.

"You're so fucking good with that dirty mouth," I mutter

wrapping my hands in her hair so I can watch her suck me off. "I've missed your fucking tongue," I add thrusting a little faster.

She gags and pulls her head back, leaning it against the cabinet behind her. She pulls the straps of her tank top down, exposing her pretty titties to me as she continues to stroke me with the most perfect 'fuck me' eyes.

"Cum on me," she moans before swallowing me again.

"God damn, Ebony," I groan as her greedy hands cup my balls, playing with them.

She manages to get me completely down her throat twice before I'm about to cum. She can tell. It's written in her eyes as she shoves my dick back down her throat and I'm done for. I spill my cum down her throat and watch her pull my dick out and show me.

She swallows it, adjusts her clothes, then pulls my pants back up. She nudges me to walk past me and I grab her, pulling her into a deep kiss.

"I thought you wanted me to cum on you," I whisper against her lips with a smile. I bite at her bottom lip.

She giggles. "Guess I got too into it." She kisses me again. "I have to wash my face," she adds with a laugh.

"I don't know why you would need to," I say playfully. My eyes locked on her as I roll my tongue around in my mouth suppressing a smile.

She laughs, nudging me away from her and disappears into her bedroom. I lean against the counter laughing to myself. I just had my whole dick down this girl's throat and she walks off like it didn't happen.

I take a long drink of my wine, grab both glasses and the bottle, then sit back on her floor looking at my blueprint. Silver nudges up against me.

"Your mom is a bad, bad girl, Silver," I whisper to him as I scratch his chin.

"Hey, don't tell him things like that," she sits beside me and tosses her paper to the side and starts trying to draw again.

I study her for a moment and lean against the couch with my brow furrowed.

"I feel like I was used." She looks at me confused. "You swallowed all of my dick and you're just…" I gesture to her and she laughs.

"Do you want to talk about it?" She asks with a smile on her face. She's mocking me a little.

"No," I say looking at her. "I want to return the favor."

She can't say anything else before she's on her back with my body on top of hers. My hand is already down her pants with my fingers plunging inside of her.

My tongue is in her mouth. I can taste the toothpaste she just used and I growl. "You don't like the way my cum tastes?"

"I do," she whispers while she pants and moans for me.

My fingers are back inside her thrusting hard. The sounds of her wetness make me hard again. "When you swallow my cum keep the taste on your fucking tongue," I growl in her ear before kissing her hard.

She whimpers against my mouth.

I tear my lips away from her and move between her legs taking one long swipe with my tongue. Her back arches and I dive in head first. My tongue swirling around her wetness until I start sucking it up. My hands undo my pants so I can fist my dick.

I groan into her pussy and suck harder. Her hands are tugging at my hair and she's moaning my name in an endless loop. I insert one of my fingers and she cums for me at that moment. My name tumbling out of her mouth like a prayer.

"You wanted me to cum on you?" I ask kneeling in front of her. I pull my dick out more as I stare down at her.

She nods, her chest rising and falling as she catches her breath. "Please," she whispers and pulls her tits out, playing with them for me.

"That's right, baby. Play with those pretty fucking nipples," I groan.

She's rubbing herself again. And I lean back to get the full view. She dips her fingers in and moans my name.

"That's my pussy," I groan.

She moans and I use my free hand to rub her clit gently to my rhythm and she starts shaking. Her head lays back on the carpet and she cums moaning my name again.

I move closer to her shooting ropes of cum on her stomach and tits with a low groan. I look down at her as my chest heaves before using my finger to write my name on her using my cum.

"Mine," I whisper against her lips.

She laughs, kissing me softly with her hands in my hair. I lean back watching her.

She laughs more laying back against the floor, while I slowly adjust my pants with a laugh of my own. I lay beside her staring up at her ceiling.

"I am so fucked," she says to herself mainly. She puts her hands over her face stifling her giggles.

I look over at her, still laughing with her.

You and me both, baby.

26

Ebony

I stare at the blank canvas on my laptop before giving up and closing the screen. Leaning against the arm of my couch, I watch as Silver basks in the sunlight. Golden beams brighting his dark fur from his tower.

Kane went home to visit his parents for the weekend, but has been texting me on and off since he left Friday after class. I look at my phone and dial my father's number. I listen to the line ring. I chew at my nail bed and watch the dust dance around Silver's relaxed face.

"Hello?" My mother sounds tense and angry. She always does.

"Hey mom," I greet her softly. "I was calling to check on everyone."

"Everyone's fine. What did you need?"

"I just miss you guys."

Silence occupies the space where conversation should exist.

"Your Dad's not here and when he comes back we are going to Europe for vacation, so we won't be available."

"Oh, that sounds fun. You and Dad deserve a trip away."

She hums her response to me, then fusses at someone. "I'll have him call you back." She hangs up before I can say anything else.

"Love you too, Mom." I put my phone on the couch beside me and go back to watching Silver. He looks over at me with his bright green eyes shining in the sunlight.

"Such a beautiful boy aren't you, Silver?" I gush at him with a small, sad smile.

My phone chimes as a text message comes in. I check it and see a picture message from Kane. I smile at the picture of him, his mom, and Miya at a lake. I can see the resemblance in each of them.

He sends another picture with him and his husky, who looks annoyed that he's interrupting her sunbathing. Her white, black, and gray fur is full and beautiful.

I get another picture of his whole family: Mom, Dad, Miya, Han (his little brother), and Akemi, who looks much happier.

I send him a video of Silver sun bathing before as he blinks slowly at me.

> Saturday mood = Silver

> I want to be as relaxed as him lol

> Going to the gym later. Want pics of that too?

I laugh to myself before sending him a sexy picture of my own.

> … I shouldn't be visiting my parents.

He sends me a topless picture showing off his v cut and his muscular torso. I bite at my knuckle, tracing all the lines of his beautifully sculpted body.

I want to top that picture, but I know I barely can. I go into my room and dig through my drawers finding lingerie that I forgot I purchased. I snap the tags off and slip into each one taking pictures and sending them, then add a video of me in a lacy black one for good measure.

I should really be at home… Fuck, Ebony.

I can't go to a family dinner like this.

He sends a picture with the outline of his hard dick before video calling me.

"Hey," I say, laying back on my bed with my phone over me.

"You play dirty," he groans, still shirtless.

I sit the camera on my nightstand and lay on my bed.

"I've got like 5 minutes to 'talk' to you" he says with a smirk.

"Oh?" I sit on my bed and play with the strings of my black, lacy lingerie outfit.

His breathing changes as his eyes take in the image on his phone screen. His right forearm flexes and relaxes.

"Show me," I say, my voice low, aroused knowing exactly what he's doing. He moves the camera showing me a little bit.

"I'm so hard it hurts," he laughs, giving his dick a slow tug.

I stand up and do a slow sexy dance for him. I sway my hips and shake my ass.

"Fuck," he groans as his movement speeds up. "Make yourself cum for me."

I take my top off and cover my breast with my arms.

"Move your hand," he groans.

"Say please."

He laughs, closing his eyes. "You stress me out, woman." His eyes fix on me and I only lean back with my breast still covered. "Baby, please."

"Good boy."

He shudders and I take the rest of my clothes off. I start with slow steady circles before speeding up. My fingers grab rub across my sensitive nipples and I moan his name.

"That's right, baby. Make yourself cum for me," he groans.

I watch him stroke himself before laying on my belly and giving him the back view of me playing with myself.

"Fuck you're so damn beautiful." His head lays back as he stifles a moan.

I get lost in his rhythm, dipping my fingers inside of my hot center and get swept up in an intense orgasm. Burying my face in my sheets, I moan his name as I cum on my fingers.

He groans my name, spilling cum on his stomach. He lays his head back and sighs.

"I should have stayed at school if you were going to do all this to me," he laughs out as he leans to the side, out of the camera's view.

He reappears with a shirt and cleans himself off, giving himself one last tug before getting up. He brings the phone with him to the closet and props it up as he starts getting dressed.

"I'm going to let you go," I say drowsily, still laying in my bed undressed.

"No the fuck you're not," he states looking at the phone screen. "We're going to talk until I get to the restaurant with my family, then you'll be able to take a nap. After that, I'm gonna call you again tonight."

"So demanding," I laugh.

He continues to stare at the camera half naked and beautiful. His pants are half on and unbuttoned. His hand rests on a black button up top.

"Fine." I feign annoyance. He smiles, leading us into a deep conversation until he's at the restaurant.

And he does exactly what he says.

27

Kane

Tonight's the night of the Halloween party. I'm masking my excitement as I pre-game with my friends, who came to visit for the weekend. Zeke joins us fumbling with the ties of his toga.

"I've been seeing you with Ebony a lot lately," Zeke says to me, wiggling his eyebrows.

"We're working on a project together, Zeke," I announce, rolling my eyes.

I'm sure he knows there's a little more to it. We don't exactly hide our attraction for each other. It's not like either one of us are in relationships. Just two attractive, single people that occasionally drop hints about wanting to fuck in various places on campus.

Her costume selections don't help either. All skin tight and form fitting.

I may have cum to a few of the pictures to keep from fucking her while we worked on our project over the last couple of weeks. And that shit hasn't been easy to keep from doing, especially when she's cumming on my damn fingers every chance we get.

Rainn stepping close to me snaps me out of my musing.

She has her makeup palette and a brush in her hands to add scars and gashes to my body. When she finishes, I stand and adjust my toga in the mirror, thankful that it's loose enough to hide anything that's going on below the waist when I see Ebony in one of those sinfully sexy costumes. Based on how my body's been reacting just by being near her, there'll be a lot of something going on below the belt.

We all arrived at the party shortly after prepping. The small brick colonial style house is lit up from the outside. The music pounding through the speakers spills onto the lawn. People litter the front yard drunk. Discarded cups and plates scatter across the lawn. We step over a dude with permanent marker all over his face and step through the threshold.

People mill around, a few dance. My eyes immediately look for her and I see her. Black leather suit, tits perked up and spilling over the zipper, and cat ears. That leather makes her ass look fatter. I groan internally.

"Hey!" She greets everyone as the song changes and more people start to dance.

"Everything looks so good! You should have let me help!" Miya, my younger sister, says to Ebony, hugging her.

I had no idea they were this close before this moment. I'd be lying if I said I didn't slightly enjoy their familiarity.

"You had other plans. I'm more than happy to get every-thing finished up. Clean up crew's gonna come tomorrow night. Gives people time to get out." She laughs and nudges Zeke.

A loud thump startles her and she turns to look in the

crowd.

"Get the hell down!" she shouts over the crowd. Sure enough, someone stands on the landing upstairs getting ready to jump over.

I don't know what face she gives the guy, but he immediately climbs back over the rail apologizing.

Zeke laughs beside me. "E, you seriously have that 'eat shit' look down."

She rubs the back of her neck. "They've been trying to break themselves or something in this house all night. The party just started!"

We laugh as she moves out the way, grabbing wrist bands.

"Omg! They came out so good!" Miya gushes as E shows her the colors.

"For mixing and mingling" She explains to us as she smiles at Miya. She writes hearts on Miya's purple bracelet, which matches hers. "If someone needs an organizer they'll know to look for a purple band." She says to the group then points to the wall with a projection of what the colors mean.

"These are VIP!?" Zeke is giddy beside me.

I look at the bright yellow band that matches my friends. She grabs my band, writes my name quickly then adds a heart at the end before writing on Zeke's. I admire her professional mode as she tucks the marker in her hair, which is pinned up in a high ponytail.

I could wrap that around my hand pretty easily.

"I'm going to show you where to go," she says to the group before addressing Miya. "We had to change where we had everything set up because they moved stuff around and none of the people that signed up to help showed up."

She motions for everyone to follow her as she and Miya talk about the party plans and changes. Her hand innocently grabs my wrist lightly. I wiggle my wrist shifting her hand down enough to intertwine our fingers. She's so engrossed in conversation with Miya that she doesn't realize it.

Zeke nudges me and looks at our hands then at my face. I shrug nonchalantly as we take the stairs, her ass a perfect view for me. It takes everything in me not to grab a handful or bite it.

Today is my lucky day.

At the landing, two black leather sofas sit next to each other with a small white dorm fridge in the middle. A dry bar sits in the farthest right corner. The music is less loud and the air smells cleaner. A fan rotates slowly overhead. A few people sit around making out or drinking.

"Where can I find that?" I hear Miya ask and Ebony points her down the hall. Miya's little legs rush off towards the other end and round the corner, disappearing.

She notices our fingers are interlocked and quickly pulls her hand from mine blushing. I lean against the wall behind me watching her fumble.

"You guys can basically come back here any time downstairs becomes too much." She grabs keys on black ribbons and hands one to each couple. "Room keys. I suggest taking the back ones. Front ones are clearly the go-to here," she states.

"I don't get one?" Zeke asks. "You planning on having your

way with me? I'm willing and ready." He outstretches his arm. His off white toga exposing most of his chest. He flexes for her.

"No," she says pointedly laughing. "Miya and I have a key for the cleaners. I'll have to find the others, but there are a few in the back already unlocked." A moment passes and her face lights up.

"Oh! Hot box." She smiles real big. She nods down the hall and heads in the direction Miya went. We follow, intrigued.

Stock art hangs on the white walls. At first, the smell of fresh paint overtakes the smells of the party until we round the corner. An immediate punch of weed smoke fills the air.

"Holy fuck," Sanjay exclaims laughing. "That's a hot box."

Ebony tries the handle, then bangs on the door. "Stop locking the fucking door."

She pulls out her key and unlocks the door and a curtain of smoke falls out of the room. She coughs. "Whoever locked this door, your mom's a hoe."

"E!" an inebriated, delayed voice rejoices. She opens another door and more smoke clears out the space enough to let us see the couches and bean bags around the room.

"Gotta air it out sometimes or you'll end up like Eli. Stuck."

Eli leans in a chair somewhere between wanting to sit and needing to lie down. A smile is glued to his face, but he's lost in another realm. His eyes are just slits. My man is completely faded.

She tosses out some cups and walks back to the door and does a little dance. "That's it. Nothing too extravagant."

"Cap," Zeke states laughing. "Shit's more organized than

the frat's stuff."

"Getting locked into the bathroom and shit," I add, laughing. My eyes study how her hips sway. My palms tingle as I ache to touch her, grab her and pull her to my body. As everyone else shifts to leave, she makes a small sound that gets our attention again.

"Test your drinks with your wrist bands. If it changes color, throw your drink out. Miya, the chemistry students, and I are beta testing it before presenting it to the board again."

Zeke and her exchange a quick glance. His face is laced with concern, but she shies away from his gaze. I don't think too much on it, he said there was some traumatic shit that brought them together. And she's very vocal about not wanting him as more than a friend. Not that it matters or anything.

"Have fun!" She waves as she lets everyone walk past her.

She hip bumps me and I grab her, pulling her to me, getting close to her face.

"Go have fun!" She giggles as she weakly tries to pry my hands off her.

"You're coming with me," I say, grabbing her hand following behind Zeke. "What was that look about between you and Zeke?"

I ask more out of curiosity than jealousy.

"Long story. Everything's okay though." She smiles at me and I slowly back her into the wall. I dip my head and kiss her lips once my friends round the corner. She kisses me back a few times. "What happened to having fun?"

"Kissing is fun." I drag my tongue across her bottom lip

and she sighs, wrapping her hands around my neck, opening her mouth more for me. She pushes me back gently.

"I want to dance. Come on." She drags me back downstairs. As I stand waiting for our drinks, she dances beside me as she explains the concept of the wrist bands and their plan to transition to a more tech based bracelet once the department signs off on it. I admire the glow and animation in her face as she talks about the project. This girl is fucking brilliant.

She grabs my hand after getting a refill and pulls us into the crowd, her cup high in the air as her hips move. I grab them when we find a clear spot and pull her against me so we can grind.

Zeke bounces over and dances in front of her. She laces their fingers together and keeps her hips moving in sync with mine. Zeke puts his hand on her other hip, getting closer to her. As she laughs, she leans her head on my chest.

The crowd starts singing along with the music that thumps through the sound system and someone catches Zeke's attention.

He fist bumps both of us before walking away towards some guy that's eyeing him.

She gets my attention as she faces me dancing. Placing her cup to her lips, she downs the rest of her drink and I grab at her ass.

My lips find hers as the lights dim and flicker around us. My tongue tasting her mouth, pulling her close to me. Pressing her hips into mine, I grind my erection against her and feel the vibrations of her moan.

"I need you to myself," I whisper to her, interlocking our fingers and weaving through the crowd, heading up the stairs.

She follows behind me to one of the last rooms, the sounds of my friends and their girlfriends taking advantage of their key access greets us.

"Miya said they may need it," she says through her giggles.

I laugh, pulling her to me and backing her into the room. I kiss her and kick the door closed. Our tongues dance as I unzip her costume.

"You look so fucking sexy in this thing,"

I kiss her deep with my hands on either side of her face. She reaches between us and tugs at my stiff dick and I groan into her mouth. "Do that again."

She wraps her hand around it and strokes it slowly. "You like when I grab you like this?" She's teasing me with her tongue. Barely putting it in my mouth, but grazing my lips and my tongue before backing away from me.

I grab her ass and hoist her up. She wraps her legs around my waist and I deepen our kiss, putting her down on the bed. My hips grind into hers and she moans. I kiss down her neck, palming her tits.

"Wait, your sister might need my help," she sighs as I kiss the side of her tits.

"How many organizers are there," I ask, kissing her lips softly. She holds up four fingers. "She can ask them. You're mine."

She giggles as I peel her leather suit off of her, laying her back on the bed. A black lace thong and matching bra knock the wind out of my lungs. I stand back for a second, admiring how it looks on her body before crowding her. My fingers flip, unlatch her bra and I toss it to the side.

Our lips fuse together again and my hand slips down her black lace thong and she moans loudly.

I bite at her bottom lip, rubbing circles around her clit, her pussy dripping wet for me. I suck on her neck and dive my middle finger in her then slowly add another. Her body shivers as I run my tongue down her body.

She lays there in nothing but her sexy black thong. Her back arches up as I wiggle my fingers a little.

I drop to my knees and put her legs on my shoulder, running my tongue up and down her lower lips.

She lets out a soft moan for me as I move my fingers in sync with the flick of my tongue. Latching on to her clit, I give a gentle suck before releasing it.

"This pretty pussy tastes so damn good," I groan.

She moans as her hands run through my hair. "Right there, Kane."

She digs her heels into my back as I continue. Her moans get increasingly louder until her phone starts to ring beside her. I stop tasting her but continue fingering her. "Check it."

I take this moment to lick her off my lips before kissing from her stomach to her neck.

"It's Zeke," she pants. "Keep going." She drops the phone beside her as I dip my head back between her thighs.

"Answer it," I say, planting a kiss on her pussy lips then on her thigh. I wait until she does, then use my tongue to make her breathing shaky. My tongue moving in slow circles around her clit before I suck on it.

"What's up, Zeke?" She tries to keep her voice even but I insert another finger. "I'm fine…" I wiggle my fingers inside her and she covers her mouth stifling a moan. "I promise I'm okay—" I grab her phone with my free hand.

"She'll call you back," I say with a smirk, then hang up.

"You are so fucking bad," she laughs out as I climb on top of her. I kiss her slowly.

"Where are the condoms?"

"You don't have pockets in your toga?" she giggles.

I bite and suck at her neck, grinding against her. She moans and points to the nightstand, getting the point. There's a few packs of condoms in the drawer. I grab a ten count and rip it open pulling out one and leaving the box on the nightstand.

She unpins my toga and lets it fall to the ground. She touches my chest appreciatively and kisses her way down. Taking my dick in her mouth, I groan, moving my hips to get deeper in her mouth. Her tongue swirls around my thickness. She looks up at me, pulling the tip out with a loud pop. She places a hot, sloppy kiss on the tip.

I grab her neck, pulling her up to me, kissing her aggressively, sloppily. I pull at her thong, ripping it in the process, and look her deep into her eyes. "These are mine now."

I shove my tongue in her mouth, sheath my dick in a condom and enter her body roughly.

She groans and grinds her hips against me. I start rough and hard. Pushing deep inside her, listening to the sounds I'm pulling from her.

"You're so fucking big," she gasps as my body slams into her. Fingernails rake across my skin, digging deeply into my flesh and it turns me on more.

I take her nipple in my mouth, using my thigh to hitch her leg higher over my waist, then on my shoulder so I can thrust deeper. She moans louder. I let go over her nipple and look down at her. Her eyes are closed and her mouth hangs open.

"Eyes on me, baby," I groan. She opens her eyes and I kiss her deeply. "That's right, baby. Let me see that pretty fucking face."

"Harder," she moans.

"Say please." I slow my thrust down and start rubbing her clit. She moans, swearing. I pull out of her and gently tap her clit. "Say. Please."

She reaches down to rub her clit, but I grab her wrist and pin them both over her head. My hips hovering over hers.

"Please, Kane. Harder *please*."

"You're such slut for me, E." I shove my dick deep inside her again, pounding into her harder. She whimpers in my ear as she fists the sheets.

"This is mine," I grit out in her ear, grinding against her slowly before bringing our sweaty skin together hard. "You hear me. Your pleasure is mine."

Her hand gently touches my stomach pushing me back.

Bringing her into a sloppy, uncoordinated kiss, I slow the rhythm in my hips. Slowly pulling out and pushing my dick back in hard. My tempo increases when her moans turn to soft whimpers and as she catches my tempo.

My name fumbles out of her mouth in breathy moans, then she moans it louder.

"That's right, baby. Let everyone know who's making you cum."

Her body shakes as her pussy squeezes me, damn near knocking me on my ass. I grind my hips into her, feeling myself pulsating as she milks me. I moan her name in her ear.

"You feel so fucking good," I whisper to her.

She moans softly and pulls me into a slow, messy make out session. I brace myself over her body, tasting her mouth. Our hips start grinding into each other, starting us right back up again.

We can't keep our hands to ourselves and end up running through the rest of the pack by the end of the next day at her apartment.

Yeah, luck really is on my side.

28

Kane

With our final game qualifying the team for the playoffs approaching, I spend more time in the gym conditioning. Zeke spots me as I bench press trying to max my previous weight.

"'She'll call you back,'" Zeke mocks as he helps me rack the bar. He rolls his eyes and scoffs. "Still waiting on that call back," he mutters.

Ever since the Halloween party, he's been playfully huffy with me. Taking every chance he gets to complain about me taking over the phone call. He has an idea of what was going on, especially since he also commented that neither one of us were seen for the rest of the night. There's no point lying to him. Again, he's my best friend, he knows me better than my parents. Which is why I don't miss the ghost of a smile on his face as he turns away from me.

"Jealous, Zeke?" I wipe the sweat from my forehead then toss the towel over my shoulder. I don't hide my smirk.

"Naw," he adjusts the weight and grabs the bar. "I'm just trying to figure out what happened." He gives me a pointed look.

He wants me to confirm his assumptions, but I won't. I

like keeping her and what we do to myself. No locker room talk, even though Zeke is friends with the both of us and would support us regardless.

Us. What am I saying? There's no us.

But you want there to be, Admit it. The small voice in my head taunts me more now that Ebony and I reconnected in the way we both have been trying not to.

I ignore him and pull my phone out to text Ebony.

> Still sore? ⊠

> Ha. Ha. Ha.

> Took two ibuprofen and went to work.

> Hm, then maybe I didn't do my job right.

> ha-ha-ha . I have a bruise AND hickies all over my body. You did enough. I have to work, ttyl.

I put my phone in my pocket laughing to myself.

"You're smiling at your phone again," Zeke says leaning on the bar before sitting on the bench. "Just admit that a special someone caught your eye and I'll leave you alone."

"You've never left anything alone when you got some information from me."

"I just want to know if you and Ebony are a thing now."

"Why? You're gonna stop flirting with her?"

"Hell no. I'm going to flirt with her more!"

I swat Zeke with a wet towel and he howls with laughter.

He sits on the bench and starts his set. My hand ghosts under the bar.

"I'm just saying," he starts once he pauses and takes a deep breath in. "Ebs is cool. It's not such a bad thing to like her."

I help him rack his bar with a snort. I'm not going to admit anything. At least not to him.

I leave him for the pull up bar and start my set. He watches me, trying to see if I'll drop a hint before going to the free weights. I love my friend. Trust him with my life. I'd eventually tell him, but not right now. Mainly because I'm not really ready to admit it to myself.

You can't trick yourself, dumbass.

Zeke is on his phone smiling as his thumbs type a message. "E's performing tonight. Think I'm going to go see her. Want to tag along?"

I focus on my last few reps before dropping down off the bar. I shrug my shoulders cleaning off my equipment. "Sounds cool with me."

He chuckles typing in his phone then putting it in his pocket. "You're always cool with going to see her." He makes a whipping sound.

I flip him off and then run on the treadmill as excitement starts to build in me. I barely get excited for anything but football, but this girl really does a number on me.

29

Ebony

Liam's shoes squeak as he paces the black speckled linoleum floor backstage while we wait for Clint to emerge from the dressing room. Liam had the *brilliant* idea to get us costumes. Vest with fringes for the guys and barely anything on me.

"This is just fabric, Liam!" my Gramps' husky voice growls as he looks over my outfit, then Liam's.

"I thought they'd fit differently," Liam says defensively.

"Get your money back," Gramps grumbles, shaking his head.

"Funny story…" Liam starts.

"You're kidding? Again!?" I groan.

"In my defense, I had them for a while."

Gramps groans, then storms off as I adjust the shorts under my black leather skirt for the umpteenth time. My adjustment does little to keep it from creeping up in places they shouldn't.

The white top he got me was entirely too big, but I managed to find scissors to cut the sides to make a tight wrap around effect. And if we're all being honest, we don't look all that bad.

I wear all black high top converse, even though he wanted heeled boots. He must have lost his damn mind. Performing on stage with them is very different than as a femme fatale.

Isaac walks over, his chest out and glistening with baby oil and vaseline. He used both because he wanted to make sure he looked good under the red lights. His leather pants squeak as he walks.

"You sound like a bag of rubber duckies," I giggle.

"I feel like I'm about to shoot a porn scene."

I cackle holding my guitar tightly so it doesn't bang into the wall behind me.

Clint emerges in too tight pants, a loose fitting vest, and a scowl. "Liam, what the fuck?" he grunts.

Isaac and I try not to laugh as I pull out my phone and take a picture.

"Ebs, I will kill you if you post that picture," Clint warns as I try to contain my giggles.

I hide my phone in my bookbag behind the stage after sneaking a few more pictures. I check the mirror and give my hair a swoop bang effect and pull it in a high ponytail. My locs are a little curled from the braids I came in with.

Dj Shel gently pulls me towards her, securing my mic pack to my skirt then helps me slide my in-ear monitors in my ear. Another new purchase courtesy of Liam. This one I don't mind so much, it works better than the old ones we got on wholesale and tried to make ourselves.

"Okay, kids," Liam says with a nervous chuckle, "how are we feeling?"

"I am alive!" Isaac shouts with a big smile. He gives a little spin. "These fringes make me want to do the Tina Turner shimmy number." He attempts it before giggling.

There's a long pause before Liam responds with "right…"

He scratches his head then looks at me. "Alrighty our little femme fatale. You're taking lead tonight."

"Excuse me, what?" I gawk, immediately feeling anxiety grab me by the throat and slam me into the wall. My knees shake a bit. "Liam, it's always been—"

"But tonight it's you." He puts his hands on my shoulders and smiles at me. "You are incredible and you always rock it out there. If you feel yourself slipping, you have us right behind you to back you up."

I notice Clint and Isaac flank him and nod.

"Just breathe and take that first step," Liam reassures me with a gentle squeeze. I slowly nod and he releases me from his hands. His guitar strap flying over his shoulders.

Clint looks at me and grins. A smile he hid after we reached a certain age. It warms my heart seeing it now.

"You're gonna kick ass, Ebs." He kisses the top of my head and retreats. His too little pants pop a little from his movements and he grumbles again.

We step out once the curtain opens. I do my best to not look out at the crowd, but two faces in particular catch my eye—Kane and Zeke. I've performed in front of them before, sure, but things feel different now. At least to me.

Kane leans in his seat, a beer in his hands. His eyes are hungry as he takes a sip. They roam over my body taking in my outfit. He places an elbow on the table and puts his hand over his mouth. His free hand gestures for me to spin.

I look away blushing, then slowly turn. Kane shakes his

head, adjusting himself in the seat.

"So, tonight, we're gonna do a little something different," Liam says looking at me with a smile.

There's more people than usual as the cheers get louder. I roll my shoulders and head around as Liam keeps talking.

"We think our little vixen needs some back up," Liam states.

A loud whistle erupts from the crowd.

Liam still eyes me wanting me to take the bait for our little bit. I take a deep breath and laugh softly.

"I'm a vixen?" I look at the guys, then at the audience. "You guys think I'm a vixen?"

Kane nods slowly as Zeke cheers beside him.

"Awww, you guys," I say, giving my best smile and feigning bashfulness. Then, I laugh backing away from my mic as the crowd gets louder.

"Only if I feel like Thor the Thunder God again," Isaac says to something that Liam says and I laugh. Isaac flexes and gets whistles.

"And you guys call me the vixen."

"Cause you are!" Denise's voice shouts from one of the tables and I laugh leaning away from the mic.

My in ear monitor starts counting me off and I get my guitar pick ready as Liam introduces our first cover song for the night, then we seamlessly move into a more sultry song. Wiggling the mic off the stand, I walk to the other side of the stage where more people are. I kneel at the edge singing to someone. I get up and go to the other side dancing with Liam who moves his shoulder as he plays. I mimic him before walking away laughing. By the time we end the song I'm out of breath and drenched in sweat. My eyes land on Vin, who now sits with Kane and Zeke.

30

Kane

Vin is talking our ears off when Liam walks over to talk to Ebony. She's messing with her shirt before walking off stage. Zeke glances at me, then back at the stage. Before I can get up, she's back out with even less clothes than before. I'm caught between being annoyed that she's half naked and very fucking grateful that I get to see it.

Vin finally stops talking when he notices too. "Damn. I forgot how good she looks."

To keep from giving anything away, I take a long swig of my drink. Him checking her out after telling me she's chaos irritates me.

"I think she mentioned Isaac likes you," I whisper to Zeke.

"Yeah, I tried. He's faithfully taken," Zeke rolls his eyes. "I think he just finds me attractive anyways."

I laugh, drinking more of my beer. "Don't let it get to your head."

"Coming from you, pretty boy?" he laughs looking at me. He leans closer so Vin can't hear. "I think we're tied body count wise"

I laugh, rolling my eyes. "You double mine."

"Equal opportunity, my friend." He tips his beer to me and

laughs.

"Don't get too drunk tonight. Got it?"

"It helped the last time, no?" He gives me a pointed look before looking back on the stage with a smirk.

"Asshole." I laugh.

Ebony and Liam have been playing for a few seconds and she sings with her eyes closed as she sways to the melody.

"They sound good together," Vin comments leaning forward. "Didn't know she sang like that."

"Then sit back and enjoy, my man," Zeke quips.

The song ends and they step off stage after thanking the crowd. I notice Clint, E mentioned his name one night we worked on our project, mixing drinks as people head over. Isaac shows up shortly, still in that weird vest. He's glowing, emotionally and under the lights as he passes.

Ebony steps from the back still in that short ass leather skirt, but with a graphic tee on. A look that I strangely like on her. She sees me and smiles before Vin steps in front of her and pulls her into an awkward hug. She gently taps his back then pushes him off with a confused glance.

"I didn't know you had a voice like that. Shoulda told me," he says laughing.

She shifts, creating more space between them. Her face is tense as he attempts to talk to her. I remember him claiming they're friends, at least they had been after breaking up, but this… this is painful to watch.

"Hey, E?" I ask downing my beer and walking up beside Vin. "I needed to ask you something about the project when you got a minute."

She looks at me, relief softening her expression.

"Yeah," she says to me. "I'll be back," she says to Vin before nodding towards the back. I follow behind her keeping my face even.

The hallway we walk down is dark, even with the low lights that rest in the ceiling. The wooden floor boards creak under my footsteps. The faint smell of beer and vodka floats around us. I look over my shoulder before grabbing her and pulling her to me.

She laughs, placing her warm hands on mine. "Thank you," she says, looking at me.

"For saving you from Vin?"

She nods. "I've been seeing way too much of him lately."

"Put that down on the list of things I hope you never say about me," I laugh, ghosting my lips over hers.

"I'm still sore," she mumbles against my lips.

"I just want a kiss," I laugh. "Just one."

"When has it ever been just one anything with you," she laughs, looking into my eyes.

"Not my fault you have soft lips."

She laughs stepping up on her tiptoes kissing me. She's right, one kiss isn't enough.

The way she taste swims in my mouth, fucking with my thoughts. I push her up against the wall and lift her into my arms. She giggles running her fingers through my hair pushing it out of my face, then fisting it.

"You are liable to get fucked right here if you do that

again," I mutter against her lips. I roll my hips against her for good measure. "Especially in this fucking piece of fabric you call a skirt."

She laughs, kissing me again. "Liam picked this out and fucked up everyone's sizes."

"Remind me to thank him and whoop his ass." I trail my lips down her neck and she sighs my name when I suck on the base of her throat.

"I have to work the bar, don't give me a hickey," she wiggles against me and I groan.

"You absolutely have a bar you need to work and it ain't out there." Her chest rises and falls against mine before she wiggles enough to make me let go. She grabs my hand, pulls me into a small dressing room and pulls me down to kiss her. I lift her back up, then press her back into the door. Her hands playing in my hair.

"You're gonna fuck up my hair and they're gonna know I'm fucking you."

She laughs. "I don't care." Her voice is raspy, low with anticipation and arousal.

I kiss her again, tugging at the shorts she's wearing under her skirt and toss them to the floor. I struggle holding her up and rolling on a condom as she kisses my neck. I groan finally sheathing myself. She winces, squeezing onto my arms as I slowly slide myself completely into her. She sighs in my ear moving her body with me. Soft moans trickle out of her as I get the position just right.

Wedge my hand between us and rub her clit, thrusting

quickly into her, bringing her to a quick orgasm. She buries her face into my neck, moaning my name as her pussy clenches and unclenches around me. I give a few more thrusts before following behind her.

We laugh out of breath as I ease out of her. She looks at me as she steps into her shorts.

"I don't like when you're quiet," she says watching me button my pants.

"I made some noise, a little 'mm' here and there," I laugh.

"I like when you talk dirty."

"Oh," I look at her thoughtfully. "So when I call you a dirty slut?"

She nods as I walk over towards her. I kiss her, gently nudging my tongue in her mouth. "When are you going to let me try again?" My hands rub her thighs, hips, and ass as I wait for her response.

"My place tonight?" she asks, looking into my eyes.

"Such a dick hungry slut," I groan, kissing her again. "I'll be there."

"I know," she says smiling.

She kisses me again, then walks towards the door before I grab her hand and pull her back to me.

"I was thinking," I say. Awkwardness settles in my chest as she looks up at me with those bright eyes and I focus on intertwining our fingers. "You should come to my game."

"I don't know," she starts, fidgeting a bit. "For playoffs?"

I nod. "Think on it?"

She smiles at me as she nods and I smile back at her.

"Let's go," I urge, pulling her with me to the door.

Once in the main room, she dodges Vin to go help Clint and Isaac behind the bar. Zeke hands me a new beer, then looks me over.

"You smell like Ebony," he whispers to me and takes a drink of his beer. He gives me a knowing look before looking at Vin. "Ready to get your ass handed to you?"

Vin laughs, rolling his eyes as Zeke escorts him to a pool table. I watch Ebony work for a second. She glances up and smirks at me before giving her attention to another customer.

31

Ebony

I watch out the window as colorful leaves fall off the trees. The dry erase marker squeaks against the board as the instructor writes on it. Denise sighs beside me scrolling through her phone. Mine buzzes and I take a look.

> U better bring your sexy ass to my game tonight.

> I'll think about it.

> I'll give u something to think about.

> I think about that too much.

> Never too much. Let's indulge.

I shake my head trying not to laugh or look back at Kane.

> What's the game plan???

"Who we texting?" Denise asks, leaning towards me. "You got dicked down didn't you? You got that glow to you." She smiles knowingly. "It still better be from homie in the back."

"Ms. Winston, how do we complete this problem?"

I cover my face trying to hide my laughter as Denise solves the problem and stares at the teacher. Our instructor nods, but warns her to pay attention and continues with her lecture.

"I know my shit," Denise whispers, leaning back in her chair with her arms crossed. She holds her hand out and I give her a little five trying not to giggle. We avoid each other's eyes covering our faces so we don't laugh.

I steal a glance back and catch Kane's eye. He's in a long sleeve ACDC tee shirt. Black denim jeans and brand new black Vans on his feet. His hair is pinned back with a headband showing off his fresh undercut. I notice the head band he's wearing is one he took from me (jerk), and his new gauges with gemstones flash a little in the light. He subtly nods to the door with a cocky smirk.

I have to study after this.

I can help u.

We'll work based on a reward system.

Reward system?

I'll kiss any part of your body u want. Maybe walk around in a towel for good measure.

That'll distract me.

Good. I rather have u screaming my name.

In the bleachers.

So, I'll see u at the game?

I grab my stuff as the instructor dismisses us, pocketing my phone. I adjust my jeans and throw on my sweater.

"I'll see you later," Denise says, giving me a hug. "If you go to the game tonight, cheer for me too. I gotta work." I pout, but give her a nod and notice she's glancing behind me.

"I'll make sure she does," Kane says as he leans on the table. She smiles and waves rushing out of the room. "Even D wants you there."

He has a cocky look on his face as he leans closer to my face. I start to swing my bag over my shoulder and he grabs it, throwing it over his shoulder instead. Girls watching behind him scowl at me. I'm still not used to the attention he brings me.

"I might for Miya," I answer, looping my arm in his and walking. He takes my hand instead and intertwines our fingers.

Look, I said I didn't like *their* attention. His attention sends fire through me. I happen to like fire.

"Just for Miya? My sister is great, but I'm better."

"I beg to differ."

"Did I not do that thing with my tongue right," he whispers, making me laugh.

"You have to do a lot more than 'things with your tongue,'"

I whisper back, nudging him.

We stand outside and he pulls me out of the way of the door and looks down at me. "You came to the last three home games, why not this one?"

"I also went to the last three away games," I add, crossing my arms over my chest and tapping my foot defensively.

"Okay, okay, but it's not tonight's game," he reasons with a smile that makes his eyes twinkle.

My heart flutters and my stomach gets excited. "Might be the last." He pulls me to him and puts his hand in my back pocket. An action that might look funny since I'm about a foot shorter than him.

"Cap. You guys have been running through every team."

He leans down hovering his lips over mine. "Please," he says, trying to give me his best puppy dog eyes.

"I'll think about it," I peck his lips and attempt to walk away. He yanks me back, planting a kiss on my lips, then my neck. He drops his arm over my shoulder walking me to my next class.

"Don't think, just show up," he laughs. "What's one more game gonna do?"

"I could be working on our project," I look up at him and he rolls his eyes.

"We both know we're way ahead because you can't not work on it."

Crossing my arms over my chest I scowl. He's right, I can't. I don't like worrying about getting it done. Even though we're ahead of schedule.

We stop in front of the math building and he kisses me

slowly. I suck on his tongue before pulling myself closer to him. He plants another soft kiss on me.

"I'll see you at the game." He helps me shoulder my bag, then rushes off to Zeke before I can protest. I shake my head as I watch the two play fight. People dodge them as they shove each other.

"E!" Zeke shouts and waves when he pushes Kane over. I wave back with a wide grin on my face. "See you at the game!" Kane turns with a panty dropping smile.

Subtly bracing myself, I give one last wave before I walk in the building. That damn smile gets me every time.

32

Ebony

Miya's in the office looking over flyers when I enter the student life office. I peek over her shoulder. "What's that?" I put my book bag under the desk and take a seat next to her. She sighs and tucks some of her hair behind her ear, then slides me the papers.

"We're doing a fundraising event with the football team. Profits from ticket sales go to support both departments."

"The football team gets enough donations," I protest. She nods in agreement and leans against the desk.

"They have everything planned out. We start practicing with them soon." She glances at me.

"I suggested that you and I be on the team against my brother." She smiles playfully.

"He doesn't stand a chance," I laugh, opening my computer.

After a few moments of us working silently, she huffs near a filing cabinet.

"We have to pick a day to plan Family and Friends Week," she says, pulling out a folder and sitting it on the table. She tucks her hair again. "Make sure my brother knows that you have other obligations."

I laugh, looking back at her, "He shouldn't be a problem."

"Shouldn't doesn't change the fact that he *is*," she jokes. "If he does, we'll just put him to work. Him and Zeke."

"We should do that anyways," I laugh.

A moment passes as she shuffles through the paper. The clicky part of her pen clicks before she drops it down on the table with a huff.

"What are you doing for Thanksgiving?" she asks, still going through the folder. Papers are stacked in neat piles in front of her. Her hands crawl through another folder, then she watches me.

"Probably just staying around here," I confess. "What's that?" I walk over to her and look at the folder.

"Records from the chemistry department's test. Some of the chemical bonds aren't lasting like we hoped. Technology department made a new suggestion." She pauses then looks at me again. "Why are you staying here for break? Aren't you sick of being on campus?"

"I am, but my parents are busy all the time. I don't mind."

I study the results and grab a notepad writing some things down.

"You should come home with Kane and me," she offers with a bright smile on her face. An offer that only she would extend. Her eyes plead with me. She doesn't know much about my family. Not the fact that I haven't talked to them in a while or that they've been ignoring my attempts.

"I don't think that's a good idea," I say with a laugh.

"What's not a good idea?" Zeke asks from the counter

behind me.

I spin my seat and wave at him just as Kane comes into the room. He leans on the door frame with a small smile on his face.

"She doesn't want to come home with me for Thanksgiving," Miya says pouting.

"Yep, terrible idea," Kane states sarcastically, nodding. Walking around the desk, he takes a seat by Miya.

"I thought you'd at least agree," Miya grumbles.

Kane shrugs his shoulders, then ruffles his sister's head. She slaps at him with a glare before straightening her hair out using a pocket mirror she pulls from her tiny purse.

Zeke sits beside me and glances at the papers on the table. He picks up one of the documents and reads over it. "Family and Friends Week proposals? You guys really plan this stuff?"

"Yes," I say, snatching the paper from him and putting it back with the others.

"I was thinking of a gala. Get all fancy." Miya pushes the folder over towards Zeke and he looks it up.

"Prom on 'roids?" Miya flips him off, making him laugh. His eyes scan the picture.

"It's fun and it allows people, especially us, to pretend we're important."

"You may not be important, but I am," Kane says, leaning back in his chair.

"Mom and Dad don't count, moron," she pokes, sticking her tongue out at him.

"Such a brat," he laughs, then focuses on me. "You should come with us for break. Mom would adore you."

"Probably because the only girls you've brought home were the ones she caught you sneaking out," Miya giggles.

"Good thing I don't have to sneak her out then," Kane says smugly.

"Because I won't let you sneak her in your room. She's coming as my guest. I asked first." Zeke and I sit back watching them bicker. I grab the glass candy dish and offer some to Zeke. He takes a handful laughing to himself.

"I think I take priority."

"Why? Who are you to her to take priority?" He pauses. His mouth opening and closing before sighing defeatedly. He laughs, shaking his head. Miya flips her hair over her shoulder. "It's settled. You come with us and you're *my* guest."

"You two are more alike than I thought," I mutter.

"Oh, yeah. Carbon copy," Zeke agrees.

The two scowl at us.

"It's true," Zeke defends, taking some more candy from the bowl, then holds it out to them. "Candy?"

Kane snatches some and shakes his head stifling a laugh.

33

Ebony

Bright stadium lights flood the green football field below. Cold seeps into my jeans as I sit on the metal seat of the bleachers. I pull my arms closer to me, shivering, my long sleeve shirt and jeans not keeping me warm. Miya sits beside me pulling on her high school letterman jacket, reminding me of the hoodie beside me. Opening it up, I shove my head through and stand to pull it over my body when it engulfs me. I'm accosted with his sweet, warm scent.

"Did he really take my hoodie?" I groan. "I look like a toddler."

Miya laughs hysterically as my body disappears in Kane's hoodie. The hem ending at my upper thigh as his sleeves dangle over my hands. I roll them and grumble.

"Does he have yours?" Miya asks with a giggle.

"I hope not, he'll stretch it out."

I sit beside her, joining her laughter and silently relishing in Kane's scent. We finally settle and talk about some other ideas for Family and Friends Week when the crackling of the speaker catches our attention.

Music booms out of the speakers as our team is introduced. We stand on the bleacher seats screaming loudly. Miya uses an air horn as she shakes a pompom vigorously. I see him and the guys come out of the locker room shouting into the air getting the crowd hyped.

I dance to the music with Miya, screaming for them. Kane sees me and blows me a kiss I pretend to catch. He holds up a half of a heart and I complete it making him smile wider. He shoves his helmet on, while my heart flutters as Miya squeals.

Bodies collide and crash violently as the game starts. Helmets crackle together and against other plastic pieces. Kane's team is up by five. I cheer Kane's name loudly, setting the crowd off. He looks in my direction before charging towards the opposing team to defend the ball.

As the winning play is completed, I jump up screaming and shaking Miya's pompom. The players run off the field to the locker room as Miya and I follow the crowd before making a beeline to the locker rooms.

"Everything set up at your Gramps' bar?" Miya asks as we find a place to stand. During our time planning, we decided to celebrate the team's potential win.

"Yes! Clint, Gramps, Liam, and Isaac should be putting up decorations now. Isaac said the food is already there and set up."

"And the wristbands?"

"Delivered and with Liam and Isaac. They'll be at the door passing them out for us."

"This is exciting! We're going to the playoffs AND we're doing another trial on the bands."

She squeezes my hand excitedly. Cheers and applause capture our attention as players exit the locker room.

Kane walks out, his hair wet and his shirt clinging to his body. I gently nudge Miya forward as she launches into his arms squeezing him. He kisses the top of her head, then smiles at me

"I knew you'd make it."

"It was all for Miya," I smile back at him as he rolls his eyes. He drapes a heavy arm around his sister's shoulder, but she shrugs it off.

"I was actually going to wait for Zeke," she says sheepishly.

"He's gonna meet us there," Kane states.

She gives him a pouty look and he sighs. Placing his bag down at my feet, he walks back into the locker room, then reemerges with Zeke tucked under his arm.

Zeke laughs, shoving him off before hugging Miya, then me. "Are we going to celebrate or what?"

***

The smell of beer and hot wings fill the air of my Gramps' bar as we stand in the back. It's packed. People from the game huddle at pool tables or dance to the music playing over the speakers. Clint mixes drinks behind the bar, passing out our yellow wristbands. Our table is piled high with discarded food containers, napkins, and beer bottles.

Isaac brings over a fresh tray of fries smothered in ketchup as an old school 80s song plays. He looks at me before we start singing along. I squeeze my pool stick using it as a mic. I move my hips to the beat. Miya grabs my hands singing with me.

Kane watches us from the stool he's sitting on eating a cold fry. An amused expression on his face.

Isaac walks over, singing along with us. He grabs Miya and pulls her close. He dips her then spins her around. Dancing over to Kane, I sing the lyrics to him dramatically making him laugh. Pool balls clatter and scramble across the table as Zeke breaks, starting our game. He looks up with a laugh, then makes another shot.

"I hope you're not a poor sport when you lose," he says cockily.

He leans over the table, lining his stick up with the cue ball and connects it with another, but doesn't sink it.

"Watch and learn," I wink at him leaning over. I line up the cue ball and look up at Zeke as I hit the ball into the pocket and get another. I sink two more and line up to make another.

"Dammit!" Zeke groans. "Kane, you must have taught her."

I miss one of my shots and pout.

"I had no idea she could play," he laughs.

I dodge a dancing Miya and Isaac as I walk over to Kane and lean against him. He circles his arms around me pulling me closer. I grind my hips against his.

"I'll fuck you in the back again," he whispers, making me snort. He plants a kiss on my cheek. He slides his thumbs through my belt loops. "Thank you for coming to my game." He sits his chin on my shoulder.

"Like I had a choice," I tease.

He chuckles, "You didn't."

He looks me deep in my eyes. " I love—d seeing you there,"

he says, stopping himself. His face looks a bit conflicted, but he pulls me closer to his chest. Surrounded by his warmth, I feel his heart beating into my back.

"You good? Anxious your boy's gonna lose?" I smile widely at him as I wiggle out of his tight embrace.

He rolls his eyes with a ghost of a smirk.

Zeke groans from the table as he misses his shot.

"My turn!" I kiss Kane's forehead before walking up to the table. I line up my pool stick again and sink all my balls. I point to the pocket I plan on making the eight ball go into and win the game. I hold my hand out and Zeke puts a twenty dollar bill in my palm. "Thank you!"

"I want a rematch later," he grumbles as I pass my pool stick over to Isaac.

"Make sure you have my money ready," I shoot back, sticking my tongue out and pocketing my newly acquired loot.

I take my spot back in Kane's arms and lean my head back on his shoulder. He kisses my cheek softly swaying me to the music. His eyes fixed on the pool table as Miya and Isaac play.

He takes a deep breath in and releases a tense sigh nuzzling into my neck. He lifts his head, tracing my ear lobe with the tip of his nose.

"I love you," he whispers softly by my ear before sitting his chin on my shoulder. He releases a controlled breath physically relaxing his body.

A chill runs through me. My mind takes a moment to process what he just whispered to me. I peek over my shoulder and see his vulnerable eyes as he smiles at me.

Yeah, he said it. Holy shit. He said it.

"Wanted to tell you before I chickened out. Again." He laughs and rubs his hands over my thighs and pulls me closer. "You don't have to run away," he says with a nervous chuckle.

Anxiety creeps into my body, taking hold of my heart and making it work overtime. The pounding in my chest making me fidget. My teeth gnaw at my lip as I pick at the skin of one of my fingers. Kane catches my hand and interlaces our fingers to get me to stop. A thousand thoughts race through my mind and all land on one singular thought. It terrifies me, excites me, and humbles me all at once.

"Breathe, baby," he encourages softly. His voice is laced with concern. "You don't have to—"

"I love you, too," I finally whisper back, relaxing my body against his. I laugh to myself and squeeze his hands before looking into his eyes. "I love you, too, Kane."

A lazy grin slowly forms on his face and he pulls me in for a kiss. "You had me going for a minute," he laughs before kissing me again. His tongue sliding into my mouth as he drapes both his arms over my shoulder. My hands rub his sides.

"Get a room," Zeke teases from the opposite side of the table. We flip him off laughing into another kiss.

34

Ebony

Kane holds me close to his body as his tongue explores my mouth. The shower water cascades over his broad shoulders as I run my hands over them. He fists some of my hair, backing me into the cold shower wall, then lifting me into his arms. I wrap my legs around his waist as I run my fingers in his wet hair, pushing it back and leaning away to look at him. My thumb caresses his cheek before I place soft kisses over his face, then back to his lips.

He pulls back, kissing my neck and down to the tops of my shoulders, then back up my neck.

"I don't have a condom in here," he pulls back letting me go. I cling to him pulling him back in for a kiss. "Are you on–"

"Yes."

"Thank fucking God," he groans pressing my back into the wall again and notching himself into me. He pushes his hips, filling me, with his hand around my neck. "You look so fucking beautiful like this. All wet and filled with me."

I moan, leaning my head against the wall. His lips drag across the skin of my neck before he runs his tongue over my exposed skin. His mouth stops at my ear as I hear his ragged breathing.

His name tumbles from my lips in sensual whispers as he grinds his hips into me every time our bodies connect.

"You ready, baby?" he asks, rubbing my throat with his thumb. I nod and feel his finger add pressure and his thrusts intensify. He kisses me deeply before releasing my neck.

A ragged moan falls past my lips as I breathe in and feel the pressure again. The sensation between my legs intensifying as he pushes deeper, harder. A low buzz tickles my ears as the pleasure builds.

"I love the way you look when I take your breath away." He bites into my shoulder and releases his hold. A shaky breath escapes my lips and I whimper at the intensity of the orgasm building inside of me. "One more, baby."

I breathe in and he clenches my neck and increases his speed. I hold his body tightly as I fall over the edge. My legs shake around his body and when he releases my throat his name comes out in a jumbled cluster of words and phrases.

"Oh my god," I finally articulate repetitively as my orgasm hits in blinding waves. My fingernails dig into Kane's skin as he follows me over the edge and crushes his lips to mine.

"I fucking love you, Ebony," he groans into my mouth. "So fucking much."

"So, so fucking much," I pant out as he kisses me slowly.

He eases me down and we wash each other, periodically entering into a slow make out session until the water grows cold and we hop out laughing.

I'm walking around in a towel while he works on our project. It's late at night, but we're both wired.

I grab a bottle of wine and two glasses and put it at the kitchen table where he works. I pour him a glass, then me one and put the bottle on the table.

Silver hops up and chirps at Kane before brushing against his bare chest. He idly runs his hands over Silver's fur, focused on the screen.

I grab my phone and snap a few pictures and he smirks.

"I'll let you keep those pictures, only if I get to take some of you." He looks at me eyeing my towel.

"Like this?" I ask, turning around.

"Abso-fucking-lutely." He reaches for me and pulls me to him. "I've wanted you like that so bad," he states laughing.

"And you say I'm trouble." I kiss his lips.

"You are." He looks up at me lovingly. "I never said it was bad trouble."

Silver jumps off his lap and lounges on the couch.

Kane grabs my leg so I'm straddling him as his tongue explores my mouth. I laugh pulling away from him. He looks at me with a smirk on his face and kisses the tip of my nose.

"You're incredibly sexy," he leans his chin on my shoulder. "Especially when you cum as hard as you did in the shower."

I kiss at his neck, rubbing my hands across the smooth skin on his arms before looking at his tats. Using my index finger, I trace the lines and rub the shadings His arms cage me in, moving as he types before he nips at my shoulder.

"Are you mine?" I whisper against his neck. One of his hands rubs my thigh then up my back before he tugs my hair and looks me in my eyes.

"All yours." He kisses me deeply. "Let me show you."

I giggle as he lifts me up, slapping my ass in the process. He tugs my towel off and drops it to the floor, carrying me into the bedroom where he makes love to me all night.

35

Ebony

Beakers clink against the thick, black table top in the science room. Miya and I observe a new round of testing for the wrist bands, getting everything perfected for our presentation scheduled during Family and Friends Week.

"So, we had to change the formula in the bands. Over time the internal liquid became unstable," one of the third year chemistry students states.

"How different is the formula?" I ask.

"Not much," he states as he pulls out the formula log. Miya and I look it over and notice the differences in a few of the elements.

"How does this impact the color feature?" Miya asks.

"Colors are actually bolder. It comes in contact with a molecule of the drug and it immediately changes colors. Tech department is discussing including the formula in a capsule for a band that will alert the wearer. Have you guys seen that prototype yet?"

"Not yet, but that's our next stop," Miya responds, looking back over the formula log. Her eyes read over the notes.

"How long has this one been holding?"

"About three weeks so far. This was something we worked

on in August but ultimately chose the latter during testing."

"Has there been degradation?"

He shakes his head. "Not even when we dilute it with what broke down the original formula."

"That's a relief. Will these be ready for Family and Friends Week?" I ask.

"Should be. We have a batch that's going through a quality check. We should have a confirmed answer before break."

"Send us a text when you know for sure," Miya says with a warm smile.

He nods, returning her smile. The beaker scrapes against the table as he focuses back on testing the formula and recording his findings.

Miya and I exit the science lab after hanging up our protective gear. I pull out my phone and write a few notes in my notepad before shoving the device in my pocket.

"Tech just sent an email about the new bands," Miya shows me as we walk across the white linoleum floor. We take the stairs down to the main level and exit the building into the frigid air, winter rearing its head early. I shiver against the wind.

"Will the new bands change colors?" I ask as we pick up pace.

Other students mix and mingle in the courtyard. Steaming cups of something in their hands as they laugh loudly and shiver in clusters.

"The first set did, but the second set doesn't say. It does check vitals. It scans the skin and records body temp and heart rate. It can be connected to multiple devices via Bluetooth. At least that's how it's being constructed. You'll have to review the code to make sure it does exactly what we need," Miya responds.

I nod as we shuffle into the building basking in the warmth. We head to the tech office and knock, catching the student assistant's attention.

"We wanted to speak with Dr. Goodwin?" I say. The student nods and disappears, then reappears with a tall black woman. Her hair is slicked back in a sleek ponytail. Deep purple paints her lips and the lids of her eyes. She smiles, showing us gleaming white teeth.

"What do I owe the honor, you two?" She shakes our hands.

"We got an email about wristband updates. Are the prototypes ready?" Miya chimes in softly.

"Yes! I actually just got it on my desk. Let's head to the lab."

We follow behind Dr. Goodwin. Her heels click against the black tiles on the floor as she passes computer labs, server rooms, and everything a tech department could ask for. She knocks on a lab door and walks in.

It's a standard computer lab, but this one has a large counter in the back. A few sealed boxes sit on it.

"Here it is." Dr. Goodwin reaches for the box and pulls out a sleek black band.

"The band has solar and battery powered LED lights. They change colors based on body temperature, heartbeat, and body steadiness," Dr. Goodwin informs us.

She slips the band on and it lights up. She shows us the

digital screen and it shows her heart rate.

"This is so much better than I imagined," Miya gasps, touching the band on Dr. Goodwin's wrist.

"It works like any smart watch. The tips of the band can be dipped in the liquid, then the LEDs light up and send a report to the database."

"This was in budget?" I ask, looking at her as she slides the device back in the box. She tucks it under her arm and grabs her keys.

"Not exactly, but I talked to a few people and explained the project. They provided some donations. I'll send that over for your records. We're still on budget. This was the tech department's 'thank you.'"

"We should be thanking you," Miya gushes. "This is incredible."

"Absolutely, we're pushing the limits, making these more than a drug preventative. The designs you both proposed can help so many other people." Dr. Goodwin smiles at us.

"Could you email us the timeline for when those bands may be ready and shipped? We were hoping for Family and Friends Week to test the final product," I ask.

"Based on our production schedule, we should have them by then," Dr. Goodwin answers before looking at her phone. "I hate to cut this short, I have a meeting in a few minutes. Walk with me."

As we follow her, Miya speaks up first. "Do you have access to student count records to get a guesstimated headcount for Family and Friends Week?"

"It will take some time, but I'll see what I can do." Dr. Goodwin stops at one of the conference rooms. "I'm going to present these and I'll send you the results."

We thank her and watch as her slender frame slips into the room, then smile giddily at each other.

"Dinner at my place!" I gush, linking our arms and dragging her with me.

36

Ebony

Sparks fly off the metal I'm welding, the heavy apron and mask keeping my clothes and skin safe. I stop, lift the mask, then rotate the piece in my hand. I grab a mallet and bang on the metal.

"I didn't know we had a rage room on campus," Zeke comments. He leans against the table with a smile on his face.

"I wish," I laugh, putting the welder and metal down. I embrace him tightly. "What brings you here?"

"Wanted to see you. Kane's been keeping you to himself," he snorts.

"Aw! Missed me?"

"A little," he says, nudging me. He roams around the room looking at the work of other students, his hands in his pockets. "I think you should tell them," he says softly.

"Tell who what?" I sit on the stool, looking over my terrible sketch. I grab my pencil and scribble notes in the corner.

"Miya and Kane. They're asking questions and we both know you have some of those answers." Zeke pulls up a stool and sits across from me with soft eyes.

I sigh, looking back. "What good would it do, Zeke? I barely have answers."

"I know," he grabs my hand and gives it a squeeze. "They have more connections than I do. They can help us find those answers."

Rapid breaths fall from my mouth as I think of what he's saying. Confessing to Miya and Kane that I'm the Jane Doe in articles they've scoured scares me. Paralyzes me to the idea that I'm broken because I let it happen. I know there's nothing I could do, but my mind still tells me there was *something*.

When my parents and Vin found out, they blocked all news articles immediately. I thought it was for me, but it wasn't. They didn't want to be asked questions. That was the attention they didn't want until election time, which was coming up. Then, my story will be plastered everywhere with sentimental music, nauseatingly false remorse, and a vote for Vin's Dad, Ephraim Cross. All without them consulting me. My past edging the line of repeating.

"Hey," Zeke's voice is soft. His eyebrows are bunched together as he looks at me closely. "It's up to you. I won't tell them."

I nod with a sigh. "I know I'll have to eventually, but I don't know."

"I get it." He hugs me tightly, then releases me. His finger drums against the table and he smiles at me.

"What?"

"I can't get it through my head that you and Kane are fucking." He laughs.

"I don't want to have this conversation with you," I groan.

"I mean, public make out sessions at a bar in front of people that matter? It's pretty serious. Let me know when to get my tux," he jokes with a chuckle.

"Like you haven't made out with people publicly," I state, rolling my eyes.

"We're talking about Kane," he says with a laugh. "My partner in crime that also had a harem of women to make out with publicly. Now, it's just you. How does it feel?"

"I don't think you want to know what making out with your best friend is like. You had more access to try and then some," I joke. I laugh as Zeke flips me off.

I start back arranging pieces of aluminum parts for the drone's body.

"I'm asking about you being the final girl." He wiggles his eyebrows.

I look at him, my eyes roaming over his face trying to stifle a smile. I roll my eyes at him with a soft laugh instead. "I may not be the final girl," I respond softly, focusing back on the parts.

"Who's not the final girl?" Denise asks, walking in with food and drinks. "Hey, Z!"

"Hey, D," he greets her and gives her a hug. A loud pop echos in the room. "Don't start that shit, boy."

He laughs rubbing the back of his hands. "I was telling our friend that she's Kane's final girl."

"Let me guess, she says she isn't," Denise rolls her eyes as she sits on a stool.

He nods and they both stare at me. Their eyes prying into my thoughts. I pretend to be busy so they can't see the blush on my face.

"Girl," Denise says, sucking her teeth. "That man is in *love* with you. Wrapped around your pretty little fingers."

"Love is fleeting," I defend, giving them my attention. Zeke shakes his head and huffs.

"You're hopeless," he groans, "he literally left our bachelor pad to basically live with you."

"Shacking up is not something hook ups do," Denise adds, eating a piece of fruit. "You wake up next to each other!"

"We're having fun," I shrug.

"Just cause he didn't slap a label on it doesn't mean he doesn't feel it," Zeke says. "He looks at you the way my parents look at each other."

"Can we talk about anything else," I groan, rubbing my temples. "How's working with Miranda?" I ask Denise.

She shrugs. "You were right. She's good with her hands," Denise takes a sip of her drink.

"Are we talking good with her hands or *good with her hands,*" Zeke asks.

"Boy," Denise throws a fry at him. "She's good with building stuff. Nasty."

Zeke catches the fry in his mouth and chews, nodding thoughtfully. He scratches the back of his neck and laughs to himself. "Maybe I should think a little more," he mumbles.

"You think!?" Denise shrieks before laughing. "Don't change, Zeke. I actually like you like this."

"So, you're saying I have a chance?" Zeke gives her a flirty once over.

I cackle as Denise's face morphs into a glare.

"Well, do I?" Zeke asks.

37

Kane

I've never known peace like this. I had a decent childhood, but this moment right here, wrapped in silk sheets with this beautiful fucking goddess in my arms takes the cake. Today I get to train her and her team for this charity event we're doing in a few weeks, but honestly I'd rather stay here. My eyes look over her sleeping frame. Her back rising and falling peacefully. The sheets only covering below her waist. I kiss her shoulder and she moves closer to me with a sigh. My eyes trace the lines of her tattoo on her back. Flowers blooming on the outside of two fine lines that follow her spine.

"Kane," her startled voice calls. She pushes herself up, then looks behind her.

"I'm here, baby." I pull her to me and kiss her forehead. She lays her head on my chest. "You okay?"

She nods into my chest and places a soft kiss on my neck. Her fingers tangle into my hair as she listens to my heartbeat. "I thought you left," she says softly.

"Kicking me out already," I say with a laugh and she pops my side.

"You usually have football early," she states, tracing circles on my chest.

"Not until the group practice." She groans and rolls her body off of mine, but I pull her back making her giggle.

"I have to pee," she squeals before I let her go. She slips into the bathroom and I lay back in the bed with my hands beneath my head.

The door opens after a minute or two when she's washing her hands. I watch her, a slow smile crawling on my face as I watch her brush her teeth. She hums a song as she studies herself in the mirror.

I throw my legs over the bed and walk over to join her. We stare at each other in the mirror as we brush our teeth naked.

Her eyes drink me in entirely and mine do the same to her. She washes her face off and stands behind me, circling her hand around my dick and stroking me while I brush.

My eyes close as a groan escapes my throat, thanking God I finished brushing my teeth. I wash my face off, then reach for her. She moves to the side, my dick still in her hand, and runs her other hand over my chest, facing me forward.

"I want you to watch." Her voice is muffled by my back. She brushes her lips softly against my muscles then places a small kiss on my spine as she strokes me.

"Making my ego bigger, baby?" I chuckle watching her hand stroke me.

"Mhm," she laughs softly into my back. Her free hand rubs up my abs to my neck, then back down. "Your dick is so fucking pretty," she says catching my eyes in the mirror.

"Oh? You like it?"

She smiles at me. "You know I do."

She tightens her grip slightly and moves her hand faster. Soft kisses tickle my back as her hand keeps touching my chest and my nipples. I grip the sink, my eyes locked on myself in the mirror. My balls tighten as she strokes me faster.

"I'm almost there."

She bites at my back, squeezes my nipples harder, then cups my balls.

"Cum for me, Daddy," she moans.

I lose it. I cum so fucking hard my knees buckle. My cum hits the mirror, the counter tops, the faucet head. My hands squeeze the countertop tightly as she finishes milking me with her hand. She walks around to my side with a smile on her face and licks cum off her hand, then plants a kiss on my temple as I lean over the sink.

I lay my head on my forearm laughing and panting, "What the fuck, Eb."

She shrugs with that sexy ass devious smile and walks into the room getting dressed.

"No. No-no-no. Take those off," I demand walking over to her once I regain composure.

She laughs. "We have practice."

My jaw ticks as I stare at her. "Fuck that."

I toss her over my shoulder and slap her ass. She's laughing all the way to the bed. I drop her down on it and hover over her, my nose an inch from hers.

"I will rip your clothes off," I warn, my hand at the hem of her tank top. "So, you can take them off or…" I tug at the hem of her shirt making some of the seams rip. She pops my hand before I dip my hand underneath, touching her soft, warm skin.

"Practice isn't optional," she giggles, pushing my hands out of her shirt.

I lean over and kiss her neck. "Practice may not be optional, but neither is me burying my dick so deep in you that you cum every time you think about it."

She gasps, pushing against my chest. I look down at her. My eyebrow arched and a ghost of a smirk on my face. She's breathing a little heavier, something I notice she does when she's very turned on. She pulls me to her lips and I immediately slide my tongue in her mouth. Her hands are in my hair as I yank her shorts down and groan.

"You were really gonna waltz your pretty ass out there with no panties on?"

She furrows her brow and laughs a little. "I normally go out without them. You couldn't tell?"

I drop my forehead to hers with a groan, then shake my head in disbelief when I look at her.

"Fucking trouble. When you danced on me?"

"Yeah, I was performing," she pants.

"Us planning our project?" I'm kissing her neck, suctioning the skin as I make my way down to her shoulder.

"Nope. Not at any point during our project."

I lean back looking at her face, "Such a dirty little slut."

A smile lights up her eyes as she beams up at me before pulling me into a kiss. I position myself between her legs and enter her slowly. A groan escapes my mouth into hers and I pull my mouth back to look into her eyes. They close slightly as I push myself deeper into her.

"I love the way you look when I'm inside you." I kiss her, setting a slow pace. Her mouth hangs open slightly. Then, I kiss her eyelids. "So fucking beautiful."

I thrust harder and she finally moans for me. With a groan, I push into her harder again. "That's it, baby. I want to fucking hear how good I make you feel." I intertwine our fingers and pin her hand above her head, moving faster. She moans louder for me. Her eyes finally open and so full of lust.

"Just like that, Kane. Fuck me just like that," she gasps. Her free hand grips my arm. "Faster, please, baby faster."

I pick up tempo, driving my hips into hers. She releases my arm and grabs my ass, making me push deeper, harder. A loud moan spills from her mouth as she throws her head back.

"That's it, baby. You fuck me so fucking good," she moans in my ear when I kiss her neck.

"Your wet pussy feels so good."

Little gasps escape her mouth as we move together. There's a euphoric look in her eyes as her back arches.

"Fuck, Daddy. I'm so close. Make me cum."

I've been called Daddy plenty of times, but something about the way she says it, there's a desperation in it. Like I'm the only one that can make it happen. The only one she wants to make it happen. That desperation knocks my ass right over the ledge and I'm instantly filling her pussy up. I groan into her neck, trying to keep the pace.

She's calling me Daddy still and she cums hard right behind me, moaning out my name like I'm some kind of God. Some kind of savior.

My hips are moving slowly as her clenching pussy milks me. I brush my lips across her sweaty skin, thanking everything in the universe for having mercy on me for this moment. I could die between her legs, buried deep inside her. God damn she feels so fucking good. I lay my head on her chest feeling her fingers play in my hair. Her heart pounds in her chest, but her breathing is steady. "I could fall asleep right here."

"We have to go," she says laughing. Her fingers still brushing past my scalp.

"Fine," I pull out of her slowly and get her something to clean up the mess I made between her thighs. "But you're wearing panties. I don't want anyone to get close to touching that pretty pussy."

She laughs from the bed and I admire her. The way her skin glows in the sunlight. How her smile stays on that gorgeous face even after she's done laughing. How peaceful she looks. I'm so uncontrollably in love with this woman. "Hey, E." She looks over at me. Eyes twinkling in the sunlight as she rolls to her side to get a better look at me. "I love you."

She tries to hide her smile, but her cheeks rise up and the skin around her eyes crinkle. "I love you, too."

38

Kane

Ebony walks with me as I show her to the training room together. Giving me a quick wave, she leaves my side and takes a seat next to Miya.

I enter the locker room with my teammates shortly after and quickly change into a dri-fit shirt and gym shoes.

"Bro, she's so good with her mouth." Vin's voice rounds the corner catching my attention. I pause and listen for a second, slowing my pace.

"You serious?" Someone groans. "She's got lips that look like she gives bomb head," the same person finishes. Sounds like Sam, the second year.

"Ask Kane," Vin suggests, laughing. "They're always together claiming they're working on a project or some shit. Just gotta wait your turn."

I'm up on my feet before even thinking about it. I round the corner catching Zeke in Vin's face.

"Chill the fuck out with that shit," Zeke growls.

I stand beside him eyeing moron number one, Sam. Cutting my eyes, I narrow them at Vin, quirking my eyebrow.

"The fuck is your deal?" I ask, moving Zeke back. He pushes against me. His eyes fixed on Vin, then Sam like he's ready to cave their faces in. After me though, I'm ready to stomp their heads in on this cement floor.

Vin holds his hands up laughing. "I saw you two walk in together. They were asking about her."

"I don't see what the fuck is so funny," Zeke growls.

"Oh, that's right, you had a go at her too. Maybe you can tell them how good her pussy is."

Zeke launches, but I'm faster. Vin's pinned to the lockers with my forearm on his throat. "Keep her fucking name out your mouth," I growl.

He holds his hands up with a lazy, arrogant grin. "Guess you two are a thing."

"It don't fucking matter. Keep her fucking name out your mouth." I push my forearm further, daring him to say more.

"Or what?" Sam snickers like the idiot he is. Zeke's quicker than I am. He grabs him by his collar, pulling him close to his face.

"I'll make sure it's the last fucking thing you say, bitch," Zeke spits. Sam shrinks back. There's a deranged look in Zeke's eyes as he stares Sam down.

Coach's hands push us apart forcefully. I reluctantly stand next to Zeke glaring down at Vin and his dumbass friends. He still has an arrogant smile on his face.

"We need to run drills?"

"Naw coach, just getting some things straightened out," I spit.

Coach pointedly looks at Vin. "We good, Coach. Just a misunderstanding. Won't happen again."

"Better fucking not," Zeke growls.

"Ezekiel!" our assistant coach shouts. "One more of those and everyone's running drills. Clear?"

"Crystal," Zeke grits. With one last look, Coach steps out of the locker room. Vin walks away clapping his friends back and Zeke and I walk out behind them.

Tension fills the training room when we enter together. The student life kids shift uncomfortably. Vin looks at Ebony and blows her a kiss. She flips him off then turns back to Miya.

"After this I got you, E." He adjusts himself eye fucking her. He looks at me with a smirk.

"Vin," Coach warns.

"I'll behave, coach." He stifles a laugh.

My eyes land on Miya and Ebony who look between Zeke, Vin, his dumbass friends, and me. Clearly piecing together that there was a problem. Any person smart enough would know that some shit popped off that's got us all riled up.

"Alright, we're gonna talk about the basics and then get on the field," Coach starts. "I got Zeke and Kane here to teach you all the stuff you need to know, but I got rules, so listen up!"

As he continues, I calm myself down visualizing all the ways I could shove Vin's scrawny ass in a locker or the sewer where his ass belongs. Coach divides us up into teams and hands the floor over to Zeke and me.

We do a quick rundown of what to do on the field, show them a few moves and then use the whiteboard. I'm setting up a drawing as Zeke talks. I look at Ebony and her eyes are roaming over my body. Her tongue dances against her cheek as her leg shakes. She meets my eyes with a suggestive look before looking over at Zeke.

Trouble. And I love every bit of trouble she brings me.

"We're gonna talk about formation and proper technique," Zeke says.

"Ebony knows all about that," Vin laughs. His punk ass friends giggle.

"Vin, go suck a dick," she spits back.

"Not when you do it so well, baby." He winks at her and blows her a kiss. A few of Vin's friends laugh.

"Vin. You'll be doing suicides if you don't cut the shit," Coach threatens.

"I'm just joking, she's a perfect angel," he stifles a giggle.

Zeke and I exchange a look before we continue. We attempt to keep our cool as we show them different formations, then break out to go on the field. Coach hands us belts with flags attached and I help my team secure theirs. Vin, who's unfortunately on my team, stands back with his arms crossed, staring Ebony down.

Ebony, unaware of this creep, secures her belt and adjusts it, then gives my sister the biggest smile. I'll gladly knock this guy's head off with my bare hands to keep that smile on her face.

We step into the cold. Snow flurries spiral out of the sky as the grass crunches under our feet. I get in front of Ebony before Vin can and look at her.

"Wassup, mama."

She laughs looking at me as she uses a rubber band to pin

her locs back.

"This feels unfair," she mutters, getting in the formation we taught them in the room.

"How?"

"You're way bigger than me, Kane."

"I thought you liked that," I say with a smirk.

She rolls those pretty brown eyes and laughs. "You know good and damn well that's completely different," she whispers through her laugh. I smile at her, then look down the line.

"I'll be back," I whisper to her before checking everyone's positioning. A few of the guys that I'm cool with step in to help the student life kids beside them, making this job easier.

"Hold your places." My voice booms out as I help adjust a few of the newbies on my team. I catch Vin's glare as he squats in front of a scrawny kid from student life.

'That's right, bitch. Can't fuck with her when I'm around.'

Sam is in front of my sister attempting to stare down her fucking shirt.

"Sam, switch with Paul," I growl.

He goes to protest, but visibly pales when he looks at me. As he scrambles to switch, I give Zeke a nod.

"Question, shouldn't the training captains be guarding each other," Vin asks standing up. A devious twinkle illuminates his face.

"This is flag football. Ranks don't matter as long as you get the flag," Zeke says. "Your captain told you to hold. You can run suicides until your knees buckle if you don't know how to follow orders."

Vin shoots Zeke a murderous look before getting back in his spot.

"When we get you guys set, this is where you go. You stick with your partner. Keep them away from the ball and your flags. Do not hold belts and no tackling. It may get a little aggressive, but save the actual football techniques for the playoffs." I say, strolling back to my spot.

"All yours, coach," Zeke calls out, getting back in his spot.

"So serious," E playfully mocks my tone. She giggles looking at me.

"That's funny to you?" I look at her amused.

"Hysterical." She smiles at me before looking back at the grass.

"On the whistle," coach states.

The whistle blares into the air and we're off.

Ebony is fast. She darts off towards our quarterback and reaches for one flag before I grab her. She laughs as I keep us from falling over.

"There are other people you can guard," she pushes trying to get back to her team, but the play is already over.

"You don't like seeing me in action," I joke, walking back with her. She breathes heavily beside me. "Don't tell my team I'm telling you this, but use your energy wisely." I bump into her and she stumbles laughing.

Miya groans on the other side of the field, her face red and stray hairs sticking to it. "This was a terrible idea," she pants out. Zeke laughs walking beside her.

"You're just not used to playing hard," he says, helping her back to her spot. He squats down talking to her and she nods before tumbling to the ground. He laughs and helps her up.

"I think those two might have a crush on each other," Ebony says beside me.

I grumble as I watch them interact. The two of them exchanging looks and smiling at each other. I think Ebony's right.

I pull at her hair, earning a glare. She pushes me away. A smile passes between us as she gets to her side and drops down. I lean real close to her face. "I think we have an audience."

She looks down towards Vin, then back at me trying to conceal her smile.

"He looks so pissed," she whispers in my ear.

The whistle blows and we dart off. She dodges me, going straight for the quarterback and I grab her as she snatches a flag and tosses it down. She sticks her tongue out. I toss her over my shoulder, and walk her back to our spot making her giggle.

"I don't think that's part of the game," Miya shouts, laughing. She stands with her hands on her hips, unaware of Zeke. I shrug at her with a smirk as he scoops her up and tosses her over his shoulders. Her shriek pierces the air, then her giggles follow.

"Let's not pick each other up please," Coach says, shaking his head. "This is supposed to be fun."

"We're having fun, Coach," I shout. "Right, babe. You're having fun?" I whisper to E. She giggles as she slaps my back to get me to put her down. I slap her ass in return, making her yelp. Vin's head whips around from talking to Sam and I smirk at him. I feel E's body twist as she struggles on my shoulder.

"You're gonna make him even more mad," she giggles as I put her down, intentionally sliding her down my body.

Vin is a few players away from us, a glare pasted on his pathetic face. I look back at E, her playful brown eyes on me as she pushes off my chest.

"I wonder how mad he'd get if he knew I cum in you," I whisper with my hand on her waist.

"Don't do that," she laughs, getting back in formation.

There's heat in her eyes. A heat that's always there when I say dirty shit to her in public and when I grab her waist to keep her close to my body. It excites and frustrates her in the best ways. And I secretly love that shit, too.

I squat down looking at her. She blushes looking away. The whistle blows and I go for her, pulling her to me and pressing our bodies together. She giggles pushing away, but I pull her back. When no ones looking I adjust myself and she eyes me.

"Having a hard time?" she asks with a devious smile.

"The hardest," I say smirking, letting my eyes roam over her body. She adjusts her top a bit, giving me a good look at her tits. Devious eyes meet mine as she noticeably checks me out.

Antics like that continue, especially when no one important is looking, as I get closer to her. Ghosting my lips over hers after we complete plays. As it gets darker, I find myself gripping her body more, letting my hands grope parts of her that would get me thrown off the field.

She doesn't mind, even returns the favor giving me heated

looks. Especially when I pull her to me. Her hand will slide over my shorts when she guards me from getting the ball or taking her flag. A subtle movement that looks like coincidences but by the way her palm squeezes me I know it's not.

Eventually, I use my body to block her from the prying eyes of others as we laugh. Those are the times she gets bold, sliding her hands down my pants, giving me a few good strokes before leaving me there even more turned on.

Tangible heat rises from our bodies as we play hard, but sexual heat burns hotter as she inches closer to me. Stealing kisses from my lips in the shadows and a mini make out session right before the field lights kick on. More than one of my teammates have watched us interact. Especially Sam who reports back to his master.

As the moon ascends into the sky, bright and beautiful, we get ready for our last practice play. Getting into our position, she shifts her thighs uncomfortably. A habit she has when she's needy and hot, trying to get alleviation from her arousal. A smoldering heat lingers behind her eyes when they lock on me. Femme Fatale on full display. I lean close to her as we get into our positions. My lips ghost the shell of her ear as I whisper in her ear.

"I'm going to fuck you so hard when we get back home." I lean back, my playful expression gone.

The look in her eyes and that sound she makes has me ready to end the game immediately. A mix between a desperate whimper and a moan. She wants to be fucked, fucking needs it. A sound that tells me that I could tell coach I needed to help her in the locker room and she'd ride my dick until I filled her pussy and no one would know. Unless I hit all her spots just right, then she's letting everyone, including that fucking bitch Vin, know that my dick's making her cum. And yes, I'm always going to hit all the right spots whether he's around or not. Fuck that, her pleasure is my job. I take pride in it.

When the whistle blows, she jogs wanting me to get her, and I do. Pulling her waist and bracing our bodies so we don't fall. I may end up inside her then. Give everyone a little show.

Her hand grips my back as she stumbles, bringing us closer and a sensation that has me thinking of this morning.

Coach blows his whistle and I tell her to follow me in the locker room. We follow behind Zeke and Miya, who are standing closer together and covered in grass and sweat. She taps my arm with a ghost of a smile, looking at them. I shake my head, leaving it alone.

I change my shoes and toss her my hoodie. A few of the guys on my team talk to E, gravitating towards her naturally. Vin's gang stares as we leave the locker room together. I catch Vin's glare and smirk as I drape my arm over E's waist.

Yeah, dumbass. She's mine.

39

Ebony

Whirring from the printer drowns out the music playing around us. With three weeks left until Family and Friends Week, we finish getting signs and plans put together. Well, Miya gets the signs while I work on coding the data from our wristbands from the bar celebration a few weeks back.

Miya is excited as she walks into the room humming a song. She has her arms full of arts and crafts materials and I look over the computer screen at her.

"All that for signs?"

"Yes! Consider it motivation to beat the other team!"

We haven't been practicing long, but we are fairly good thanks to Zeke. I feel faster and lighter on my feet compared to my first practice. Even Kane had a hard time catching up to me for a bit. With our team, we have a chance of winning, which is surprising.

"You robbed several troll kingdoms, Miya."

She laughs and sits the stuff down on the table. "A necessary evil for us to kick ass."

I laugh with her, letting the music fill the air as I get back to coding. The door clicks and Kane steps in, kissing the top of my head and sitting next to me.

"Did a troll throw up in here?" Zeke asks as he kneels beside Miya.

"No, we're making signs. And by we, I mean me and you."

"Joy," Zeke grumbles before Miya nudges him with her elbow.

"What are you doing here?" I ask, looking over at Kane.

"Coding. I told Miya I'd help you guys get some things flushed out for your project."

"He wants to save a friend from eternal damnation," Miya says, squirting glue on a navy blue poster board. "I figured you wouldn't mind an extra set of hands to get the coding done."

"You trust him to help me do our job?" I ask.

His jaw drops as he turns his head to look at me. "You forget my skills so easily." He laughs looking back at the screen.

"That's too much glue, Zeke!" Miya shrieks.

"I thought you'd need a lot!" Zeke sounds panicked. His hand scrubs against the paper.

"That messes it up even more!" Miya pops his hands.

I giggle, putting my hand over my mouth. "That's how I feel coding with your brother."

"Keep talking shit," he says looking at me with a hint of amusement in his eyes.

"I give you permission to hit him with anything you want," Miya says, getting back into gluing.

"That's not for you to decide."

"Well that's too damn bad!" Zeke says, making us laugh.

"So, um, E," Miya starts before sitting back on her heels. "I couldn't find the article you told me about that got you started on this project. Where'd you find it?"

Zeke looks at me. Everyone does at this moment. I stare at the keyboard trying to remember how to swallow, how to breathe. My fingers hovering over the last few keys I pressed for my code.

"Um..I…" I chew at my lip. *Now or never, E.* "I researched everything and wrote it…" I say softly.

Feeling the energy shift in the room isn't something I'm too fond of when it deals with heavy topics. And this particular topic leads to several different types of energy. Since last semester, I've dealt with them, those energy shifts. Navigated them in ways that stifled me. I drowned in them most days. Zeke never lets me drown, never lets me wallow. Neither does Denise or Isaac, but that doesn't help me when new people hear about the incident. And silence is a force that makes the energetic shift feel so fucking heavy. I want to vanish from the face of the Earth.

I don't want this to be a part of my story. I never wanted it to be, but it is. I struggle to accept it. Struggle to deal with *how* to exist with it. So, I ignore it. I avoid the topic. I bury it deep into projects and proposals, then lock myself in my apartment terrified to trust anything beyond my bubble. I can control what happens in my bubble, but these three people… they want to help. They want to exist in this space I carved for myself. They've made themselves beacons in this fucked up world, this corrupted university, so I suck in a breath and decide to spill my guts.

"I was at a party last semester," I start softly. My mind goes back to that moment. My favorite song, a song I can't listen to now without having a panic attack, played and I was dancing with a group of people I just met. "I was dating this person, Eva, and they went and got me a drink because they spilled mine. And when I drank it, I blacked out."

My chest aches and I shift uncomfortably. *Tell them more.* My conscious urges, tugs and pries at the door to the darkness. My throat is tight, so tight that it's painful. I push through it, reciting the images as they play in my mind. They always play in my mind.

"They disappeared and when I started to feel out of it, I stumbled somewhere. People laughed, said I was wasted and left me there. Eva found me, and I thought they were going to take me out of there, but they didn't."

Mixed in with grief is usually rage. It sits in the corners of my mind, wanting to wreak havoc, to hurt, to cause chaos. It's out for blood and revenge. At least mine is. And my rage steps forward as I start tumbling down with the thought that someone that was supposed to care about me left me in a shitty situation.

"They took me to a room and there was a guy. I barely knew him, I don't even remember his name. Not then and not now." My eyes scan the keyboard as I try to remember the details. I take in a shaky breath, pushing rage aside.

Not here. Not yet, you'll get your turn, but not now.

"I begged Eva to get me out of there and they left me. I don't remember anything after them picking me up off the floor and leaving me in this bed that smelled so bad." The smell comes back into my nose and I cringe before taking a deep breath. "I don't know what happened after that."

I look up and notice that Zeke and Miya shifted closer. I shy away from looking at Kane. I can only imagine the haunted look on his face, like I'm broken. Like I'm *tainted*.

"I remember parts every now and then. I remember Zeke helping me. He dragged me out of the party into a cab, I think." I look up at him and he nods. His face is grim, but strong.

Keep going.

"The doctors and nurses poked and prodded when I came to. They never said a word. Not *one* word." A tear falls down my face before I can stop it. Anger rising in my chest as I remember how distant I felt. "They marked it as alcohol poisoning even though traces of ketamine and GHB were found in my system. But, thanks to Vin, they never took me seriously because of my record."

I wipe my face and sigh. "And that is why it's important for me to do all of this. No one should ever feel lost or hopeless." I pause and chew my lip. "I still have black spots in my memory so I can't explain what happened. Only what people tell me and clearly people make shit up." I scratch at my head uncomfortably. "And that is the tragic story of Ebony Young." I let out a pathetic laugh.

Shame is the heaviest energy that sits on my shoulders now. Blame a close second. They hold hands, and take turns riding on me like twins at a fair. They've rooted themselves so deep that I burrow in deep dark corners and pray the sun scares them off.

It never does.

They only linger and I'm stuck in the vicious cycle of fighting, caving, and hiding.

With a quick wipe at my eyes, I stand up and walk out. Rushing out to avoid the 'I'm sorry's, 'I didn't know,' 'What did you do to get it.' I don't make it far down the hall before a sob rips its way out of me. I kneel on the floor covering my face. I *hate* this shit.

There's heat beside me and I feel his wide hand rub my back. He pulls me into his arms and I resist. I don't deserve affection, love, or care. It's fleeting, conditional and I'll become too reliant on it.

"We'll figure it out." His voice is even, calm. The way that Zeke's was. The way that Isaac's and Denise's were.

I look at him and he kisses my forehead. His eyes search my face as he wipes away my tears. "Don't think this means you get out of helping me code this shit," he mumbles, making me laugh.

"Thank you." My voice is thick from the tears. "For not treating me like I'm fragile."

"You're not. Never were and never will be," he confirms. "So why are we letting them have a glitter war without us?"

"Glitter war?"

He shows me the sleeve of his shirt and I laugh again.

"War of the glitter fairies," he says with a shiver. He looks at me seriously. "You aren't alone in this."

I nod, kissing him gently. "I love you."

"You fucking better. I threw glitter for you," he confesses.

"You started it?"

He nods with a wide grin. I laugh, getting to my feet and dragging him back into the room where there is in fact a glitter fight going on.

These people are pretty fucking incredible.

40

Kane

Six. That's how many washes it takes me to get most of the glitter out of my hair. My clothes are covered in a rainbow of colors, which I'm sure will sparkle for at least a year. Ebony's clothes and hair aren't any better, but she's smiling and laughing again, that's all that matters.

I walk out of her bathroom with a towel around my waist and one in my hair, still removing glittery speckles. "I regret throwing glitter," I groan, sitting on the edge of her bed.

She responds with a laugh, then the bed shifts as she moves to help me dry my hair. My eyes are on her, studying her closely. My t-shirt hangs over her frame, brushing past her thighs with each movement.

Her focused face is one of my favorite faces she makes. Her lips look fuller when relaxed and even though people say she looks like a bitch, which I absolutely fucking love, I can tell by her eyes that she's a soft person.

She drapes the towel over my shoulders as she blow-dries my wet hair. She's gentle and tentative. Her fingers run through my wet tresses and I relax. It feels like our normal routine. Shower, dry off, then bed.

Silver peeks from behind the dresser, his green eyes wide

and alert. His little black ears pinned back until she turns the device off. After a minute or two of silence, he creeps on black paws sniffing around.

"All done?" I ask, looking at her. She nods and I pull her into my lap. "We should skip class tomorrow. Go do something fun."

"Tomorrow is a work day and I have tests in my other classes." She lays her head on my shoulder drawing circles on my chest.

"We should take a break from both projects. Invite the gang over, just chill. You and Miya have been working hard. Zeke and I—"

"Have been annoying me," she says looking at me.

"I annoy you?"

She nods her head vigorously, a playful smile tucked in the corners of her mouth as she lays her head back on my shoulder.

"When?" I arch my eyebrow up before laying back. She shifts her weight, laying on my chest.

"Your excessive flirting on the football field."

"Oh. That. You didn't seem to mind if I recall correctly." She snorts.

"I mind when Vin glares at me from the other side of the football field. The entire team seemed to notice."

"You want me to stop?"

She's quiet for a moment as she looks at me. I wait for her response and she laughs to herself, then shakes her head.

"Clearly, I'm not annoying."

"You drive me mad," she growls, slapping at my chest. She

straddles me and I adjust my position so we're more on the bed.

"Only madness you should have around me is in love."

She rolls her eyes at me.

Silver hops on the bed and lays on my chest, swaying his tail. She smiles at him, rubbing his fur.

"Such a good boy," she smiles down at him then locks eyes with me. I'm sure she can tell that her saying 'good boy' affects me. In fact, she shifts her weight to help me adjust. A new kink I didn't even know existed and trust me, I've explored a lot of them.

"You want to be called a good boy too?" she asks me.

"The best boys," I laugh, rubbing her thighs. I watch her admire Silver as she scratches his chin. "I think I was at that party."

She looks at me. Her hand rests on Silver's back as she watches my next move. Her smile falls and I notice her breathing picks up, almost like she's panicking, drowning in dark memories. She's alert, waiting for something to happen. Something that's going to shatter her. It won't happen here, not in this space.

"Zeke and I went. It was Sanjay and Zeus' last year so we went to celebrate. To think while I was having a good time, you were in hell."

"You don't have to—"

"I'm not trying to make you feel bad." She shifts her weight on my body then puts her attention on Silver.

It must be easier distancing herself when talking about something this heavy, this weighted.

I rub her thigh wishing it could help take the pain away. I'd do anything to take the pain away.

"My friend gave me some details that will help. I texted them while you were in the shower. They want to help. To meet you and combine evidence," I add after a moment or two.

"There is no help. The school won't listen," she starts in a soft, raspy voice. "I had a meeting with Dr. Sumner and he told me that if I keep trying to investigate, I'll be expelled for the rest of the semester and potentially next. They claim they can't share the details of their investigation. I even tried looking, the records are sealed."

I hum for a moment, brainstorming our next move. With no solution, I muse to myself, "That was you there that day."

Shifting the conversation's easy when you can avoid verbal landmines. I had to do it as a kid to keep my Dad off my ass. I've even done it a time or two for my friends. It helps, according to them, to not be so wound up about the real shit going on. Especially on the brink of a panic attack, and by the look on her face, she's starting to feel one coming on.

"What?" she looks at me with furrowed brows.

"I did some shit. Harmless pranks. They didn't like it so I landed in his office with academic probation and a bunch of stipulations."

She's less tense as she looks at my face so I do my best "beats me" expression and she laughs a deep belly laugh.

"Harmless pranks like?"

"I uploaded the entire semester book list online for free. Redirected all students to the 'portal.' Then crashed a golf cart."

"A golf cart?"

I shrug my shoulders. "It killed the Koi fish. I'll take it as a sign though." I scratch behind Silver's ear. "You probably know my sins and think I'm one of you, don't you Silver."

He purrs on my chest and she laughs more.

"It was the koi fish," she says. "They're punishing you for the Koi fish."

"I think so too."

We talk a little bit more until she falls asleep.

I admire the relaxed expression on her face in the moonlight. Her eyelashes kissing her cheek bones. I trace the lines and slopes that create her beauty. I'm not a praying man, but I silently pray her dreams are as peaceful as she looks.

Brushing my fingertips softly across her face, I plant a kiss on her forehead and wrap my arms around her.

Maybe this is her safe space, here with me, like this. If only we could bottle this, preserve it on a shelf to open up and use on bad days like today, like *that* day.

She shifts in my arms, bringing her warm body closer to mine, then mumbles something. Leaning closer, I place the shell of my ear near her mouth.

"You're being weird," she says softly.

I chuckle, looking down at her. Shadows kiss her skin and overs some of the shaping of her eyes. Even then, her beauty still prevails even as she stretches and looks around the room briefly.

"You should get more sleep," I whisper, pulling her back towards me.

"Only if you stop watching me," she looks at me.

"I read one of my mom's romance books. Ladies *love* it."

"In fiction," she laughs, then lays back on me.

Silver shifts at the foot of her bed, then stills. His soft snores filling the silence of the room.

"Sometimes," she mutters. "You make me feel like I'm not so fucked up. Like there's not something wrong with me."

"Because you aren't and there isn't," I rub her back, staring at nothing in particular but feeling everything.

"I know, but you and D, Isaac, Miya, Zeke… my cousin and Gramps… you guys just let me exist outside of what you expect. It's nice."

"We don't do expectations. It limits people."

She plays with my messy hair that I'm sure still has fucking glitter in it. She doesn't respond. She's lost in her thoughts for a moment, but I let her exist in there. I'm just here so she doesn't feel so alone.

"You don't have to be afraid of me," she says softly.

I look down at her with my brow furrowed. Instead of responding, she brushes her finger across my lips then places her palm on my cheek. My lips touch her warm palm before I lean into her touch. We move in sync as she straddles me and I shift in bed so she's more comfortable. I slide my palms up the smooth warm flesh of her thighs.

"I know you don't mean to move like you're timid, but you are. You don't have to. You being at that party doesn't mean you have to feel guilty for what my ex and someone else did. You didn't give her the drugs. You didn't carry me to a room."

"You shouldn't be comforting me," I say, pulling her face to mine and she kisses me softly.

"I want to."

"It's pointless. Just know, I'm thinking of several different ways to fuck up any and everyone that put you in that situation."

"Even me?"

I pop her ass and she lets out a short yip before glaring at me. I pin her with a glare of my own.

"Don't do that," I say firmly, looking her right in her eyes.

"Do what?" she asks, folding her arms over her chest.

"You're blaming yourself for going to a party. You went. We all did. Half the school went. You didn't ask for any of that shit, so cut it."

She pouts, staring me down like a brat wanting to have their way. I laugh a little, then pull her mouth back to mine.

"Sleep," I murmur over her lips.

"I can't."

She gets up with a sigh and tugs the shirt she's wearing down. "I think I'm going to try and get some work done."

Silver jumps off the bed and walks into the living room, I'm assuming to get water or sick of us talking. Anything goes with him.

I sit at the edge of the bed and pull her towards me.

"Let me try to replace it," I offer, giving her a thoughtful look. We interlock our fingers and I kiss each of her knuckles looking up at her hopeful.

She looks at me skeptically before laughing. "You can't

replace memories."

"But I can give you better ones."

"Then give me better ones." She's being sarcastic, defensive. I get it. What I'm offering won't take shit away, but it could help. She doesn't want me timid to kiss her, touch her, fuck her, *love* her. And all those things I want to do at her pace.

I kiss her, pulling her to me and tugging my shirt over her head. Fervent kisses greet me as she kisses back immediately. As her hands cup my face, I suck on her bottom lip then kiss down her chest. She releases a soft sigh.

"This is helping," she whispers with a soft laugh as I suck her nipple. I chuckle against the tightening bud, then run my hands up her curves before pulling our mouths together. "Kane."

I pull her onto my lap so she's straddling me before I reposition us more on the bed. My hands run up her soft skin and back down.

"Yeah, babe?" I kiss her neck, then her ear before biting at her shoulder.

"I love you." Her voice is thick, weighted with emotions as she recalls darkness that I want to guide her out of. I pull her face to mine and stare into her watery eyes.

Take my hand.

"Let me make it better."

"You can't," her voice is a broken sob.

"Let me try," I say, wiping her tears and kissing her face. "Is that okay?"

She nods, pulling my mouth back to hers. A salty, desperate

kiss that I slow by putting my hand on the back of her neck, anchoring her to me. I let her lead everything else as she reaches between us and slides me inside her. She sighs into my mouth, biting on my lip.

Her hips grind against mine before she bounces slowly, letting her adjust to my size. I groan in her mouth, grabbing her waist to help her move.

"Harder," she gasps through a sob. I tighten her grip and bring her hips down on mine hard and she moans. "Talk to me."

"You feel so good," I groan, leaning my back to her headboard watching her body move.

"Dirtier," she gasps, moving faster. "Fuck me like a whore, Kane. *Please.*"

The desperation is back, but more intense than ever. Adjusting our position, I pick her up and steady myself on my knees. I hoist her legs into my arms, widening her for me. My body slaps into hers.

"You take all of me so well," I groan. "Always so greedy for my dick."

She moans, opening her eyes and staring into mine. I lay her on her back, keeping her legs on my shoulder and fuck her harder. She gasps my name, digging her fingernails into my back before pulling my hair.

I ease back, grinding against her as her body trembles. I tease her with my strokes until she whimpers, begging me in panted words to keep going.

"I love to hear you fucking beg,"

She mutters 'please' over and over as I move my hips slowly. "Daddy, *please.*" She's a withering, desperate mess for me.

Her pleas are close to sobs, like she needs this. The aggression, the roughness and I want to give it to her. Anything she wants she can have, especially when my dick is buried deep inside her like this.

"Good girl," I groan in her ear, fucking her hard.

Soft, silk skin brush past my sweat slicked shoulders as she wraps her arms around my neck, making me her anchor as she cums hard.

A mixture of her professing her love for me and telling me how good my dick feels falls from her mouth. I trip over the edge with her, cumming so hard inside her that I shiver.

I pull her into a heated kiss, tears spilling from her eyes. The silence speaks for us as she covers her face and cries. I clean her up listening to the ragged, raspy sobs and my heart aches. A sharp pain that I've never really experienced until this moment. I can't fix what's hurting her inside and it fucking kills me.

Her sobs continue as I pull her into my arms and kiss her forehead, her temple, her cheek. I tell her I've got her. That she's safe. That I love her for being all the things that make her, her. When her sobs subside, I kiss her deeply. Anchoring her to where we are right now, in her bed together.

A place where she's safe.

41

Ebony

Sunlight trickles in through the curtains of my room when I wake up. The keys of Kane's keyboard tap noisily from the living room and the warm fragrance of coffee wafts through the door. Silver's collar jingles as he hops on my bed. I pet him, rubbing the top of his head until he guides my hand down his body to his tail.

"Good morning, handsome," I whisper to him before climbing out of bed to brush my teeth.

I opt out of clothes and walk in to see Kane focused on the computer screen. His muscular back flexing with his movements. His boxers peak from beneath his black sweatpants. I walk over to him, planting a kiss on his shoulder, then up to his neck.

"Morning," I whisper in his ear.

He smiles, pulling me around and pausing. His face is a mix of surprise and lust. I smile at him.

"No 'good morning'?" I tease and his eyes drift up to my eyes.

"Fantastic fucking morning," he leans back, eyes glued to me. "I could watch you like this all day."

I hum a response turning away to go into the kitchen, he

grabs my arm and pulls me back to him.

"I wasn't done."

I laugh, pulling my arm from his hand then sitting on his lap. "What are you working on?"

"Trying not to cum in my pants apparently," he kisses my shoulder, then my neck. "I'm coding for our project. That way, I can help you and Miya more. I'm thinking cross coding."

"Cross coding isn't a thing," I say shifting on his leg.

"No, but my idea is you finish your codes, I finish mine and we overlap them."

"Creating like a back door or a firewall?"

"Yes, we link the codes. Use specific wording and trigger codes so it's seamless. The point is for the code to repair itself."

"Codes can't be perfected that way, even with a team of people."

"You're right, but we've been working on this to the point that we could essentially hack our way back into our system, enough to repair the gaps in the code."

"Making it harder to penetrate."

"Yep," he looks at the screen then back at me. "Speaking of penetrate…"

He kisses me hard and I laugh, shying away. "I should get some work done too."

"I have plenty for you to work on, let me just get you back in that room or we can use this table. It looks sturdy enough." He grabs it and gives it a shake making me laugh.

"I just wanted to see where you went."

"About to dick you down. Don't play with me, girl," he

kisses me pushing his tongue in my mouth. I ease up off his lap.

"I gotta meet Miya in an hour."

"Tell her you'll be late. She'll get over it."

"You can handle not fucking me for a day."

"Nah. I need to be in you all the fucking time. Especially if you're walking out like this." He kisses my neck letting his hands roam. "Just give in, you'll get a bomb ass orgasm and then get to work with my cum in you."

I pop his hand, laughing. "Later. I promise."

He groans then slaps my ass hard. "I'm not being gentle when this 'later' comes."

"I like when you're rough."

His nose flares as he gives me a heated glare. He adjusts himself as he rolls his tongue around his mouth. "If you don't get your sexy ass in some clothes, I'm going to fuck you on this table. And I will stop every time you're about to cum. Begging won't help."

A chill shoots through me as I stare at him. He's being serious. He loves when I beg so denying me an orgasm seems like something he'd gladly do. He's mentioned it a few times when I playfully annoy him. His eyes look over me again as I reach for his coffee and take a sip. He stands, positioning himself behind me.

"I meant what I said," his voice is low, raspy as he drags his hands over my hips, up my back, then in my hair. He pulls me back to him from the nape of my neck and a moan escapes my mouth. He drags his hand across my breast, down my stomach, then in between my thighs. He slaps my clit and I push back into him from the shock.

"Don't be an asshole," I moan as his fingers move in slow circles, dipping into my wetness periodically.

I reach behind me, but he steps back. My breathing comes out in staccato-like exhales as I feel myself building up. I try to control my breathing, keeping it even so I can steal my orgasm from him, but he stops. A frustrated whimper expels from my mouth.

"What did I say?" he whispers in my ear. He kisses me before putting his fingers in his mouth and groaning. "You're gonna be the death of me. Why the fuck do you taste so damn good?"

He slouches on the couch, his eyes still on me. He runs his hands through his hair. Glitter flutters down and a frustrated groan rips from his chest.

"I'm so sick of seeing glitter. Why is this shit so hard to get rid of!"

I laugh, kissing him. His hand creeps up and circles around my neck as he pushes his tongue in my mouth and slaps my ass.

"If you don't leave now, I'm locking us both in that room."

Laughing again, I kiss him again, then walk in the room.

He huffs and mumbles to himself before his keyboard keys start clicking again.

Once fully dressed, I step into the kitchen. As I grab a bottle of water, I catch his less heated eyes on me. "Meet in the computer lab?"

"Very weird way to say bedroom." He smiles softly and

nods. "After your second class."

With a smile, I grab my book bag and give him a kiss. I pry his hands off my thighs and rush out the door. Leaning against the door, I laugh.

I'm beginning to like waking up next to him.

42

Ebony

As promised, Kane meets me in the computer lab so he can look over my codes. I stand at a work table putting together components for our drone. Smoke tendrils dance into the air as I melt and fuse wires to the metal casing that I welded together.

Kane stretches, then walks over to the table I'm working on, checking out my work.

"You're much better at this than you are at coding."

I hold the soldering device up and glare at him.

"I'm kidding. Damn," he laughs, kissing my temple.

"All of this is durable. Got it from the art department. Lightweight and flexible."

"So, we should have a working drone by the time this class is done?"

"That's the plan. If I work on it over break." I get back to my work.

"Good, my Dad has better tools in his garage."

My head pops up and I look at him. He's focused on the computer screen typing again.

"Why would I be in your Dad's garage?"

"Because you're coming home with me and Miya?" he says

slowly looking at me with his brow pinched together.

"I didn't agree to it!" I put the soldering machine down.

"Well, my mom is excited to meet you."

"Does she—"

"No, she doesn't know that we have anything going on other than this project." He pushes back from the computer. "Miya told her before I could. We're basically fighting over who calls dibs on you, but since I'm driving…"

His smile touches his eyes in a beautiful way. They shine in the light like rain puddles shine to someone that enjoys puddle hopping. The deepest, most amazing eyes.

"Is Ebony in there?" Vin's voice trickles through the cracked door.

Kane's smile fades into a dark grimace.

I grab his hand and rush towards the servers. He stumbles as he follows me reluctantly. Pushing him into one of the bays, I tug him with me to a dark corner. With him positioned in front of me, I watch through the cracks in the plastic partition.

Kane lays his forehead on my temple laughing softly. "Eb why are we hiding," he whispers in my ear. "I can tell him to get lost."

"And witness you beat his ass *and* get expelled? No." I whisper back. "He won't leave either. It's Vin. He doesn't like the word 'no'."

"E?" Vin looks around. "Eb? Look if you're hiding from me that's some childish shit."

Kane mocks him in my ear and I stifle a giggle.

"I have to talk to you. It's about Kane. Look, you two being all over each other on the field didn't sit right with me and something happened in the locker room with him."

"You must have done a number on him," Kane whispers before biting at my ear. "Too bad you're mine."

He runs his tongue up my neck. A small noise escapes my mouth and I cover it as Kane laughs into my shoulder.

Vin's head snaps around. "Ebony?"

"He's gonna catch us back here, stop," I whisper to him, still watching Vin.

"We're not even doing anything," he whispers. His nose traces up the side of my neck before his lips take over. "You smell so fucking good."

My eyes look into his now. I shift in the little space that we have to make some room. He stops me with his hand on the metal shelf and looks at the end of the bay as Vin passes by. Kane puts a finger to his mouth before kissing my neck again. His fingers slip down my pants and I cover my mouth, stifling a moan. He smiles as he drags his tongue up my neck. "Naughty girl."

I shudder as his thumb circles my clit and his fingers curl in my body.

"Let's see how quiet you can be, baby," Kane whispers in my ear as he removes my pants as I unfasten his. Then, with my legs balanced in the crook of each arm, he penetrates me deeply.

I muffle my moan in his chest as he hisses in my ear. "Such a dirty little slut for me."

He pushes in slowly, moving his hips against mine.

The awkward position and tight space gives my body the friction it needs. His thick hand covers my mouth as I moan his name. "Maybe we should let Vin know who fucks you this good."

He bites at my neck and his hand captures my intense moans.

"Ebony?" Vin's voice echoes in the bay. "Come on now, stop fucking playing."

"You want to stop fucking playing?" Kane whispers in my ear, shifting our position and pushes deeper.

I continue to moan in his palm, then lean into Kane, giggling softly.

"He's gonna catch us," Kane whispers, laughing in my ear before kissing me.

"Eb!?" Vin's voice is close, but I'm more focused on Kane's thrusts.

His hand's around my throat, stealing my breath away. He releases and I inhale deeply before he does it again. The way he knows my body turns me on more. I release control over to him as he continues.

"You want him to know?" Kane whispers in my ear, kissing my neck. "Cause I'm going to make you cum so fucking hard."

Vin stands at the end of the bay we're in. Kane and I stare down at him in the shadows as Kane continues to thrust, his mouth at the shell of my ear.

"I bet it turns you on to think he's watching you get fucked like a slut," Kane whispers.

Vin takes a step forward before the opening and closing of

the main door catches his attention. He hesitates then goes back into the computer lab.

"Ebony?" He rushes around the room and I cum so damn hard. Flashes of white light burst behind my eyes as my muscles squeeze and shake. I'm floating. Suspended in the air. Transcending to the sky and my only thought is how fucking good it feels to fly.

Kane's hand is around my mouth when I moan his name through my orgasmic high. He moans into my ear, releasing himself inside of me, then helps me down.

We get ourselves straightened out and go back into the main computer lab area and laugh once our eyes lock.

"He almost got an eye full," Kane says laughing. He sits in the chair he was in.

"Wouldn't be the first time."

Kane's laugh turns into a coughing fit. He stops, shocked.

"Story for another day," I say with a smile and a shrug. I force myself to continue working on our project.

"And you say I'm bad," he mumbles. Amusement lacing his tone before the clicking of the keyboard takes over. I look at my phone and groan.

"I have class. Are we meeting back here or our apartment?"

"Our apartment?" he smiles at me.

I stand there looking like a fish out of water. "Forget it."

"No, don't forget it." He pushes away from the computer, taking long strides to me and kisses me.

"I will be here when you're done with class, then we will go to *our* apartment together."

I smile at him, kissing him again, then leaving for class. A silly grin on my face. My head is swimming with happy thoughts.

43

Kane

Something about Vin popping up to talk to Ebony doesn't sit right with me. Not because I'm possessive. Not completely. I just know there's more to him. My Dad taught me how to read people, their body language, their facial expressions. That's where the truth sits and not even the best trained manipulator can fool everyone.

I save the code I'm working on and embark on a search of my own. First using Vin's name, only learning information I know. For one, his father's the mayor of our city. Next, I try a combination of keywords. Out of curiosity, search Vin and Ebony together and find old articles from when they were together.

I read them. "Sent to juvie for possession… In the passenger seat…."

I print the article and keep digging and printing more. So engrossed in my search, I barely hear the door open as Zeke walks in. I nod to him, then go back to my search.

"What's up, man," Zeke greets me then looks over my shoulder.

"How much do you know about Vin?"

"Not much. He's an arrogant bitch just like his Dad. That's

about it."

"E ever say anything about doing cocaine or any hard drugs?"

Zeke scoffs and shakes his head. "You know like I know that girl will only smoke weed. The best shit. Why?"

I move my chair out the way so he can read the article. "She was charged with possession of cocaine? She was trying to sell? But why would she be in the passenger seat of his Dad's car?"

"Exactly. And where would she or Vin get that much cocaine?" I move back to the screen as Zeke pulls up a chair. He watches over my shoulder. "That's not the only article that pins blame on her and everything is a direct quote from the Mayor or Vin."

"She's their scapegoat," Zeke looks grimly at me.

"Even in the article from last semester. He claims he saw her take the drugs and he took her out of the party to the hospital. And for everything I found, the police reports are sealed at the request of some unknown person."

"Someone's burying her story."

I nod. "Vin is a fucking problem. Her parents clearly don't believe her. The school is indebted to the Mayor. He's basically untouchable. She's a pawn and he's got her backed in a corner."

"Then we need to find a way to expose him and get her out of that corner."

"His Dad won't go for any bait we lay. We'll have to get them both."

I lean back looking at my friend, then an idea hits me.

"I have a plan, but I need you on board with me."

"I'm not going to seduce Vin," Zeke grimaces. "I've bitten bullets for you before, but not this one."

"I wouldn't ask you to stick your dick in crazy. I told E I was going to meet her here, get some work done with her, then go to our apartment. I'll let my sister know the plan just in case she can't make it here. I need them both on board for this to work."

"Okay, who's apartment? *Ours* or *hers*?" The arrogant fucker has a smug look on his face after he asks. I pop him in the back of the head, laughing. "It's a valid question. The kids miss you," he says, laughing.

"Stop that shit," I save everything to my computer and get up. "She should be out of class in a couple minutes. Let's grab some food and I'll tell you on the way."

I'm not entirely sure if I can pull this off, but if I can show them the connections I made, their project will open Pandora's box. And the only thing they'll have to do is sit back and watch the cards fall.

Good news, might have found something to clear your name. Will update u when I know more. Sit tight a little longer.

44

Ebony

Oranges, reds, and pinks decorate the sky as the sun begins to set. The cold settles into the atmosphere, getting worse as the wind blows more. Denise walks with me, our drinks in her hand as I struggle with my broken backpack strap.

"I just got this bag," I sigh, sitting my bag on the bench and looking at the damage. I sling one of the straps over my shoulder and grab my drink.

"When? Cause it don't look just purchased, boo," Denise comments poking her finger through one of the holes in my bag.

"Okay, not brand new, but it shouldn't have broke."

"Baby, this been broke." She holds up a piece of my bag strap that's still attached with her eyebrow quirked. It's mangled like a chew toy."

I laugh, snatching the piece out of her hand. Slowly, her face morphs into a look of disgust. Following her line of sight, I catch a glimpse of Vin running towards me.

His eyes are fixed on me as he rapidly approaches, it's too late for us to run. I groan internally, crossing my arms over my chest.

"Eb, I've been looking for you," Vin says loudly before he

comes face to face with me.

A few people stop talking to observe what's going on. That's how loud he is. Denise stands beside me as he approaches.

"Hey, D."

She scoffs giving him an eye roll before looking him up and down in disgust.

"Okay," he mutters before looking at me. "You have a minute?"

"No, I gotta run to meet with D's mom." I grab D's arm, walking us rapidly through the thick crowd before breaking out into a sprint. We dodge people on bikes, clinging to our stuff. She laughs, running beside me as we enter other buildings before making it to the computer lab. Safe inside the lab, Denise and I burst out with laughter as she collapses in a chair and I lean over the work table.

"Girl," Denise pants from her rolling chair. "I have never had that much fun running. Ever."

We continue laughing for a moment, then I realize the space around us. Residual laughter bubbles out of me as I look around the large room. Kane's and Zeke's bags lay in the corner of the room. The computer Kane works on is still open, but the Knight University screensaver bobbles around the screen.

A soft rapping noise from the door has Denise and me scrambling to find some place to duck off to, but we're too late. Isaac and Miya walk in, eyeing us both strangely. Both carrying trays of hot cocoa and coffee.

"Are you two good?"

Miya slowly enters the room, sitting her tray on the table. Her eyes looking between Denise's and mine as we start giggling again. We embrace them before collapsing in chairs rehashing the events that took place a few minutes before meeting up with them.

"He was behind us talkin' bout some, 'Yo E! Wait up!'" Denise laughs leaning against the wall.

"Did he chase you here!?" Miya asks, looking between us more shocked than amused.

"I think we lost him back in the math building, but who knows," I shrug, glancing at the door.

"Maybe it's because of that rumor I heard," Isaac says, taking a sip of his drink, still laughing slightly. "Allegedly, you and Kane were all over each other on the field."

"They were!" Miya groans. "Attached at the hip. It's so weird. He's gross."

"I'm not that gross," Kane says, carrying bags of food. He sits them on the table and kisses my forehead, then scrunches up his face. "Why are you sweating?"

"These two raced across campus to escape the big bad Vin," Isaac giggles.

"Did he hurt you?" Kane and Zeke ask us at the same time.

"Naw, we left him in the dust before he could decide what to do," Denise said, rubbing her calves. "I'm really outta shape."

"Did you see him when you guys came in?" Miya asks, pulling a few things out of her bag. She sits at a vacant table neatly stacking her things

Zeke shakes his head, pulling a chair out to sit with her.

"No, just the usual transition."

Kane sits beside me and looks between Denise and me. "Did he say why he's looking for you?"

"Probably to tell me what he wanted to tell me earlier?"

Kane leans into my ear and whispers, "That I make you cum harder?"

"He wouldn't know that," I mumble back, blushing. I push his chair away and get to a computer myself.

Denise looks at her phone for a moment before digging in the bags and boxes of food.

"OMG! Pizza!?" She groans, grabbing a slice. "Keep him, E."

I scoff looking at her. "You're giving me away for pizza?"

"Yeah? At least he's cute." She shrugs with a smile.

With the door propped open, we all start respectively working on assignments. Isaac plays music softly making a medley of keyboard keys clicking, pencils scraping across paper, and papers shuffling.

I glance through the propped open computer lab door and freeze. I shouldn't be surprised to see Vin walking in to look for me. He's always had stalker-like tendencies. I duck my head in the workstation catching a few furrowed brows.

"What are you doing?" Denise asks me, looking at me strangely. Isaac and Kane roll over to me giving me the same confused look.

I look her in the eye and nod. All three look and she drops down with me. Isaac slowly kneels beside us looking even more confused, but Kane stares down at us like we grew three heads.

"He must have a tracking device on you," Denise whispers.

"That's Vin!?" Isaac hisses close to Denise and me. Isaac pops his head over the workstation wall. "THE Vin?" he whispers.

"Yes, now will you both get down." I hiss, yanking at them.

"Hey, Kane. You seen—" Vin pauses looking down at Denise, Isaac, and me. "…Ebs"

I give a pathetic wave and the three of us scramble up.

"Ohhh, bitch. There's my contact. Thank you for helping me look." Denise pretends to blow it off and put it back in her eye.

"When did you start wearing contacts?" Vin asks.

"You in my business," Denise says flatly before nudging past him to sit down.

Zeke eyes the situation, tense. Miya sits beside him furiously looking on. Her eyes go between him, me, and a very defensive Kane.

"Why were you looking for E?" Kane asks, leaning against the workstation wall and crossing his arms over his chest.

"Wanted to talk to her about something. I wanted to talk to you too."

"Well, talk now," Isaac interjects.

There's a tense silence as everyone stares at Vin. He shifts uncomfortably.

"It's a private conversation," he says with a nervous laugh. He scratches the back of his neck.

Kane looks at me now, his eyes searching me. "What did

you need to talk to me about?"

Vin sighs. "I wanted to apologize for the shit back in the locker room." He looks at Zeke. "Just wanted to make sure you guys were good."

"Why wouldn't any of us be?" I ask with my brows furrowed.

Vin stares at me. "Because your pops called mine pissed. He thinks you're fucking a mafia man's son. He's talking about pulling you from school."

"How would your Dad, let alone my Dad, hear about any of this shit," My voice is quiet. I'm lost in thought for a second before my eyes fix on Vin. "You took *rumors* to my Dad!?" I'm almost shouting.

Denise and Isaac hold me back. I'm an inch away from Vin's face. He holds his hands up and Kane's arm is between us as he looks at Vin, then me.

"My pops asked how you were doing. I let it slip."

A bitter laugh slips out of my mouth. "Right. Just like all the other times. Jesus Christ, Vin. Do you ever know when to shut the fuck up and mind *your* fucking business."

I grab my things and dial my Dad's number in a panic. "Did you ever tell them the shit you did? No? Just all the shit I do so you can keep the fucking *golden boy* crown."

I shove past him, muttering under my breath.

"Where are you going?" Vin asks behind me. His desperate voice makes me roll my eyes. I hate him. I never hated him more than I do now.

"To do damage control. Again." I don't stop walking.

"He doesn't want to talk to you," Vin says firmly, but there's a shake in his voice. "He said if your decisions make him look bad and cost him his reelection, then he doesn't want to be associated with you until you get it together."

I stop mid stride and turn to look at him. I suck in a lungful of air and hold it until my lungs start to burn. "Then fuck him. He doesn't want me around, especially after what you've done? Fine."

"Ebony…" Kane speaks softly, but firmly as he shoulders past Vin.

"You know it ain't like that," Vin says rushing over to me.

"Oh no? What's it like? You and your Daddy fuck up *families.*" My voice breaks but I can't stop my words. "*My family.* You ruined *my* life, Vin."

"No one told you to go wild after we broke up. Or get high."

"And no one told you to get me high or leave me in those situations. No one told you to sell drugs to people and get *me* arrested."

"Don't do that. Don't pin that shit on me. You practically begged for all that, begged men to fuck you," he shrugs with a sarcastic chuckle.

"I was sixteen and drunk."

"And a fucking cock hungry slut. You begged for all the dick you could get, dirty bitch," he spits out.

My vision fills with red as my fist collides with his nose. It cracks loudly. I swing again, but my body is lifted in the air and flung over Kane's firm shoulder as he quickly walks me out of the computer lab. Denise and Isaac scramble behind him with my stuff in their hands.

"Put me down, Kane." Instead of it being firm, it's a sob because I'm crying. And his shoulder's digging into my gut and the only thing I want is to set the world on fire and watch it fucking burn.

He puts me down and looks me in my face. I try to pull away to charge back towards Vin's crumpled body, but Kane uses his large hands to force me to look at him. He wipes my tears with his thumbs. I look back one last time as Zeke and Miya leave the room. Zeke's arm over Miya's shoulder, escorting her out of the room with a satisfied smirk.

"You want to burn the world, I'll burn it with you, but not here," there's truth that lingers in his eyes. Partnered with concern and a softness that urges me to breathe.

"We gotta go," Denise says, looking at us anxiously. People peer into the computer lab as Vin continues to groan, blood dripping down his arm. "We can't do this here."

I look around at my group of friends and nod.

Regret starts to fill my chest as we walk out of the computer lab like nothing happened. Kane intertwines our fingers as we walk across campus.

"My bitch gotta mean right hook," Isaac muses before laughing.

"Knew you had it in you, E," Zeke says from the other side of Miya with a smile. Kane squeezes my hand with a satisfied smile on his face.

45

Ebony

"Girl," Denise says before laughing. "You knocked that ass out."

Isaac doubles over with laughter. "Dude had big balls. 'You're nothing but a cock hungry slut!' Pow!"

Kane sits next to me studying my hand. "You need ice for that hand, Rocky. Remind me not to fuck with you."

Soft laughs fill the room as I lay my head back on the couch.

"I fucked up," I groan putting my hands over my face. "I'm sorry, Miya. I wasn't thinking." I look at her alarmed eyes and she smiles.

"For what? He got what was coming for him."

"You're invested in this project."

"And there will be others. Plus, my 'mafia boss' Dad would do anything to make sure I'm happy." She shrugs, sitting in the chair beside me. She takes my hand and squeezes it.

"If he tells his Dad, there will be no way to get this project finished." I stare at her.

"His Dad isn't that powerful," Miya says, playing with Silver.

"He has ties to the people that make the drugs," I confess softly. "I found it out snooping before today. It was a tip I got from the police department before the files got sealed."

The room is silent as everyone but Zeke stares at me. He clears his throat, nodding slightly.

"The drugs found in Ebony's system are the same drugs connected to him," Zeke confirms. "That was in the doctor's report."

I stand up, walking into my room. I unlock my safe and pull out a thick yellow folder and bring it back out to where everyone is. I drop it on the table and it lands with a loud slap.

A tense feeling settles over my entire body as an ache in my fist reminds me of where I am. "Everything is in the folder. The test results, a few of the police records, anything I could get my hands on…"

I look at Miya, "The anonymous documents you have that we used for the case study… those are these. They're mine. The only documents I know for a fact can be tied to them."

She shifts in the seat and covers her mouth. "Ebony…"

"I'm missing something," Isaac says, scooting closer to the table. "What's in those files?"

"Her blood test came back with a lethal amount of some unknown substance. It was like an allergic reaction. Her body attacked it hard. They used some form of Epinephrine to counteract the reaction, making it worse before it got better," Zeke adds.

"My heart stopped," I state with a shrug, "and they had to bring me back in that room because a dead girl looks much worse than a drugged one."

"You better be fucking lying to me," Isaac whimpers. His

eyes are wide as he looks up to me. There's a glossiness to them as he forces himself to take deep breaths.

"It's true," Denise confirms. "Zeke called me that night and I got to the hospital. I was able to pretend to be her sister to get the information. It wasn't just the date rape drug, it was like a fucking drug cocktail."

"You're the perfect victim," Kane says softly, looking at Zeke.

"Told you I'd talk to her," Zeke confirms with a nod.

"I was able to swipe the original documents before they were altered and sealed. These are what they sent to the Mayor."

"I'll kill him," Kane growls. "Vin and his Dad are as good as dead."

"He didn't give it to me. Everyone has access to this shit." I say looking at Kane. "I have proof that they make it, but not that they supplied it. And I can't find a way to get the proof that they transported it without getting caught."

"You won't get caught," Kane says slowly, looking at me. "I did research after the first time he went looking for you." He sucks in a lungful of air, then fixes his eyes on me. "I think we should combine projects."

"That wouldn't work," I say looking at Miya. She looks at Kane with hopeful eyes.

"He told me about the idea. You two should hear him out," Zeke says from the table.

I sit on the floor beside Isaac.

"We do the coding for everything, Zeke and I hacked the system to override a lot of shit so I know how to get in undetected."

"You're on academic probation for that," Miya comments. "Don't be dumb."

"I'm on academic probation for destroying the golf cart and killing the Koi fish.'

"What the hell did the Koi fish do!?" Denise shouts looking at Kane.

Zeke, Kane, Miya, and I stifle a laugh as she covers her mouth. She waves her hand for him to continue looking at an equally confused Isaac.

"Dad said whatever I needed for this project I have access to. I can get all the information, digitize it and put it on the drone, then upload it online and make the link reroute to a database with the information."

"I have access to projector parts and hard drives," Zeke adds.

"We'll do it the last day of Family and Friends Week. We'll upload everything and then project it at the Gala." He looks at his sister.

"Wait," Isaac says, looking at Kane. "You're planning on exposing more than just Vin."

Kane nods. His sister glares at him.

"That's dangerous," Miya fusses.

"The man isn't untouchable," he defends. "You just have to get him backed in a corner."

"He's not a person that should be backed in a corner," Denise warns. "They're psychotic."

"Lucky for them, I'm eager to see how far they're willing

to go."

"Kane," Miya starts. Her voice is tense, there's a warning in it. "We have one chance."

"Don't put yourself at risk, Kane," I say, catching his attention. "I can handle this."

My ringing phone disrupts us. Isaac looks over my shoulder, then at me.

"Don't pick it up," he says softly.

"I have to," I say softly, picking up the phone and walking into my room.

"Ebony Imani Young, what the fuck has gotten into you!? You attacked Vin?"

"Not technically," I say softly, sitting on my bed. Kane walks into the room and cracks the door. He sits beside me and I put the phone on speaker.

"What the hell happened?"

"He came in and said you were mad. Called me names and I hit him. I don't think you'd like for your only daughter to be called a cock hungry slut," I roll my eyes knowing good and damn well it's a name he calls me frequently.

"If you're acting like a slut, then he has every right to call you that."

Kane's hand, which is rubbing my back, pauses. He looks at me.

"You will apologize to him. You broke his nose, Ebony. All over him calling you names!?" He scoffs. "I bet it has something to do with that mafia guy that he says has been lurking around you."

"She's fallen from grace, Bobby. She should have been cut off back when she went to juvie."

Kane grabs my phone and hangs up. "I'm with Isaac. Don't answer these calls anymore."

My phone rings and he powers it off, then tosses it on the bed. "I feel bad for not telling you," I say.

His eyes are thoughtful as he looks at me, standing up and pulling me to his chest. He kisses my forehead.

"We all have skeletons. Yours just happen to fall out and surprise the fuck out of me."

I laugh. "Gotta keep you on your toes."

"Doing a good job with that," he laughs. He takes me in for a moment. "Sleep on the idea. I don't want to force you to do something that you're not comfortable with. Just know, Vin comes around you with that slut shaming shit, I'm doing more than breaking his nose."

"Let's see if we can get this drone working first," I say walking past him. He grabs me.

"You actually should be packing. We're leaving tomorrow."

He kisses my lips and leaves me stunned in the room.

I forgot about that.

46

Kane

Miya's phone blares musical soundtracks through my car speakers as we speed down the freeway. I groan as her and Ebony scream lyrics at the top of their lungs. Ebony air drums as my sister plays the air guitar. Zeke, who sits in the back, shakes his head looking between the two of them amused.

Ebony laughs as Miya attempts to hit a high note and ends up squawking.

"That's enough Scuttle and Ariel," I say, glancing at them as I change lanes.

"Did you just call me Scuttle!?" Miya shrieks at me.

"He has a point," Zeke says with a laugh and my sister glares at him in response.

Ebony takes over the music as Zeke silently apologizes by handing my sister his phone. She laughs leaning closer to him and a slight groan passes my lips. Ebony places a hand on mine catching my attention.

"Relax," she says as softly as she can to me. She turns the heat down a little bit and leans back in the seat.

"Kane, pull over I have to pee," Miya whines.

"We're almost there."

"I will pee all over these leather seats if you don't pull over now!"

I grumble curses at my sister as I find an exit and pull over at a gas station. Everyone climbs out, stretching their limbs before Miya and Zeke head towards the bathroom talking. I start pumping gas in my tank for good measure, then take a step around the hood of my car to follow, but Ebony grabs me, pulling me to her body and kissing my lips softly, effectively distracting me.

"You did that on purpose," I mumble. She smiles at me, then kisses me again. "I'm still going to see what's going on."

"You're going to watch Zeke pee?"

I slap her ass, gripping it in the process. She laughs, pinching at my side. "You setting them up?"

She shakes her head, sliding her hands in my jacket and up my back. "It's naturally happening."

"Don't like it."

She hums her response as her eyes explore my face, then she lays her head on my chest. The wind blows, sending a howl through the air and she hugs closer to me. Her body shivering against the cold's roughness. I wrap my arms around her.

"You should get in the car," I kiss the top of her head. "To at least get out of the cold."

"Are you going to make things weird between them?" She asks, leaning back to get a better look at my face

"It *should* be weird, he's like my brother and she's my sister."

"Don't make it weird!" She slaps at my arm for good measure as the gas pump shuts off with a pop. She steps away from my body and I put the pump back. She steps in the car with me and we sit in the warmth.

She smiles at her phone.

"What's got you smiling?" I ask, looking at her.

"My Gramps," she says, showing me an image of him and Clint decorating the bar. "He loves the holidays."

I smile at the thought, then let a few moments pass watching as she continues to text.

"I want to ask you something," I start. She casts me a side glance before putting her phone down and gives me her attention. "Is sex uncomfortable for you after everything?"

She thinks for a moment, chewing at her cheek as her eyes go unfocused, then she shakes her head.

"Not exactly," she starts, clearing her throat and looking out the window. "I have my reservations about it, but there's like this switch in my brain and I get so hyper-fixated on chasing the dopamine that it gives me." She looks at me, her eyes searching mine bashfully. "Sex with you recently," she says more softly. "Is different."

"What about when you perform? There's a lot of touching there."

"That's something new. A persona that I created."

"Persona?"

She nods before chewing at the skin around her thumb, "I've been looking for a way to bring both parts of me back together."

I don't say anything as I watch her mind work. Instead, I pull her finger from her lips and give her hand a squeeze. The back doors open and a gust of crisp air greets us as Miya and Zeke slip into the car with snacks.

With one hand on the steering wheel and the other on her warm thigh, we restart our journey. I give her a squeeze as Miya and Zeke strike up idle conversation.

47

Ebony

As a little girl, I was always amazed at the large houses in the rich neighborhoods tucked just outside of town. I always wanted to live in one. That was until my Dad got his big break and moved us into one. Long corridors with so many doors you could get lost in. I was in heaven, then I met Vin and the bad shit took over. I was sent away before really enjoying it. Something I had a feeling my parents had always wanted to make happen since I showed up at their doorstep, but I looked good for political campaigns.

The only big house I managed to stay in, after they basically kicked me out, was the reform school for girls. I had my own room, bathroom, and walk-in closet, but that was the extent. The headmaster made sure to let me know they weren't my family. They were there to get me into shape, teach me how to be a proper lady, and set me free into the world prim and proper.

They clearly failed.

I rarely come across large houses like the ones I saw as a kid, that is until Kane pulls into the curved driveway of a beautiful large house. Gray stones stack one on top of the other. Two large navy blue doors greet us at the top of the gray steps.

"We'll meet you guys inside," Kane says from the driver seat.

"Uh huh, sure," Zeke mutters, hiding a smirk. Kane rolls his eyes and shoots him a pointed look.

Zeke planned to stay the night here tonight for Miya's movie night. I'm sure their shift in friendship encouraged both her asking and him accepting, quickly might I add.

They walk inside the house as Kane drives around the side. Large trees line brown grass. I imagine how beautiful and green everything looks in the spring. A large garage sits in the back, echoing the structure of the house. Several cars are parked in the garage when we pull in. Finding a spot, he stops his car in it, then turns it off.

"There's a lot of cars in here," I comment poorly as the sound of my shoes echo in the vast space. A large black SUV sits beside Kane's car. A sleek, black motorcycle is parked beside that.

"Yeah, my Dad, little bro, and I love cars," Kane says with a chuckle, putting his arm around me. "With the snow threatening to come, we're gonna switch to the one I parked next to."

"Is that one yours?"

"Yeah." He grins. "And the bike."

Leading us to an exit, we step out on a small path that snakes towards the house towards a large pond with lilies floating on it.

"Told my mom you liked lilies so she had some flown in," Kane says with a hint of shyness in his tone. A slight blush rises in his face.

"That's very sweet." I kiss his cheek.

We stop walking and gaze at the lake from the path before he tugs me towards the house. Large windows expose me to the cozy interior, the bedrooms, the offices. The patio with an expensive grill set and the sunroom.

"Your house is beautiful," I say softly as we get closer.

"My Dad had it custom built for my mom," he says with pride as we walk in and take off our shoes.

"Lucky mom," I say softly, looking around the beautiful house. Hardwood floors cover every square inch of the house. They shine brightly even with the overcast weather. We kick our shoes off and sit them neatly by the door we entered. The floor is cool beneath my feet. Kane calls out to his mom in Korean, then switches to Japanese, pulling me behind him. I quickly step to keep up with Kane's excited footsteps.

"She went to the store," a voice calls behind us. I slip, tumbling into Kane as I turn. He steadies me with a laugh.

Kane's younger brother, Han, sits up on the couch, a video game playing on the screen. He looks like Kane a little bit, but his hair is short and smoothed to the side. He eyes me suspiciously before looking at Kane.

"Ebony?" he asks.

"In the flesh," Kane says with a smile. "E, this is my little brother, and Miya's twin, Han." Unlike his photos, his face is more defined like the lean muscles on his body.

I wave to him before taking in the game he's playing. "You like zombie games?" I ask. He breaks into a large grin, his dimples display themselves.

"Yeah! I'm playing this one again. There's a hidden room somewhere that I missed the first time I played it."

"Oh! I think I remember where to find it." Han hesitates before offering me the controller. I lean over the back of the chair and break a few things before revealing a door. I hand him the controller with a smile. "I'll let you do the honors."

Kane's hand rubs my back as his brother opens the door. "Didn't know you played."

"On occasions," I nudge him.

"Hey, kid, Dad still here?"

"Office. Might be on a call," Han says idly. "Thanks for the help, Ebony." He says with a small smile. I smile back at him as Kane drags me away by my waist, up a set of hidden stairs.

"Secret lair?" I whisper looking at him.

"My Dad's study," he laughs, leading me up the stairs. A long hallway greets us at the top as he walks through. Light spills in through the windows before he stops at a door and knocks on it.

There's shuffling on the other side then it opens, revealing a tall man. Kane smiles widely, hugging his father briefly before turning to me. "I don't know where Miya went, but this is Ebony."

"The friend you two were fighting over?" Mr. Yamada's voice is deep and playful. There's a sparkle in his eye as he looks at Kane suspiciously before shaking my hand.

"It's nice to meet you, Mr. Yamada," I say awkwardly.

"Nice to meet you too, Ebony. I've heard amazing things

about you," he says with a warm smile still on his face.

"That's a relief," I laugh, scratching at my arm.

"Apparently, you keep this one here on his toes." He leans towards me. "Thank you for challenging him. He'd just coast his way through life otherwise."

I laugh and nod.

"While you're here," he starts. "Feel free to use any parts you might need for your drone."

"Thank you! We're hoping to have it done soon."

"I hope so, I'd love to see it."

"You'll be the first call, Dad," Kane says. "We'll let you get back to work."

His Dad nods to him, placing a large hand on his shoulder, then shooting me another warm smile before going back into his office.

"He likes you," Kane whispers as he walks me further down the corridor, then takes a right.

"What's not to like?" I ask, smiling at him.

"I haven't seen anything so far," he says with a smile.

48

Kane

After showing Ebony the rest of the house, I lead her to her room, which is a few doors down from mine and right across from Miya's. She looks around, finding her bags sitting neatly in the corner.

"If you don't like it, I can bring you to my room," I say with a smile.

She laughs at me shaking her head. Her teeth scrape against her lip before she turns to look out the window. I wrap my arms around her. With my chin on her shoulder, we look out at the backyard. Soft fingertips brush my hand as she caresses it, then intertwines our fingers.

"I may not want to go back to our apartment," she sighs. "This house is big enough for me to stay and not be found," she finishes laughing.

"You may change your mind by the end of the week," I comment, laughing. I place soft kisses on her neck. "I'm glad I could help you get away."

"Says my knight in shining armor," she says wiggling her eyebrows, pulling at my Knight University hoodie. I roll my eyes, shaking my head.

"No, E," I laugh.

"I think I deserve a kiss for that," she mumbles, shrugging. "It was a good one."

I laugh, pulling her face to mine for a kiss. My tongue brushing past her bottom lip. She opens her mouth, meeting my tongue with her own. Her arms snake around my neck as she pulls me closer to her.

"There's a bed right there," I mumble across her lips. She kisses me through a smile. My fingers ghost over her skin as I inch underneath her shirt.

"The door is wide open," she whispers against my kiss.

I hum kissing her as I pull us back towards the bed. "Don't really fucking care right now," I whisper back, pulling her on top of me as I sit on the bed.

She laughs, pushing away from me. "The door."

I pull her back into a kiss. "We can always just make out," I suggest, putting my hand at the back of her head as she lays beside me. Her lips are soft and her tongue is gentle as it brushes against mine. I pull her closer to my body, pulling her leg over my waist, grinding against her.

She pushes away, shaking her head and sighing. She paces the floor. "Me on a bed with you doesn't ever mean just making out," she whispers to me laughing.

"You don't want to?" I ask, pulling my shirt off and standing up.

"Oh. My. God, Kane," she laughs, covering her face and turning away from me.

I toss her over my shoulder and take her into the bathroom. With the door closed, I sit her on the counter kissing her neck.

"What about now?" I mutter into her warm skin. Her pulse throbs against my mouth and I suck on her neck. Her flesh is sweet on my tongue. My hands rubbing her thighs. A soft moan falls from her lips as she pushes her chest into mine. I pull her shirt off, running my hands over her hot, smooth skin before I unlatch her bra, then place gentle kisses to her neck as I toss her bra to the side.

Her nipples are hard against my chest. The balls of her nipple rings gently brush against my skin. A sensation I've grown to love. My lips find hers while my hands slip up her thighs and grab at her ass. A soft moan vibrates in her chest and she scoots forward, providing friction against my erection. I groan into her mouth, teetering the line of pushing this much further and keeping it at this agonizing torture.

A knock on the door has her covering a giggle and slipping off the counter. Gathering up her discarded clothes, she disappears in the closet. Laughs bubble out of me as I stand at the counter with my hands bracing me when Zeke walks in, my shirt in his hands.

"I interrupted, didn't I?" he chuckles, tossing it over so I can pull it on.

"Yes, you ass," I playfully punch his arm.

"Sorry, E," he calls behind us as I close the bathroom door.

"Your mom is wandering the halls looking for you and Ebony," Zeke whispers as we wait for Ebony.

"Has she come down this way?" I ask sitting in a chair in the room.

"Once, but that was to talk to Miya." Zeke leans against the wall with his arms crossed.

"What did I do?" Miya asks, waltzing in wearing sweatpants and a tank top. She drops on the bed before hopping back up. Zeke nods to the bathroom and she looks at me in disgust.

"Please don't. She's right across from me," Miya whines.

"Who is?" Ebony asks as she exits the bathroom.

"Let me convince you not to mess with my brother anymore. He's gross, I can find you someone less… related to me," Miya looks at her with pleading eyes.

Ebony laughs.

"I can make a whole presentation," Miya continues. "Starting with baby pictures."

"That's a low blow," I groan. "I was a cute baby anyways."

"With a big head," Miya argues.

"My head wasn't big," I argue back. "That was yours."

Akemi runs into the room, her fluffy white and black tail wagging as she runs around the room greeting everybody. I run my hands against her soft fur and give her scratches all over, she flops on the floor and rolls on her back.

"Such a good girl," I praise rubbing her belly.

"I'm going to introduce you to my mom," Miya says as she links her arm with Ebony's. I stand, taking a large step over Akemi and wrap my arm around E's waist.

"I got it."

My sister pulls E towards her and I pull E back.

"Guys!" Ebony gets away from us. "Not a tug of war rope."

Akemi sniffs around Ebony's legs and gets a scratch behind her ear. "Such a sweet girl," she says to Akemi before looking at us. "You both can take me."

Me and my sister glare at each other before we shove each other trying to get to Ebony. Zeke throws his arm over her shoulder as the two of them laugh at us.

49

Ebony

Those two bickered the entire way down the stairs until we met his mom in the sunroom. The red, purple and blue streaks in the sky make her look like a portrait. Zeke gives my shoulder a reassuring squeeze as I hesitate.

"She's cool," he whispers, pushing past Miya and Kane giving their mom a tight hug. She laughs, kissing his cheek.

"If it isn't my third son," she holds Zeke's face. Small thumbs brush against his cheek before she looks over at her children. "These two." She laughs before standing and embracing Kane.

"I want to—" Kane starts.

"No, I'm going to introduce Ebony to Mom," Miya cuts in. "Mom, this is my—"

"Miya," Kane groans. "Come on."

"Mrs. Yamada, this is Ebony. Our friend," Zeke says, rolling his eyes at both of them.

"The infamous Ebony. These two bicker like this all the time when one of them brings you up," she says as she kisses my cheek and gives me a brief hug. "Don't let that scare you off."

I laugh looking over at the two of them. "I won't."

Mrs. Yamada's face holds a youth to it. Her skin is smooth,

vibrant underneath the dying light. Her hair is short and full. Brown eyes fill with love as she looks at her children. She's about my height and petite.

"I bought popcorn," she informs us. "I'll place an order for dinner soon." She smiles warmly at all of us.

"Thank you," Miya and Kane say in unison.

As we enter the kitchen, I peer out at the shimmering lake, then scan the vast space until I spot the piano in the foyer. Slowly breaking away from my group, I take a closer look. The polished black instrument is smooth and cold beneath my fingertips.

"You know how to play?" Kane asks, looking over my shoulder.

I shake my head. "Never got to learn."

He sits on the bench and pats the space beside him. I slip in as he puts his fingers on the keys, then begins to play, filling the foyer with a beautiful medley that swells and echoes off the walls. His calm face looks at the sheet music in front of him. His thigh flexing as he hits the pedals before he finishes playing.

He looks over at me with a smirk. "I could teach you."

"You flirt with her anymore and I'm going to think she's not into you," Miya groans walking up to the piano.

He rolls his eyes.

"Shouldn't you and Zeke be working on your gains any-way?"

"No," Zeke interjects, laughing. "We don't work on gains, we maintain what we have." He flexes and wiggles his eyebrows. Miya blushes, but rolls her eyes.

"I need a shower," I whisper to Kane, sliding off the slick piano bench. Meandering up the stairs, I examine the doors trying to remember what side of the house I'm on.

"One up, to the left," Kane's voice startles me.

"Jesus," I say, laughing.

"Were you expecting Him?" Kane jokes.

"Don't be a dick," I laugh, walking into my room. The queen sized bed sits in the center of the room on top of a gray area rug. My computer sits on the small desk near the bathroom. A small sitting area claims a section by the window. "You keep following me," I comment.

"Clearly you needed help." He laughs. "You keep disappearing." He leans close to me letting the tip of his nose brush past mine.

"Don't want me finding the dead bodies and your sex dungeon?"

"Maybe," he smiles at me.

Pulling clothes out of my bag, I put everything I need for a shower on the counter while Kane leans against the door frame.

"You're doing that creepy thing where you watch me."

"Trying to stay on this side of the room," he says.

I step out of the way of the open bedroom door and pull my shirt off slowly. "That's a good idea," I say. I latch my fingers underneath my sweat pants and drop them to the floor.

He sucks in a deep breath through his nose. His tongue rolls around in his mouth as he crosses his arms over his chest. "A very, very good idea." His voice is deep, laced with desire.

I unsnap my bra and throw it at him. He catches it with

a smirk, tossing it over his shoulder. I take slow, steady steps towards him, but stop. "Where's the line?"

"Dangerously close to where you're standing," he grumbles looking me up and down.

I inch closer. "Here?"

He shakes his head, licking his lips. "If you want some dick, all you have to do is beg." He smiles.

"What if I want you to beg?" I ask, stepping closer.

He arches an eyebrow before grabbing me. I giggle as he lifts me up in his arms and kisses my neck. "I like when you beg better."

I laugh until his lips find mine. His tongue slides into my mouth brushing against mine. He closes the bathroom door. "In here again," I mutter against his mouth.

"Mmhmm. You need a shower." His hand brushes up my side as he slips my nipple in his mouth, rolling his tongue around then giving it a gentle suck. His other hand palms my other breast, squeezing and massaging before giving it attention.

My hands pull at his hair as I pull his face back to mine. Our lips are slow and soft in this kiss, taking our time to explore the depths of each other in ways we've never done before. His hands grab my waist.

"You're still going to beg," he murmurs, then smiles against my kisses.

"Why?" I ask against his lips, pulling away from him. I smooth his hair out of his face.

"Because I love the way you sound when you're desperate

and needy for me."

"Desperate and needy?" I trace circles around his neck with my tongue.

"Very." He pulls my lips to his, kissing me again. He pulls my hips towards him, sliding me off the counter.

"What are you doing?" I look up at him with furrowed brows. "Kiss me."

He drops a kiss on my lips, then walks towards the door.

"You're just going to leave me like this?"

He smiles at me. "Are you going to beg?"

"You're such an asshole." I laugh, shedding out of my underwear and throwing them at him.

"Thank you," he says, smelling them, then putting them in his pocket. "You smell so fucking good."

"Probably taste even better." I wiggle my eyebrows at him with a devious smile.

"One hundred percent," he walks out of the bathroom after one last look.

"You're so annoying," I grumble.

He laughs on the other side of the door, then the latch clicks as he closes it. With a frustrated huff, I step into the shower grumbling the entire time.

50

Kane

Regret sits on my chest as I stand in the shower letting the water run down my body. She didn't really have to beg me, but there was too much going on to give in. Zeke sneaking up on us, which was best case scenario, didn't help either. I don't want to risk changing my parents' perspective of her. I want more of this, her coming to visit. Me thinking with only my dick would have taken that option away. She's not that good at staying quiet when I'm with her and I absolutely love how unfiltered she is.

I also really fucking love the way she sounds when she begs.

With my shower done, I get dressed in black lounge pants and a ribbed tank, then run my fingers through my wet hair as I make my way to the theater room. A popcorn machine hums, making the room smell like butter. Shelves with snacks sit on the back wall. Four rows of red leather seats face the large screen where Zeke sits by himself scrolling through movies

"Had fun?"

"Didn't do shit," I respond, dropping down beside him.

"You think she'll be… okay?" he asks softly after a moment.

"I think so. She can always sleep with Akemi in the room

with her or with Miya."

"You're not offering your bed?" Zeke playfully asks wide eyed.

"I don't want my parents to have a reason not to like her," I say, grabbing some blankets from a closet.

"Woah," Zeke says softly. "What have you done with Kane?"

I respond by throwing a blanket at his face, sitting back down.

"We should watch a rom-com," my sister says as she walks in with Ebony. Both wearing baggy pajama pants and tee shirts. Ebony's is a bit shorter, showing off the skin of her stomach.

"No," Zeke and I say in unison. I grimace at the idea of some sappy love story. Gag. Bore.

"An action movie," I state and Zeke agrees.

"What about a thriller," Ebony asks, sitting at the end of the middle row. "I heard there's a really good one that just came out."

"Thriller movies freak me out," Miya whines a bit, sitting next to Ebony. "You'll have to hold my hand through it." She holds her hand out to Ebony, who laughs taking it.

"Deal."

"Uh-uh. I'm not sitting next to Zeke." I walk over to my sister. "Beat it."

"What the hell did I do?" Zeke asks, looking confused as hell. Ebony covers her mouth trying not to laugh.

"You were already sitting next to him," Miya argues.

"To find a movie."

"Damn, am I really that unloved?" Zeke asks.

"Shut up, Zeke," Miya and I say in unison.

"I'll sit with you Zeke. These two clearly need a 'get along' shirt for whatever this is," Ebony says, getting up and sitting next to Zeke. She lays her head on his shoulder, then pops his hand. "Hands, dickhead," she scolds with a faint chuckle in her voice.

My sister and I glare at each other as she takes the seat next to Ebony and sticks her tongue out at me. With an annoyed head shake, I sulk in a new seat. Movies scroll on the screen as Ebony gets up, looking over the snacks.

"You sneaking away to sit with me?" I whisper to her and she hides her smile.

"I'm going to sit by myself if you two don't get it together," she whispers back. Then, she grabs the popcorn scoop and slowly fills a bag. And when she's done, I grab her, pulling her to my seat.

"I'm supposed to sit with those two," she whispers.

"They'll live," I throw a blanket over us, rubbing her arm as she leans into me.

"I thought you wanted to keep them apart?"

"I'll worry about that later," I say, kissing her. "You should have picked a movie we've seen."

"Why?" she furrows her brows.

"So we could make out," I say against her lips. My tongue nudges past her lips as the movie starts. Our mouths explore each other as I shift her closer to me, but she pushes away with a giggle, nodding towards the screen. With my arms wrapped around her, we watch the movie, stealing kisses once Miya and Zeke fall asleep.

51

Ebony

I can't sleep.

I lay frustrated in the softest bed I've ever been in staring up at the ceiling. And counting sheep doesn't help. They just bleet in my mind, roaming around the fields I create for them. I turn to my side, facing the door and force my eyes closed, but I'm consumed by the urge to open them. Climbing out of bed, I slip into the quiet, dark hall. Soft snores greet me as I creep to Kane's door. I knock softly.

He opens it slowly, peeking out. His bare chest greets me as his door widens. My eyes drag from his thick, defined torso to the large smile on his face.

"Sorry, I can't sleep. Did I wake you?"

"Nah, was laying here." He wraps his arms around me kissing my forehead, then my cheek. "You good?"

"New environment things. I remember people saying silence can be loud, but out here…"

He laughs. "It gets real quiet out here. My parents love it. You want Akemi in the room with you?"

"Why when I'm here with you?"

I nestle into him as we lay in his bed, using my fingertips to trace shapes in his skin. The soft light of his lamp reveals posters of models, sports players, and musicians. A full bookshelf with trophies and pictures at the foot of his bed. Game consoles sit on racks beside a large, mounted tv with shelves lined with games.

"Your family is great," I say, looking up at him. "They're so funny."

"Sometimes," he laughs. "Normal family dynamic here." He pauses before quickly adding, "not that your family life is abnormal."

"It is," I shift my weight so I'm laying on my stomach. "Gramps and Clint are my normal."

"Big guy that plays the bass?"

"He's my cousin. I have more family, but they're estranged."

"I was wondering why you two seemed so close," he murmurs, brushing a finger down my face.

"Jealous?" I ask with a small laugh.

"No," he says a little too quickly. "Okay, I thought he was competition."

I snort, leaning my forehead against his warm chest again. I run my hands over the toned and defined muscles before looking at his tattoos.

"That thing with Vin," I start softly. "It's always chaotic. You should know before this, whatever this is, goes any further. Don't get wrapped up in me."

He rubs my back, his eyes searching my face. "My life isn't chaotic?"

"I'm not saying that," I sigh. "I'm saying that bad shit

happens to people around me."

He takes a deep breath. His thoughtful brown eyes never leaving mine. "Why does he scare you so much?"

"He's vindictive. He knows how to twist a story to benefit him. He could ruin your life."

"Fuck Vin," he groans. "I don't give a fuck about him. I give a fuck about you though. So, tell me, what do I have to do for you to understand that I'm not going to let him hurt you anymore?"

"There's nothing you can do, Kane. He will find a way. It's how he is."

Kane looks up at the ceiling quietly. His jaw ticks as he clenches and unclenches it. I study his face before shying away. He grabs me and pulls me back to him.

"I don't want to make you mad," I say softly.

"I'm not mad at you, E."

We sit in silence as he stares up at the ceiling, stewing in his frustration. His hand aimlessly brushing against my skin.

"I apologized to him." I chew at my lip looking at him. "I texted him as soon as we got here."

His hand stills and he closes his eyes slowly. A heavy exhale escapes his nostrils. "Now I'm mad at you," he shifts to look at me again. "You didn't *have* to apologize to him. I don't like that you're letting him control you."

"I can't put this project in jeopardy. Miya and I are so close to figuring something out. If they shut us down, I won't have the answers I'm looking for."

"And apologizing to him helps how? I can get you and

Miya the answers you need. Give me time."

"I don't have time." I push away from him and sit up. I frustratedly rub a hand over my face. "I've never had time."

"You've always had time." He sits up staring at me.

"You're being so overbearing with this. Please just follow my lead."

"Overbearing? I'm being overbearing because I want to expose that asshole?"

"*You* want to expose him, I want to do something completely different."

"Because you're too intimidated to fucking do it."

Regret is the first thing I notice after the words are out of his mouth, but it's too late. He can't take them back. My heart aches at the fact that he was angry at me for being scared. Something in the way he said it made my spiraling mind speed up.

"Wow," I stand up, pushing away from his reaching hands. I look back at him, at a loss for words. "Wow."

Storming out into my room, I softly close the door which only makes me angrier. I wanted to slam it, let him know he fucked up, but this isn't my place and I don't want to wake anyone up. I pace my room before sitting on the bed, then hop up, pacing again. I hear him on the other side of my door before he knocks. Instead of answering, I stare at the door willing him to go away. He opens it anyway.

"Get out."

"No," he says. "I don't like that we're fighting. Not about this. Not when you're here."

"This is going to get a lot worse if you don't leave."

"I'm not going to argue with you about Vin. I don't agree with what you did, but I'm being an asshole about it. I'm sorry. You need me in your corner to figure this shit out. I'm here."

He crosses the room and sits on my bed staring up at me. He runs his hands through his hair before grabbing my hand. I pull away needing space. I walk towards the door taking deep breaths.

"Don't shut me out, Ebony. Please."

"I'm not intimidated," I turn and look at him, anger still bubbling in me. "I tried exposing him. Every fucking time we broke up. And you and everyone else don't get to judge me."

"You're right. I was crossing a line," he admits.

"That's it? No smart ass remark about me texting him."

"I have one," he shifts. "As your boyfriend, I don't like that you're texting your obsessed ex."

I roll my eyes and scoff. "You're not my…" I look at him and laugh to myself. "You have the worst fucking timing."

"Feels like perfect timing to me. Gotta claim my spot." He gets up, pulling me towards him as he eases back to my bed.

"Look, E, everyday we talk about Vin and both of the projects we're working on… there's so much more than that in life."

"I don't make enough time for you…"

"You do. Just… while you're here. Just be my incredible, sexy girlfriend spending time with my family."

"I'm still mad at you."

"You're very fucking sexy when you're mad."

"I hate you," I laugh, moving away from him.

"You don't. I pissed you off, but you love me." He moves closer to me. "I really am sorry. I crossed the line judging your choices."

"I will let you know when I need you to take charge. For now, follow my lead."

He nods. "Can we please stop arguing now? I don't like it."

I laugh at him nodding. He sighs and pulls me into his lap.

"That was intense," he says, leaning in and kissing my temple. "So?"

"What?"

"We're making us official?"

"There was an us?"

"Don't be an ass. " He laughs. "There always was, even if we didn't want to admit it." He looks at me thoughtfully.

I groan. "Why are you being so cute?"

"I'm not all muscle, looks, and strength."

I laugh, pulling his mouth to me. "I'm ninety-five percent okay with making us official."

"What's going on with the other five percent?"

"You have to apologize to all of me."

He smiles against my mouth. "Make up sex?"

I pull my shirt over my head and straddle him. "Might help me sleep."

"I'm all for helping you sleep," he says looking over my naked body. The tenor of his voice is low.

"That's what a perfect host does," I say, ghosting his lips.

"The best host," he mutters before pushing his lips onto mine.

He deepens the kiss as he rolls his body over mine. He sucks on my tongue, removing his pants and pulls the covers over us.

52

Kane

Movement from Ebony's room has me out of bed and at her door in less than a minute. I don't bother knocking. She sits on the bed rubbing her eyes, her t-shirt rumpled and pulled up to her hips. A fresh hickey sits on her thigh and on her neck.

"Morning," I close the door as I step in. "Sleep well?"

A ghost of a smile sits on my face as I look at her.

She squints looking up at me, then nods as she shuffles to the bathroom. A frustrated groan follows.

"Dammit, Kane." She points to her neck, glaring at me. "I don't have anything to cover this with."

"I got carried away," I shrug, hiding my smile.

She mocks me before grabbing her clothes from her bag, shoving her legs in her sweats. "I swear you want me dressed like a damn nun," she grumbles.

"I think they look good on you."

"Because you put them there!" she growls, snatching her toothbrush up as she aggressively brushes her teeth. I wrap my arms around her and kiss her temple.

"I can leave more if you want," I whisper in her ear, catching her eyes in the mirror. She shoves me back with her hips then spits the toothpaste out of her mouth.

"We are at your parent's house." She glares at me as she brushes her teeth. A hint of a smile tugs at her eyes.

"That didn't stop you last night when you came all over my dick. Twice."

She spits and laughs into the sink. Her hand covering her face. "You're terrible." She glances at me through the mirror. "How long have you been up?"

"An hour or so. Worked out, then waited for you."

Hoisting herself up on the counter, she pulls me towards her, then wraps her arms around my waist with her head on my chest. She runs her fingers through my hair. Her eyes are filled with affection, no longer searching, but seeing. My heart warms as my fingers brush past the skin on her face, then she places a soft kiss on my lips.

Akemi's collar tings as she walks into her room. Her nails clicking against the hardwood floor as she looks around. She sees us and giddily prances into the bathroom jumping up on my leg, her tail wagging happily.

As Ebony scratches, Akemi moves her head right where she wants to be scratched. I watch the two of them interact before giving Akemi a rub.

"You still have to cover the hickey on your neck," I say looking at Ebony as she groans.

"I hate you," she growls, looking at me in the mirror.

"You weren't saying that when you were—"

She covers my mouth, laughing. I kiss her palm before removing it from my lips.

"'I love you, I love you, oh my God, Kane, I love you.'" I mock her with a smile on my face as she uses her hands to hide her blush.

"You're annoying," she says through a laugh. She decides on a hoodie to cover as much of the hickey as she can, but grumbles when she thinks about it as we make our way downstairs, Akemi hot on our heels. Zeke's already in the kitchen with a plate in his hand as he picks from a wide spread of food. Grabbing a cup for Ebony, I fix her water as my mother walks in covered in sweat. "Morning," she says, sounding out of breath. She kisses Zeke's cheek, then my temple and smiles at Ebony. "I'd give you a hug, but…"

Ebony laughs. "It's okay. Good morning."

"You sleep okay?" she asks, grabbing herself a glass of water and drinks it.

"A little. Had to get used to the quiet."

My mom hums with a smile on her face. "It takes some time, but when you get used to it, it's wonderful. With Kane and Miya gone, it's so much more quiet."

"My mom misses us. Everyday it's her wanting us to come visit more."

"I think she regrets asking that every time you guys come back," Zeke says, laughing. I pop him in the back of the head making him laugh harder.

"Don't hit Zeke," my mother scolds. "Boys. So violent," she whispers to Ebony. "Alright, I'm going to get ready for the day. Kane, your Dad left the keys to his workshop somewhere around here." She leaves with a wave.

Ebony stands next to Zeke as she takes an idle sip of her water, he leans into her, positioning his mouth towards her ear. "I heard you two arguing."

Ebony chokes on her water as her wide, horrified eyes look into Zeke's. "He is overbearing," Zeke concludes as he shoves fruit in his mouth.

"How much did you hear?" she whispers, looking around the kitchen.

"Not much. Are we still mad at him? 'Cause I love a good cold shoulder. Drives this guy nuts."

"Aren't you supposed to be on my side?" I ask, leaning against the marble countertop.

"I am. I just like knowing there's someone that gets you flustered," Zeke says with a grin. "I gotta go, my parents just pulled up so we'll see everyone tomorrow night."

He shoves his last piece of fruit in his mouth, tosses his bag over his shoulder, and leaves a very flustered Ebony. I laugh walking over to her and rub her back.

"Was I loud?" she asks, whispering to me.

"He didn't hear *that* much." Her shoulders relax as she resumes fixing her plate.

"I was thinking, we can finish up the last bits of the drone today," she finally says.

"How much is left?"

"Motor and projector. Zeke helped me piece them together before we left."

"That's why we had to wait for you," I say thoughtfully. "You decided to work and not pack."

"I was packed," she pouts, taking a seat. "Just nervous. I'm meeting your parents," she whispers.

"Didn't need to be," I reassure her as she eats. Pulling the stool beside her closer, I sit with my face leaned in my hand while I study her.

She shoots me an incredulous look. "They raised you to be this incredible person. Big deal."

"Careful now, I might think you love me," I say with a smile.

"Ew," Miya groans from the doorway. Her hair is a mess, tangled and rearranged from wildly sleeping. "I didn't think breakfast would come with Ebony turning into a sap."

"I'm always like this," Ebony says laughing. "Morning!"

"I feel like I was hit by a bus," she groans, grabbing some fruit, then dropping into a chair. "I don't remember getting to my bed."

"Kane carried you," Ebony offers, smiling between the two of us.

I steal some of her fruit, keeping quiet.

"He has his good big brother moments," Miya grumbles looking over at me with a small smile.

"Let's go out later," I say to Ebony. I brush my finger up her bare arm.

"Like a date?" I nod.

Miya's head perks up. "Let me dress you up!"

"Oh... um... Okay?" Ebony agrees, reluctantly. She looks at me, then at Miya as she happily scarfs down the rest of her food.

"Kane, tell me the details later!" Miya runs off with a giddy squeal.

Ebony looks at me slightly horrified. Kissing her forehead with a laugh, I grab more of her fruit, shoving it in my mouth.

"That was my favorite!"

"Come get it," I say, leaning towards her.

She nudges me, rolling her eyes, "that's gross."

"What? It's like kissing, but with food," I argue.

"Gross," she articulates, laughing. "Come on."

53

Ebony

Kane and I manage to get the drone's motor and projector running, but still want to run more tests. After a hot shower, I sit at my desk working on coding when Miya enters. An arm full of makeup threatens to tumble to the floor as she walks in, then dumps everything on the bed.

"What are you going to wear?" Miya asks with a smile.

I stand showing her my jeans and midriff graphic tee. Miya groans and points to the bed. She storms out the room and knocks loudly on Kane's door. The two exchange words, then she comes back, closing the door.

"Dump your bag," she states.

I grab my bag, dumping out all my clothes. Miya looks them over, moving items to the side with a shake of her head until she pulls out a black skirt. She grabs one of my graphic tees then tosses it to the side, then settles on a corset silk top with long flared sleeves.

"Tights? Heels?"

I hold up a pair of platform heels earning an approving smile. She bounds out of the room, then returns with a pack of thigh high tights. Once everything is laid out, she assaults my face with mists and brushes, even hiding the hicky on my neck as she mutters under her breath, then instructs me to get dressed.

The mirror reflects back the neutral tones and highlights kissing my skin. Brown lip liner blends with gloss beautifully. Adjusting my outfit, I pick out jewelry, rearrange my locs, then give Miya a spin.

"You look so cute!" she squeals.

Mrs. Yamada softly knocks, then eases into the room. She smiles warmly at us. "Are you two going out?"

"Kane's taking her out on a date," Miya gushes.

"So he *does* have a crush on her," Mrs. Yamada utters thoughtfully. There's an infectious giddiness in her voice.

"They're probably going to make it official tonight," Miya speculates with pride.

"He'd be a fool not to," she smiles. "Now, let me make sure he's on his best behavior."

Miya cringes as her mom slips out of the room. "We might have to end our friendship. I don't like hearing about you and my brother in the same sentence."

"You'd prefer someone you don't like with your brother. Noted."

She thinks for a moment then sighs. "Okay, but it's awkward." She smiles. "He better make it official."

"He did," I share, sitting on the computer chair.

She gasps. "Seriously?"

I nod with a smile, then grab my bag and a jacket. After a quick hug, I head downstairs to find Kane. Once on the bottom step, I see him in a black button up that hugs his muscles. The sleeves are rolled and bunched on his forearms showing off his tattoos. Black dress pants cling to his defined thighs and kiss down his thick, long legs. He shoves his hands in his pockets as his mom fusses over his hair, which has a fresh undercut.

"Mom, breathe," he says, laughing. "You were like this when I went to prom."

"You're going on a date. I have to make sure you don't run her off," she scolds, adjusting his hair. "Pin this back."

"What's wrong with my hair?"

"You should show off your handsome face."

"You don't think I look good like this?" he looks at her baffled.

"Fine, have it your way," she touches his face with a smile. "Don't keep her out too late."

Han enters the foyer, then stops short. His eyes fixed on me as I gawk at his brother. "Uh… Kane," he calls, nodding over to me.

A wide smile spreads across Kane's face as his mother steps back taking pictures.

"Mom," Kane murmurs.

She shushes him, waving us together. Shyly, I meet him in the middle, "You look nice."

He kisses my forehead then whispers in my ear, "You look so damn sexy." He smiles at me. "Okay, See you later."

54

Ebony

Our date feels perfect, he had a bouquet of lilies on the passenger seat when he opened the door. He took me out to one of the nicest restaurants I've ever been to. We were able to see the river flowing through town and the lights of the skyscrapers. We stargaze now, laying in the back of his SUV with the back and the panoramic sunroof open. A blunt passes between the two of us. I pull my thick jacket off and use it as a pillow as I watch a plane pass.

"Hot?" His eyes are low as he blows out the smoke and passes it back to me.

"Very," I look at him with a smile, then straddle him. I lean into his ear. "Suck," I whisper, taking in a lung full and blowing the smoke into his mouth.

"Still the sexiest thing you've ever said," he says, rubbing my thighs.

I close my eyes and roll my head back enjoying the sensation of his hands caressing me. They drift from my thighs to my ass, then he squeezes at it. The smooth texture of his shirt greets my palms. A heated expression passes between the two of us, then he's up, tossing the butt of the blunt out and kissing my neck. Moans bubble out of me as I rub up his muscular arms, over his shoulders, then into his hair. I tug his head back and move my hips in slow circles. "Kane?"

He groans his response, then squeezes my waist. His eyes on mine.

"Make love to me," I whisper, bringing my mouth to his. I push my tongue into his mouth and start unbuttoning his shirt. He groans into my mouth, separating our lips and pulling his shirt over his head and tossing it in the front.

I wiggle my shirt over my head, dropping it beside us as his lips kiss down my chest. He reaches behind me, closing the door. Moonlight trickles in giving a soft light guiding us to each other. He pulls me back to his mouth. My clumsy fingers fumble with his belt for a moment until the clasp finally gives. I whip it out of the loops with a loud snap making him laugh.

"Slow down, we've got time," he whispers.

I kiss him deeply, slowing my mind to enjoy this time with him. He takes his time unbuttoning his pants.

"Kane, hurry."

"Desperate and needy," he murmurs against my lips as he pushes himself in me. I gasp into his mouth, digging my nails into his back. A smirk crawls on his face. He watches me, rocking his hips slowly.

"You look so fucking perfect taking all of me," he whispers against my lips. His hands tighten on my hips as he helps me move. "You can do it, baby. Nice and slow."

I moan as I move my hips in circular motions, rubbing my clit against his lower abs.

"Bounce that ass on Daddy's dick, E," he growls, slapping

my ass so hard I yelp. He tightens his grip, bouncing me roughly against him, meeting my hips with the same amount of aggression. "Just like that."

I grab onto the seat behind him, using it to help me ride him. His eyes are locked onto mine as he slaps my ass more. I moan, leaning into him for a messy kiss. He grabs my neck, squeezing.

"Such a good fucking girl," he groans, releasing his grip, pulling me back to him. "Open your fucking mouth."

I do, caught up in the moment of his intense strokes and rough slaps. He spits in my mouth, making me moan. He uses one hand to squeeze my tits and tweak at my nipple.

"You're so fucking deep," I moan hoarsely.

"Turn around. Ass up for me, baby," he commands, helping me off of him. I lay my head on the pile of clothes we made and arch my back.

"Such a pretty pussy," he says, kissing my clit. His tongue flicks across as he takes long licks, then sucks on my clit. He adjusts, pulling his pants down more, then pushing deep inside me. His hand bracing me while the other slaps my ass as he thrusts. I push away from the intensity, but his grip tightens on me as he pulls me back.

"Where you going, baby?" he chuckles, slapping my ass. "Take Daddy's dick, baby girl." He leans over me, pulling me back to his chest. His ragged breathing in my ear, the way he knows I like it.

I groan, throwing my arms around his neck. "Harder," I gasp. "Please."

He eases me back down into my makeshift pillow. The sound of our skin meeting making me moan, but he only intensifies his thrusts.

"Fuck," I whimper into our jackets. He slaps my ass hard, sending a tingling sensation across my skin.

"This pussy mine, baby?" He slows his strokes, teasing me with his pace.

"Kane," I whine. "I'm so close."

He pulls out of me, using his finger to bring me back to the edge, then stops. "Who's pretty pussy is this?"

"Mine," I giggle and he slaps my clit with his dick, then his hand. "Fuck, Kane," I moan.

"Who's pussy is this?" he asks again, firmly sliding his tip in me.

"Yours, Kane," I moan. "This pussy is yours."

"Good girl," he growls, thrusting himself back into me. "This is your dick. Only yours," he groans.

The tension in my belly is like a twisted rubber band wound up tightly. When it snaps, I cum hard, feeling my body clenching around his rough strokes. I tremble as my orgasm rolls through me, pulling me into a state of bliss where I can barely hear or see anything. And when I come back down, another one hits me as his finger circles my clit. His hand is on my back as he uses slow strokes to make this one last longer.

"Breathe, baby. Just like that. Ride that fucking high," he groans, his fingers back circling around my clit as he brings me back up.

I've never been surfing, but I assume this is as close to riding a wave as I'll ever get. He manages to turn me onto my back, rubbing my clit when my third orgasm hits. His tongue circles my nipples as I grip the clothes sprawled around me, then his arm on reflex.

"I can't, I can't," I sputter out in a soft whimper as my orgasm subsides. Ever since we figured out how to make them happen back to back, he's always done it, making each one more intense than the last.

He kisses me deeply, his tongue exploring my mouth as he strokes himself. I moan into his kiss, reaching for him with arms that feel like jelly.

"Let me make you cum." My voice is breathy.

He chuckles against my lips as he brings my mouth to his dick. I lick the tip, then shove the whole thing in my mouth, tasting myself off of him. I moan around his girth and a groan rips through his chest.

"You're so fucking good with your mouth." He moves my hair out of my face, watching me swallow him. I place his balls in my palm and roll them around as his hips start moving. "I'm cumming," he moans with his eyes squeezed shut.

I pull him out of my mouth stroking him. "Open your eyes."

His pleasure filled eyes meet mine as I bring him to release, getting his cum on my face and my breasts. He groans as I suck him back in my mouth getting what's left until he moves his hips back with a shudder.

"Fuck, E," he pants.

He lays beside me laughing. "Your face is a mess." He grabs

his shirt and cleans my face off, then writes his name using his cum on my chest.

"Stop writing your name on me with your cum," I laugh, popping his hand.

"You can write your name on me," he says with a smile. He wiggles his eyebrows.

"I love your annoying ass," I sigh, looking up at him.

"I love your sexy ass right back," he responds with a smile, then kisses me.

"You're gonna get cum on your chest."

"I can always shower," he says as he continues kissing me even as his phone starts ringing. Peeking at the screen, he sighs. "It's my mom. We should get back."

I yawn nodding my head before getting my clothes back on. "I'm never fucking in the back of a car again," I groan as we both climb out the back to head to his house.

55

Kane

I use the time Ebony's out with my mom and sister to work more on our project. Even with the motor going, it won't fly. Frustrated, I look into the codes and back at the build. I check her notes, then go back to my computer.

"Something I can help with?" my Dad calls out as he enters his workshop.

"Maybe?" I move out of the way as he approaches. He puts on his glasses and looks over our notes and the code. "What if… may I?" he gestures to the keys and I nod.

He starts typing inside the overlapping codes. "We were thinking of adding some firewall and backdoor protection by overlapping codes."

"The code itself is fine, strong really, but this code right here was just missing an additional layer." He finishes, then shows me. "The code I added prevents the drone from being immobilized."

I feel his eyes on me as I look over the code. "I didn't think of that," I scoot back, then look over the drone. "She's better at building this thing than I am." I chuckle and run my hands over my head.

"She did an amazing job constructing it," my Dad says. He

picks it up looking over all the components, then the blueprint letting out a low whistle. "It's not flying?"

"I think we forgot something we needed. It's hovering. Let me show you."

I pull my phone out once my Dad puts the drone down. He steps back as I use the app we built to turn on the propellers. The drone lifts eight inches from the table and hovers before sputtering back down.

"I can send you some robotic parts from work that might solve the problem." He slides his hands in his pockets as he looks over the device again. He then takes a seat and looks at me. He shifts uncomfortably as he clears his throat. "Your mom said that you and Ebony went on a date last night? That you two are dating?"

"Yeah, made things official a few days ago," I nod and my Dad looks around tapping at the table. "Uh, Dad? Mom gave me the birds and the bees talk already…" I grimace. He laughs a deep belly laugh.

"We both know you are very aware of how all that works. We just want to make sure you're both being cautious," he says softly. He's uncomfortable again, but he isn't the only one this time. I laugh nervously and nod.

"You two look happy together, but your mom feels she's too young for grandkids and of course you two have your whole lives ahead of you."

"We aren't quite there yet," I reassure my Dad, laughing again.

"Good, good." He takes a moment before speaking again.

"I looked into her. What I read is very different from what I'm experiencing, but looks can be deceiving. Be careful."

"She created the project Miya's working on," I state looking at my Dad. "She confirmed that the school is hiding something. She's got reports and records to back up what she's saying. And I think once we get more, everything you read will be proven either false or taken way out of context."

My father gives me a thoughtful nod. "Can I ask you something, son?"

I nod, running my hands through my hair.

"There's nothing going on with you and Ren right?"

"What? No." I laugh in disbelief. "Ren is very into women, Dad."

"I just wanted to ask. You and Ren were close for a while. And having two people in love with you can be chaotic," he gives me an anxious chuckle.

"That won't be a problem," I answer. "I really care about Ebony. I wouldn't want to do something like that to her. She's been through enough already."

"Okay," my Dad sighs, releasing the tension. He rubs his palms on his dress pants. "How was the date?"

"Fun," I smile. "We went out to dinner, then watched the stars while we talked for a little while."

"I remember my first date with your mother. We went skating."

"You can't skate."

"Exactly," he says with a smile. He starts laughing again. The sound lightens the mood and his face. "Take chances like that and you will enjoy every moment with her."

I give my Dad a thoughtful smile before hugging him.

"Love you, son." He kisses the side of my head.

"Love you too, Dad."

I pull at my phone while he explores our project and reviews the plans.

> Do you know Ebony Young?

> Only by name I guess. Why?

> Wanted to ask.

"Hey, Dad."

He hums his response looking up at me over his glasses. His arms are crossed behind his back as he leans over the device.

"I asked Ebony if I could share this with you because it's not just a harmless project."

He looks at me and nods. "Is it going to hurt people?"

"Not as much as the people that are involved. Her being one of them."

"Talk to me," he says more firmly as he adjusts his glasses.

I tell him everything I know. The connections we've made, the suspects we have evidence on. He listens to it all with a straight face. And when I finish, he nods.

"Tell me what you need help with," he offers with a warm smile.

56

Ebony

Zeke's parents, Yasmin and Alejandro, are incredible and sweet. I can see where Zeke gets his carefree and compassionate traits. And when Zeke ranted about my band, they, and everyone at the table, suggested the band and I perform at the Gala.

Sitting on my bed after a hot shower, I look through a list of cover songs we know and write a quick text to see if they want to perform. My headphones are in my ears as I listen to the songs and pretend to play the notes. Kane, who slipped in at some point, sits on the chair across from my bed. As I look through my phone, I jump when I see him move. On reflex, my phone goes flying at him.

"Oh, shit." He dodges with a laugh. "I didn't mean to scare you."

"I'm so sorry," I rush over to him, looking him over before slapping his arm. "I could have hurt you."

He continues laughing as he picks up my phone. "Good news, you didn't hurt me and your phone is in the same condition as it was when you chucked it at me."

"Thanks," I say, making a face at him, then check a text in the band's group messages.

Isaac

Yes. A thousand times yes. Get me away from my parents.

Liam

I'm in.

Clint

I guess that means I have to go?

Isaac

won't be the same without you.

Liam

I mean, Eb might be able to play the bass parts.

I want you there, Clint. Fuck what Liam says.

Liam

Hey!

"Guess I'm performing at the Gala," I say to Kane, laughing. I chew at my cheek, looking at the black screen of my phone lost in thought.

"What's up?" Kane asks, sliding his hands over my shoulders, rubbing them.

A soft groan passes my lips as I close my eyes, enjoying the kneading of his thumbs. "Have I ever told you how good you are with your hands?"

"It doesn't hurt to hear it more," he says arrogantly with a chuckle. "Are you going to tell me what's on your mind?"

"I have to come up with a playlist now and Liam wants me and Isaac to do some duet."

Kane hums running his fingers up the base of my scalp, then up and down the nape of my neck. "If it's too much, you know you can always say no."

"I like performing. I hate the stares. Other than being with you, D, everyone, it's the only time I feel like myself. The me before."

"Have they suggested songs?" he asks.

I shake my head. "I told them I would do it because I think the performance should be when we broadcast the articles and records we have on the drone."

He sits on the chair and pulls me to him. He leans his head on my arm before looking at me. His mouth a tight line and a crease forms over his eyebrow as he tenses up.

"You really want to use your performance as a gotcha moment?"

"Yes. Send a message through music, then boom. It's projected on a screen right in front of everyone."

"I don't want you to get hurt. You being on that stage, sending a message, is going to get you hurt."

"Just a few days ago you complained I was too intimidated to do something and now that I'm telling you my plan you're telling me to not do it. Giving mixed signals here."

"I'm giving clear signals. I don't want you to get hurt. Me is a different story. You, no."

"What's so different about you getting hurt than me?"

He stares at me, then sighs. "I don't want to argue, E," he

says softly, grabbing my hands.

"You're not going to pacify me by saying you don't want to argue," I state, staring in his eyes. "I'm not fragile, Kane. I won't break."

"No, you're not fragile, but I watched you break down on two different occasions because of the shit they did to you. You won't break, no, but I don't want you to go through any more pain. If I'm wrong, then I'm wrong."

"Do you trust me?"

"What does me trusting you have—"

"Do you trust me, Kane?"

"Yes," he says with a sigh. "Just know, if anyone hurts you, I'm willing to spend the rest of my life in jail."

He places his hands on my face, caressing it. "E, I love you. Knowing what they've done to you… I don't want that for you again. It feels easier to not have you in the middle."

"I already am. Whether I wait or I do it during the performance. I am always their target."

"We should have a back up plan, too," Miya says from the doorway. "I agree with my brother. It's real dangerous to have you in the center, but we can have people in place to make sure nothing happens."

She sits opposite Kane and looks between us.

"So, we're exposing everything?" I ask.

"Everything," she confirms, looking at me. "The more people we expose, the better."

"Can we agree to do subtle messages through songs, only if it's necessary?" Kane asks. "We want to at least have the element of surprise."

"Is the drone ready?" Miya asks.

"We forgot something that we need to make it fly. One of the control modules. Once that's in we should be good to go," Kane says, leaning back in the chair he sits in, rubbing his hands over his face.

"I looked over the codes when we got back in. Everything's loaded. Key loggers are running and anytime I try to break through the code it reroutes me."

"Are your parents coming to Family and Friends Week?" Miya asks softly. "I know your relationship with them is rocky, but they're your parents."

"I don't think they will. Especially with Vin painting you guys as children of the mafia."

Kane snorts from his chair. "If we were, he isn't very bright to fuck with you."

We're quiet, each of us chasing the thoughts in our minds about what's going to happen. We formulate ideas, plans to make sure we're safe, but successfully achieve our goal.

"Zeke was right, you two arguing makes me feel things," Miya's voice breaks though the silence as she pouts. "Don't fight." She looks at the both of us. "I actually like you two together," she mutters before getting up and walking out.

57

Ebony

The final few weeks leading up to Family and Friends Week are busy. Besides double and triple checking records and codes, I'm practicing 24/7 with the band. Kane and I see each other in passing or right before bed. We text often, but texting isn't the same as spending time together outside of class or practicing for the flag football game. It helps though.

Loud music plays through the speaker, while Miya and I get decorations stored.

"Need help?" Zeke asks. She shrieks, almost dropping a box that I manage to catch on my knee. Painfully.

"Oh, shit," Miya says, rushing to grab the box.

"I got it," Kane says, hoisting the box on his shoulder like it weighs nothing. "Where's it going?"

"I'll show you," Miya says walking towards the backroom. Kane follows behind her as Zeke picks up another box and follows them. Limping, I'm reorganizing my office when my phone chimes. Absent-mindedly, I check my message and my heart drops.

Vin

With an annoyed eye roll, I shove my phone in my pocket as I limp in the stockroom. Kane and Zeke balance boxes as Miya strains, balancing herself on a shelf.

"Do you need help, Miya?"

"No, I almost got it!" A soft click sends a giddy smile on her face. She climbs down, moving to the side so Kane and Zeke could put the boxes back.

"That's it?" Kane asks.

"Yep. All the brochures, schedules, planners, maps… everything."

"Practice ended early?" I lean against the door frame.

"Yeah, coach wants us rested for the flag football game next week," Zeke answers.

"Does that mean you guys get to help us set up?" Miya says with a hopeful smile.

Kane looks at me with disdain, but I shoot him a thumbs up resulting in a sigh. "We'll help."

"You're volunteering my services?" Zeke complains, looking at Kane.

"You got something else better to do?"

Zeke sighs, then groans. "Fine."

"This weekend we should be able to start setting up," I say.

I pull my phone out of my pocket. "I have late night practice. We learned a new song. You guys wanna tag along?"

★★★

The bar is nearly empty when we enter. Pool balls clatter from an occupied table in a corner. On stage, Issac and Liam assemble various equipment as Clint fusses with a cable. I break away from my group to get myself setup.

"I'm going to get some back track in here," Liam starts as he plays a song over the speaker.

My mic stand groans as I adjust the height. I nod subtly, pushing in my in-ear monitor.

Isaac hums the song, air drumming. "Which way are we swaying first?"

"Left shoulder," Clint's gruff voice says through his mic as he mimics the movement.

"Okay, Clint with the little two step!" Isaac cheers, spinning his drum sticks.

Clint glares at Isaac, flipping him off before turning back to face the front. He tries to conceal his smile.

"Ready?" Liam glances around the group. The tapping of Issac's drumsticks count us off. Liam's voice brings our band to life as we play, our bodies swaying along with the melody. The few patrons that play pool, or drink, grab a vacant chair listening to the song. Miya's infectious smile beams from Kane and Zeke's favorite table. Once we're done, Liam bounces off to the computer.

"I can't hear your vocals," Liam addresses Issac and Clint.

"I was supposed to sing?" Clint asks bewildered. He looks among us as Isaac and I try not to laugh.

"That's how it works." Liam stares blankly at him then sighs as he clicks on the keyboard. "Ebony, I'm pitchy, can you hit the high notes instead?"

"For five dollars," I say smiling. He shoots me a middle finger as we laugh.

With a tap of the spacebar, the vocal bar resets as I take over where Liam sat. I work my magic adjusting the levels, then layer my voice where we need it, then edit the entire track and play it back.

"Hell yeah," Isaac cheers.

"I like it!" Miya shouts, getting Kane's and Zeke's eyes on her. She shrugs. "It's cute. A little love song."

Kane shakes his head laughing. She says something else that makes Kane blush. Something I'm still surprised he's capable of.

"How are we ending?"

"Can we pin 'Happier Than Ever' the Kelly Clarkson version?"

"Sending a message?" Isaac asks.

"You could say that," I shrug at him.

"Her voice sounds so good singing that one. Heard her recording the backtrack in the studio. Fucking chills." Liam gushes, clicking around on his old laptop. One of the drives makes a rattling sound while it hums.

"You should get that checked," I say to Liam with a laugh

as I glance at my phone.

"Why the fuck do you have 120 texts?" Isaac whispers to me. "Babe, if you need help, call me."

I push his shoulder laughing, pocketing my phone. "I need sleep."

"Liam, are we done?" Isaac whines, giving me a wink.

"For today," he idly says as he fusses over something on his screen.

With a grateful whoop, we all pack up, slipping our equipment in their cases and parting ways. Kane, grabbing my guitar case after helping me off the stage, slings his arm over my shoulder so we can finally call it a night.

58

Kane

Ebony's phone buzzes on the table beside the couch while she showers. I scroll through mine idly as it buzzes a few more times. Reaching over, I press the button to mute it, but the screen lights up. Snatching it up, I go through the messages.

> Not afraid to show up.

> or post the vids n pics I have. I don't care how old they are.

> Okay, that was wrong. I shouldn't have said that. I just… this shit with yu and Kane. Is it true?

> Yu don't have to use him to get to me, E. He's not real competition. Dudes a privileged kid.

> E. Come on.

> I could end your entire life. yu'll be nothing but a whore on the street and even then no1 would want yu.

Yu're starting to piss me off.

n I hate that it's turning me on. My dick is hard
as fuck. I need yur mouth.

I stop reading the messages, clenching and unclenching my jaw. I lock her phone, leaning back on the couch. Apparently, this fucker has pictures *and* videos of my girl. Then has the balls to try to sext her while threatening to leak them. It takes everything in me to keep me from finding him and beating his ass tonight.

"I was thinking," Ebony muses from the room, "when we get a new apartment, we could get a two bedroom so I can practice more. Record a few songs." She pops her head out of the room. "What's wrong?"

"Why is Vin texting you?" I ask, trying to keep my voice level. I'm not mad at her. She can't control what he does. I'm pissed that he threatened her a few times and she hasn't told me. I'm pissed that she feels like she has to deal with his shit alone.

"Because it wasn't a big deal. I wasn't responding." She pulls on an oversized t-shirt then pauses. "You went through my phone?"

I roll my tongue around my mouth. I know I fucked up. What's the use in lying? "Yes," I look at her. "I went to mute your phone so I can spend some fucking time with you and saw he messaged you. Why didn't you tell me he fucking threatened you?"

"Kane, what the fuck?" she stares at me in disbelief. "What

the fuck? I thought you trusted me to handle this *my* way?"

"He's threatening you. I'm not going to let him threaten to leak anything of my fucking girlfriend."

"I get that, but you didn't have to go through my fucking phone, Kane." her voice is more frustrated than angry.

She's guarded because she can't read my anger. She's told me her relationships have been chaotic, toxic. Like me, but I don't want to scare her off. I want to let her know that she's safe, loved, wanted.

"Were you going to tell me then?"

"You didn't really need to know," she states. "They're just empty threats."

I take a deep breath and look at her. She stares at me with her arms crossed over her chest. It's a protective stance, even if her eyes are filling with anger.

"I think I should know when someone's shit talking me to my girlfriend."

"He didn't say anything about you," she spits, walking over to her phone and unlocking it. She scrolls through and sighs. "These were from today. I didn't read these." She sets her phone down and it clatters to the floor. She stares at it for a second, then picks it up and tosses it on the couch.

"I'm not mad that he's texting you. You can't control that. I'm upset you didn't tell me."

"Snooping isn't going to do shit but cause fights. Like right now. He can't do shit he hasn't already done."

"What are the pictures and videos of?"

She falters, scratching her head and avoiding my eyes, then

she retreats to the bedroom. I follow behind her, closing the distance quickly, but not closing her in.

"Ebony. What are the pictures and videos of?" My voice is a bit softer, but the anger adds an edge to it that I try my hardest to conceal.

She flinches a little, still avoiding my eyes. I stay away from the door to let her know she's not trapped. I just want to understand. I don't want to fight, not with exposing Vin, his Dad, and everyone else so close.

"Don't judge me," she says softly. "He has nude pictures and videos of me from a year ago, maybe two."

"How'd he get them?"

She chews at her lips. "We had messed around when we reconnected, then I ended things. He threatened to get me expelled and ruin my chances at other schools." She opens her mouth then closes it. Her eyes drift up to mine as she takes a deep breath. "He's not as bad as he used to be. Let's drop it."

I open my mouth to say something then stop myself. Instead, I walk over to her and place my lips to her forehead. I rub my thumb across her cheek then look her in her eyes.

"You forgot that you have a secret weapon right here."

"There's nothing you can do," she says guardedly.

"There is," I take her hand, leading her to the living room where I left my computer. With a few programs on the screen, I write a few codes, then create a link. She's quiet beside me, observant. Her fingers are intertwined tightly in her lap. She chews at the skin on her lip. Shallow breaths escape her lips before she pops her knuckles.

"He clicks this link," I start. "It tracks what he's doing. Opens his picture app? Pictures deleted and spam texts." I hover the mouse over the 'run code' button. I look over my shoulder finding her eyes.

She's chewing at her fingernails now as she studies me before taking a lungful of air. Her hand trembles as her finger hovers over the key. Swiftly, she taps the key and stares at the screen.

"That won't make him stop," she mutters.

"Nope, but it will fuck up his phone, and track wherever he goes from there." I turn her face towards me. "Any picture or video he has of you, will be deleted permanently."

"You can't promise that," she whispers. "but thank you for trying."

"Trust me."

We sit staring at each other for what feels like eternity. I place my arm on the back of the chair near her, then play with the ends of one of her locs.

"You're stressed," I say evenly. "I'm stressed," I confess. "What's about to happen has so many different outcomes. It scares you. It scares me. I can't guarantee that shit won't get a little crazy, but just like you need me to trust you, I need you to trust me."

"Do you trust me?" she asks. Her voice is still soft, like a prayer laced with sadness, pain.

"If I didn't, the argument we had would have been completely different," I say honestly. I place my hand on the side of her neck, using my thumb to caress her cheek.

Tense silence separates us as her eyes sort out whatever's going on in her mind. I wish she'd share it with me. Open up a bit more, let me love all of her. Show her that perfection is just a word in this fucked up society that has no weight, no validity. I pull my phone out and hand it to her as an olive branch. A moment for her to trust me.

"I don't need to go through your phone," she says as she pushes it away, then leans into my hand. "Why are we arguing so fucking much?" she groans, looking at me. A pained expression carving its way deep in her eyes. I hate it.

I shrug. "After this weekend, we'll be caught up in a bunch of shit, but I have your back. Me, Zeke, Miya. Everyone. We have your back."

She breaks eye contact with me, staring at her hands, then looks back at me. There's a hint of playfulness behind her eyes now. "Do that shit again and I'm throwing your computer out the window."

"I can always get another one," I say with a small smile.

"Maybe, but you'll have to remember what happened to the original every time you open it."

I pull her into my arms, adjusting my position so she's laying on me. I kiss her softly, rubbing my hand up and down her back. "We've got to stop arguing," I mutter against her temple. "Shit is stressing me out even more."

"Stop being a dick then," she pushes herself up to look at me.

"Then talk to me about what's in that beautiful fucking brain of yours. You don't have to do anything by yourself anymore. Especially when you know I can knock Vin out for fun."

She snorts, laying her head back on my chest. "You said no Vin talk."

"I said no Vin talk while we were at my parents. Now is a different story."

She hums her response and gets more comfortable on my chest. "Baby?"

"Yeah?"

She swallows, her hands fisting my shirt.

"I'm so fucking scared." Her voice is a whisper, but I hear her. "I don't know what we're doing. I don't know if it's going to make sense or work."

I hold her tighter to my chest attempting to absorb her fear. Give her the courage, arrogance that I have to know that whatever Vin attempts to do, will never amount to what he has coming for him. No matter what happens, I'll get him.

Instead of telling her that, I tell her the next best thing, something that won't send her too deep in a spiral. "Let's spend time together tonight, get your mind off things. We'll take it one day at a time. You decide we don't do this, we won't."

She nods, her head back on my chest. She laughs softly. "I got the drone to work." Her voice still sounds heavy, preoccupied with navigating this situation going on. "Meet me at the workshop tomorrow?"

"Can't wait," I say with a smile. I plant a small kiss at the top of her head as she grabs the remote to put something on to watch. We steal as much time as we can in this space, wanting to exist here forever.

59

Ebony

I normally don't skip class, but I made an exception for today. After Kane and I called it a night, I tossed and turned, waking Kane and Silver up multiple times. I attempted to slip into the living room and clear my head, but Kane woke up and wouldn't go back to bed until I went with him.

Kane

> be there in 10. Just got out of class.

> Take your time. Doing a few more tweaks.

> Give me 5 then.

> Kane.

> tell me you love me and you'll see me in 5 mins.

> I hate you and take your time.

> I'll bend you over that table until your legs give out.

> You know I like it rough, Daddy.

> … I'm wearing sweatpants, Eb. Come on…

He sends a video from the guy's bathroom, a noticeable bulge in his sweatpants. He pulls his pants down a little, showing off the thick base. Before "adjusting" and turning off the video.

I watch it again, admiring his body. Clicking my camera on, I give the room a quick glance, then send him a video of my own. Standing the camera up, I flash the camera, gyrating my hips as I play with my nipples. Satisfied, I send the video, watching as the bubbles appear and disappear.

> Are you alone?

> Yeah, why?

> because you're getting dicked down.

> Right.

Snorting, I put my attention back to the drone, flying it around the room and turning on the projector. Smoke tendrils snake from somewhere and I groan. Landing the device on the table, I search for the source.

Kane's lips on my neck startles me. "Sorry," he chuckles. "What happened?"

"One of the components is backfiring," I pull out a few parts and he reaches over to help me. "How was class?"

He looks at me. "A waste of time. Wanted to sleep instead."

"That's what you get for using all your free days."

"You can always donate yours," he says, cocking an eyebrow. "You still have two to spare."

"Not when I was responsible."

He snorts, rolling his eyes. "Found it."

Moving quickly, he rearranges a few wires, then puts the pieces back together. Whirring from the wings greets my ears. Using the controls, the device darts around the room as images flicker on the blank wall. I land it and Kane pulls me into a hug.

"Holy shit we did it!" I squeal, dancing in his arms.

"You knew we could," he kisses my forehead, then my lips. "I have to show my Dad."

I smile, then start the process again, displaying each feature as Kane follows my movements with my phone until we're satisfied. With a smile on my face, he embraces me.

"When was the last time I told you how smart you are."

"Last night when you were half asleep," I smile at him. "But you can tell me again."

He kisses me. "You're so fucking smart."

He lifts me on the workstation table, kissing me more intensely. His hand snakes up my shirt, cupping my breast.

"Here?"

"I told you I was going to," he laughs against my mouth, pulling me closer to him. His tongue brushes across my bottom lip. He tugs at my shirt. "Arms up."

"Anyone could walk in," I gasp, pulling my shirt from his greedy fingers.

"Door's locked." He kisses my neck, tugging at my shirt again. "I'll rip this off if you don't take it off."

With an anxious glance towards the door, I lift my arms up as he pulls the hem over my head. Warm palms brush up the sides of my neck as his fingers tangle in the back of my locs. Tilting my head back, he deepens the kiss.

"You'll be the death of me," he groans as he frees my legs from my pants, my bare lower half greeting him. Discarding his pants, he pushes himself deep inside me, giving rough, urgent thrusts.

My first orgasm is fast and intense as he leans me back on the workstation as my body shakes around his.

"Such a good slut for Daddy," he groans.

Tossing his shirt to the side, his thick hands rub up my body. Urgent fingers unlatch my bra, tossing it somewhere. A soft whimper escapes my lips as his hand encloses my throat.

"Ready?" I nod, taking a deep breath in. He squeezes my throat, giving me agonizingly slow thrusts. He releases my throat and a desperate, raspy whine escapes my lungs.

"Harder."

"Say please," he kisses my chest, sucking my nipple into his mouth.

"Fuck me," I groan trying to move my hips to speed him up.

"Not until you say please," he says, pulling out of me and slapping my clit. My body jolts and I whimper.

"Kane," I whine.

"My slut needs to be fucked good, huh?" He smiles, putting

his lips to mine. "Say please."

"You're such an asshole." My voice is breathy. He places his hand on my clit.

"Grind," he commands as he lightly circles my clit with his knuckle. He keeps his knuckle close enough for me to feel the pleasure building up, but far enough to keep me from cumming again. "Good girl," he growls, kissing me. "Now, beg for me to fuck you, baby."

Someone bangs at the door as soft moans spill from my mouth. Too caught up in the moment to answer, I close my eyes feeling my body shudder.

"We're busy," he growls loudly towards the door, his eyes still on me. He leans into my ear. "They're going to know you're getting fucked in here if you don't quiet down."

"I don't care," I moan, pushing my hips forward. He moves his hand back smiling at me.

"You look so fucking beautiful on display like this," he whispers against my lips. He uses his hips to spread my legs more. The hand at the back of my neck eases my body back, pushing my breasts forward. His eyes drink me in. "So damn beautiful."

"Then fuck me so you can see how beautiful I look on display and satisfied."

"Say." He slaps at my clit and I jolt. "Please." He taps it again and I moan.

"Please, Kane."

"Good fucking girl," he growls, turning me around placing my chest on the table.

He spreads my legs and enters me slowly. A hiss escapes him before he starts pushing into me deeply.

"Beat this pussy up, baby," I moan, grabbing on the edge of the table to keep myself steady.

He snakes his hand over my thigh and rubs my clit, making me cum hard for the second time.

"Breathe," he instructs, keeping his pace. "Come on baby, just like you showed me."

I follow his instructions and feel a third orgasm before the second one finishes. Hot white light flashes behind my eyes and my whole body tenses. His hand covers my mouth as I scream his name. He chuckles, slapping my ass, slowing his thrusts.

I lay against the table, wobbly legs and sweaty. "I can't take anymore," I laugh as I brace myself against the wooden surface.

He pulls out of me and turns me around. His tip brushing against my clit and I shiver.

"You sure?" He rolls his hips, getting the same reaction. I nod before kneeling in front of him and taking him deep in my mouth.

A low groan rumbles from his chest as he watches his dick disappear and reappear in my mouth. I roll my tongue over the head and lick down the base to take his balls in my mouth.

"You look so fucking perfect with my dick on your face," he groans.

I pull back and spit on his dick, stroking him before sliding him back down my throat again. I wiggle him further and he moans.

"That fucking mouth," he groans.

I pull him back and plant a wet, sloppy kiss on the tip, then roll my tongue around, stroking him roughly. His breathing hitches as he grips the table.

"I'm about to cum," he groans softly. His eyes locked on mine.

I take him back in my mouth. His dick swells as he groans, releasing into my mouth.

Pulling back, he covers my face, chest, and bits of my hair with his cum. His half lidded eyes meet mine as I use the left over cum to write my name across the length of his dick.

"Damn right," he says smiling. "You look so pretty covered in my cum."

I laugh, wiggling in my sweatpants. "I didn't think this through."

"Me neither," he whispers laughing. His eyes scan the room as his hand grips my waist. "Shit, I have to go to the other building for paper towels or something. I'll be back."

I nod moving out of the way of the door as he opens it and slips out. I see the soggy napkins from my lunch and use the crumbling pieces to wipe my chest and some of my face.

I slip into my bra and my shirt, cleaning up the mess from our project.

"Found a new hiding spot?" Vin's angry, yet sarcastic voice startles me.

My head shoots up as I stumble back. His face is bruised from his broken nose. A clear nose brace distorting his features slightly. He smiles at my reaction.

"Your parents are coming next week," he says, his smile

getting wider. "Not to see you though."

"Why are you telling me this?"

"You know, E, they were pretty pissed you didn't come home with me for break—groveling." He inches forward and I step behind the table creating space. He moves quickly, pulling me to him. "You're mine, Ebs." His fingers brush a loc out of my face. "Don't get me wrong, I'd never be with you. Even plan to marry someone *so* much better, but you will *always* be mine. Nothing more than a fucking cum dumpster at my disposal. A throat to fuck and a warm hole to cum in. I *own* you."

His face ghosts over mine and a whimper escapes my lips as he squeezes my arm tightly.

"Let's be clear, *no one* can have you. You understand?"

"Let me go," I growl, pushing away.

His grip tightens. My arm starts to tingle. He twists it to an uncomfortable angle. A gasp falls from my mouth as I wince.

"I can do whatever the fuck I want to you," he whispers laughing. "Kane'll be done with you soon and you'll come crawling back to me."

"Go fuck yourself," I shove against him and he pushes up against me. His erection poking into my side. He rolls his hips before reaching for my pants.

"Stop!" I fight against him as he tugs.

He slaps me, then pulls his lips over mine shoving his tongue down my throat and I gag.

He steps back and licks his lips. "New lip gloss?" He chuckles against my lips before shoving his tongue back in my mouth.

Kane's hand grabs him, shoving him back into the shelf. The items clatter and tumble to the ground noisily. Vin laughs, pushing himself up off the concrete ground, then dusts himself off.

"The fuck you doing here?" Kane growls, blocking me with his bulky body.

"Just reminding Ebs of a few things. Don't worry, I'm not going to interfere."

Kane steps forward, his fists balled.

"Do it," Vin chuckles. "So your sorry ass can get kicked off the field."

Keys knocking on the door stop their standoff. "Everything okay?" A feminine voice asks as she halts at the door. Her badge waves, flashing sunlight back to me.

"All good," Vin says as he licks his lips. Blowing a kiss, he waltzes out of the workshop like nothing happened.

60

Kane

Vin's as good as dead when I get my hands on him.

Rage simmers at the surface of my brain every practice to the point where I have to run suicides for almost knocking his head off. I'd do it again. Anything to make sure he never lays a finger on her.

I walk into our apartment late and find her sitting on the couch with Silver on her lap. She scratches behind his ear as he purrs. A sight I've realized has the tension in my shoulders releasing. The two of them have quickly become my happy place. Shrugging my bag off my shoulder, I place it on the floor of the entryway, kick off my shoes, and walk over to her giving her a kiss.

"You're wet," she laughs.

"Showers," I grumble sitting beside her and rubbing Silver's fur. He swats at my face as I lay my head on Ebony's lap. A soft growl vibrating in his chest. "Share," I laugh, scratching his fur.

"He doesn't like to share, just like you," she laughs, giving him another scratch before turning her attention to me.

She reaches over for the tv remote, turns it off and studies my face. Soft hands brush across the stubble on my cheeks as she leans over giving me a deep kiss.

"What happened?" she asks as her fingers brush against my skin.

"Had to run suicides. Knocked the wind out of Vin a few times."

She snorts looking at me with a ghost of a smile on her face. "Babe," she starts.

"I'm trying. I promise. Just seeing his face pisses me off. I can't get the fucking image of his hands on you out of my mind."

"Can I tell you something," she asks.

"Am I going to like it?"

She shrugs. "Your cum was on my lips when he forced me to kiss him." A soft giggle slips past the hand she uses to cover her mouth. The joy in her eyes has me joining her.

"Did he know?"

She shakes her head. "I couldn't get it all off, so when he forced his mouth on mine, he just so happened to get what was left."

"You were saving it for later?" I ask, wiggling my eyebrows.

"No!" she laughs covering her face.

I chuckle as my large fingers circle her wrist. With a gentle tug, I move her hand from her face and kiss her palm gently. She sits her hand in the middle of my chest and gives me a soft rub. Warmth spreads through me.

My eyes scan her face, loving the small smile that she gives me. The way her eyes look so clear, so gentle, so kind. Finally seeing something in me, at least I hope she does. Something that she had been searching for months ago. I wonder what it was? Whether it satisfied her emotionally, like I know I can physically. Maybe she created it, unlocked a door that I had buried deep inside me until she dove in deep and found it. Unlocking it to bring me to the other side.

Her skin is warm beneath my touch, warming my palm. There is nothing I wouldn't do for her. Including destroying heaven and hell just to keep her happy. I touch the back of her head, gently bringing her mouth down to mine and kiss her slowly, intentionally. I use my lips, my tongue, my hands to pour the love I feel throbbing in my chest for her. A kiss that's meant to read like a love letter from me to her. She smiles against my lips, a sensation I love. One I plan on keeping there no matter what I have to do. She's worth the effort.

"When are your parents coming in?" she whispers against my lips. She pulls her face back and runs her hands through my drying hair.

"Sunday night with Han. I think they want him to come here for college."

"He doesn't want to?"

"Not really. He wants to go his own path. He thinks he's following mine and Miya's too closely by coming here."

She hums her response as her fingers run over my chest slowly as she thinks. She licks her lips then plants a kiss on my forehead.

"Where does he want to go?"

"Military," I answer flatly. "Mom is a mess thinking about

it."

"How close are the two of you?"

I shrug my shoulders thinking about how often my brother and I spend time together. "We talk here and there."

"You should spend time with him," she suggests. "There might be something his big brother can tell him."

"He's not going for it," I say, shifting more on the couch. "I tried when he started getting into trouble. But he's not going to listen to someone that gets into shit too."

"Then involve him in some fun shit. We built a fucking drone, baby. Could you imagine the shit you could show him that keeps him out of trouble?"

"Damn I'm lucky," I say laughing.

She rolls her eyes kissing my forehead before shifting. I lift my head so she can get up with Silver in her arms.

"I'm going to make something to eat, want anything?"

"Let me help." I push myself off the couch and follow her to the kitchen.

She puts on music and starts dancing with me as we cook. Perfection, that's what this moment feels like. It solidifies my thoughts about her. She's the most amazing woman that's ever entered my life willingly.

And I'm so fucking lost in the depths of her.

61

Kane

When my parents arrive, they demand I take them to see Ebony. We go out to dinner and my mom and Miya offer to take her dress shopping for the gala. Her face lit up immediately, which gave me time to show my brother around the school to pick his brain.

Best thing about Friends and Family Week is no class. The school treats it like a holiday because most parents that come are people who have sunk millions into making the campus what it is now. Even if the school doesn't openly admit it, my parents are one of the top donors. It was my grandparents' company that created the blueprints back in the day.

My brother has his hands shoved in his pant's pockets as we walk. The cold wind blowing his normally neat hair all over the place. He sinks deeper into his leather coat as we head towards the chemistry lab.

"Miya tell you about the project her and E are working on?"

My brother shakes his head. His face is long and uninterested, but he follows me anyway.

"You remember that chemistry set we had to share?" I ask, looking at him.

"The one you broke," he says with a smirk.

350

"Bullshit," I chuckle.

Silence follows as we watch chemistry students work on projects in the lab. I slide my hands in my pockets as Han shifts beside me.

"What's Miya's and E's project?" he looks over at me then back into the chemistry room.

"They're making wristbands," I state, facing him. "To make sure people's drinks aren't laced."

"Oh," an internal light flickers in his eyes.

"You see the yellow band on that table?"

"Yeah," he answers, looking at me. "Is that it?"

"It's one of them. Miya and E came up with this idea where the screen is digital. Some type of connectors run through the band, and when it comes in contact with a substance, it changes colors."

"I didn't think that was possible," Han says, looking into the room more. "Are they testing them?"

"Yeah," I glance in the room.

"Party jewelry like those candies people wear at raves," he states with a small smile on his face. "That's fucking cool."

"Come on, I think they'll show you what it looks like."

Swiping my card, the door hisses as I lead Han in towards the beakers. Passing him goggles and protective gear in the process. Chemistry students demonstrate the process of the old and new bands. Han, even though not enthusiastic, admires their work.

"Do you guys have to get to a certain level to do experiments like this?"

"No, in the chemistry department, you get immediate access to the labs. We work with some incredible chemists that rather take that approach," the chemistry student answers. "Are you thinking about coming here?"

"Uh, no," my brother says quietly. He gives a nervous chuckle. "Thanks," he adds, looking at me.

I nod to the student as I put our gear in the sanitation station and head out the door. "You seemed interested in that."

"I haven't done anything with chemistry in a long time."

"There's more than chemistry here," I say nodding down the hall with a smile. He follows me, curiosity filling his eyes as we walk down each department so he can explore the labs, projects, and speak to whoever's available. After a few hours, we head back to my apartment to meet my parents for the rest of the events for Sunday evening.

62

Kane

No matter how many times Family and Friends Week happens at this school, it always feels like a circus. Normally, Zeke and I sit back and watch the chaos, but because Miya and Ebony are running this event, we willingly jump in to help. For the first two days, we focus on checking and registering bands to the system. Occasionally, we provide directions until campus security is free to use their golf carts to escort people to events. Golf carts that I am instructed not to touch, not that I want to. By Wednesday, everything is running smoothly, which gives me time to bother Ebony about her dress for the Gala, which she's hiding somewhere in our apartment. She claims she wants me to be surprised. I'm not a fan of surprises and plan to find it or see a picture of her in it before then. For now, I'm more focused on keeping her busy and away from Vin. He's been circling her with his family. Thankfully, hers aren't with him which helps.

"Has she heard from her parents yet?" my mom asks as we walk over to the fashion display. Her arm is linked in mine as we stroll through the small room. Fresh wax permeates the air while making the floor glow under the bright lights.

"Her and her parents aren't close," I offer as we stop in front

353

of a blue dress with high slits. It rotates on the platform and reveals that the dress is backless. The swoop diving dangerously low on the back of the mannequin. Jewels glitter underneath the high display light.

My mother glances at me before looking back at the design. "I can only imagine how she feels," she finally says as we move to the next display.

I nod walking in step with my mother. "She doesn't seem to mind that they're not here."

"She's pretending she's okay with it," my mother says looking at the display plaque.

"You think that's what she's doing?" I ask as she progresses to the next one.

My mother admires the next design, but her face is pensive. She's deep in her mind. A crease forms between her eyebrows as she looks at me. "Watch how she interacts with us, then watch when she's watching us interact with each other. You'll see what I see, my love." My mother gives me a small smile as we head for the exit. "I'm going to meet up with your father before Miya's and Ebony's presentation."

"Do you remember how to get to the auditorium?" I ask as I lead her towards the parking lot.

I slide my free hand in my pocket as the cold whips past us. She huddles closer to me, ducking her head between the collar of her jacket to protect her face.

"We went with Miya yesterday and she gave us a special map to make sure we remembered," my mother finally laughs. Her teeth chatter together slightly afterwards from the cold. A snow flurry drifts from the gray sky.

"Han wants to spend some time with your group, if that's okay?"

I give her a soft smile. "He's more than welcome."

She smiles back at me and pats my arm as we near my black SUV. I help her into the car, then get in.

Heat blasts through the air vents when I turn the car on. Relief washes over me as my body adjusts comfortably to the heat.

"I think he is starting to warm up to the idea of coming here," my mother says looking out the window as I pull onto the main road. "He was really interested in the theater department when he was with Miya."

"He might be in the next binge-worthy series," I say with a soft laugh.

"Maybe. As long as he's happy," my mother says through a smile.

The drive to the hotel is short, but we spend the time discussing future plans after I graduate college. Even if my Dad owns a data protection company, he and my mother still want me to make a name for myself. I may have a position available, but they expect me to earn it. I respect it, even if that means I may have to work harder to show them that I earned my position by knowing my shit. Proving myself has never been something I cared for, but because my Dad's name and legacy is attached to this, it's something worth giving a damn for.

After dropping my mother off, and seeing her inside, I drive back to campus excited to see E. I did my best to spend time with my parents so she and Miya could focus on their presentation.

Silver greets me when I finally make it in. I place my keys on the front table by the door, kick off my shoes, and head for the room when I don't immediately see her.

The sound of the shower leads me to her. Her silhouette moves against the shower curtain as she washes her body. Her voice echoing off the walls as she hums a song.

I lean against the door frame crossing my arms over my chest with an appreciative smile on my face. I watch her figure move, listen to her calm her nerves.

"I'm back," I finally call out, pulling my shirt over my head.

"Shit," she gasps before she pops her head around the shower curtain. "You scared me!"

"It's easy to scare you," I chuckle, taking off the rest of my clothes. "Move over."

"I'm almost done!" she groans, but makes space for me. She holds the shower curtain open as I step in, then rinses herself off. "Had fun with your mom?"

Hot hands caress my cool skin as she touches my arms and drags them up to my shoulders. I bend down kissing her softly before getting under the hot water. My skin turning red under the high heat.

"This water feels like it comes straight from hell," I laugh, turning it down some.

"You're going to make it cold!" she shouts, a pout forming on her lips as she crosses her arms over her chest.

"It's still hot," I defend grabbing her hand and putting it

under the water.

"Not the way I like it!"

"Little displaced demon." I poke fun at her as she nudges me.

"Turn," she instructs as she squirts shampoo in her hands.

I grab her hips, steadying her as she steps on her tiptoes to wash my hair. I study her face as she focuses on the task. She's gentle, thorough. Her fingernails scratch against my scalp gently and I close my eyes, enjoying her heat and gentle touches. A soft nudge from her finger tip has me tilting my head back so she can rinse the shampoo out. Her body brushing against mine, sending electricity through every nerve in my body.

I pull her closer to me, making her giggle against my skin. I look down into her warm, rich brown eyes. I place another kiss on her lips, deeper than the first. Her hands rub down my chest, around my waist, then up my back as she pushes her tongue in my mouth.

This is the first time we're alone since my parents have been in town. And we've both been busy shuffling between weekly tasks, prepping for her presentation, and spending time with all of us and our families.

Her chosen family. An argument that she fought hard to debunk until D laid out the facts for her until Ebony agreed that each of our respective families were in fact her family. An argument I stayed silent during, but completely sided with D on.

They love her nearly as much as we do, but I know for a fact no one tops the love I have for her. The diamond ring I bought spontaneously that I tucked in one of the drawers she cleared out for me is proof enough.

We kiss for a while, enjoying the heat from the water and our bodies intertwining in the space we share. A slow, steady kiss that leads nowhere, but here. Not to say our bodies didn't want them to go anywhere, they do. I feel it in the way she pulls herself closer to me, brushing past my erection and sighing in my lips when I roll my hips against her.

I'm not a fan of quickies with Ebony, but all things considered, I crave the feel of her. I lift her in my arms and push my dick deep inside her. Adjusting her position in my hands, I roll my hips into her slowly as she moans, getting used to the feeling, which I enjoy. She always needs a second to adjust to how my body fits inside of hers.

I wait for her, holding her tightly as I suck on her bottom lip, then slipping my tongue into her mouth brushing it against hers.

She starts moving, her hips swiveling in small figure eights to create friction between us. I rock my hips into her slowly at first, then pick up speed losing myself in the action.

Sounds of our pleasure fill the bathroom as we get more intense. Our bodies slapping together under the cascading water from the shower head. We say nothing in our moment of intimacy. Only moans into desperate kisses as we chase each other's pleasure in frenzied circles.

I place my hand on the shower wall behind her, using one arm to keep her steady as she shudders. An orgasm running its way through her body as she moans my name so fucking beautifully. I can make this last, but not much longer. I'm nearing the edge as I move faster, harder bringing out her second orgasm moments later, then tumbling over the edge with her.

We pant into each other's mouths, my hips slowly grinding our bodies together as the lingering effects of our orgasms subside. I help her down with another kiss and we finish our shower in cold water, stealing kisses and laughing as we shiver.

We dress quickly and I fight the urge to make her cum again. Her skirt is tight, showing off the roundness of her ass and the gentle curve of her thighs and hips. She throws on an oversized sweater, tucking it under to let it fall over in a midriff looking style. Her heels are high as sin and I already plan to have her keep those on the next time I get her alone.

She grabs her things before she notices my eyes on her. My shirt is halfway buttoned, exposing my chest. The look on her face tells me she's thinking the same thing I am, just more in control of those thoughts. She tears her eyes away from me and steps into the living room and plays with Silver as I finish getting ready.

Miya, Zeke, D, Isaac, and Han join us as we step out of the apartment. All of us dressed like we own the school. We could, if we cared enough. The way we turn heads though, they tell a different story. We're a force. Power, strength, determination.

Inside the auditorium, I kiss her forehead as she steadies her breathing. Anxiety taking over her calm demeanor.

"Just pretend you're talking to me," I offer, kissing her temple. "You know this. The both of you do."

I look over at my sister and pull her into the huddle.

"I think I'm going to be sick," Miya groans, leaning over, placing her head between her knees. Zeke rubs her back as he squats beside her whispering something in her ear. Isaac on her other side listening in. I catch her eyes.

"We'll be right in the middle with Mom and Dad. You both just look for us if you feel like you're going to panic."

They nod at me as they take each other's hands. They give each other a tight squeeze as D instructs them to take deep breaths. I notice Han looking at D, his eyes bright and curious as she leans in continuing to help E and Miya control their breathing. Zeke catches my eyes and raises his eyebrows trying to conceal his smile. He nudges me as I shake my head, focusing back on Miya and E.

The MC tells us it's time and we leave them after giving hugs. I find my parents in the audience and notice Isaac's, Zeke's and D's family are with them. We sit together, staring at the ruby red velvet curtain as it flows with the movement behind it. Then, the curtain parts, other students that helped with the project stand on stage on either side of E and my sister. Soft claps resonate in the large auditorium.

The presentation begins and Ebony kicks off with a synopsis, leaving out details that only those closest to her know. My sister follows up with breaking down the trials.

I admire them in their element as they explain every important piece of their project and how the bands will be used in the future. And when they finish, the audience erupts in cheers as they smile and thank the audience.

E's eyes land on me as she smiles wider. I stand with our friends and family clapping for her. I send her a wink as I listen to the cheers from those around us.

"They did amazing," my mom gushes as the curtain closes. We scoot out of our section and make our way out of the auditorium. We depart from the crowd and wait for them outside the backroom, prepared to celebrate their success and get ready for our flag football game. A day I've worked hard to distract E from.

As E walks out with Miya, her face is bright, but she falters, stopping right where she stands. Her mouth hangs agape as she stares a little to my left and I turn. An older man with light skin and a woman of the same complexion stare at her. Neither looking happy. In fact, they look disgusted as they stare back at her. Hate filling the space around them. Ebony's eyes dart towards me as her parents give me a disapproving once over. Vin walks up, embracing them and their demeanor changes as they walk off with him.

"I'm so glad you guys finally made it!" he greets them with a laugh as they depart. "My parents are this way."

Miya, who's trying to get Ebony's attention, looks at me with desperation in her eyes. Ebony's eyes search for something in the space in front of her. I know that look. She's trying to calculate something. Pain etches on her face, as she looks at Miya.

"Those were my parents…." she says. She tries to smile, but it doesn't reach her eyes. Instead of letting her fall apart, I wrap my arms around her.

"Do you know how amazing you were up there?" I whisper to her, kissing her temple. "A fucking goddess."

Her eyes are glassy, but she blinks it away. Standing back, I watch as all of her chosen family embraces and congratulates her and Miya.

"What happened?" Han asks from beside me.

"Her parents showed up," I mutter with a sigh.

"Vin's up to something if he brought them here today," Zeke says from my other side. His hands shoved deep in his pockets.

"Vin?" Han asks, looking between us. "Who's that?"

"Ebony's ex," I answer, looking at my brother. "Come on, let's go save Miya and E."

I cup my brother and Zeke on the back as we walk over to Miya and Ebony. Their body language more relaxed, but there's still lingering tension in Ebony's body as she looks around in the direction Vin ushered her parents. I hate the look of hope and despair that linger when no ones looking. And in that moment, I realized what my mother meant. There was still a little girl trapped inside of her, still seeking love and acceptance from assholes that will never see her strength, her beauty for what it is.

But we do.

63

Kane

"Game day!" Miya shouts from the doorway. Her hair is a mess on top of her head. Creases from the couch are etched into her face as she wraps a blanket around her. The gang ended up staying the night to keep Ebony company. They didn't tell her that, but I can tell she knew.

Ebony groans from the mattress beside me as she stretches, then rolls into my chest. She hides her face from the sunlight that trickles in.

"You can always forfeit," I offer, kissing her temple and holding her.

"You'd love that wouldn't you?" she mutters into my chest.

"It would save you the humiliation of losing," I state laughing. She pinches my side. "Ow!"

"You earned it," she snickers as she rolls out of bed and adjusts the t-shirt she's wearing. One of my t-shirts.

I get up, slipping into the bathroom with her and closing the door softly, pulling her into a heated kiss. I sit her on the counter and have her cumming on me as many times as she can handle. I have to keep her mouth covered so no one can hear her.

We head to the field moments later. My parents meet Han,

D, and Isaac by the locker rooms and head to their seats. The girls part ways to go to the girls locker room as Zeke and I enter ours. I shuffle in my locker, the door hanging open as I dig for my shoes and the gear one of the donors gifted us.

I'm partially dressed when my phone buzzes from the wooden bench behind me. An image of Miya and E posing together in their uniform sits in our group chat.

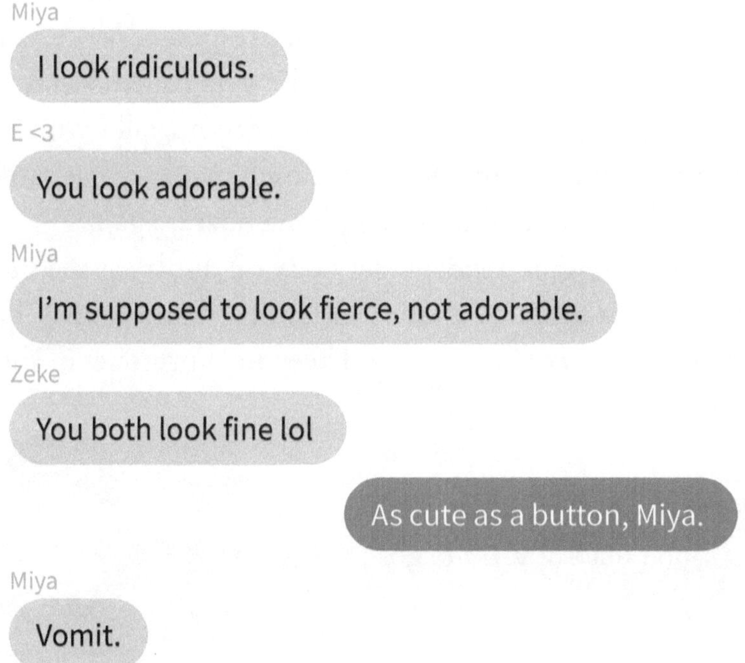

Switching over messages, I send E two different pictures. One tame and one more risqué.

I'm supposed to be focusing on winning!

You are winning. Your bf looks good af.

My boyfriend is trying to throw me off my game.

Never

I laugh to myself as I wait for her response. More voices mix with the existing ones as everyone gets ready. Vin, being tame and staying on his side of the locker room, talks with Sam. He glances my way and nods. Ignoring him, I turn back to my locker pulling on my shirt as my phone buzzes again.

Ebony sends me a video. Her body on display as she shows off that she never put on any panties this morning. My hand grips the top shelf of my locker as I keep my hormones in check, poorly.

put them on.

Don't have any. Gotta go, I love you! BYEE. ⊠

Ebony.

My message doesn't deliver, meaning she turned off her phone. I grumble as I shove my phone in my bag and adjust my shirt. It's hard to play when you've got a whole Eiffel Tower in your pants.

Zeke walks up to his locker, his hair all over the place and his uniform barely on. The muscle in his jaw is tight until he unclenches just to clench it again.

"You good?" I ask him as he reaches his hand out. We slap our hands together.

"Yeah, my parents are driving me *crazy*," he groans sitting down. "They caught a guy sneaking out of the apartment Wednesday, before the presentation, and have been asking a ton of fucking questions."

"Ready for you to settle down?"

"No. Thank God. Not that you and E help in that department." Exasperation sits on his face for a second before he shakes it off with a laugh. "I think they'll start asking soon."

"Me and E haven't done anything," I laugh, closing my locker door and shoving my feet in my shoes.

"You guys look at each other like Gomez and Morticia Addams. It makes all of our parents all sappy."

"No, we don't," I argue as I tie my laces.

"Bet," Zeke says, pulling out his phone and showing me a picture of me and E very much looking exactly like he said we looked. "You were saying?"

"Okay, see," I stumble out before admitting defeat with a laugh.

"Exactly," Zeke says laughing and pushing his phone and other items in his locker and closing it. "They assumed that guy was my boyfriend."

"They just wanna see you happy, man."

"I am happy, slinging dick to anyone that wants it. You know how it is," he laughs looking at me as I nod. A small laugh falling past my lips.

"You know I do."

There's shuffling to the exit of the locker room as both coaches enter the space. Clipboards are shoved under their arms and a whistle dangles from their neck

"Guys listen up," Coach calls out. "Gotta couple guys out so we'll have to shuffle you all around a bit."

Zeke and I listen closely as he pairs us up with the other team. He moves me from being near Ebony to the other side of the line up, but thankfully he pairs her with one of the girls from student life. Vin shouldn't be near her.

"All set?" he asks looking towards Zeke and me.

"Yeah coach," a chorus rings back as we get up and head to the field. I roll my shoulders, getting my head ready for the game. My teammates, the ones I get along with on and off the field, walk over to Zeke and I, subtly tell me they have my back. I'm hoping they won't need to do anything out there to show me that they do.

64

Ebony

Kane keeps glancing my way like he wants to pounce on me, again. I have to turn away to keep from blushing. Thank God he's not on my team because then he'd really find a way to have me close to him. Like he did when we were practicing, which ended with me coming so hard I caught a cramp in my leg.

He still laughs about it. Asshole.

The bleachers are packed and loud from where everyone sits. I pay no mind to see where anyone is. I know it'll make me want to throw up.

Wind rushes past us as we all make our way to our respective sides of the field. The girls and boys passing each other to get to their teams' side. Zeke high fives me and Miya with a smile.

"If it's not my two favorite ladies in the world," Zeke gushes.

"We better be," I retort back with a smile and a wink. Miya giggles beside me as she links our arms and huddles close to me for some much needed heat.

The uniforms we got are nice, but they feel like they're more for the aesthetic than they are to play. The light blue, nylon material of the shirt holds the cold closely to my skin and the skin tight, black cotton bottoms barely repel the chill. My nipples stiffen uncomfortably as another gust of wind pushes past.

A gray cloud of smoke billows from the opposite side of the field, somewhere near the center of the courtyards, where a bonfire is planned. The warm, smokey scent of maple and ash intermingle with the air. It reminds me of a time from long ago when I was a child. One that knew some form of love. That was when I lived with my Gramps and my Grams, when she was alive, and they kept me safe, happy.

The coaches approach the center of the field and motion for us to huddle together. We slowly gather shoulder to shoulder, using our individual body heats for warmth.

"Reminder for my boys, this is flag football not tackle. You snatch the flag, not tackle the players. This is supposed to be fun, have fun. Got it?"

A weak chorus of 'got it' rings around the huddle.

I smell Kane immediately as he approaches my side. He presses his hot body against my side helping me stay warm. I notice Vin looking in our direction. His eyes are normal, less aggressive and menacing. He looks away, staring at the coach who continues talking through the rules of the game and what he expects from everyone, then sends us to our respective sides.

Kane's warm hand taps my ass before he walks off with a smirk. He breaks into a soft jog as he pats a few of his teammates on the back getting them riled up.

"Alright guys, who's ready!?" the coach asks towards the

stands. Cheers erupt from the crowd. The metal rafts clang and bang as people stomp their feet, adding to their excitement.

We get in formation and I see Vin's shoes behind the line of people. I keep my eyes focused on the gate that sits in the distance. He stops in front of me and gets in our starting formation. I look at him startled before looking at Zeke and Kane, they both glance at each other, their jaws tense as they look at the coach. He says something to them with a shrug and they look even more angry.

Vin smirks. "Hey, princess," he greets me cockily, "thought you could avoid me all week?"

I glance at Miya and she shrugs her shoulders looking between Zeke and Kane. Neither one moves. I shoot her a weak thumbs up.

"Good girl," Vin mutters softly, his voice laced with venom.

I thought he was chill, when I should have remembered that he was only waiting for this moment.

Fear rushes through me, heating my entire body and twisting my stomach into tight, violent knots. My ears burn as I stare at the ground in front of me. My heart pounds painfully as the blood rushes through my ears, drowning out the cheers from the stands. The whistle blows, calling the ball in play and I dodge Vin with a spin. I know of a few of his tricks from practice and before. I rush towards the quarterback dodging other players, letting my legs do the work.

Strong arms wrap around me and spin me in the opposite direction. I smell him immediately and relax as he sets me down with a soft chuckle. I growl looking at Kane through squinted eyes as his eyes warm up looking at me. Cheers get louder as I watch Zeke charge towards the quarterback. I cheer from beside Kane. Zeke's fast and agile, moving his body quickly as people dive for his flags before he snatches both flags at the same time. He smiles, holding up the black flags.

Kane gently nudges me with a smile. "He's not trying anything is he?" We walk towards our spot as I control my breathing.

"All good," I say through my pants. I smile at him as he leans down watching me.

"I love you," he mouths as I turn to look at him again.

I send him a wink before getting into my spot. My fingers touch the crunchy dead grass as I place my fingers in front of me.

"Thought I said Kane's no good for you," Vin grumbles as everyone slowly gets set.

"Thought I said to stay out of my business," I snap, sending him a glare. He chuckles to himself, then gets set.

The whistle blows loudly and I'm off. I fake Vin out, making him dive onto the ground, and head straight for the person with the ball. Zeke and Miya are in hot pursuit, dodging people as their eyes meet mine. If I don't get it, they have it.

We move in sync charging towards the man with the ball until I'm grabbed. Vin's fingers dig into my side as he yanks me back roughly. I fall to the hard grass, feeling the frozen earth beneath me. He stumbles over me, his face too close to mine than I care for it to be. He pushes up off the ground quickly, then extends his hand to help me.

Ignoring his helping hand, I push myself up off the ground and dust off. Watching as the person with the ball makes the touchdown.

"Damn," I groan.

My breathing is labored as I place my hands over my head, trying to take in lungfuls of air.

"Should have picked a better team, dolly," Vin tries beside me.

I can tell by his playfulness that he's trying a different approach. That he wants me to be accepting of his friendliness before he attacks. It's the method that used to work often. I can hear the smile on his face that makes his voice sound less tense, less threatening. It still is though, I can hear it clawing its way to the surface.

I roll my eyes at Vin who insists on walking beside me. I don't engage with his trash talk as I get back in formation and look down the line. Kane catches my eye as he smirks at me and sends me a cocky wink. I blush looking down at my tennis shoes.

"You two really a thing now?" Vin asks, nodding towards Kane.

Kane's focused on the person in front of him now. Hunched over with his tattooed arm positioned in front of him like a statue. Fuck that man is sexy as hell.

I don't answer Vin because I'm sure he knows the answer. Kane and I aren't subtle about our relationship status. We're basically always together and if we're not, you can always find either one of us in the vicinity.

A growl rips through Vin's chest when he doesn't get a response. I steady myself thinking of which direction to run. I didn't take his bait, and by the way he growled, I know he's not going to make this game fun. He hates being ignored. I may have just made things worse for myself.

The quarterback calls out for everyone to be in motion, but I'm too slow. Vin quick steps in front of me, pushing all his strength into his elbow that he sends into my sternum.

His strength knocks me on to the frozen ground below. The wind is knocked out of me for a second as I groan involuntarily.

This is only the beginning.

He'll do anything now that he knows I won't speak to him.

He grabs my wrist and yanks me up from the ground. My shoulder pops and I pull my hand back. He used to get this way when we dated. Unnecessarily rough when he's angry. He's liable to pull my arm out of the socket. It wouldn't be the first time.

"Can you chill the fuck out," I snap at him rubbing my arms. I roll it around in the socket, trying to alleviate the throbbing pain in my muscle.

"Chill the fuck out? I'm just playing the game, *babe*," He growls, getting in my face.

"This is *flag* football not tackle, asshole," I growl back.

My eyes locked on him like a target. Mixed in with fear is my own rage. Both intermingling within me as this ass continues to try to dominate me on the field.

The dying grass crunches under the feet of the coach as he approaches us. Vin glares at me one last time and steps back looking away. I rub my arm and turn away from him, getting back on my side of the invisible line.

"We need to separate you two?" Coach threatens.

He's not going to give me another opponent, he's going to throw me off the field if I say 'yes.'

Vin will find an excuse to leave too, which gives him more opportunity to bother me with questions he has no business asking. Bother me or worse.

The crowd is silent now as everyone, including both teams, look on. I avoid their eyes, giving my shoulder another squeeze.

"We're good. Getting really into the game," Vin says with a fake laugh.

"Right," I spit with a bitter laugh.

My shoulder continues to throb. Tingles skitter from my shoulder joint to my fingertips. My arm feels weak now, forcing an old memory with Vin to the surface and I wince. That night was bad. I look up to the sky and take in a ragged deep breath before forcing myself to face him. He'd be dumb to do anything more than jostle me around on the field with people watching.

The coach gives us one more look before running back off. His whistle jingles as he moves. As the memory lingers, anger and panic fill my chest. I realize that Vin is much, much stronger than he was in high school. I knew this already, but feeling his strength takes me back into a space I dug myself out of a while ago. The shit that left bruises can now potentially render my arm useless for a while.

The game continues for a little while, Vin doesn't engage as much, but I feel his glare every so often. He's simmering in his rage, letting it grow. I can feel it radiating off of him. Despite that, I ignore his glare as we switch sides as my team gains the ball. I give my arm one more stretch, massaging into the muscle before I get down in position. The wind picks up and I shiver, but squatting down like I was taught. The energy around Vin shifts negatively. He growls, startling me.

"You're fucking him," Vin hisses."I can fucking smell him all over you."

A bitter chuckle comes out of his mouth. I look up at him, masking my emotions, shoving fear and panic down deep inside me. Willing rage to take the front seat to keep me safe as he begins to unlock the dark doors his shadows and demons linger behind. There's this look that gets in his eyes when he's on the brink of checking out. Like the night he beat some guy an inch from being on life support.

His rational mind has left his body. The brown in his eyes shifting, darkening like shadowy phantoms forming in dark corners of rooms. I'm not safe. This man would kill me if he could get the chance. He's said many times before that he wanted to. Got off on the idea of being the one to watch me take my last breath. He meant it then, and based on how things are going on this field, he'd do it now. He'd have the perfect cover story, too. The thought makes me sick.

Vin toes forward. "I know you fucking heard me," he whisper-shouts through clenched teeth. His voice drops to a menacing, almost a gravelly growl that pulls from the deep depths of hell that are locked in him. Immediately, my internal alarms go off as I realize there is no way away from him. At least as long as I stand on this field in front of him, and maybe for as long as I live.

Somebody help.

The desperation in my mind takes me even further back to the night I was drugged. I swallow a sob as my anxiety makes my body hyper aware of everything around me, which overstimulates me dangerously. My hands shake uncontrollably as I stare at the ground. I feel cornered, caught in a trap with nowhere left to go. I thought this was over. I thought I had healed, but here I am, standing right in front of him, potentially knocking on death's door.

My quarterback shouts and I sprint past Vin, using my fear to push me in the open portion of the field. The ball spirals towards me and I catch it. Cheers burst from the stands as I sprint towards the end zone. My flags flapping against the wind as I run for what feels like my life. Somewhere back there is Vin, gunning for me like a bat out of hell. He wants blood, my blood, and I'm terrified. Me having the ball puts a bigger target on my back for his violence.

I hear people screaming for me to run and I push forward. Someone charges towards me and I falter, side stepping and almost losing my footing before using the balls of my toes to push me closer to the end zone again. I'm so close until someone's arms encircle me and I scream. My flags are ripped off and Kane's lips are on my cheek.

"Gotcha," he says playfully as he puts me down.

I put my shaky hands on my knees, catching my breath. A weak chuckle escapes my mouth. My mind still telling me to run. I use my rapid breathing to mask the fear induced tears that choke me up. I can't tell Kane I need his help. He would fight him and get kicked off the field and out of school trying to help me. I can't let him get in trouble protecting me from my shitty decisions from the past. I have to figure out how to get through this. If only my brain would kick it into gear.

"You okay?" he asks, squatting down to look at me. I lift my face, camouflaging my tears with my sweat.

This part of me that I'm hiding from him, it's for his own good. No one wants someone that's broken. Hell, my family doesn't even want me. He may know the gist, but he doesn't know the real story behind Vin and me. The events, the plans, the why's that make me so afraid of Vin.

I look at him and force myself to laugh, pushing back those dark thoughts. "That's not even fair," I laugh through a sobby-pant. My sides ache and my lungs burn as the cold air flows through me when I take in a deep breath.

"How?" he asks with a laugh.

His eyes study my face. I notice the concern that's surfacing. I turn my head away from him, looking at the other players that walk to their spots. Despite him not knowing, he can sense it. Kane's been around me long enough to know my quirks, my behavior. We set in our new location and I slow my steps. Kane follows suit making this moment last a little longer. I'm grateful for it. How he seems so in sync with me, but I have to be careful. Kane doesn't know the dark side of Vin. And I will do anything to keep Kane safe.

"You can't pick me up," I continue to fake laugh, but the fear is leaving just as quickly as it came.

He leans into me, "You being out here not wearing panties is unfair." I genuinely laugh this time. His face is down right tortured and pathetic.

I walk away with a residual smile on my face. A few of my teammates, ones I met through Kane, give me words of encouragement and 'good job' remarks as I pass. I give them a grateful smile, then make it to my spot, leaning with my hands on my knees finally evening my breathes out. My eyes are fixed to the ground. Zeke shuffles next to me. His hip bumps into mine, catching my attention. "That was fucking dope, chica!"

I smile at Zeke before Vin comes storming over and takes his spot. A scowl on his face.

"Get it together, Vin!" someone gruffly shouts from the crowd, probably his father or mine. There's no telling, not when I barely remember what either of them sound like.

The brown grass is sharp beneath my fingertips. I stare down at it, watching it shimmy as the wind blows past. I peek down the line to my quarterback. He calls the play and I'm moving, but not for long. Vin shoves his bulky shoulders into my gut full speed. The force he uses lifts me slightly off my feet and slamming us both to the cold ground. The wind is knocked out of me before my head knocks on the ground hard. Stars shoot up behind my eyes and the edges of my vision go black. His heavy body crushes me, strangling any lingering air out of me. Panic rises in my chest as I feel my body lay limp beneath his.

"Dirty fucking slut," he growls.

A whimper escapes my lungs as I roll to my side. I can't breathe, I can't move anymore than what I've already done and everything hurts. Blackness fades, but my vision is still blurry as I attempt to catch my breath. Then…

Chaos. The moment he's thrown off of me players collide. Some separating Kane and Vin, who are shouting as close to each other's face as anyone will allow, and others who are taking sides. Kane pushes past people helping me to my feet, looking me over as I finally gasp, getting a valuable lungful of air. He stands in front of me as the team breaks out into a fight. Student life students run back to safety as the football team morphs into an angry ball of fury.

This is what Vin does.

Zeke and Kane push me farther back out of the way as players collide. Miya rushes over, grabbing on to me as she watches in horror. Her eyes just as wide as her mouth as she squeezes onto my arm.

Fists hit into flesh and I clench Kane's shirt in my fists horrified. The mass grows angrier, less controlled as shirts are ripped and limbs collide with other bodies. Each player going after another like men with a vendetta. Vin stands back with an amused smirk on his face. Kane sees him and tenses before taking a stride towards him. My fingers grasp his torso in a panic. His skin is hot and slick beneath my fingers until I grab his shirt again. The fabric tears slightly as he takes a step forward. He falters, grabbing my arm and pulling me to the sideline where the medic stares at the riot.

The referee and coaches charge towards the group, whistles blaring. I wince, trying to find solace in something, but getting no relief. The crowd stares in awe, some of them on their feet and others sitting still as stone. This isn't what they paid for, but they're willing to enjoy this violent show anyways.

"She needs to be looked at, she hit her head on the field," Kane's voice is muffled amid the yelling and the whistle's tweeting.

"I'm fine," I grumble, wanting to go someplace else.

Exhaustion sweeps over me. My entire body feels heavy. I trip over my feet for a moment and Kane pins me with a dominating look. He's not taking no for an answer, not when I hit my head as hard as I did. I sigh, letting him lead me to the bench near the medic. My head spins. The *world* spins. A groan passes my lips as I lean my head into my hands.

Tension increases as Kane's hand leaves my back. Approaching footsteps have me looking up and I see Vin. Walking over like he didn't spear me to the ground with his entire weight. He holds his hands up in the surrendering motion.

"I come in peace," he says with an anxious chuckle.

Miya places her hands on me as she glares at him. In fact, we all glare at Vin as he stops in front of me.

65

Kane

That arrogant bitch, Vin, has the balls to approach her like he wants to make amends. Her hand is around my wrist before I can get in his face. I can see the eyes of the other team members on us as Coach chews them out.

"You better get the fuck back," I growl.

"I just wanted to check on her. She hit her head pretty hard."

"You fucking think," Zeke spits.

Vin rubs his hands together and shrugs. "I got too into the game. Look, back in the day, Ebs and I… We used to play rough like that. And you guys know me. I don't like to lose."

I pick up on the double meaning behind that. I would think it's for me, but his eyes stay focused on Ebony. The way she grabs my wrist lets me know she gets his message loud and clear.

I don't like to lose what I think *belongs to me.*

I step in his line of sight. "And?"

"Can I at least talk to Ebony without you two. What are you guys anyways, her bodyguards?"

"Close enough," Zeke growls, staring daggers at Vin.

"Oh, so you guys are like, what, in a poly situation?" Vin

pries. "Or is it just you, Kane?" His head tilts to the side and I know better than to fall for this trick, but I still do.

"You're so fucking interested." I chuckle and step closer.

"Yeah, she's mine." My voice drops to a growl. My eyes size him up before I smile, leaning closer. "I make her scream my fucking name every fucking night when she's cumming on my dick." I step back. "The fuck are you going to do about it, bitch?"

"Kane," Ebony's voice is weaker than it normally is when I'm going in at this asshole.

I look over my shoulder at her and grab her hand, making a statement. I will protect her no matter what.

Vin looks at our hands and smirks. "That's cute," he says mostly to himself before narrowing the distance. "How does my dick taste then, *bitch*?"

Zeke reaches for him, but I side step in front of him.

"Wouldn't know, but you know how mine tastes." Ebony's weak laugh comes from behind me.

Unimpressed, confusion is the first look on his face, then he looks at Ebony. I feel her body move, then his face falls. The color draining from it as his eyes shift from her to me.

"You said you liked my lip gloss," she says from behind me. "So, how does it taste?" Her voice is still weaker than I'd like for it to be, but she's on her feet, using me to keep her steady.

I smile, wiggling my eyebrows at him, driving the point home. He retches, covering his mouth. Another gag escapes him and he runs to the nearest trash can, emptying his stomach.

A megaphone crackles to life in the center of the field.

Coach stands in the center, the old, dingy device close to his mouth. "Sorry about the disturbance. The players are a little on edge. We'll have to cancel the game until further notice," Coach calls out.

Footsteps bang against the metal bleachers as some people leave. Others slowly collect their things, watching the field as players begin to run suicides. A murmur grows as people talk about what happened while others share their disappointment about the canceled game.

"Do I even want to know?" Miya asks, stepping up beside Zeke looking between me and Ebony. I shake my head before looking at Ebony. Her eyes are bloodshot red, one of her pupils is dilated. She looks like she's about to pass out. I grab her waist, but she resists.

Her eyes fixed on the opposite side of the field. I feel her heart hammering in her chest and I follow her line of sight.

The light skinned man and his wife are stomping towards her. A scowl etched deeply on his face. The woman swears, a look of pleasure flickers in her eyes.

"Ebony!" the man's thick, gravely voice booms from the middle of the field.

The mayor, Vin's Dad, is with Ebony's parents. His eyes attempt to stare through me to Ebony, who is more tense. She cowers behind me squeezing my hand.

"Please get me out of here," she whispers. We act quickly, scooping our things in our arms. I lift E in my arms as we head off in the opposite direction.

Not today, assholes.

66

Ebony

Kane's parents pick us up before we make it to my apartment. I lean my head against Kane's shoulder, the throbbing at the base of my skull getting increasingly worse. I close my eyes, earning a nudge from Kane.

"Can't sleep," he whispers to me.

"I thought you guys were playing flag football, what the hell did he tackle you for?" Han asks. Anger adding an edge to his voice as he leans against the back of the seat Kane, Miya, and I are in.

"I don't know," I say softly. It isn't completely a lie. I don't know what Vin's problem is, not exactly, but I also know he's trying to gain control over me. Control like he had before.

"Vin's just a bitch," Kane mutters looking over the seat at his brother. He looks down at me, pulling me closer in the process.

"Are you okay?" Han asks me, leaning closer.

"Yeah, I'm fine," I say, trying to sound normal. My voice waivers as the pain increases.

My phone vibrates from my bag. I check the caller ID and see my father's number. I ignore the call, shoving my phone deep in my bag. It stops ringing, then starts again.

"We should go to the hospital," Miya says from beside me. She looks over at me, then picks pieces of grass out of my locs.

"Can we just go back to your hotel? I don't want to chance seeing my parents," I mutter.

Kane's father nods as he heads towards the hotel. His mother glances at me, then checks on everyone else in the car. The silence is tense, weighted with confusion, anger, and frustration. The game was supposed to be our way to unwind, but leave it to Vin, and me, to make it more hostile than it needs to be.

The hotel comes into view a few minutes after leaving the school's parking lot. We head up to the suite and take up space on the two couches that face each other. Kane and Miya's parents leave the room to call a doctor.

My phone continues buzzing in my bag. I pull it out and see a few missed calls and texts from Clint. I respond to him letting him know I'm okay, then shove my phone back in my bag.

We all take turns washing up. Thankfully we packed spare clothes in our duffels for the showers after the game. Miya is the first to go, then Zeke, Kane, then me.

I'm still unsteady on my feet, but I manage to get through a hot shower and sit back on the couch with no problem. Kane hovers, watching my every move until the doctor comes and checks on me. I'm diagnosed with a moderate concussion, but I'm given the green light to sleep, which I desperately need.

The sun starts setting by the time everyone dozes off. The room is a cacophony of heavy breathing and soft snores. I lay against Kane's chest. His heart beats slow and even as he holds me in his arms. Normally, I'd be asleep too, but the incessant buzzing of my phone keeps me up.

I slowly wiggle out of Kane's grip and grab my phone. I make my way to the balcony and answer the phone. I sit on a fancy wooden seat with soft gray cushions. I tuck my feet beneath me. My head has eased up considerably making this conversation a bit more bearable.

"Where the hell are you?" my father growls at me through the phone. I can hear the wind through the phone as he drives.

"Safe," I say steadily. Thankful that my voice is even and firm.

"Safe?" He scoffs. "Where the fuck are you?" His voice is deep, impatient.

"No," I say, looking out at the trees in the distance. A moment passes as he fusses with someone in the car.

"Tell me now, Ebony," he demands. "That shit you caused on the field today, that scene, Vin's dealing with it and you should be too."

"You could at least ask how I am. And, I didn't ask him to power drive me into the cold ground, Dad. It's flag football, hence the bright blue flags on a belt around my waist."

"If you hadn't been flirting with that guy on the field, then he would have been able to control himself."

"Don't flirt with my boyfriend? Make it make sense."

My peripheral vision captures movement and I look. Kane sits in the chair beside me, his hair finger combed through to one side of his head. He rubs his eyes, then slides his thick hand on my thigh.

"Your boyfriend?" My father releases an exasperated sigh. "We need to have this conversation in person."

I let the silence edge into the conversation. There is nothing I can say over the phone or in person that would make this situation easier. He's mainly concerned about Vin's image. Always has been.

"He's kind to me," I mutter looking down. My fingers pick at the fabric of my pants. "He doesn't yank and pull on me because he's angry. He doesn't raise his voice. He protects me. I've never been happier."

Kane gives my thigh a squeeze and my eyes find his. There's a lightness to them, anchoring me to this moment. They're soulful, protective, *loving.*

The sun has almost completed its descent, painting the sky in vibrant colors. The chair scrapes the ground as he stands up and walks inside and comes back out with a blanket. He pulls me into his lap, wrapping us both in the blanket.

My father laughs, a deep bellied, bitter laugh. "Just because he's getting what he wants out of you, showing you what you want to see until he's done, doesn't mean he's kind. He's a man."

"Eb, face the facts. He's using you and you're too stupid to realize it," my mother spits. She snickers with my father as I pull the phone away from my ear and hang up, blocking their number in the process.

Kane kisses my temple and tights his grip on me. "Whatever they said isn't true," he whispers against my skin. His warm breath a stark contrast to the cold that settles around us.

"They're mad I don't want anything to do with Vin," I say softly.

"They'll get over it," he states, leaning his forehead on my temple.

"I was supposed to marry him," I snort.

"Is that what the all girls boarding school was for?" he asks looking at me amused. I nod and brush my fingertips gently across the stubble on his jaw. It scratches the pads of my fingers sending tingles up my hand.

"Sending me to boarding school was to make me the proper wife. Quiet, complacent, willing to do anything he asked whenever he asked, no matter what it cost me."

"You didn't," Kane says with a smile.

I shake my head. "Nope. Little Ebony realized there was much more to life than mediocre sex with no orgasms. So, Vin was right, I went away to school and I went wild." I laugh to myself at the memories I have.

"Wild how?"

I look at him with a smile still on my face. I lift my eyebrows. "I couldn't get enough of the people in my school. Girls, the boys that found a way to sneak in, the people in between. Then, when I turned eighteen, a few teachers."

"Naughty girl," Kane says, shaking his head. He runs his hand down my back.

"They were a distraction. Just like I was a distraction for them. And then I came here and met Eva. My very first official queer relationship."

"Eva," he studies my face. "What was it about her?"

"They were gentle. Rough around the edges, but I was used to the kind of roughness they offered."

"Did you love them?" he swallows. I've never seen Kane afraid of anything until this moment. I look deeper, searching for what he was afraid of. Was it me? The past version of me that entangles herself in the woman I am right now?

"No," I sigh. "I thought I did, but after them, I realized love is something much different. I met you and felt everything I learned after Eva."

The fear disappears. His eyes are warmer, less distant, less guarded. "You're just saying that," he chuckles.

"I'm not," I lay my head on his shoulders. "It actually started with making better friends."

"And then you told Zeke you liked me."

"I told Zeke I wanted to fuck you," I correct with a laugh.

"Oh? You were going to use me?"

"You had your reputation, I had mine."

He laughs, his shoulder shaking underneath my head. "The feeling was mutual."

"And you gave me a hard time," I laugh against his chest.

He laughs, tapping at my thigh.

"I would see you on campus pretty often. We had a few classes together, too. That good girl persona, I saw right through that shit."

"I am a good girl," I argue looking at him.

"Good girl for people like me, yeah. But anyone else, you'd walk right over them. Leave them completely worthless." He looks deep in my eyes. "You have this fucking power and I swear you can drown the world with it. Me included."

"I don't want to drown you," I whisper.

"I'll only drown if I don't let you, be you," he mutters against my temple. "And I'd be a dumbass to not enjoy who you are. You're fucking incredible."

"Never took you for a sap," I joke laughing.

He laughs with me, squeezing my thigh. "Asshole."

"You were getting sentimental. Had to give you an out."

"I don't want one," he says looking at me. "Not with you. Never with you."

"You say stuff like that and I might think you want me to stay around for the rest of your life," I lay my head on his chest.

He's silent for a moment and I slowly ease back looking up at him. His eyes are warm, thoughtful as mine meet his.

"I do," he says softly, pulling me into a deep, dizzying kiss.

67

Ebony

Steam fills our bathroom as I shower. Hot water runs over my body, relaxing me as I go through the playlist for tonight's gala in my mind.

With my parents not able to reach me, I know they'll show up. I make sure to text Liam the songs I want to switch out, thankful that we practiced all of them before this moment. I want to send one final message before I ruin their lives. My sweetest revenge.

Kane pulls the curtain back, stepping in. He kisses the back of my neck. His arms circle around me as the hard ridges of his body touch my back. His hands run over my breasts, down my belly and over my thighs. My body internally warms up to his touch, his kisses, as he grasps the hair in the back of my head and tugs it back. I gasp looking up into his eyes. He smiles at me, placing a deep kiss on my lips.

"Are you going to finally let me see your dress?" he whispers against my lips as he rolls his hips against me.

"When I'm on stage." My tongue slides across his mouth, in between his lips.

"Even if I beg?"

"You'd beg?"

His eyes burn hot with lust as he nods.

"It's a surprise," I turn in his hands when he releases my hair.

My hands come in contact with his warm, wet skin as I touch his abs, up his chest, then link my hands around his shoulders.

"Why is it such a surprise?" he asks as his hands grab my ass, pulling me back towards his lips.

"Because I know you'll really enjoy this one." My voice is breathy as our hips grind together. His dick leaking pre-cum on my stomach in the process. A soft groan escapes his lips as my hands unlock and my fingers graze his shaft and tip.

"Bed," he orders, turning off the shower.

I step out, wrapping my body in a towel and walking to the bed. I feel his heat behind me. He smacks my ass, grabbing a handful before pulling me back to him. His teeth drag across my shoulder before he bites down.

A gasp escapes my lips as the pain from his teeth heighten my arousal. Releasing my towel, I let it fall to the floor as I face him, pulling him towards the bed.

The back of my knees touch the softness of the mattress and I sit back, my eyes locked on his. My fingers wrap around his shaft, giving it slow, tight strokes. He groans, his hips thrusting with my movements. I push my face closer to his shaft, running my tongue around the head.

"Keep playing and you'll be tied up," Kane groans. His watchful eyes are filled with a heated warning.

I smile at him, his tip just a breath away from my mouth.

I blow warm air on it before wrapping my lips around it. He pushes deep to the back of my throat and I gag, using my hand to push his hips away so I can readjust. His hand grabs the back of my head, pushing me down further.

"Just relax, baby," he groans. His hips finding a rhythm he likes.

His dick pops out of my mouth and I pop his hand, glaring up at him playfully. "Now who's desperate and needy?"

"Open your mouth," he sternly states, looking down at me. I roll my tongue around the tip and lean my head back as he attempts to push past my lips. "Open."

"Beg," I say softly, giving him painfully slow strokes.

His hips rock into my hand and I tighten my grip, slowing him. His eyes locked on mine as I shift our position and push him back against the bed. "You want me? Beg for me."

Hot, thick hands grab my thighs, digging into my flesh as he feathers kisses across my stomach. Leaning into the sensation, I tangle my hands in his hair. Soft sighs expelling from my lips as his tongue follows his kiss trail.

"That's not begging, Mr. Yamada," I say slowly.

His body reacts to my voice with a shudder as he looks up at me.

"You're making me think things, Ms. Young," he responds, burying his face between my breasts. His hand groping the sides as he smothers himself with them. He takes one of my nipples in his mouth, then the next one. Seductively looking at me as he goes back to take the right one back in his mouth. I step back out of his reach and he stares at me.

"Stubborn are we?" I ask, running my hands over my body.

"Ebony," his voice is low, a warning, a caution.

When he begs, he's rough like he urgently needs to make me cum to show me who's in charge. Dominating me in the best ways that make me squeeze my thighs as I think about it.

"Come. Here." he demands.

We're battling to take charge and I love it. The look of pure dominance and lack of self restraint on his face. He stays on the bed, liking this battle just as much as me.

"Ohh, baby," I purr, "that's not how you beg."

I slide my fingers between my thighs and sigh as I brush my index past my clit. My other hand grasping my breast as I rub my thumb over my nipple.

His dick twitches as he watches me before he palms it.

"Hands off." I pin him with a look I know gives me exactly what I want. He releases himself slowly, letting his finger tips brush against the veiny underside. "Good boy," I smile at him.

A groan, mixed with the rough edges of his growl, escapes his chest as he watches me. "E," his voice is impatient, demanding. A playful heat dances in his eyes.

"Kane," I respond back before sliding my fingers inside myself and moan his name. "Oh, Daddy, you should really feel how wet I am," I moan.

"Bring your fine ass over here," his voice is less demanding. He's close to giving in or maybe getting up and claiming me against the wall. He's done that before, it's a memory I use when he's not around.

"You know what I want." My voice is breathy as I give

myself slow teasing rubs.

"Ebony," His voice is desperate. "Baby, come here."

That's as much as he begs before he's aggressive again, which is how I know he'll claim me on the wall.

I consider challenging him as his chest rises and falls with every steadying breath. Instead, I walk over to him. His thick hands grab my hips, then begin his exploration. Soft moans fall past my lips.

"I know, baby," he mutters against my lips as he guides one of my legs over his shoulder. "It's going to get so much better."

His lips switch from my upper lips to my lower ones as he places a gentle kiss on them, pushing the tip of his tongue against my clit, making me jolt.

"You tease me," he says, blowing against my bundle of nerves. "I tease you." He gives me another soft lick.

"And then you give in," I say softly, pushing his head closer to my pussy. He doesn't resist, but chuckles as his tongue takes a long, grateful lick. Devouring me like I am the best tasting thing in the world. I grasp and squeeze at my breast as he sucks on my clit. He releases it with a soft suckling pop and looks up at me.

He's always been good with his mouth, making me cum before he enters me. Always taking his time to taste me, torture me with his expert tongue techniques before showing me he knows how to work magic with every part of his body.

His hips lift to meet my rocking hips. My thighs trembling as I release shuddery breaths. His mouth suckling as he moans against my clit and looks at me.

"Cum for me, Ebony," he breathes against my clit before giving it a hard suck.

And I cum. Spiraling down the tunnel of pleasure as my pussy clenches and gushes into his mouth. He groans, slowing his movements, easing me down from my orgasm as he pushes my hips down to his. He enters me before I'm fully back in the present.

He's rough, pushing deep inside me, hips slapping into mine urgently, desperately. I hook one of my arms around his neck, the other bracing myself on his thick thighs as I give in to him. My head leans back as my breast bounces into his mouth. His hand slaps my ass hard and I moan.

"So fucking big," I moan.

"Yeah? You like this dick?" he growls, gripping my ass cheeks to guide me back down on him.

"I love this dick, Daddy," I moan as my fingers grasp the hair at the nape of his neck as pleasure takes over.

His thrusts are ragged, his tip bumping into my cervix a time or two making me dig my nails into his thigh as I try to push away.

"Uh-uh, baby. Take all this dick." he chuckles.

"You're so fucking deep," I gasp as he hits it again.

Pain and pleasure battle inside me as I lay my forehead on his shoulder feeling limp, weak against his roughness.

His lips find mine for a sloppy kiss. He rocks my hips as he pulls me down giving me the friction he knows I need and I cum, groaning into his mouth as he slows his speed, helping me coast through the pleasure. With one arm bracing my back and the other gripping my thigh, he lifts me.

We stay connected as he lays me back on the bed, covering my face and chest in kisses as he slows his strokes. We make out as the ripples of my last orgasm fade. His hips rolling as his forearms dig into the bed, caging my face in. My fingers dig into his scalp as I wrap my legs around his waist, locking my ankles, effectively pushing him deeper.

"You should be getting ready," he laughs against my lips, rolling and grinding his hips a little faster, but making no effort to stop. His lips release mine as he kisses down my jaw to my neck. He sucks on it.

"Kane, no," I groan trying to wiggle away from him. He chuckles against my skin, nipping at my flesh.

"I should," he whispers into my ear. "So everyone knows you're mine." His thrusts get harder again, rougher, claiming me in this space we created. A bubble that contains our pleasure alone, but the bubble is tightening, squeezing as his thrusts go unsteady.

His breaths are shaky breathes in my ear before his groans take its place. He's so fucking close. I squeeze my walls around him, feeling myself tilting, tipping.

Fireworks explode behind my eyes as my body releases around him, pulling him down towards me. With me in the tornado of orgasmic high that has no real direction.

He releases inside me digging his teeth into my shoulder before kissing up my neck. Shuddery hip thrusts greet mine before he stills. He kisses around the shell of my ear before our faces meet for a deep, passionate kiss.

"I swear if you left a hickey…" I say through pants as my skin buzzes.

He laughs his response, kissing my forehead before tilting my head up towards him. He places a kiss on my lips. "I got something for you," he says, sucking in a deep breath. He taps my shoulder and I move, sitting in the bed as he grabs a washcloth, wets it, then helps me clean up. Not that I need help, but I'd be lying if I said I didn't enjoy the care he puts into it.

Then, he reaches into his drawer and pulls out a flat square box and pulls me into his lap. His body still hot, skin still sticky.

He places a dazzling, glittery diamond tennis bracelet on my wrist. My wide eyes find his bright ones. Small diamonds line the entire band. The small clasp blending into the side.

"This is beautiful," I gasp.

"I thought you'd like it," he kisses my temple, then my cheek. "Since I can't claim you with a hickey," he adds with a laugh.

I nudge him with a chuckle, glancing at him, then back at the bracelet. "Now I feel bad for not getting you anything."

"I mean, you could show me your dress," he tries with a smile.

"No, I promised your mom and sister I would show you on stage."

"I should have known they'd be in on this," he laughs, helping me to my feet. "You ready for tonight?"

I release a calming breath as I pull out something temporary to wear, "As ready as I'll ever be," I respond as he wraps me in his arms to calm my nerves.

68

Kane

She's on stage in a gown I can't keep my eyes off of. Shimmering under the bright stage lights, her rose gold dress does not disappoint. There's a high split that shows off her thick thigh, the one with the tattoo she got early this semester, and a dangerously low neckline that shows off the perfect curves of her tits. Ones I had my face buried in not even an hour ago.

She steps to the side, helping Isaac with his drum set, setting the shimmering in motion grabbing attention, like I'm sure this dress was meant to do. She knows she doesn't need any help with that. She's a damn force with her smile alone. Material hugged curves tempt me in ways I know would make her blush, mainly because I can picture her sprawled out whimpering beneath me in it. Especially with the long bottom that pools around her feet, which are in black stilettos that show off her pretty toes. I'm not a foot guy, but hers do something to me. Everything about her does.

She grabs an empty black bag and turns her back to the audience, exposing the zig-zags that tie the back of her dress. Her back tattoo on display just beneath her curled locs. I clench my jaw keeping myself in the seat. I don't mind that she's showing off her perfect body. I mind that I didn't get a chance to preview it up close.

Miya nudges me from her seat with a knowing smile. "Told you, you'd love it," she whispers.

I nod giving her a grateful look, then finish visually appreciating Ebony in her full glory. She and Isaac smile for a picture while everyone else continues to set up on stage.

Chairs scrape against the floor as more people file in and take their seats. The noise gradually increasing as more bodies are added. Music plays overhead giving everyone a chance to sip their champagne, eat their dinner, and enjoy the company.

Ebony's shimmery dress catches more attention as she walks down the stage steps to a guy at a table covered in wires. He says something back then helps her secure her mic pack and in-ear monitors.

When he's done, she climbs the steps and gets her guitar ready. I glance around the room locating Isaac's family at the second table to our right, Denise and her family right next to ours and Zeke's family on our immediate left.

Han leans over, talking to Denise. His lips close to her ear as she smiles and nods at him. I glance at Zeke and Miya who look from them to me.

Miya smiles then looks towards the door. Her smile falls.

I follow her line of sight, adjusting the sleeves of my black suit jacket and see Vin enter covered in red velvet. His father and mother following close behind. Ebony's parents behind them. All dressed in glamorous designer clothes and sparkly jewels.

Isaac

> They look stank.

Miya

> What are they talking about?

D

> My sister says they're talking about stocks and stuff.

> We've got people here. They'd be dumb to try something.

Isaac

> Oooooo. Mr. Mafia.

Zeke

> HAHA

Miya

> we're not a part of the Mafia!

I look up at Ebony, who stares at them for a moment, then turns away. She's masking her emotions for the most part, but I can see the anxiety creeping in slowly.

"Give me a second," I whisper to my parents and push to my feet. I walk up to the stage looking up to her.

"Hey, you," she says with a big, beautiful smile.

She climbs down the steps and I notice she's wearing the diamond bracelet I got her. Each finger, but the ring finger on her left hand, has a ring on it. If we hadn't just started officially dating, I'd change that tonight, but I need to slow down. We have time.

"You like?" She gives me a little spin.

"I fucking love." My eyes take her in gratefully.

I know people are watching us, so I keep it tame for the most part. I lean to her and whisper in her ear. "Let me talk to you backstage for a few minutes."

"We wouldn't be talking," she says with a laugh.

"Body language. My body needs to *tell* you all the ways I appreciate you in this dress," I whisper and pull back.

"That was the point," she winks at me, then giggles.

She takes me in now. My partially buttoned shirt showing off the top of my chest, my black dress pants that cling to my muscles. Her eyes trace the lines of the muscles underneath my clothes.

"Be careful, they might think they're getting a very different show," I mutter leaning against the stage so she can get a better look. She scoffs, but heat still lingers in the depths of her eyes.

There's a hint of a smile on her face as she looks at me. "Is everything set up?" she asks softly, stepping closer to me.

I nod. "Just give me a signal if you want me to do it."

She shakes her head. "Thanks, but I think it would get the message across if I do."

I rub my hand down her shoulder, finally touching her warm, smooth skin. She steps towards me placing her hands on my waist and I pull her in to me, kissing her forehead, then her lips. I cup her face in my hands and steal a second kiss. I'd go for more, but I can feel her hands shaking against my side. Nerves probably. A lot is about to happen in less than a few minutes.

She smiles up at me. "I love you."

"How much?"

She snorts, shoving me playfully. I laugh, sliding my hands down to hers, intertwining our fingers. "So fucking much."

Her eyes look behind me and she smiles. Gently, she pulls me towards an older gentleman. His face aged slightly. The edges of his hair graying, but he's still tall. A traditional suit on his broad shoulders. His gray eyes fixed on us as he smiles. Ebony lets my hand go and embraces him tightly.

"Gramps, I want you to meet someone," she says as she glances at me.

Smoothing my hand down the front of my suit jacket, I reach my hand out and shake his firmly, "I'm Kane. Nice to meet you." I smile at him.

"It's nice to finally meet you. I was beginning to wonder," he says with a soft chuckle. His voice is deep, rich with an edge to it. I can see the resemblance between him, Ebony's father, and her.

"Not imaginary, Gramps," Ebony says with a laugh. Her arm hooked in the crook of his.

I laugh. "I play football for the school, so I was always busy."

"I used to play football," he laughs. A thoughtful look passes his eyes. "She says the team has been undefeated since you've been on it? You and someone named Zeke."

I smile and nod. "Yeah, the team was great already, but I guess we helped."

"Keep up the good work," he says, reaching for my hand again. I shake it gratefully.

"Ebs," Liam calls from the stage, getting her attention. "Hate to cut in but…" he taps his watch.

"Yeah, be right up," she says with a smile.

"Have fun up there," her Gramps says, kissing the top of her hair. "Your Grams would be an absolute mess if she saw how beautiful you look tonight."

"Gramps…" she says softly. Her eyes, getting misty. She hugs him tightly.

"I'm so proud of you, little one," he whispers against her hair. He gives her one last squeeze, sends a salute to Clint, then moves his way to Denise's table.

I smile thoughtfully as I kiss her temple and lead her back to the stage, using my hand to provide her support as she walks up the stage steps and depart after another kiss.

With my hands pushed in my pants pocket, I get back to my table and take a drink of my water, halfway listening to the conversation going on around me. I watch as Ebony moves her guitar, grabs her mic, then walks backstage disappearing behind a thick black curtain. Isaac adjusts in his seat as everyone shifts to get ready.

The room quiets down as the in-house lights dim. The sound of glasses clinking on the glass table tops slows as we sit waiting for the performance to begin.

Isaac stands, moving to the front of the stage with his mic as the band plays. He begins to sing in a style similar to Ebony's. His raspy voice blends in with the music as he looks out to the crowd somewhere by the doors, then at the crowd. Liam and Clint play, nodding their head to the beat the new drummer plays.

I look for E for a second, then her voice joins in before we see her. She steps through the door, her dress shimmering in the light. Walking near our table, she stops in front of me and sings sensually. Soft fingers touch my face, then she's in the center of the dance floor looking up at Isaac.

He steps down the stairs towards her with a smile, he takes her hand and pulls her to him moving their hips together. They back away and she moves her shoulders and hips mouthing his part before singing her ad libs. They end the song and she hugs him before walking up the stairs to the stage.

"So," Ebony says into the mic a little breathless, "on behalf of the school, thank you family and friends for joining us this week." Applause fills the space. She smiles as the band shifts behind her positioning themselves and their instruments.

"With that being said," she lets out a breathy laugh. She rubs her palms down her thighs. She smiles as the guy that played the drums begins playing the piano, while Isaac takes his spot drinking water with a warm smile on his face.

She begins singing a love song, her eyes locking with someone. She gestures with her head, and a young couple dances in the middle of the floor. The song continues as Liam and Issac sing back up vocals, admiring the people joining the couple in the room.

Her voice gives me chills. I've always loved listening to her sing, loved when she performed. Especially how she captures everyone's attention no matter how hard they fight it. I look over at her parents who stare dumbstruck at her. I safely assume they didn't know she could do anything to this scale. Maybe they would have exploited her in a different way.

The thought disgusts me more.

She loops her guitar over her hand and adjusts the strap with Clint's help. My mother's hand finds mine and I look at her. A smile on her face as she watches the two kids embrace. I smile at her as she takes a sip of water.

"She's so good," my mom whispers, giving my hand another squeeze.

After that, the band breezes through their playlist as Ebony's fingers move through chords.

She finds my eyes a few times with a sexy smirk. By the time the end of their set comes up, Ebony is more relaxed. The guys shuffle, rolling their shoulders for their last song. She sets her guitar down and shifts her mic stand.

Clint gives her shoulder a squeeze, shooting her a reassuring smile, one I've noticed he only gives her when she's on edge. He sits at the piano on the stage next to her. His fingers ghost over the keys, then he starts playing.

I've never heard them practice this song, but I recognize it. The piano begins to play the opening notes of "Happier Than Eve" and Ebony starts, putting her own spin on it.

Her voice is strong, yet haunted. She looks in the direction of Vin and her parents as she sings the song. Disgust seeping from her eyes. She's bitter, hurt, so beautifully angry. Lyrics meant to send a message and she does it so powerfully. Her hands are on the mic stand keeping her steady.

Clint stands, slinging his bass on, as Liam and Isaac join in. She's belting the lyrics letting all her emotions out in every single note. Grabbing the mic tightly, giving them a very pointed "fuck you" with the last note. Her eyes glisten and then she presses the button on her mic stand. Our drone whirrs to life, lifting into the sky and illuminating on the black curtain behind her. She takes a staggering step towards the back as she lifts her head to the sky.

Anger, rage pulsating through her body, then relief as her shoulders relax. The lights go out and she's gone. Each member of the band filing out behind her.

People gasp as images of various bruised body parts show up on the screen next to threatening video messages to her from Vin and the mayor. Then, video clips of Vin or his father doing something questionable.

I'm up on my feet rushing towards the back to find her. Pride and concern mixing together as she exposes the people that caused her years of pain. Miya is behind me, Zeke to my left. Denise has already disappeared behind the curtain by the time I make it back there.

We see Isaac first, a smile on his face as he embraces each of us. I don't hear what he says until my eyes find her. She's pacing, panicking. I excuse myself and embrace her tightly.

"You fucking did it," I whisper against her hair. She hugs me back, squeezing me tightly in her small arms. "I'm so fucking proud of you, baby."

"Is it still playing?" I nod.

We planned to have my brother live stream everything on throwaway accounts. I show her the feed as the view count increases.

"Why are so many people tuning in," she whispers.

"We tipped off some pretty important people. Mayor Epharim and his family have no other choice but to answer for what they did."

She puts a shaky hand over her mouth and laughs. "Holy fuck."

There's sounds from behind the curtain and her mother appears. Her anger suffocates the happiness out of the room as everyone stops and stares at her.

She walks up to Ebony, pulls her arm back and slaps Ebony across the face.

"Your mother should have dropped you anywhere else, but here," her mother starts. Everyone gasps into the silence as her mother stands over her. I stand back, shock riddling me useless.

Ebony covers her face as she straightens her head and looks at her mother.

"You're the biggest mistake in any of our lives," her mother spits through gritted teeth.

"Vivian," Clint's voice is hard, loud in the small space. He takes a step forward, but her glare pins him.

"Careful, Clint," Ebony's mother hisses with a threatening glint.

"Don't threaten him," Ebony's voice is quiet, but fierce. "You can be ashamed all you want for *your husband's* mistakes, but those are his burdens to bear, not mine."

She looks her mother up and down, then laughs bitterly. "You can throw in my face how you didn't want me. How my father didn't want me. You're the pathetic woman that used me for popularity anyways. My mother will have her day to answer for abandoning me, just like you'll have to answer for the shit you put me through."

"I raised you to the best of my abilities, Ebony."

"You hated me. Admit it. Every time you had the chance to ship me off somewhere, you did. Never once did you think about the innocent child in the middle."

"You embarrassed your father *and* the mayor with your lies," she hisses.

"Official documents aren't lies, Viv."

Her mother breathes roughly, opening and closing her mouth like a fish out of water, then she scoffs. "You're done. Don't reach out anymore."

"Should I cry about it?" Ebony spits back before laughing.

She leans close to her mother, "You probably should have stopped Vin that night he tried to sell me off like a piece of meat for his drug habit."

Ebony turns, leaving her mother stunned in the spot she's standing in and I follow quickly. I grab her wrist gently and tug her towards me. She wraps her arms around me tightly. Her eyes find mine and she laughs to herself.

"I don't know where that came from." Her voice is soft. The sound of shuffling behind us catches our attention.

My brother has a large grin on his face. I drape my jacket around her arms and face the group. Snow flurries flutter out of the sky. I catch a few before Han's giddiness captures my attention.

"That was incredible. There are already a ton of people coming forward saying something similar happened to them when they were around Vin's father," my brother shares.

"We should check the database to see if anyone tried to disable the broadcast," Ebony suggests after a moment. She glances at me as she takes my hand.

"My friend, Ren, is supposed to be here soon. From there, we can take the information to the nearest DA's office."

"I already sent it," Ebony confesses. "After the argument with my parents at the hotel, I sent them everything in an email."

"That was incredible," a soft voice and the sound of clapping responds behind us. Ren steps into the clearing, their all black suit helping them blend in the shadows. Their heels scrape against the concrete as they step forward. They tuck their hair behind their ear.

I release Ebony and embrace Ren tightly. I turn to introduce them to everyone, but notice D's, Isaac's, and Clint's glares fixed on Ren. Their body language angry, protective. Then, I notice Ebony, whose face is visibly paler. Her jaw is hanging open as tears trickle out of her eyes as she blinks. She looks at me, then at Ren. Her eyes doing that searching thing again. Something isn't adding up to her.

"What is this?" Her voice is no more than a whisper.

I open my mouth to explain who Ren is, but they step forward instead, still smiling but it's different now. A smile that makes me feel like I've made a huge mistake.

"Kane," Ebony's voice trembles. Her eyes are wide, terrified. "Why are *they* here?"

I'm still not grasping why Ren looks so predatory and Ebony looks like she's about to run away.

Ebony sucks in a ragged breath before a shudder escapes her as Ren takes a step forward.

Then I see it, the devilish grin that climbs across Ren's lips as Ebony takes a retreating step backwards.

Ren's sinister voice alerts me, "Hi, E. It's been a while, *baby*."

The pieces fit together. Reneva, Ren's full name. *They're* Eva.

They were linked to the same people and I missed all the evidence that told me that Eva and Ren were the same person.

Looking at Ebony hyperventilate now, I panic.

I think I just made the worst mistake in my life.

Acknowledgements

First, to all of you who took a chance on my book, thank you! I hope you enjoy this series and you stick around to see what happens next for these two (be mindful of triggers).

To those of you who believed in me, thank you for the unwavering support and uplifting me every step of the way. A special shout out to my sister, Toni, and my niece, Taliyah "Tia", for listening to me ramble. A lot.

To my kiddo, your pride and excitement when you tell people that I wrote a book means more than you know. I love you more.

To my writing partners: Haley Hamilton (*The Elflaine Chronicles* | @haley.h.writes) and Eve Miller (*The Astrian Trials* Forthcoming | @evemiller_author).

Haley, this journey, from querying to self publishing would not have been the same without you. You've pushed and encouraged me in ways I don't even think you're aware of. Congratulations on your debut and I'm proud to be a part of this journey with you.

Eve, who would have thought a random follow on instagram would have led to late night writing sessions with us mostly talking about books, the publishing industry, and everything in between? Thank you for that. I'm excited to share your beautiful writing with the world.

Thank you both so much for taking a look at these pages and falling in love with my characters just as much as I have. Without your support, guidance, and advice during this journey, this book would not be what it is today. I can never thank you enough and I won't stop trying.

To my Alpha readers, Kyra Hammond and Kevin Bomely – LeDoux, thank you for being the first two to meet Ebony and Kane. Your suggestions and feedback helped this story evolve in beautifully resilient (hehe) ways.

To my first beta, Cristina, thank you for taking a chance on this book. You helped me figure out the story from a readers perspective and I appreciate you for it.

With all the adoration in my heart, thank you.

About the author

Aneka Bailey lives in Marietta, Georgia with her daughter. As a lover of fiction of all kinds, you can find her mostly reading dark romance, dark romantasy, romantasy, thriller/suspense, or horror books in her free time. Her interest in writing piqued when she discovered indie authors in social media groups and finally decided to start, and finish, one featuring a Black female main character. Thus, the Pretty Something Series was born.

You can connect with Aneka on her social media pages.

Instagram and Threads: @anibwriting
TikTok: @anigoeswhoa and @anibwriting

To access the books playlist and stay updated, scan the QR code below.